Samantha Parks is the pen name of Sam Gale. Her pen name comes from her late grandmother Velma Hobbs nee Parks, who was one of Sam's greatest role models. Sam was born in North Carolina but now resides in Bournemouth, UK, with her husband Alex. She owns a successful marketing company and is enjoying her slow descent into "crazy plant lady" status.

The Summer House in Santorini was her first novel.

BB bookbub.com/authors/samantha-parks

THE SUMMER WEDDING IN SANTORINI

SAMANTHA PARKS

One More Chapter
a division of HarperCollins*Publishers*
1 London Bridge Street
London SE1 9GF
www.harpercollins.co.uk

HarperCollins*Publishers*
Macken House, 39/40 Mayor Upper Street,
Dublin 1, D01 C9W8

This paperback edition 2023
First published in Great Britain in ebook format
by HarperCollins*Publishers* 2023
1

A catalogue record of this book is available from the British Library

ISBN: 978-0-00-841810-6

This novel is entirely a work of fiction. The names, characters and incidents portrayed in it are the work of the author's imagination. Any resemblance to actual persons, living or dead, events or localities is entirely coincidental.

Printed and bound in the UK using 100% Renewable Electricity
by CPI Group (UK) Ltd

For Alex, the man who always makes me feel like my dreams are the most important thing.

Chapter One

Anna felt instantly at home as she stepped through the doors of the airport terminal and the Santorini heat hit her skin. She used to hate it, but over the past four years she had come to miss it when she was away. The humidity of the Philippines and the huntsman spiders in Australia had helped her learn to appreciate the comparably pleasant Grecian summer.

Anna had been travelling for years as a professional photographer. It was only possible because of her ex-boss Marcus, who also happened to be… well, her ex. But they'd been working together successfully for years now, and Anna had gotten to shoot all over the world on some truly exciting projects.

But this trip hadn't been to the sunny shores of California or the cobbled streets of colourful Barcelona. Instead she was coming from three weeks in the Tierra del Fuego, an archipelago on the other side of the world from the one she was on now. Her winter parka weighed heavily in her duffel bag, and her paler-than-usual skin told the tale of weeks without summer sun. She could practically feel the vitamin D absorbing into her as she made her way towards the bus stop, the way she would normally get home, but as she was about to cross the street, an arm wrapped around her waist, and she startled.

"Hello gorgeous," Nikos said as he hugged her waist and buried his face in her hair, kissing her neck. Anna closed her eyes and smiled, letting out a contented sigh. She sure had missed him. It was hard on both of them when she was gone for that long, but the reunion was always worth it.

She turned to face him, wrapping her arms around his neck and kissing him, letting him spin her around. As she pulled back, she could see his deep brown eyes scanning her, taking in every detail, like he did every time she came home from a long trip, and she did the same. It never stopped delighting her, how seriously sexy her boyfriend was. His long black curls were usually swept up into a rough-and-ready man bun, but now they hung around his face, tickling Anna's jaw when they kissed. He was tall – especially tall for a Greek man – and strong enough to easily pick Anna up, which he loved to do. His olive skin was extra dark this time of year because of how much time he spent outside, and it wasn't hurting his physique either.

"It's good to see you," she said, sinking further into his embrace, feeling the press of him against her, grounding her, welcoming her home. "That was a rough one. I've been sitting around doing nothing but travelling for three straight days, but I feel like I could sleep for a week."

"Well it's been three straight *weeks* since I've seen you," Nikos said, planting a kiss on the underside of her jawline, his voice low and husky, "and I'm going to need a few other things from you besides sleep."

Anna threw her head back and scoffed, mocking offense, but Nikos just smacked her bum and threw her duffel bag over his shoulder, leading her towards the truck.

As they drove over the hills and around the bends that Anna had come to know so well over the last two years, she slid across the seat and snuggled up close to Nikos as he drove, taking in the scent of him – a rich earthy smell that told her he'd been in the vineyard or the garden before he came to meet her.

Anna only had one other trip scheduled for the summer, and she knew, snuggled up to the man she loved as they climbed the hills of Santorini, that a longer stretch at home was well overdue. After just a few minutes, they pulled into the driveway of their tiny summer house. She let out a deep breath, taking in the sight of the house she'd renovated with her own two hands, where she now lived with the love of her life. She was home.

Anna's father had left the summer house to her and her sister Lizzy in his will, surprising everyone – especially his parents, Anna's grandparents, whose garden the building sat in. It was a bit of a loophole that it was deemed a separate property at all. It had taken Anna months to find out about the house, nobody having wanted to hand it over to an estranged family member who had never even visited the island, but the moment she came to claim it and decided to start renovating it, she started to fall in love. With Santorini, with her family, and with the little summer house. She'd tried to distance herself from all of it, navigating secrets and revelations about her family and about Nikos, but eventually she realised that the life she had built there was far more meaningful than the one she'd left behind. In the end, her choice was easy. She had decided to make Santorini her home for good.

But that was nearly four years ago. And nowadays she spent more time away than at home, her career having taken off, but the summer house was always her safe place to return to. She had a partner she loved waiting for her. She had a family she finally knew ready to welcome her home. She had friends and community on the island that she'd never found anywhere else. It had truly become her home over the past four years, no matter how often she was away.

Nikos had moved in on their second anniversary, though it hadn't been planned that way. His cousin Elena, Anna's best friend, had moved in with her boyfriend Vasilis, and Nikos's mother's house, where they both had lived, seemed too big and empty for just him. He was spending most of his time at the summer house, anyway, so he sold the house and moved in full-time with Anna. They only realised afterward that it was the second anniversary of Anna's decision to move to Greece permanently.

When Anna's grandfather Christos announced just a month later that he was retiring, he offered his construction business to his then-employee Nikos. Despite inheritance being incredibly important in Greek culture, nobody expected or wanted Nikos to accept the job – it was a lovely gesture from Christos, and a message that he considered Nikos part of the family. But, in the end, it was Christos who convinced Nikos to follow his passion, instead. So, their friend Kostas took over the business, and Nikos vowed to follow his dream.

The abundance of time to himself also seemed to have cultivated a new passion: gardening. He had taken over the space between the main house and the summer house with raised beds and trellises, planting courgette and aubergine and tomatoes and artichokes until there was barely any room left to walk. He'd even managed to rescue some olive and lemon trees that were being torn down at a nearby construction site and transplant them into the ground outside. The first year it had looked like the trenches of some war, with mounds of soil and stray ladders everywhere. But now it looked like a proper Eden – all that was missing was a naughty apple tree and a talking snake.

His pride and joy, however, was his vineyard. In typical Nikos style, he had gone all in on his plan, using most of his money from the house to buy up half of an existing vineyard with a crop ready to go. He met up regularly with a few winemakers on the island to get their advice, and he went out every day to prune and soil test and measure. The club he was in had even started travelling within Europe every couple of months to meet with distributors and top sommeliers. Two vintages in, Nikos's wine was getting better and better. Or so she'd heard; Anna hadn't been able to try this year's yet.

"The garden looks amazing," Anna said as they walked towards the front door. Much of the produce had been just starting to ripen when she had left, and now she could see a rainbow of veg amongst the jungle of green.

"Thanks, I've already done a harvest for today. It was extra big since I've been away for a few days." Nikos had been in Tuscany with his winemaking friends, taking a three day course all about how soil PH impacts bouquet.

Nikos ducked under the bougainvillea cascading down from the trellis over the patio and unlocked the front door.

When Anna stepped inside, she was immediately hit by the smell of garlic, black pepper and lemon. Baskets of vegetables covered the worktops and the table, and she could see a chopping board and bowl already set out.

"What's that?" she said, sniffing the air.

"That's our dinner," he replied. "Lemon chicken with orzo and some of the early courgette crop."

Anna's mouth started watering. He hadn't even cooked anything yet, and it already smelled fantastic. "That sounds so good. I'm starving."

As she turned around towards the bed to start unpacking, she gasped. Hanging over the bed, where a cheap, store-bought painting used to hang, was a huge black and white photo of boats anchored in a small bay. Ammoudi Bay, in fact, right here on the island – Anna would recognise it anywhere, because she had taken the photo. It wasn't for a shoot, or for a client, but just for fun. Anna had been experimenting with shooting in black and white instead of converting it later. Nikos must have found it on one of her memory cards, which she usually kept in a bowl on the dresser. She didn't even know he looked at them.

"Nikos, this is amazing," she said, admiring the perfectly paired gold frame and gallery-style light hanging above it. "This is one of my favourites. How did you know?"

He came up behind her and put his arms around her waist, nuzzling his chin into the space between her shoulder and neck, planting a kiss on her collarbone. "I didn't," he said. "It's my favourite too."

"Really?" she asked, hugging his arms in hers. "Why?"

He stood up a bit more and tilted his head, and Anna leaned back to watch him examine the photo.

"I think it's because even though it's in black and white, you can almost feel the vibrance of it. The light levels add just as much depth and visual interest as colour could."

Anna nodded as Nikos settled into her. She had taught Nikos a bit about photography over the years, but it helped that he seemed to have a natural appreciation for it. "That's why I did it," she said. "If your intention is to end up with black and white photos, then, sometimes it's better to shoot that way to begin with so you can find where the light works best to your favour. It's not always easy to tell what will look good once you convert it."

With his cheek pressed to hers, Anna could feel Nikos grin. "You're sexy when you talk about this, you know," he said, kissing her shoulder.

"Oh, yeah? How sexy?" she asked, turning her head to kiss his forehead.

He didn't spin her around to kiss her, but, instead, moved his kisses up her neck, tickling the side of her ear with his tongue. Anna sighed, pushing back against him. Her chest rose higher on each inhale, and her head tipped back as she exhaled deeply, baring her neck to him.

Nikos continued to kiss her, keeping his touch light as a feather. In contrast, his hands moved to her hips and grabbed her firmly, pulling her back into him even more. She moved her hips in response, and she felt him harden. She began to run her own hands along her body, unconsciously circling her breasts as his kisses deepened. She wanted to grab his hands and put them right where she needed them. The reality of three weeks without his touch suddenly seemed impossible, and she needed to fix that. Now.

As if reading her mind but not quite ready to give her what she wanted, Nikos brought one hand up under her tee shirt and then down beneath the waistband of her leggings, running his fingers over her ever so lightly – infuriatingly so. He was trying to tease her, and she was falling for it hook, line and sinker.

"Please," she murmured, the sound more like a gasp as it escaped her lips.

All of a sudden Nikos was properly touching her, rubbing her, his other hand tugging on the hair at the nape of her neck, then squeezing her breast hard, and she was writhing and rocking against him. She could feel him get harder as she did, which just encouraged her, his hands barely keeping up as she moved against his touch. And as she came, he pulled her against him and gripped her tightly, his fingers pulsing against her as the waves of her orgasm radiated through her body.

After they had subsided, she led him to the bed, and they

made love until both of them were sated, lying in a tangle of sweaty limbs, trying to catch their breath.

"I sure missed you," Nikos said as he ran a finger along her hip, making her shiver.

"I always miss you," she said. "Though these reunions really are something."

"That they are," Nikos replied, planting a kiss on her mouth and standing up abruptly. "And now for dinner. Everyone will be here in a couple of hours."

Anna frowned, both at the fact that Nikos had left the bed and at what he'd said. "Everyone?" She couldn't remember inviting anyone over, though maybe she'd forgotten about a double date with Elena and Vasilis? But something about the way he'd said "everyone" felt like more than just the four of them. "What do you mean, 'everyone'?"

Nikos grinned as he pulled on his clothes. "We're having a little party tonight," he said. "Big surprise, remember?"

Anna fell back onto the pillow, going over what he could mean. Their calls whilst she was in Chile hadn't been reliable, and she suspected he had told her and she'd managed to forget, which meant she would have to play along. But whether he'd told her or not, if guests were coming, she needed to clean up a bit – both the summer house and herself.

After she'd taken a bath, whilst still in her robe, Anna tossed her bag onto the bed and unzipped it. Better to start unpacking now, instead of just stashing it somewhere still full, otherwise her bag would sit in the corner until she needed it again. Anything left inside would be abandoned until she started packing for the next trip.

As always, the first order of business was her memory cards.

She had made a routine of always keeping them in the same place so that she never misplaced them. She pulled them out of the small pouch in her bag and put them in the left-hand half of a little ceramic double bowl on the dresser. The right-hand half was full – nearly overflowing, in fact – with memory cards she'd already backed up, and these would join the pile tomorrow. Though, from the look of it, Anna would need to find a way to consolidate soon.

Then she pulled out her parka, gave it a sniff, decided it was acceptably hygienic, and hung it on the footboard. She would have to ask her grandmother Eirini if she could store it in the main house; she didn't suspect she'd have much need for it on the island, but she suspected it would come in handy on future trips.

The rest of her clothes went into the hamper to go into the main house on laundry day, and the duffel bag went in the drawer at the bottom of her wardrobe.

The last item in her bag was a pair of socks – Anna had accidentally taken some of Nikos's with her, and despite trying them on thinking they would work well with her snow boots, they were laughably big. So they had sat otherwise unworn in her bag for three weeks, reminding her of home every time she looked at them.

She took the socks out of the bag and walked over to Nikos's dresser, sliding open the drawer. But as she tossed them in, she saw a small, bright patch of red peeking out from between his things.

She pushed his things aside to see a small red velvet box sitting at the bottom.

Anna's heart was suddenly in her throat. As she stared down at what she knew was a ring, she felt emotions welling up in her. Nikos wanted to marry her. She felt her mouth spread into a grin so wide it hurt her cheeks, but she couldn't stop smiling. She brushed her fingers over the velvet, debating whether to take a peek—

A noise from the kitchen made her jump slightly, and in less than a second she shut the drawer and stepped back over to her wardrobe. She looked over her shoulder to make sure Nikos hadn't seen her, but he was fully focused on the lemons he was zesting. He was still making dinner, but several trays of food had materialised whilst she was in the bathroom, possibly from the main house. She watched him for a couple of minutes before he even noticed, wondering what the night had in store. Clearly, he thought he'd mentioned it, but whether he had and Anna forgot or he was mistaken, she didn't know for sure. Could the big party have something to do with the box she'd just found?

Anna's heart soared at the idea of marrying Nikos. They'd talked about it a few times over the years, but it had always felt so far away with how much she travelled. Sometimes, she worried he resented how much time she spent away, but if he was going to ask her to marry him, surely that was his way of saying that he was happy with her the way things were, right?

"What are you looking at?" he asked, wagging his eyebrows at her suggestively. She laughed.

"Just wondering about this mysterious party," she answered. "Do I need to dress up?"

Nikos shrugged. "Wear whatever you'd like, my love. You always look wonderful."

"How many people are we expecting?" Anna asked, looking around at all the food that was out and wondering if her summer house could handle the army it would feed.

"About fifty," he said. "But it'll be worth it, I promise."

She rolled her eyes jokingly. "As long as you're making bougatsa, I'm in."

Nikos made a big show of lifting up a tea towel covering a tray of bougatsa, and Anna made an equally big show of gasping and clapping her hands together. She grabbed his face and kissed him deeply, tasting spices and lemon and the tang of sweat on his lips. As she pulled away, she held his gaze for a moment. Good food, good friends, and quality time with the man she loved – this was the homecoming she looked forward to every time she was away. Anything else was just a bonus, no matter how sparkly.

And then there was a knock on the door.

Chapter Two

One week ago

Anna barely had a spare moment in Chile to think about her life back home in Greece. Not only did she have a job to do photographing the new range for an American camping gear company, but she was working with one of her idols, landscape photographer Patrick Farr.

That's how Marcus had convinced her to take the job, in fact. Normally, she didn't enjoy product photography, but with Patrick working on the stills for a documentary with the same company at the same time, and all of them staying on the same remote island, Anna knew she'd be able to rub shoulders with him and, hopefully, learn from him along the way. She couldn't have imagined though how much time she'd actually get to spend with Patrick.

Well, with him and with Marcus. But Marcus was unavoidable these days – as Anna's agent, he came on almost all of her trips unless they conflicted with something he was working on. Nikos didn't love the idea of her spending so much time with her ex-boss and ex-lover, but working with him had launched her career, and his connections were helping her grow it, so she'd agreed to let him manage her on a trial basis for a few months. She'd expected it to be a disaster, but it had actually gone so well that she'd signed with him indefinitely. He kept her very busy, but she'd loved almost every job she'd been on.

He also, importantly, never tried to hit on her again. Now that he saw her as a peer, he didn't seem as into her. Anna tried not to think about what that meant about his respect for her before – or lack thereof. At the beginning, she figured that at least this way, with them travelling together, she could keep him from preying on PAs and interns. But he had really reeled it in on the excessive womanising, to the point that, sometimes, Anna felt like he was a completely different person, and most of the time she was truly grateful for everything he did to help her succeed. She suspected he was sacrificing a lot to do so.

In the two weeks she had been gone, she had spent three days of it travelling to and from the island. To get there, she had to take four different commercial flights – connecting in Mykonos, Frankfurt, and then Buenos Aires – before joining the crew on a boat ride through the archipelago to their base camp. By the time they got there, Anna was already exhausted. Then she had two weeks of two four-hour shoots per day, one during the day and one at night, carrying around twenty pounds of equipment and wearing more clothing than she thought was possible in a desperate bid to stay warm.

During the limited amount of time she had off, she was either learning at the feet of Patrick Farr – he'd already let her shoot second on one of the day shoots when his normal second had shown up hungover – or arguing with Marcus about their upcoming itinerary. He didn't love that Anna wanted to take some time off over the summer; the longer days meant bigger shoots, apparently, which equalled more money and more exposure. But

Anna was insistent. She knew she and Nikos were in desperate need of some quality time together after how busy they'd both been. Just one more week and she would be on her way back home, and then she'd be back with Nikos.

Anna had managed to FaceTime with Nikos twice, but the signal was atrocious, and the time zones meant one of them was drifting off mid-conversation. But it was probably for the best – Anna always felt herself having to pull away from the action to make time for Nikos when she was on shoots. She'd have loved to have him along on her adventures, but simply put, she was busy..

It didn't make it any easier, though, and she did feel a pang of guilt every time she got to the end of a long day and realised she hadn't thought about him in hours.

On one of their FaceTime calls, just a couple of days after she'd arrived, Nikos said something about a surprise for her for when she returned. Anna was on the boat because the water seemed to be the only place she could get enough signal for a conversation, but even then the call broke up constantly. Marcus and two of the crew were there unloading more equipment, and Marcus was doing a poor job of pretending not to listen.

"That boy is going to propose," Marcus said when Anna hung up, his affected, McConaughey-style southern drawl on full display.

As soon as the words had left Marcus's mouth, Anna felt the warm fuzzies bubble up inside her. It wasn't the first time she'd thought about marrying Nikos, and Elena had teased her about the possibility over a glass of wine every now and then, but it was the first time in nearly four years that anyone else had outright mentioned it. She tried to hide her giddiness from Marcus as she answered, clearing her throat and dropping her voice half an octave.

"Do you think? What makes you say that?"

"Because every time you talk to him, he lights up like a

Christmas tree. And you've been together almost four years, haven't you?"

"That's not that long..." Anna said, but she knew that wasn't true. Secretly, she had been thinking about it a lot. He'd undoubtedly plan a super romantic proposal, and maybe they could have a small destination wedding, or even elope...

"It's long enough for that boy," Marcus said, pointing the crew members towards the main equipment tent and sitting down next to Anna. "He'll be trying to lock you down ASAP."

Anna frowned.

"What do you mean, lock me down? That sounds so antiquated."

"I mean he clearly doesn't like you being away. You think he's gonna let you leave for three weeks at a time when you're married?"

Anna considered this for a beat. She knew her travel was stressful, and Nikos had made the occasional jab about her being away so much, but was it bad enough that even Marcus could tell? "Well, yeah, of course he would. He's always been super supportive."

"What about when you have a family?"

Anna paused again. She had to admit that she didn't think about family much. She wasn't sure if she even wanted kids. But she felt pretty sure that Nikos would want her to be able to do what she loved, wouldn't he?

"I don't know, but I can't imagine he'd mind."

Though she knew in a flash that that wasn't true. There had been a couple of arguments recently about how much time she was spending away. And if Anna were honest, she knew why. Four years ago, when Nikos had asked her to stay in Santorini and she'd said yes, he certainly wasn't imagining a life where she spent as much time away as she did with him. But she wasn't about to admit that to Marcus and give him the satisfaction of being right.

"Oh, yeah, that's right. I'd forgotten he doesn't work. Guess you've got a built-in trophy-husband-come-stay-at-home-dad all ready to go." Marcus smirked. "And yet you mock me for wanting the same."

Anna rolled her eyes. Sometimes, she remembered why she'd been with him all those years ago, and other times all she could remember was why she'd hated him. This was definitely the latter. He was seriously popping her bubble of bliss, and based on what? A couple of overheard phone calls?

"You really don't know us, Marcus. It's none of your business."

He held his hands up in surrender. "You're right, my bad." She stood up to leave, but he grabbed her hand and held her there for a moment. "It's just that people like you and me don't do well with being pinned down."

"You and I are not the same," Anna said, pulling away from him towards the gangplank. Outside of what they did for work, she was nothing like Marcus MacMillan, and she was certain she never would be.

"Fine. But a word of caution…"

Anna turned around, raised her eyebrows and shrugged, as if to say *what?*

"If you haven't had these conversations yet, I'd start having them now. Otherwise he's gonna ask a question you're not actually ready to answer."

Anna pursed her lips and walked away, headed back towards her tent. But as she plodded through the snow, she felt what Marcus had said melt away like the powder beneath her boots. She and Nikos were good. They were better than good – they were madly in love. And if Nikos asked her to marry him, there would be no hesitancy; no doubt.

If he proposed, she would say yes.

Chapter Three

Nikos motioned for Anna to stay where she was, which was odd in and of itself – who or what was he expecting that she couldn't see? But then, as he opened the door and began talking, Anna heard a familiar voice reply. She came up behind Nikos and saw Elena's boyfriend Vasilis standing at the entrance with a worried look on his face.

"Vasilis, what's wrong? Is everything okay?"

Both men looked her way, but they ignored her and continued talking. Anna crossed her arms and muttered under her breath. "Nice to see you, too, pal."

If they had intended for her to understand the conversation, they would have spoken English. Anna's Greek still wasn't great – Nikos, Elena, their friend Xenia, and Anna's grandmother Eirini all spoke in English, and she didn't spend enough time at home to ever feel fully immersed. But she had picked up a lot from Christos and Vasilis over the last few years, and from what she could tell, Vasilis and Nikos's conversation went a little something like:

• • •

Nikos: "It will be fine. She loves you very much."

Vasilis: "I don't know. Today is bad. Doing it in front of friends is a bad idea."

Nikos: "Elena loves attention. Tonight is the best attention."

Vasilis: "Are you sure?"

Nikos: "Yes. I am her cousin. Trust me."

Vasilis sighed, considered what Nikos was saying, and nodded. "Thank you," he said in English, which had significantly improved in the time he'd known Anna. Far more than her Greek had improved, in fact, which was saying something since they were in, well, Greece.

He smiled at her. "Nice to see you. I see you later." Then he waved and walked off down the drive.

From their conversation, Anna knew that Marcus had been right. Someone was getting engaged. But it wasn't her. And then something clicked for Anna – Elena's birthday was coming up. The party must be for her.

As soon as the door was shut, she hit Nikos in the arm. "What the hell was that about?"

Nikos shrugged. "Vasilis is just worried about the party. He doesn't want to overwhelm Elena."

"And why would Elena be overwhelmed by a party?"

Nikos nodded his head back and forth as he considered his response. "Because it's kind of a surprise birthday party for her."

"Bullshit," Anna said. "Not about the fact that it's a surprise party; she'll love that. But about being overwhelmed. You and I both know that Elena lives for this kind of attention, and Vasilis knows that better than either of us. So you'd better tell me what's going on."

Nikos shook his head. "Drop it, Anna. You'll see at the party."

As the two of them ate dinner – the baked chicken dish somehow tasting even more delicious than it smelled – Anna thought through what was going on. The ring must be for Elena, not for her. It was her party, her engagement. For a moment, Anna felt nothing but joy for Elena. Her life had been filled with a lot of loss, and she was so deserving of the happiness she'd found in Vasilis. But at the same time, Anna couldn't help but feel a little bit cheated of what she had thought might be her own big moment.

They cleared their plates, and as Nikos started to arrange the trays of food throughout the room, Anna began getting ready. Twenty minutes later, she emerged from the bathroom wearing a white linen minidress, her legs unbearably pale since her winter retreat in South America.

There were already a few people there, which was unusual for their friend group. Anna figured Nikos must have told them an earlier time to get them to arrive before Elena. Nikos had changed into chinos and a blue, short-sleeve button-up that was far from buttoned up, and now he was in conversation with Kostas and his girlfriend Katerina. He was gesturing to the drawing Katerina had done years ago of Anna and her father, which was now framed over the front door. Nikos loved that drawing. He missed his friend, and this was the closest thing to having him there.

But when Nikos saw Anna, his smile dropped and he hurried across the room. "Anna, you need to change."

"Why? I love this dress," Anna said, smoothing her hands over it self-consciously.

"Because. Just trust me."

Anna suddenly understood. She frowned and crossed her arms. "Do you wanna tell me what the hell is going on? Because if you know that my best friend is about to get enga—"

Nikos stepped forward and clamped a hand over her mouth, looking over his shoulder to see if anyone else had overheard.

They hadn't. "Keep it to yourself," he said. "Nobody is supposed to know. But trust me, you're going to want to be wearing a different dress."

Anna pressed her lips together and narrowed her eyes. But he was right. If Elena was about to get engaged, she would want to be the only one in white.

"Not sure how you're planning to regulate everyone else," she grumbled as he released her, but she obediently selected another dress from the wardrobe and returned to the bathroom, emerging moments later dressed in a grey jersey smock dress.

"Much better," Nikos said, kissing the top of her head. "You still look stunning, my love."

"Thanks," Anna said, standing on her tiptoes to kiss his mouth. "You don't look so bad yourself."

As more people began to arrive, Nikos turned into Superhost. Sometimes, it made Anna feel exhausted watching him make the rounds and jump from conversation to conversation, but tonight she felt a sense of awe for how hard he worked to make their house welcoming for others. He had clearly put in a lot of effort to make tonight special for Elena as well. She was the only family he had, and he was always thinking about how he could make her life better. In fact, he did that for everyone he loved – it was one of the things Anna loved most about him – but especially for Elena.

It was about quarter past eight when Nikos looked up from his phone and began shushing the room. It was packed full of Elena's friends from work and school and university, and the room was so full of excitement that it took a solid minute to get everyone to quiet down.

"Okay everyone, Vasilis and Elena will be here in about ten minutes. But this surprise party is going to be a little bit different. Once we've surprised her, don't rush her straight away. You'll see why."

He repeated the instructions in Greek, and then he began hiding people. A couple of times he even ran outside, checked to make sure he couldn't see anyone through the windows, and then ran back in to reposition them. Anna sat on the swing while he worked.

When he was satisfied that everyone was adequately hidden, he dropped down onto the swing outside with Anna and let out a deep exhale.

"Well done babe," Anna said. "She'll be super surprised."

Nikos chuckled. "She'd better be, or Vasilis might be too thrown to go through with..." He looked at Anna and shrugged. "You know."

"I do know," she said, "so you might as well tell me!"

Nikos shook his head. "Nope. No way. I'm sworn to secrecy. Even if you claim to already know, I'm not about to break my word by confirming it."

Anna laughed. "You're clearly such a tightly locked vault."

Nikos rolled his eyes and inhaled, ready for a verbal volley, but as he was about to respond, Elena stepped through the gate wearing a dress almost identical to the one Anna had been wearing before Nikos made her change. Anna breathed a sigh of relief that Nikos had been paying such close attention.

"Anna!" Elena shouted, running over and throwing her arms around Anna. The two of them hugged and swayed back and forth, mumbling about how much they missed each other. As they did, Anna saw Nikos pass the little red box to Vasilis behind Elena's back.

"Happy early birthday," Anna said as they pulled apart. "You look stunning."

"Thank you," she said, striking a pose and gesturing to the dress. "Vasilis bought it for me as a birthday gift. He's been properly spoiling me all day."

"Good man," Anna said, smiling at Vasilis, whose stern face almost made him look angry, though Anna was certain he was just trying to judge the moment right. Nikos said something to him, snapping him out of his trance, and he smiled.

"He's being so obvious," Elena whispered in Anna's ear. "A white dress, a clear setup for a surprise party… he even paid for me to get a manicure." She shimmied her shoulders and held up her hand for Anna to examine. Her nails were perfectly shaped and covered in subtle white glitter – just enough sparkle to catch the eye without outshining something else sparkly in close proximity.

"I assure you I have no idea what you're talking about," Anna said, but Elena wasn't even listening. She was just staring at her hand, no doubt imagining what it would look like with a diamond ring on it. These boys were terrible at surprising people, but at least Elena felt special. She deserved it. Anna just hoped Vasilis's offering would live up to her hopes and expectations.

"Well, shall we go inside?" Nikos asked, a bit too loudly, but Elena didn't miss a beat. She walked straight through the door, and when everyone jumped out and yelled "SURPRISE!" she gave the perfect impression of being shocked and startled.

But, instead of moving to crowd her, everyone stayed where they were, just as Nikos had instructed. And as Anna and Nikos stepped into the kitchen to join the crowd, Vasilis grabbed Elena's hands in his and dropped to one knee.

Seriously, she should have been an actress, Anna thought, watching Elena manufacture confused and excited expressions like a pro. Vasilis started speaking to Elena in Greek.

"You are the most beautiful woman I've ever seen," Nikos whispered a couple of seconds later, so quietly and so close to her ear that Anna felt chills run up and down her spine. Her belly tightened as his breath tickled her neck, flashing back to their reunion earlier. It took her a moment to realise he was translating for her, and as he breathed the words out quietly, Anna couldn't help but imagine him saying them just for her, his own little red box in his hands.

"The moment I saw you, I knew that I would do anything to spend the rest of my life with you. You bring joy to my life every single day."

At this point, Elena clearly wasn't pretending with the emotion anymore. Tears were spilling down her cheeks, though somehow she still looked glamorous, and her lip was trembling softly. Elena was an absolute showboat, but she was also wholeheartedly, undeniably in love with the man in front of her.

"You're the first thing I think about in the morning, and the last thing I think about before I close my eyes at night. And I can't imagine – don't want to imagine – a day where I wake up apart from you."

Nikos's voice faltered on the last part, and Anna's stomach dropped. The change in his energy was sudden yet palpable. She thought about all the mornings they woke up on opposite sides of the globe. Maybe that was bothering him more than he had let on. She hoped it wasn't getting in the way of him picturing a future together.

Vasilis pulled a box out of his pocket. "You make my dreams come true every time you look my way. Will you please, my love, make this dream come true as well, and marry me?"

Nikos's voice started to break, and Anna realised that he was tearing up. She felt a flood of affection for this man who loved his cousin so much that he would feel like this about her getting engaged.

But when she glanced at him, he wasn't smiling. They weren't happy tears.

Nikos was heartbroken. Anna had only seen him like that once before when he thought she was leaving him. And now he looked like that during what should have been the happiest moment any of them had experienced in years, and Anna knew why.

"Yes, of course I will," Elena said, bending down to kiss her now-fiancé on the lips.

And then Vasilis opened the box.

Anna couldn't see the ring from her angle, but she knew from Elena's expression that he had done well. Her eyes were as big as saucers, her mouth hanging open as she bent down to get a better look. The faces of the guests behind her mirrored her own shock and awe.

Vasilis pulled the ring out of the box and slipped it onto Elena's finger, and finally Anna could see what all the fuss was about. The ring contained a massive emerald-cut diamond with two smaller stones flanking it, and Anna was pretty sure even one of the smaller stones on its own would have been the biggest diamond she had ever seen in person.

"That's the last time we treat them to dinner then," Anna said with a laugh, turning to face Nikos.

Nikos visibly shook off his sad face and replaced it with a playful smile. How long had he been hiding these feelings behind his roguish demeanour?

Elena finally stopped staring at her new ring long enough to kiss Vasilis and immediately ran over to Anna. The two girls squealed, Anna gawking over the ring and how lucky Elena was, pretending not to notice Nikos shrinking into the crowd and busying himself with the food, instead of celebrating with his cousin. And as Elena talked about the advantages of a summer wedding versus a winter wedding, Anna saw Nikos shake Vasilis's hand, offer him a hug and then slip out the door.

After a short moment, Elena's other friends decided they had waited long enough and joined the excitement, giving Anna the opportunity to step away.

As soon as she turned away from the crowd, she felt her face collapse out of the plastered-on smile. She needed a moment to process what had just happened. She shut herself in the bathroom, put down a towel in the still-wet bathtub, and sat down inside, looking out the big picture window at the sunset over the hills of Santorini. Since her first summer on the island, this had been her favourite place to escape, in a spot that both connected her to her father and gave her a first-rate view of the place she now called home.

She didn't want to think about why Nikos was sad, because deep down she knew the answer. She knew that it was because he was jealous and hurt. Elena and Vasilis were engaged, and they weren't. And on some level Anna suspected that Marcus's words had some truth to them – that her travelling was contributing to that. She was so certain that he would be unconditionally supportive, but she couldn't shake the suspicion that her career was holding him back from taking that next step. And the fact that Nikos could feel less certain about being with her because of something so important to her was crushing.

Did Anna want to spend her life with Nikos? Absolutely. But did she want to "settle down"? Stop travelling and working and following the dreams she'd had inside her for so long – the dreams Nikos had helped her uncover all those years ago? No. She didn't. She had finally started to build a name for herself, and she had no intention of slowing down. Certainly not right now, and maybe not ever. She wasn't prepared to make any promises to that effect.

But of course, that didn't take away from her love for Nikos. If anything, feeling like the best version of herself made her even more in love with him. But was he as proud of her work as she'd hoped? As his hanging up her photographs around the house would suggest? Or was he secretly wishing that she wasn't quite so successful that it took her away from him?

Almost immediately, Anna started to mentally defend Nikos.

Of course he didn't want that. Of course he was happy for her and proud of her. Happiness for someone's success and wishing they were around more weren't mutually exclusive. Anna knew that. But she still felt a pang of doubt about how Nikos would feel if he thought Anna's globetrotting career would stay this busy long-term.

Her breath was getting faster, and Anna could feel panic rising up inside her. She could go anywhere and everywhere for work, but it only worked, only felt safe, if she knew she was coming home to Nikos. If she felt confident in her home here. If that were gone, she would be adrift at sea with no anchor. And the thought of that life made her feel seasick.

Anna pushed the thoughts away, gathering herself. She couldn't think about that now. Because as much as she was feeling in that moment – disappointment, fear, guilt – her best friend had just gotten engaged, and she was truly happy for Elena and Vasilis. She almost managed to convince herself that her heart was too full of joy for them to make room for this doubt. So Anna stood up, hung the towel over the edge of the tub, and re-entered the party.

An hour and a half later, after everyone had eaten their fill from the piles of meze Nikos had prepared, they began to filter out, planning to meet up at the resort bar for drinks. The renovation which had brought them together on that first day had been finished nearly three years ago, but it was still their spot and always would be.

Kostas and Katerina helped Anna wrap up the leftovers as Elena and Vasilis left hand in hand, waving at Anna and asking if they would see her at the bar. She didn't plan to go – she was far too jet-lagged for that, and she'd already said goodbye to Elena, so she waved them on.

Nikos was nowhere to be seen.

Just a couple of minutes later, Anna could hear muffled voices coming from outside. She busied herself sorting through the pile of jackets by the front door so she could hear better. They were speaking in English, which was strange enough.

"She'll get there, Nikos. Don't worry." The voice belonged to a woman, but Anna couldn't quite place who it was.

"I just feel bad," Nikos replied. "I'm meant to be happy for Elena, and here I am worried about my own relationship."

"That's how everyone feels at engagements and weddings," the voice replied. "No one's thinking about the other person for more than a few minutes. Most of it is either feeling sappy and in love or feeling sorry for yourself."

Nikos laughed. "I guess," he said, "I just don't know if I trust that she'll get there."

"Well, I don't know her, so I can't really say. But if she doesn't, then she's batshit crazy."

Another laugh, this time from both of them. "That's nice of you to say."

"I mean it." The woman paused for a moment before continuing. "You know, if you ever need to talk about it, I'm here for you."

"I know you are," Nikos said. "It's been really helpful having you around so much."

Anna realised she had been holding her breath trying to hear the conversation. Now all of a sudden she felt like she couldn't get enough air. She turned away from the door, grabbed a plate off the table and took it to the sink, turning on the tap but not actually washing anything. She just stood with her hands gripping the edge until her knuckles turned white.

Who had Nikos been spending his time with? Someone she didn't know who had been around long enough for Nikos to trust her and to tell her details of their relationship. She sounded English rather than American – maybe someone from university? Or maybe it was someone who came for the summer. Before they got together, Elena had warned Anna that Nikos had a tendency to fall for tourists…

She shook off that thought. She knew he wasn't flirting with holidaymakers anymore. That was years ago. But it still stung that he could have someone in his life that she didn't know about who he was close enough to for that kind of sharing. And who's to say how this woman felt about him?

She knew she should just go outside and introduce herself. Or bring Nikos inside. They clearly had a lot to talk about. But if she were honest, part of her felt relieved that she had something else to fixate on. As long as she had this, she could postpone the other conversation she could sense coming. She knew it was petty and avoidant, but in her tired state, she couldn't help herself. It was like a survival instinct. She actually felt relieved.

So in the spirit of avoidance, instead of joining them, she slipped on some shoes, grabbed her purse and keys, and stepped through the front door.

Nikos was on the swing alone. She'd half hoped for a glimpse of the mystery woman, but clearly, she'd scarpered off somewhere.

"Where are you going?" he asked. "I assumed you'd want to go to bed. You know, jet lag and all."

Normally, this comment would have been flirty, insinuating a continuance of their earlier encounter, but tonight it fell flat. Neither of them was pretending particularly well.

"Tonight's about Elena," Anna said, avoiding eye contact, even as Nikos stood up and walked over to her. "I feel like I should go support her."

"Yeah, well, I could think of better things to do," Nikos said, kissing her cheek half-heartedly, but Anna pulled away, and he didn't try very hard to stop her, or look particularly surprised when she did it.

"I'm sure you can," Anna said. "But I'm out." And then she turned and walked down the drive, leaving him standing there in the dark.

Chapter Four

Nikos

Nikos cursed as he cut himself yet again on the wire. The sun was beating down on his shoulders from overhead, and he had forgotten his sunglasses. This meant he was squinting as he wound the grapevines around the training wires he'd strung up, and every time he got close to where they were tied, he nicked his fingers on the sharp ends.

He pressed his now-bleeding finger to his mouth and sucked gently, then removed and examined it to see if more blood came. When none did, he turned his attention back to the vines.

Well, part of his attention. Most of it was focused on the party the night before, which may have been contributing to the frequency of his injuries.

It's not that he wasn't happy for Elena. He really, genuinely was – he was quite good at compartmentalising his feelings, it seemed. And when he thought about how happy Elena and Vasilis were, and how good a match they made, and what a beautiful celebration they would throw, his heart could have burst with joy.

But joy wasn't the only emotion from the night before – there was also fear, and sadness, and frustration. And it was these emotions that distracted Nikos from his work this morning.

Nikos and Anna had quite a lot in common, but one thing in particular was that they both wore their feelings clearly on their faces. So when Nikos had gotten choked up translating Vasilis's proposal, he knew that Anna would have been able to tell that it made him sad. And he knew that was true because, just as transparent as he had been, she had been, too. She had been concerned. Confused. And Nikos didn't blame her.

They hadn't talked much about marriage over the years, but Nikos knew that they were mostly on the same page. Even now, despite last night's falter, he knew that to be true. They both wanted to stay together forever.

What Nikos wasn't sure they agreed on was what "staying together" actually meant.

For Anna, it seemed to mean gallivanting all over the world with her ex-boyfriend, coming home – sometimes, only for a matter of days at a time – then jet-setting off to some other corner of the map. When she was home, things were amazing. She was just as playful and thoughtful and, of course, beautiful as the day he'd met her. But she'd grown more and more ambitious over the years, and whilst Nikos didn't mind that – in fact, it could be pretty attractive sometimes – it did sting a bit that her ambitions seemed to always take her away from him.

And that was where Nikos began to doubt their future. If Anna's deepest desires were taking her away from him, what kind of sense did it make for him to plan for a future with her? She wasn't even around for the present.

After Anna had left the night before, he'd gone inside and done what he normally did after Anna returned home from a work trip: he took the memory card out of the bowl and put it in the reader plugged into his laptop. He backed them up to his own hard drive – Anna was an organised person, but one could never have too many backups, right? – and then began to scroll through them. He'd seen every photo from every job she'd been on. Over the years, the number of photos she took had decreased; she was getting better and better at getting the shot without having to take hundreds of photos that were all the same. Her confidence was increasing, and Nikos could see it in her work.

Every time he did this, he picked out two photos: one that he thought would be the hero photo for the campaign, and one that was his personal favourite. They were rarely the same, Nikos's favourite always showcasing Anna's artistry whilst the hero piece usually showcased the product or location. But he was always right on the money.

This time, he struggled to pick a hero piece. Would it be the one of the backpacks stood up in the snow with the mountain behind them? Or would it be the one of the ice climber picking her way up a mountain with the brand name clearly visible on the back of her jacket? But his favourite was clear. There was a photo sandwiched between some product shots of the sun setting between two mountains, the sky a brilliant array of orange and purple, with a dark cloud framing the shot and providing contrast, making the colours even more vibrant. Based on where it was in the order, Nikos doubted this had been on the shot list. This was a spur of the moment photo.

He made a copy of the photo file to the folder on his desktop titled "ANNA PHOTOS TO PRINT". He wasn't sure where he'd put it, but it would be a tragedy to not dedicate some ink to the image.

Then, like he had a few times before, he swapped the memory

card out for the one labelled "HOME". But when he opened it up, he was disappointed to find that there weren't any new ones. He hadn't looked at it in months, and still the newest images were from Christmas.

Sure, Anna hadn't been around as much, but the lack of documentation made it seem like, even when she was there, she wasn't really there. For Anna, when she felt truly grounded and connected, she took photos. Always. And the fact that there were none left Nikos feeling worried that maybe she didn't feel as connected to Santorini – or to him – anymore.

"Penny for your thoughts?" Maria asked, appearing next to Nikos and making him jump.

"Jesus, where did you come from?"

Maria laughed. "Sorry, you seemed so lost in thought that I didn't want to disturb you. You've been twirling that vine around your finger for the last minute."

Nikos looked at his hands, and sure enough, he had a single vine twisted around his finger. He must have really zoned out.

"I just wanted to run through the logistics for the London event," she said.

Vasilis's cousin Maria had moved to the island around the same time as Anna, and whilst it took Nikos a while to meet her, they had become fast friends when they discovered a mutual love of winemaking. Maria worked at the vineyard next door, but she also ran the wine club Nikos was a member of, and she'd been instrumental in helping him develop his first couple of vintages. In fact, she was the reason he was out here this morning – she'd told him that he needed to be a bit more strategic with his sun exposure, so here he was, training the vines every day to make sure they had optimal sun.

Maria walked him through what he'd need for their upcoming trip to London, including how many bottles he'd need and who else would be there. Andreas, one of the other members of the wine club, would be entering as well, and Anna was even coming along. It was the first event she would be at since he'd started making wine; usually she was away, and even when she was home, Nikos always downplayed things. He didn't want her to feel like she had to spend her limited time on the island socialising with people she didn't know at an event she wouldn't understand. But he finally had a batch he was super proud of, and they were going to make a nice trip out of it.

Nikos couldn't help but feel nervous when he thought about the event.

Not because of his wine – Nikos was proud of his wine, but as long as it got a good score, he didn't really mind where he fell in the rankings – but because Anna and Maria had never met. More than that, Anna didn't even know that Nikos and Maria knew each other. And if she knew the extent of their relationship, Nikos knew she'd be hurt and confused. He would be too if the roles were reversed.

And that line of thinking took Nikos straight back to the party the night before. He hadn't meant to start venting to Maria, certainly not with Anna in the other room, but she was always so supportive, and he was seriously in his feelings about the proposal. But then the worst had happened, and Anna had overheard them.

Well, at least, Nikos was pretty sure she had. It was the only thing that could explain the way she'd left so suddenly, clearly angry with him, just after Maria had headed home. Nikos wondered how much of their conversation she'd heard.

"Nikos?"

Maria's voice cut through Nikos's thoughts, and he realised he'd zoned out again.

"Hey, are you okay?" Maria asked, stepping forward and putting a hand lightly on Nikos's bicep. He reached over with his opposite hand and put it on hers, giving it a squeeze.

"I'm fine," he said. "Just thinking about Anna."

"You two will be fine," she said, stepping closer. "You always are."

Nikos nodded. Maria was always there for him when he needed her most. He reached down and wrapped her into a hug, taking a deep breath, the smell of her shampoo mingling with the earthy scent of the vineyard. He hoped she was right.

Chapter Five

"I'm so glad you came out last night," Elena said way too loudly for Anna's liking. Her head throbbed as she stood to close the curtains.

"I'm not sure I am," Anna said, wincing as two dishes clinked together. Elena apologised.

The newly engaged Elena had brought the makings of a pancake breakfast over for the two of them to celebrate, though it was more of a brunch at this point given that it was almost midday.

The night before, Anna had stormed down the hill so quickly that she managed to catch up with everyone else, quickly losing herself in the party. If she danced enough and drank enough, she wouldn't have to think about who Nikos had been talking to or why he'd been so upset by Elena's engagement. At one point, when they were at the bar on the beach, Anna thought she'd heard the voice again, but when she spun around, there were so many people she didn't know that she wasn't sure where to begin, and she couldn't hear that English accent no matter how hard she listened.

Now, as she felt her dry mouth and her heavy head, she was regretting her night of avoidance. Nikos's early exit had woken her up as the door slammed shut, her hangover coming into crystal clear focus as the noise reverberated around her head. Part of her was convinced he'd done it on purpose after she'd woken him up when she came home in the middle of the night.

She assumed he was at the vineyard this morning, but he hadn't texted to let her know, so as far as she knew he could be out with this mystery woman somewhere.

"I'll never understand how you can be so perky after such a heavy night out," she said to Elena, sitting down at the table. As Elena set the pancakes down in front of her, the sweet, syrupy smell wafting into the air, Anna resisted the urge to pick them up and eat them with her hands. A takeaway cup of coffee quickly followed, and Anna could have cried with relief.

Elena sat down across from her. "Well, let's just say I had a little help perking up this morning…" Her eyebrows wiggled as she looked off to the side.

Anna faked being sick and rolled her eyes, then laughed. "Good for you. You've got something to celebrate."

"Hey, I'm sure you and Nikos did your fair share of celebrating yesterday, too… you were gone for a while."

Anna nodded as she thought about their reunion the day before, but she didn't respond. Instead, she took the opportunity to start in on her pancakes, but the second they hit her stomach, she felt queasy. She put her fork down, vowing never to drink again if it meant not enjoying pancakes.

She'd hoped her lack of comment would be ignored in favour of wedding talk, but Elena wasn't one to let things go. "What's wrong?" she asked, frowning. "Trouble in paradise?"

Anna shrugged. "I don't know. I'm just not so sure we're on the same page about the future." Elena kept looking at her, waiting for her to finish, so she continued. "When he said he had a surprise, I actually thought he was the one proposing – I'd forgotten about the surprise party."

Elena laughed. "Yeah, you know I would have killed you both." She turned her attention back to her pancakes but waved for Anna to continue. "So did that freak you out or something?"

"Actually no," Anna said. "Not the idea of him proposing. You know how I feel about him. But then Marcus said something that I didn't think much of at the time, but now it keeps bugging me."

Elena made a face when she heard Marcus's name. She had never understood how Anna could keep working with him, but didn't bring it up too much. She understood how important Anna's career was and begrudgingly recognised that Marcus was helping, but she had also made it clear that she thought he was capitalising on Anna's talent. "What did the parasite say?"

"He said that people like him and me don't do well with settling down."

"Well, the two of you are not the same."

"That's what I said. And honestly, until last night I would have agreed one hundred percent. But he's not wrong. I may be ready to commit to Nikos – I have been for a while, if I'm being honest – but I'm certainly not ready to settle down. And I know that Nikos loves me and wants me to be happy, but I guess it's hard to feel confident in how he feels without ever having had the conversation about what marriage would mean to him."

"Well then, you'd better have it," Elena said. "Because letting Marcus's words cloud your judgment of Nikos is ridiculous. You know those two men couldn't be more different."

"I know that," Anna said. "It's more that I'm worried Marcus and I are the ones who are alike."

Elena reached across and put her hand over Anna's. "You're nothing like him," she said. "But if you assume things about what Nikos wants and why without speaking to him, you're certainly acting like him."

Anna sighed. "I know you're right, but what am I supposed to say? 'Hey Nikos, I thought you were gonna propose, and now I'm nervous because my ex-lover reminded me how much I love to travel and I'm afraid you'll ask me to stop'?"

"If that's the truth, then, yeah."

"I don't want to hurt him though. He was really sad last night."

Elena frowned. "Was he? Why?"

"I'm not sure, I could just tell when he was translating the proposal for me," Anna said, taking another bite of her pancakes. This one went down a bit easier, so she kept eating. *Not to mention the fact that I heard him tell some sexy-sounding woman about it,* she wanted to add. But Elena was always so fiercely on Nikos's side, and she didn't want her thinking that she was making an accusation.

Elena finished her food and stood up to take her plate to the sink, the breeze from the open window catching her hair. "Well, nothing's worse than watching two people be miserable when all they need to do to fix it is just have a conversation. So I'd start talking before you make things worse. And I'd say the same thing to him if he were here."

"If who were here?" a voice asked through the window. Anna froze mid-bite. How long had Nikos been in the garden? How much of their conversation had he heard?

"Welcome back," Elena said, smiling casually. "There's pancakes in here if you want some."

"Count me in," Anna heard him say, and it sounded like he was coming around the house.

The door opened, and Nikos stood in the opening, using his heels to pry his muddy shoes off. He peeled his socks off as well, made a quick pit stop at the table to kiss Anna on the top of her head, dropped his socks in the hamper, and then headed for the bathroom.

"I'll just be a minute," he said. "Warm some up for me?"

"You've got it," Elena said as the door shut. A few seconds later the tap started running. Elena turned back to Anna. "Don't worry, he was just coming through the gate."

Anna breathed a sigh of relief and finished her pancakes.

When Nikos emerged from the bathroom, he was decidedly cleaner. He sat down next to Anna at the table, put a hand on her knee, and thanked Elena as she set a plate of pancakes down in front of him.

The two girls watched in amazement as Nikos used the fork to cut off nearly half a pancake and eat it in one bite.

"Hard morning at the vineyard?" Anna asked, laughing.

"Hey, let a man enjoy his pancakes in peace please."

Elena laughed. "A man, yes, but a hyena, no. Slow down."

Nikos made a big show of sitting up straight, using his knife and fork to cut off an unbelievably small piece, and raising his pinky as he lifted the bite to his mouth. Anna laughed, Elena rolled her eyes, and Nikos relaxed again.

"It's been ages since it's been just the three of us together," Nikos said. "Maybe since Christmas when Vasilis was in Athens?"

"That was great," Elena said. "I believe that's when we learned about the wonder and the danger of American eggnog."

Suddenly Anna's hangover felt a little bit better in comparison – and her stomach a bit worse – as she remembered how sick they'd all been after that.

"Surely it can't have been that long?" Anna said. "That's nearly five months!"

"No that's right," Nikos said. "Then you were in New Zealand for a couple of weeks, then I was in Slovenia, then you had Portugal, Barcelona and… what was the one where Marcus's intern booked you on the wrong flight?"

"Oh god, Georgia!" Anna said. "I was meant to be flying to Atlanta and she booked me a flight to Tbilisi."

"That's the one," Nikos said. "I can't believe he kept her around for so long."

"Well, he couldn't fire her," Elena said. "Then she wouldn't have slept with him anymore."

"Whatever," Anna said, not wanting to outright defend Marcus to them. "I got there eventually, and I even got to see Lizzy on that trip." Anna didn't get to see her big sister very often, so she took whatever she could get, even if it was just a quick coffee between a plane journey and a photoshoot.

Nikos laughed. "Fine, but the point is, we haven't all been together in a while. It's nice."

"Sure is," Elena agreed with a nod. "Both of you, what's your travel schedule for the next few months? I'll be planning a wedding pretty soon, and I need to know where you'll be."

Anna pulled out her phone and opened her calendar. "Well I'm in Ireland for a couple of days next week, and then we're in London for Nikos's friend's party, but I take it nothing will happen that quickly?"

"Doubtful, even for me."

"Okay, well, I'm not actually travelling for a while after that. I told Marcus I needed to work on my tan. Lizzy's here for a month, but I can be around for planning while she's here."

"Oh, perfect!" Elena said. "She can come along for the fun."

Elena and Lizzy had only met twice. Once when Anna's father Giorgos had passed away and Lizzy had come for the funeral, though Anna hadn't even been to Santorini yet at that point, and once the year before last when she'd come to help Nikos get the garden set up. Lizzy lived on a communal farm in Georgia (the one in the US, not the one where Anna had lost a suitcase and had to learn the Georgian word for "tampons") with her husband Martin, and she didn't get to leave very often, but she was Anna's best friend and they spoke every few days.

But despite only meeting for the second time, Elena and Lizzy had clicked instantly, and now Elena spoke to her almost as much as Anna did.

"But, yeah, I've just got jobs on the island this summer, and after that I've got lots dotted around for the rest of the year. When are you guys thinking? I know you haven't had much time since you got engaged, but let's not pretend like you haven't been thinking about this all year."

"Very true," Elena said, sitting up straight. "So as much as I love planning, I'm thinking about going for one of these all-inclusive deals. So the food, the venue and the entertainment all in one. And there are lots of beautiful places around here that need basically zero decoration, so that leaves me with invitations, flowers, the cake and the dress, and that's it!"

"Done and dusted," Nikos said. "Sounds like a groom's dream."

Anna and Elena both rolled their eyes, and Elena continued.

"So I've got a bit of a shortlist, and as much as I wanted a summer wedding, I think if any of them have availability this autumn or winter and can accommodate the out of town guests, we'll do it then! I'm too excited to let it drag out for ages."

"So soon," Anna said. "That's so exciting!"

"Yeah, well, we'll know more in the next week. I've already booked appointments for the next few days to have a look."

"The devil works hard, but Elena works harder," Anna said. "But good for you. Nothing like a bit of wedding shopping to celebrate."

"Damn straight," Elena said, flipping her hair over her shoulder. "Which reminds me, I'd better go. We're FaceTiming with Vasilis's family to celebrate."

"So much for our hangout!" Nikos said as Elena gathered her things.

"We'll do it again soon, I promise," Elena said. "You heard

Anna, she's around all summer! See you both this weekend for my birthday brunch, or maybe before."

Vasilis had planned the surprise party for the weekend before Elena's birthday to throw her off the scent, which meant she'd also planned Sunday brunch at a nearby resort to celebrate, just the four of them. Which was just as well, seeing as how the party ended up not being very much about Elena's birthday.

"Oh," Elena added as she opened the door, a mischievous smile on her face, "talk to him about what Marcus said!" And then she was gone.

Anna's face went red immediately. She looked down at what was left of her pancakes, willing them to swallow her, instead of the other way around.

"What's she talking about?" Nikos asked, scowling as he took another bite. "You're not going to be spending more time away, are you? Because it's already bad enough."

"No," Anna said, "it's not that." She took a sip of coffee as she processed what Nikos had said, and then frowned. "What do you mean 'bad enough'? I've been on some amazing jobs over the last year." She knew that wasn't what he meant, but she couldn't help but feel defensive.

"I know you have," he said, a bit of an edge to his voice. "I just miss having you around. It's hard feeling like you're only here part-time."

"I get that." She touched his arm. "But that's always been the case. I always wanted to travel for work."

"Not at the beginning," he said, sitting back in his chair. "You didn't start travelling until months later – until Marcus suggested it."

"Oh, so what, I tricked you into complacency and then took off? The old bait-and-switch?" Anna laughed and took a sip of her coffee, meaning it as a joke, but Nikos didn't smile. He just raised his eyebrows. "Wait, you don't really think that, do you?"

Nikos sighed and his scowl melted away. "No. Of course not. But it does sometimes feel like you'd rather be anywhere but here."

Anna instantly was transported back to her first summer on the island, when he'd taken her cliff jumping and told her he wanted her to stay, and she'd told him she didn't plan to. The same dejected look graced his face as he avoided her eye contact now, focusing on the plate in front of him.

All of a sudden, everything made sense. Just like he'd been afraid of her leaving when they first got together, of his little life on a little island not being enough for her, he was afraid that now she'd decided she'd had enough. That she was looking for an escape. It broke her heart to think he was feeling that way.

It also put her immediately on edge. Her mother had done the same thing to her father decades ago, leaving Greece unexpectedly when Giorgos was ready to commit. Now it triggered her anytime someone suggested she was trying to escape. And this was why – her mother had caused so much heartbreak and left so much devastation in her trail, and Anna couldn't imagine inflicting that on the people in her life, least of all Nikos.

She got up out of her chair, pressing on the table and swivelling into Nikos's lap, her legs draped casually around him. She put her arms around his neck and kissed his forehead.

"There is no place I'd rather be than right here," she said, resting her cheek on the top of his head. "If I could do what I do and always have you with me, I would."

He wrapped his arms around her and squeezed tight, nuzzling in closer. "I know that," he said. "But it's still hard."

They sat that way for a couple of minutes, not speaking, not moving. Anna felt their breath fall into sync, inhaling and exhaling as one. The breeze filtered in through the open window, pricking Anna's skin with goosebumps, the smell of flowers and dirt wafting in. This really was her favourite place in the world.

After a while, Nikos tilted his head back for a kiss, and Anna obliged.

"So, what was it that Marcus said then?"

"Oh, that," Anna said as nonchalantly as possible. "He just made some weird comments about us settling down."

"Like what?"

Anna looked up at the ceiling and took a deep breath. Now that she knew what was making Nikos so sad, she knew it was time to talk about it. Here goes nothing.

"That when you said you had a surprise for me, you meant that you were going to propose."

Anna expected him to laugh it off, maybe even scoff, but Nikos smiled and looked at the floor. "The thought has crossed my mind."

"Really?"

"Yeah, more than once, in fact. Ring shopping with Vasilis was particularly… inspiring."

Anna smiled. It was nice to know that she hadn't been alone in thinking about a future together. But she had more questions. Ones that would undoubtedly have a less pleasant outcome.

"But Nikos, *why* do you want to marry me?"

Now Nikos laughed. "Come on, Anna, you've never been one to need me to tell you why I love you. But I will if you need me to."

"No, that's not what I meant. I mean, why do you want to get married? A life together, sure. We have that now, and I think we both want that forever. But a wedding? Being husband and wife? Why is that important to you?"

Nikos frowned. "Are you saying you don't want those things?"

"I'm saying that I want to know why you do."

He paused and ran his hands through his hair, considering his answer. "I guess I've always wanted it," he said. "I grew up around Greek weddings, and the whole thing feels so special. So much like a celebration. And I want that for myself."

"So it's just the party part? Not the actual being married part?"

"No, I don't think that's true. It's all of it. What it symbolises." His gaze fell on her collarbone, and she swore she could feel it linger there. She loved when he got all sentimental. "You remember when we went to that wedding right after you moved here?"

Anna thought back to the first night they'd kissed. "How could I forget?"

"Well, every part of a Greek wedding is a symbol for something. But nothing is more of a symbol than the marriage itself. It's religious, but it's also deeply human. A reminder that as humans we're better together than we are apart."

Anna nodded. "That makes sense."

Nikos searched her eyes, clearly trying to gauge where her head was at. She could tell. She'd experienced it before. But if Anna was being honest, the appeal of wedding traditions had always gone a bit over her head.

"What about you?" Nikos asked, probing further, tensing beneath Anna. She knew it was nervousness, but she felt herself go warm in response. "What would marriage mean to you? A wedding?"

Anna shrugged. "I think it would be more about the commitment than the party. A statement that you're completely in love with the person in front of you, and that the life you've built together is what you want forever."

It wasn't exactly true. Anna knew that marrying someone was as much about committing to future versions of a life together as it was about affirming what already was. But she wanted Nikos to give some indication of whether marriage for him would mean her settling down.

Instead, he just nodded. "Well, there you go," he said.

"There you go," she said in reply, but she wasn't sure what exactly they were acknowledging. She was sure, however, that she wasn't in the mood to push it. She was in the mood for something else entirely.

Anna repositioned her hips to bring them even closer together, wrapping her legs tighter around him and arching her back. Her dress fell over both of them, and there was nothing but Nikos's shorts between the two of them. She felt him notice.

"So what does that mean for us?" she asked, moving her hips just a bit as she breathed in and out, feeling the blood rush to where she could feel him beneath her.

"I guess it means we should talk a bit more about this," he said, his eyes growing heavy. His hands moved over Anna's back and down to grab her from behind, pulling her tighter into him as he pressed himself upwards.

"I guess so," she whispered in his ear. "Another time, perhaps."

"Mm-hm," Nikos moaned, and as she stood up and led him to the bed, they both forgot all about Marcus, Elena, or getting married. In that moment, there was only them.

Chapter Six

As usual, the smorgasbord of food Eirini made for lunch was delicious. Greek meatballs, grilled aubergine, dolmades, stuffed olives, and more dips and spreads than Anna could name had all been spread out on the table in front of her. Now only the leftovers remained – though in this case, that was nearly half the food, because Eirini had never once failed to over-serve.

Every Friday that she was home, Anna came to the main house for lunch, and she was pretty sure Nikos had never missed one, even when she wasn't there. And every week, she knew she'd eat so well that dinner plans were rendered superfluous. Today, she was so stuffed that she suspected any attempt to eat that evening might actually be painful.

"Incredible as usual, Yaya."

"Thank you dear. I'll make you a plate to take back with you."

"Extra pita please?" Nikos asked, a childish smile plastered across his face. Eirini just laughed and nodded in response – he always asked for extra pita, and she always prepared extra for when he asked.

It usually took Anna and Nikos at least three days to get

through the leftovers after a Friday lunch, opting to snack on the leftovers to draw them out as long as possible.

Despite living in their garden, Anna really only saw Eirini and Christos a couple of times a week. She knew they were trying to give her space, especially since Nikos had moved in, and she appreciated it. It was nice to feel like they were adults building a life together, not kids living with her grandparents.

But sometimes, Anna wished she saw more of them. She'd missed so much time with them growing up. She'd never even met them until four years prior when she'd first inherited the summer house. And now, seeing them every few days didn't always feel like enough, especially when they were living so close.

Sometimes, Eirini spent time with Nikos in the garden, and it made Anna happy to know that he got on so well with her grandparents. But really, she wasn't surprised – they were as much his family as they were hers. Before Anna's father Giorgos had died, he had helped raise Nikos, who had lost everyone else close to him except Elena. They both worked for Christos's construction company, and Giorgos had paid for Nikos to attend university in London. They were best friends until the day Giorgos had died, and Anna wished every day that she could have known them both at that time.

When Giorgos passed, Eirini and Christos stepped in as parental figures for Nikos. The three were so close by the time Anna had come to Santorini that Nikos was driving their truck and eating their food most days. Once, Anna had questioned whose side they would take if Anna and Nikos broke up, in a purely hypothetical sense. In response, Eirini had slammed her hand down on the table and stated, "Family is everything, Anna, and it saddens me that you would doubt us." It was nice to hear, but Anna was always acutely aware of the loss they would feel if the relationship did end.

Not that Anna thought their relationship was in jeopardy, but it was hard to separate her life on the island from her life with Nikos, sometimes, even where her own family was concerned. Her best friend was his cousin, her other friends had been his first, and her grandparents were basically a surrogate family for him. Especially once Nikos moved into the summer house, her inheritance from her father, she became acutely aware, even if only in the back of her mind, that very little of her life was just hers, and any one thing failing could cause the rest to unravel. Perhaps that was part of why her career was so important to her.

"Where's Pappouli?" Anna asked. It was unusual for Christos to miss their lunches, especially since he retired.

Eirini sighed. "Down at the beach. Don't ask."

Anna chuckled. "Xenia tells me he's been making a fuss down there."

"That man would do well to stay home and read and watch television like any other respectable retired Greek man. But no, he has to 'find his passion,' whatever that means." Eirini was marching around the kitchen now, grabbing various containers of food, waving her hands as she spoke. "Back in my day we didn't need a life passion, we just needed a roof over our heads and food in our stomachs and a seat at church on Sundays."

A mere three days after he had retired, Christos had announced that he was going to find his passion in life. So far he'd tried surfing (he'd nearly drowned), cliff jumping (again, nearly drowned) and sailing (nearly drowned four people, including himself). Nikos had even found him picking grapes in his vineyard one day, having shown up and picked up a basket without a word to anyone, just watching what the others were doing. But, so far, nothing had seemed to stick longer than a few attempts.

Now, he had decided his calling was competitive sandcastle building. One of the hotels at Kamari Beach held a contest every year, and he had been practising almost daily trying to build something that would beat last year's winner.

A few days ago, he'd decided the black sand at Kamari wasn't suitable for sandcastles, so he'd brought a wheelbarrow full of white sand from god knows where onto the beach. Which was sacrilege enough – people came from all over the world to see the black sand beaches – but to add insult to injury, he'd wheeled it straight through the lobby of Kamari Sands, Xenia's resort, leaving piles of sand where he'd struggled to control the overfull wheelbarrow.

Nikos and Anna both laughed when Eirini told them this. "Hey, at least it goes with the name, right?" Nikos said, waiting for her to laugh. "Get it? Kamari *Sands*?"

Anna rolled her eyes but smiled.

Christos was the most genuine, kindhearted man on the planet, much less the island. No one could be mad at him for long. No one except Eirini, that was. And as if on cue, Christos came strolling through the open side door into the kitchen, completely covered from the shoulders down in sand.

"Anna! Nikos! I am sorry I am late," Christos said, bending down to plant a sandy kiss on Anna's cheek.

"Hi, Pappouli, it's okay."

"*It is not okay!*" Eirini shouted. And then she started yelling in Greek, so fast and furious that Anna had no idea what she was saying, gesturing to his sandy clothing and then to the food she was packing away. She shouted him straight into the other room and then walked back in as if nothing had happened. A moment later, they heard the shower start.

"We're so excited to see Lizzy again," Eirini said over her shoulder as she resumed scooping leftover baked feta onto a large dinner plate, pretending like she hadn't just been shouting at her husband.

"She's excited to see you, too," Anna said, exchanging a look with Nikos. They were both holding back their laughter.

Nikos took a deep breath, putting on his serious face. "We should call her and find out what she wants to do while she's here. It's tourist season, so we may need to book things."

"Oh, call her now!" Eirini said, turning around and plopping down next to Anna at the table. "I haven't spoken to her since you were in Atlanta a few weeks ago. I just want to say hello and then I'll let you talk."

Anna smiled and pulled out her phone. "Let me see if she's free."

She found Lizzy's name in her contacts and tapped the button to FaceTime her. A few seconds later, her face appeared on the screen. She was walking away from what Anna recognised as her house, a scowl plastered across her face.

"Hey Anna," she said, but her voice sounded far from chipper, her usual nickname for Anna passed over.

"What's wrong?" Anna asked. "Do you want me to call back later?"

Lizzy rolled her eyes. "No, definitely not. Martin's taken enough from me lately, I'm not going to give him the satisfaction of keeping me from talking to you because I'm too worked up. What's up?"

Nikos and Anna exchanged a look. Lizzy and Martin had been having trouble lately. Anna didn't know why, and Lizzy hadn't offered any information, but every time his name came up, she would get irritated and change the subject. When they'd gone for coffee a few weeks ago, Lizzy had seemed sad and evasive when Anna brought him up, but over the weeks since then, it had gone from sadness to fury.

"We've got someone here who would really love to talk to you," Anna said, turning the phone towards Eirini, who was grinning ear to ear and waving far too close to the phone. Lizzy's face softened when she saw her.

"Good to see you, Yaya."

"I love you, Lizzy!"

"Love you, too."

Eirini blew a kiss at the phone and then nodded at Anna, who propped the phone up against the salt canister. Nikos came around to sit next to Anna as Eirini got up to resume her leftover assembly.

"We wanted to know what you want to do while you're here," Anna said, reaching over to the sideboard to grab a pad and pencil from the top drawer where Eirini kept them. "Things might start booking up soon, so we thought we should get a list going."

Lizzy waved her hand dismissively. "I don't mind what we do, I just want to tag along with you," she said. "Elena already told me I'm invited to all the wedding stuff that I'm there for, so don't feel like you have to entertain me."

Nikos jumped in. "But the last time you were here, we just spent the whole time in the garden. And the time before that you were here for a funeral. You haven't exactly gotten to experience the island."

Anna thought back to the summer she'd come to Santorini, and how Nikos had taken great care to make sure she got to do all the touristy things, and a few things that were extra special. She had not only fallen in love with the island along the way, but with him as well. She loved seeing him show off his home.

"Don't listen to him," she said, "He'll make you fall in love with him and then we'll have to fight for him." Anna winked at Nikos, who leaned in and planted a kiss on her cheek.

Lizzy made a barfing noise. "Well, you know I'm not much for touristy stuff. I just want to eat good food and have a good time."

Anna shrugged. "Okay well, should we at least book a couple of touristy things just to appease Nikos?"

Lizzy laughed. "Sure. Whatever you need to sleep well at night, big guy."

Nikos smiled back.

They spent the next few minutes brainstorming things that Lizzy could do, from sailing around the caldera to hiking through the hills. Anna hoped there wouldn't be too much to do for the wedding so they could get to everything. Eirini suggested that they take a tour of some of the island's churches. She was on the other side of the kitchen, so Lizzy couldn't see her wink, and try as she might to keep a straight face, Lizzy couldn't help but wrinkling her nose. "No thanks, Yaya. But we can definitely do some recipe swapping!"

Eirini just laughed and resumed her tidying.

After they hung up, Anna snuggled up close to Nikos.

"I'd forgotten about some of the things we did that first summer," she said. "You really did lay it on pretty thick, huh?"

Nikos laughed. "I guess I did. But can you blame me?" He kissed the top of her head.

"We should do some of that stuff this summer, even if Lizzy doesn't want to," Anna said. "Just you and me. It's been a while since we did something exciting and romantic like that."

"That would be really nice," Nikos said softly, and Anna could feel his face move as his smile widened.

A few minutes later, Nikos stood up to leave. They were bottling the first batch of wine for the season, and he wanted to be there. Anna offered to tag along, but he said he wanted it to be a surprise.

When he left, Anna stood up to help Eirini, who was now cleaning the kitchen.

"Yaya, how did you meet Christos?" she asked, drying a plate and placing it on the shelf. She couldn't believe she'd never asked before, and clearly the older woman needed a distraction from the present struggle.

The old woman smiled, her eyes crinkling in a way Anna rarely saw. Affection was all over her face, and she looked decades younger in an instant.

"We were very young," she said. "I was fourteen, and he was nineteen. That wasn't so strange back then."

Anna smiled. The age gap was a bit uncomfortable, but the fact that they'd known each other for so long was, she thought, incredibly romantic. To know that your roots and someone else's are so entwined. That you come from the same place. You don't have to explain yourself as much, because the cultural and personal context is a shared experience. Sometimes, she wished she and Nikos had that.

"Did you meet in school?"

Eirini shook her head. "I wasn't in school. It was a different time then. Your grandfather finished school quite young too and began apprenticing for his father. But we met at church."

Anna smiled. Of course they did. Eirini was a devout churchgoer. It wasn't really Anna's cup of tea, but she loved how the traditions and beliefs permeated the lives of her grandparents. It didn't surprise her that that's where their relationship had begun.

"I grew up on Thirasia, as you know, but I was attending a new church, having moved to the main island to live with my cousins after my mother died. Sort of like Elena and Nikos. And as soon as I walked into their church, there he was, standing with his mother. We locked eyes, and something in me knew, even at that age, that my life and his would always be connected."

"How long did you date before you married?"

"Oh, we never really dated. We were friends for over seven years, and then one night, he came to my house in the middle of the night, kissed me for the first time under the stars, and asked me to marry him."

Her eyes were practically twinkling as she told the story.

"That's amazing," Anna said. "And it was happily ever after?"

"Yes it is," Eirini replied, smiling wide as she placed the last dish on the shelf. But then she turned to Anna, and her face became very serious. "But Anna, my dear, I don't think you should romanticise that kind of relationship. It's not what someone like you should aspire to."

Anna's throat felt tight. She had always thought Eirini and Christos had a wonderful marriage, but maybe it wasn't as rosy as it seemed. And what did she mean by "someone like you"?

Eirini must have seen the panic on her face, because she took Anna's face in both her hands and said, "Your grandfather is a wonderful man, and we have a beautiful life together. Do not worry."

Anna breathed a sigh of relief and took Eirini's hands in hers. "Then why wouldn't I want what you have?" she asked. "You're happy, and still together after all these years."

"Because," Eirini said, gesturing for Anna to sit down at the table, "I think you and I are more alike than you think. And I am so very happy, yes. But if I had all the opportunities that you do, I don't think I would be content being a housewife."

Anna sat down across from her grandmother, still holding her hands. "What do you mean?"

Eirini paused and looked away, her brow pinched tight and her lips pursed. "I mean," she said after a moment, "that I have a lot of passions in life. Making food, making clothing… I truly do love those things, and my family always told me that they would make me a great wife. And I believed them, because very rarely did women start businesses or pursue their passions unless they were alone in life. At the time, there was nothing worse than being alone. But if I had known that I could open a restaurant or travel the world or have a career, then I would never have been content with the life I ended up living."

"And you don't think Christos would have let you do those things?"

Eirini shrugged. "I don't think it occurred to either of us. Your grandfather is not a progressive man, but he has always wanted me to be happy. So as long as your father was looked after, I'm sure he would have been fine with it. But I didn't know that was an option for me, so I was content with what I had. What I still have."

Anna considered this for a moment. She could see where Eirini was going with this. "But I already have more. And you're saying that to give that up would be too much compromise. That I wouldn't be happy."

Eirini nodded and gripped Anna's hands tighter. "Yes, exactly Anna. You have everything for yourself that I would have wanted if I had known it was possible. Success, freedom, independence – those things aren't mutually exclusive with having a family and building a legacy. And you shouldn't have to give up one to have the other. Not if you're with the right person and doing the right thing for you."

Eirini watched Anna for a moment as her words sunk in. Anna felt like she couldn't move, lest what Eirini had said land within her and jeopardise the delicate balance she'd established; lest she have to admit that what her grandmother was saying to her was more relevant than she wanted it to be.

"When I said we didn't need passions back in my day, just food and shelter and God, I didn't mean that we wouldn't have wanted them. I meant that we didn't know they were possible. Men took over their father's businesses, and women made homes and children for those men, and raised the children so the cycle could continue. And now your grandfather has decided that passion is important, but I'm still here, making his food and keeping his home."

Tears were forming in Eirini's eyes now, and Anna squeezed

her hands a bit harder. They hadn't let go of each other the whole time, and Anna wasn't about to let go now.

"I love your grandfather with all my heart, and nothing could make me happier than seeing him happy and free. Except, maybe, if we could experience that together. And sometimes it breaks my heart that it hasn't occurred to him to ask."

Anna thought about her grandmother's words all day. She'd never said anything about her arguments with Nikos, but now she wondered if Nikos had been complaining to Eirini and Christos about how much she had been away. It would explain why it had seemed so urgent. Or maybe Anna was headed down a path that was obvious to everyone but her. Was she turning into a cautionary tale? It was so hard to take Eirini's feedback on board objectively because she was so in love with Nikos that it felt impossible that something could be fundamentally broken there.

She understood what Eirini meant. Now that she'd experienced real success, she wouldn't be content with less. But Anna was sure she wouldn't have to give up her career altogether in order to assuage Nikos's feelings of abandonment. She just needed to find a way to gauge whether he was feeling this way, too, or if she was piecing together two completely unrelated instances – Eirini's plea and Nikos's emotional reaction to the proposal.

And then, a niggling little voice popped up in Anna's thoughts.

What about the mystery woman?

She knew she was self-sabotaging. She knew she was bringing this up because it was easier to fixate on an external issue than address the real issue with Nikos. But she couldn't help herself. Somewhere on this island was a woman whom Nikos trusted with their relationship woes – woes he hadn't even articulated to Anna. And yet she knew nothing about this person.

She believed nothing was going on between them, as easy as it would be to fall down a rabbit hole of speculation. So all she needed to do was find out who this woman was and why Nikos was keeping her a secret. Then she could address things properly.

Chapter Seven

Anna's calves burned as she climbed the hill behind Nikos on their way to meet Elena and Vasilis. One downside of being away so much was that she had quickly lost her stamina. Apparently even lugging her camera equipment through the snowy mountains of Chile didn't cut it against the hills of Santorini. She had started running whilst away on jobs, and that helped, but wearing heels always cut her fitness level in half, and today was no exception.

It had only been two days since her chat with Eirini, but Anna had already let herself spiral out multiple times. Not that she could hash it out with Nikos, of course. When Nikos got home that night Anna was already asleep, and when she woke up the next morning, he was out at one of his winemaker meetups. Anna went to Elena's to help her make a list of the white clothing items she'd require now that she was officially a bride, and when she walked back to the summer house, Nikos was leaving to go play video games with Kostas. A few near misses and sliding doors, and they had found themselves having spent less than an hour together since that lunch.

All Anna had been able to think about was the Englishwoman she'd heard at the party. She knew in her heart that nothing was happening, but she couldn't help herself. It all felt overwhelming and big, and it was easier to cling to the petty. She also suspected Nikos was feeling the tension, otherwise he likely would have tried to spend more time with her over the last couple of days. Maybe it was the fact that she'd be home most of the summer, but usually they tried to cram as much quality time in as possible.

On top of her relationship woes, knowing that Elena's engagement had brought up so many feelings for Nikos had made it hard to separate her joy for her friend from her fears about her own relationship. So when she thought about the wedding, she couldn't help but feel afraid about what it meant for her. She felt like she was falling behind in a race she wasn't sure she wanted to be running simply because her boyfriend had gotten teary for ten seconds at a party. It was amazing how quickly things could change, and the lengths she would go to in order to avoid confronting that change.

"Nikos, can you slow down please?" Anna called up to him, short of breath, as they walked up a stone staircase. Nikos turned around and laughed.

"We've only been walking for fifteen minutes. You really have lost your edge."

To Anna, everything he had said the last few days sounded like a reminder of how much time she spent away from home. He came to a stop at the top of the stairs.

"Remind me why we couldn't bring the Vespa?" she asked, brushing off his comment.

"Because you trying to elegantly dismount from a Vespa in a dress is just about the most inelegant thing there is."

Anna rolled her eyes as she reached the top.

"Plus," he said, "we're here."

They walked down a small hill and through the entrance of a resort Anna had never heard of – Carpe Diem.

"What is this place? Why wouldn't we just go to Kamari Sands?"

"Trust me," Nikos said, "this place is a bit classier than Kamari Sands. No offense to Xenia, but this place is on another level. Plus, I think Elena and Vasilis wanted to check it out as a possible venue."

Their friend Xenia owned the nearby Kamari Sands resort, where they'd had celebratory drinks after Elena's party, and where Anna had spent most of her free time during her first summer in Santorini. In fact, her first photography job had been to capture the new renovation once it was complete. But as lovely as Kamari Sands was, it was more of an upscale party spot than a classy retreat.

As they walked through to the restaurant at Carpe Diem, Anna found herself gasping in a way she rarely did anymore. She had travelled the world and seen so many beautiful vistas, but from time to time the beauty of Santorini stopped her in her tracks. And she had never seen a view of Santorini quite like the one laid out in front of her.

Everywhere she turned, it looked like the cover of a travel magazine. There was a picturesque stone building behind her, a stunning infinity pool in front of her, and the northern end of the island stretched out beyond that. She could see the boxy white buildings and bright blue domed roofs Santorini was famous for dotting the landscape, the wisps of cloud overhead throwing gentle shadows across the hills. It was views like this that had made Anna fall in love with Santorini to begin with.

Anna felt a tap on her shoulder and spun around to find Elena grinning from ear to ear.

"Ah! Happy birthday!" Anna said, hugging her close.

"I have so much to catch you up on about the wedding," Elena said, guiding Anna towards a nearby table where they'd clearly been waiting, a half empty bottle of wine resting in a rose-gold chiller, with two of the four glasses in use. Nikos and Vasilis followed as the girls sat down.

"It's only been a week. How can there be that much to report?" Nikos asked, grabbing the menu in front of him and scanning it briefly. A waiter approached the table with another bottle in his hands.

"Ms Doukas," he said, nodding at Elena before popping the cork. Elena did a little golf clap as another waiter appeared with champagne flutes. The waiter poured glasses for the whole table, and Elena almost immediately started taking selfies of her ring-laden hand holding the champagne, no doubt using a filter to add even more sparkle to both. Not that the ring needed much help.

"Lunch is on us today," Elena said with a grin as she set her phone down, and Anna smiled as she remembered her joke about paying for meals.

Vasilis cleared his throat. "Well, it is on resort."

"Why's that?" Anna raised one eyebrow at Elena, looking back and forth between the happy couple. They looked at each other and then raised their glasses in unison.

"We getting married!" Vasilis shouted.

"Yeah, we know mate, you got engaged at our house," Nikos said, patting Vasilis on the arm. Anna laughed. "I helped you plan the whole thing."

"What he means is that we're getting married here," Elena clarified, grinning manically as if in anticipation.

"Oh that's great!" Anna said, raising her glass to chink against Elena's, but she didn't return the gesture.

"In three weeks."

Anna nearly dropped her glass.

"Excuse me?" Nikos asked.

"You're doing what now?" Anna added.

"You heard me," Elena said, a sly smile on her face. She clearly loved the shock value of the situation. "We're getting married right here in three weeks. From yesterday."

Anna blinked at her, not knowing how to respond.

"Surely a place like this gets booked up way in advance," Nikos said, looking around, then lowering his voice to a stage whisper. "Plus, do you really want a bunch of random hotel guests at your wedding?"

"That's the best bit," she says. "The whole hotel was booked up for a wedding. But the wedding got cancelled. We were here to see the space when they got the call. So they asked us if we fancied having the whole hotel to ourselves for four days at an absolute steal, and we said yes!"

Based on the size of Elena's ring, Anna very much doubted she needed to worry about finding "a steal," but nonetheless she felt her gaping mouth shape into a smile. This was so quintessentially Elena and she loved it. "You're getting married in three weeks," she said, nodding at her friend.

"I'm getting married in three weeks," Elena affirmed, smiling back, tears forming in her eyes.

Both girls stood up from the table at the same time, wrapping each other in a hug.

"I'm so happy for you," Anna said into Elena's hair, and she really meant it with all her heart. Elena had found someone who loved her exactly as she was, penchant for crazy plot twists and all. That was something to celebrate, no matter what else was going on in Anna's life.

After a moment of excitement, they sat down and ordered lunch. There were lots of questions – "What about all your friends abroad?" "If they want to be there, they'll be there." "How are you going to get a dress that quickly?" "I've got an appointment booked for tomorrow. Will you come with me?" "I wouldn't miss it for the world." "Where will the ceremony happen?" "Right down on the cliff side. It's gorgeous." – but mostly, there was laughter and champagne and celebration, all bubbly and intoxicating.

As the plates were cleared, Elena suddenly got very serious. She looked at Vasilis, who winked at her, nodded his head and adopted a sombre look.

"What's all this about then?" Nikos said, noticing the change in tone.

"Anna, I have something very serious to say to you, and I need you to not be upset."

Anna felt herself panic. What was this about? Had Nikos been talking to them, too?

"Why, what did I do?"

"Well, it's more about what you're going to do. Or not do, actually."

Anna gulped. She knew she hadn't done anything wrong, but she couldn't help feeling nervous. "Well, whenever you're ready, this is all very mysterious."

"Anna," Elena said, then paused, no doubt for dramatic effect, "I don't want you to be the photographer at my wedding."

Anna scoffed, forgetting instantly that this was clearly a bit. "Don't be ridiculous. Of course I'm the photographer. And I don't want any of this crap about not being able to enjoy the wedding if I'm taking pictures. You know I love taking pictures."

Elena shook her head. "I think I know what's best for my wedding. I can't very well have my maid of honour taking time away from her important duties to take pictures."

Anna stared at Elena, who deadpanned back for a few seconds until she couldn't help but smile. It took a moment before Anna understood what was happening.

"You want me to be your maid of honour?" she asked, tears forming behind her eyes.

Elena nodded.

"Are you sure?" Anna felt a tear fall down her face.

"I'm as sure about that as I am about the guy I'm marrying," she said. "No offense babe," she added to Vasilis.

"Is okay," he said, turning to Nikos. "And I would like very much you be my *Koumbaro*."

Nikos grinned and shook Vasilis's hand before wrapping him in a hug, too. "It would be my honour."

"Seriously, we couldn't imagine anyone else standing up there with us but you two," Elena said. "Thank you for being in our lives. Thank you for being our family."

The tears were falling freely now, and Anna raised her glass yet again to toast Elena and Vasilis. Between the views and the drinks and the celebratory atmosphere, she was starting to feel more enamoured by the minute.

After lunch, the four of them moved to the bar where they ordered more drinks, toasting round after round to marriage, to family, and to the future. At some point, Nikos snaked his arm around Anna's waist from behind, and she leaned her head back to look at him. They held eye contact for a moment, a knowing look passing between them – that they had some things to work through, but they'd be okay. The love was there between them and it was strong. It was all around them. And it would see them through.

Chapter Eight

The next morning, Anna kissed a sleeping Nikos on the forehead and left for a morning run. She had started running nearly three years prior on her first overseas job with Marcus. They had been in Hong Kong, and one of the crew members suggested a sunrise run along the harbour to wake them up. Marcus had called it quits after that trip, but Anna had been running ever since, to the point that now her at-home route consisted of a five-mile loop with an elevation change of over a thousand feet.

This was the route she had decided to run this morning. The hills of Santorini did not make it easy, however, nor did the pounding in her head after the previous night's celebratory drinks. After their late-lunch-turned-happy-hour at Carpe Diem, they had gone back down to Kamari Sands so Elena could ask Xenia to be a bridesmaid. Not only had she happily accepted, but she'd opened a tab for them at the beach bar, and then the rest of the evening was a blur. Anna was going to have to curb the drinking this summer if she wanted to actually remember any of it.

Nikos and Anna had tumbled into bed just after midnight but didn't go to sleep until nearly three. Now it was nearly lunchtime, and Anna knew that the only way to make herself feel up to an afternoon of dress shopping was to bite the bullet and go for a run.

As she struggled up the hills, her legs and her lungs straining against the fatigue, she mentally prepared to spend time with Elena's other friends. She had vowed to get to know other people on the island better, but Nikos was right – with all of her travels, she barely had free time for the people she did know, much less for meeting new people. When she saw Elena, it was always just the two of them or a double date with Vasilis and Nikos in tow. Kostas and Katerina had come along sometimes, as well, but Katerina worked nights most of the time, so it was rare. Occasionally she and Xenia would meet up for coffee, but it was usually work-related. Not that either of them minded – in fact, Anna was glad to have a friend she could speak to about work without feeling guilty for how much time she spent away.

From what Elena had said the night before, the other bridesmaids were her friend Thea from university, who lived in Athens, and Vasilis's cousin Maria. Anna only remembered Maria as the girl Nikos almost went on a date with when Anna had first moved to Greece; she had never actually met her. She wasn't sure how often any of them saw her.

As Anna approached the final mile of the route, she thought about Nikos lying in bed waiting for her to come home. To put it simply, they'd had a lot of sex since she got home. And as good as it was – and boy was it good – she knew that she, for one, was using it as a way to avoid the conversation she could feel coming. She wondered if maybe he was doing the same.

They had agreed to go to a meze restaurant down the road for dinner, plans made in a post-lovemaking haze at about two in the morning. *Tonight is the night,* Anna thought. She didn't like this feeling of walking on eggshells, and as afraid as she was to open the Pandora's box of discussing their future, she just wanted to get back to normal, where she would get giddy anytime someone mentioned a wedding rather than feeling a pit form in her stomach. Maybe having dinner out would help. They couldn't exactly have a shouting match over the pasta elias and pita, could they?

Anna came to a stop at the gate to the summer house, nearly doubled over with exhaustion, and stepped into the garden to cool down.

When Nikos and Lizzy had designed the layout of the garden, they had left a small grassy patch at Anna's request. And as she lay down to do some stretches, she admired yet again the work he had done. Not only was the produce ripe and abundant, begging to be picked, but the flowers were gorgeous as well. She felt a quick pang of guilt that he had done all of this without her, that he was quite literally cultivating their home in a way that she wasn't, but she reminded herself how much he seemed to love it. Even when they had fixed up the summer house together four years ago, he had gone all in on every last project. It was this level of consideration that made her sure that he had been thinking about their future, whether he was talking to her about it or not.

As Anna was coming out of downward dog, she heard the summer house door open. She looked up to see Nikos holding a cup of coffee in one hand and a glass of water in the other.

"I wasn't sure which one you'd want," he said, "so I brought both."

Anna smiled as she pushed herself to her feet, accepting the water. She chugged it in about five seconds, then reached out for the coffee. Nikos smiled.

"I've got mine over by the swing. Care to join me?"

Anna followed him over to the patio, where they swung in silence for a few minutes. Anna opened her mouth to say something a couple of times, to apologise or ask a question, but she couldn't quite find the words. She knew the conversation they needed to have was important, and she didn't want to fumble it. Plus, Nikos seemed on edge, like he was expecting a row. Clearly, the euphoria of last night had worn off, and neither of them had the energy to pretend everything was okay right now.

"When did we run out of things to say to each other?" Nikos asked after a couple minutes of silence, and Anna turned to face him, seeing the defeated look on his face. She didn't know if he meant now in the garden, or for the past week when they'd been exploring each other rather than explore the issue at hand. But either way, he sounded like he'd given up, just like he had after the party when she heard him talking to—

No, never mind that. Anna had promised herself she'd stop clinging onto the mystery of the Englishwoman. There were plenty of people on the island that Nikos knew and Anna didn't.

"We haven't run out of things to say," she said finally. "It's just that the things we would normally say on a random morning in the garden seem foolish compared to the things we need to talk about."

Nikos nodded. "I think you're right."

Another few minutes passed without a word, both sipping their coffees and gently pushing the swing back and forth. Eventually Anna glanced down at her watch and realised she needed to leave to meet Elena.

"I'm sorry, Nikos. I have to go."

"I know you do," he said. "I just hate being like this. It's not us."

"Yeah, I know it's not. But we'll get there. I really do believe that."

She leaned over to kiss him on the cheek, then left him on the swing to get dressed. And as she walked inside, that niggling voice reared its head again, and she couldn't help but remember the last time he'd been on the swing, with someone other than her.

When Elena sent Anna a location for dress shopping, she had expected it to be for a bridal shop. So when she parked her Vespa outside a small blue door in a white stone wall with no sign to be seen, she had to double check the pin to make sure she was in the right place. As she did, she heard Elena's laugh echo from the other side of the wall as if to confirm.

Anna knocked on the door, and Elena's voice called from inside to come in.

She pushed the door open to find herself in a courtyard. A small plunge pool against one side shimmered in the sun, whilst a huge shade covered the other side of the courtyard all the way to the building's front door. Under the shade was a massive sofa with blue-, white-, and terracotta-coloured cushions, on which Elena sat talking to Xenia. Both of them looked annoyingly fresh given the events of the night before. Seriously, what was everyone else doing to avoid looking and feeling so hungover? She would have to remember to ask later on.

When they looked up and saw Anna, Elena squealed and ran over for a hug.

"Where are we?" Anna asked when she pulled away. "I assumed we would go to a boutique or something, not someone's house."

"There's a tragic lack of dress shops on the island," Elena said. "But trust me, this is better."

Anna heard more voices laughing inside, and two other women exited the house. One of them Anna recognised from Elena's party, presumably Vasilis's cousin Maria, but the other one she had never seen before.

Seeing these two women, Anna felt incredibly unglamorous. Elena was always perfectly put together, and Xenia was always in a power pantsuit no matter the weather, but these two looked like absolute supermodels. The taller one wore a sleek, tailored white jumpsuit with a built-in cape draped elegantly over her shoulders, and towering white heels to match. Her hair was slicked back in a wet look like she was expected on the set of a magazine shoot. Her face was long and angular, her eyes fox-like, adding to the supermodel effect. Anna had no idea who she was, but she instantly felt like she was in the presence of someone rich or famous, or both.

The other one, the one Anna recognised, was shorter, with a more girl-next-door appeal, but still drop-dead gorgeous. Her long bouncy curls fell perfectly over her shoulders, just brushing her collarbone – Anna had never been jealous of another woman's collarbone before, but here she was – which was on display in an off-the-shoulder red floral dress that grazed the floor. The slit running up her thigh revealed that she, too, was wearing heels.

Looking at the four of them and then down at her denim shirtdress and trainers, Anna felt like the pale stepsister in a bridesmaid lineup of Grecian goddesses.

"Hi, I'm Thea," the tall stranger offered, her hand outstretched.

"Oh, hi, Thea!" Anna said, offering her own hand to shake. "I thought you were in Athens! I'm so glad you could make it."

Everyone else laughed. Anna looked around for clues to the joke she'd missed out on, feeling like she'd somehow fumbled the greeting.

"What, did I miss something?"

"Thea isn't just here for the try-on," Elena explained. "She's hosting it. She's the dress designer, and this is her temporary atelier until the wedding. She's brought some dresses all the way from Athens for us to try."

Anna's mouth dropped open. "That's amazing! I had no idea. I'm so sorry."

"Don't be silly," Thea said, then looked at Elena. "I wouldn't miss it for the world. I've been designing with this one in mind since the first time she told me about Vasilis. Plus, I'd rented this place for the season already – I'm sure you've noticed how painfully barren this island is of good bridal fashion – so now all I have to contend with is the ridiculous timeline Elena has given me…"

"Like you don't already have something incredible up your sleeve," Elena said, and Thea smiled.

Anna turned her attention to the girl in the red dress. "That must make you Maria, Vasilis's cousin?"

The woman practically glowed as she reached out a dainty hand to shake Anna's.

"Yes, nice to meet you, Anna. I was at your house the other night, but I didn't get a chance to say hello."

Anna shook the outstretched hand and clenched her jaw, trying not to let the clenching extend to her hand as Maria responded. Her reply came out in a crystal clear English accent.

Chapter Nine

The inside of Thea's house was as lush as one might expect from a Greek fashion designer's island atelier. A long, cushy sofa lined one wall, with a three-sided dressing mirror framed in gold on the other. A rose-coloured velvet pedestal stood in front of the mirror, matched by the curtain that hung across the width of the room at the back. Beyond the curtain, Thea had helped Elena slip into the first option, and then straight into the second without leaving the dressing area. Based on the muttering she could hear through the curtain, Elena was, unsurprisingly, very clear on what she liked and didn't like.

But Anna wasn't paying attention to any of it. Instead she sat on one end of the sofa sipping a glass of Prosecco whilst Xenia and Maria talked about work, actively focusing on the coupe in her hand, trying to keep her grip in check so she didn't break it in anger.

She had known that Maria worked as a publicist for some of the winemakers on the island, but she didn't know that she was an internationally accredited sommelier. It turned out she had actually started the group that Nikos had been attending so that she could scout up-and-coming winemakers for her employer. Apparently, they'd even been travelling together. According to Maria, as she told Xenia about the lack of interest on the island, Nikos's recent trip to Tuscany hadn't really been with a group. It had just been the two of them.

Anna was seeing red, and it wasn't just Maria's dress.

She'd told herself for over a week that the mystery woman meant nothing – that it was likely just a classic case of Nikos oversharing to some poor girl, and she was projecting the issue to avoid the conversation about their future. But now it was clear her instinct had been correct. Nikos had someone in his life that he was close to – very close, if Maria's words were reliable – that he hadn't told her about. And as much as she wished it didn't, it made it so much worse to know that Maria was hot. Of course it did.

It also didn't help that Maria couldn't stop talking about Nikos.

"We got so drunk at the Dordogne event," she said to Xenia, "that we ended up stealing a tray of hors d'oeuvres from a wedding at the winery and bringing them back to the group in an ice bucket."

She could barely get the last few words out because she was laughing so hard. Xenia laughed along as well, though Anna was barely managing a forced chuckle.

"I'm so sorry," she said to Anna, placing a hand on her knee. "You've probably heard all of these stories from Nikos."

Anna's leg burned where Maria was touching it. The petty person in her wanted to smack the hand away, but she just gripped her glass a little tighter, instead. Not too tightly, though. Luckily Maria seemed to care more about continuing the story than she did about registering Anna's reaction.

Not only had Nikos never told her any of these stories, but he had barely ever mentioned Maria. Her name came up in passing every now and then – Anna knew that she lived on the island full-time – but not enough for Anna to realise she was significant. In fact, it was usually Elena who brought her up in the context of her relationship with Vasilis.

She had never had a reason not to trust Nikos, but she couldn't stop the thoughts rushing through her mind.

Was it a strategic move to never mention her?

Why wouldn't he tell me a story like that?

How could I not know they were going abroad together?

Is she trying to steal him away? Or is it two-sided?

Has something happened between them? If it has, can I forgive him?

She was performing mental acrobatics to make the logic leaps, but she couldn't help herself. She was incensed.

And then, most worryingly, there was a small bit of her that hoped something had happened. Not bad enough to make her truly hate him, but enough to give her a plausible reason to keep putting off their serious conversation.

Of course, the rest of her, which far outweighed this traitorous sliver, immediately squashed the thought. Anything happening between Nikos and Maria would be devastating, and she didn't want it. She also didn't believe it had happened. Not only because she trusted Nikos – and she did trust him – but because the conversation she'd heard the other night was not the kind of conversation had by two people in the torrid throws of an affair.

But that didn't mean Anna trusted Maria, or wanted to sit here and listen to her talk about her misadventures with Nikos.

Thea peeked her head through the curtain just as Anna was losing her ability to fake a smile, and all the girls leapt to their feet.

"Her majesty has finally found a gown worthy of showing you all," she said, pulling the curtain aside and stepping through.

But it was Thea in the dress. In fact, Elena was still in the dressing area out of sight.

Thea wore a long white satin gown with the tiniest train, thin spaghetti straps which criss-crossed over a low back, a draped neckline, and subtle darts at the bust. It was stunning, but Anna was confused.

"Okay, I have loads going through my mind," Xenia said. "First of all, it's a bit simpler than I expected…"

"Same!" Anna said, tilting her head.

"And second of all," Xenia continued, "why are you wearing it?"

Anna and Maria nodded along as she spoke. Anna couldn't have said it better herself. Thea looked incredible, but it didn't exactly scream "Elena."

"Oh, that's because that's not my dress," Elena shouted from behind the curtain. "This is."

As Elena stepped into the room, chills went up Anna's arms.

If she had dreamed up the perfect dress for Elena, it wouldn't have even come close to this one. The all-over floral lace was draped with an almost iridescent tulle in an A-line silhouette, falling perfectly over Elena's hips and pooling on the floor in a long train. The tight-fitting bodice had a plunging neckline and a tiny fringe of eyelash lace edging the chest, contrasting beautifully with Elena's olive skin. A very slightly puffy shoulder gave way to long sleeves, loose around the arm and cinched at the wrist. The final touch was a satin sash around the waist delicately beaded with off-white pearls. She looked like a princess and a mermaid and a red carpet wonder all at once. She looked radiant. Stunning. Dream-like.

It was perfect. She was perfect. And of course they were all instantly in tears.

"I know, right?" Elena said in her typical showy voice, but even she was wiping wetness from her cheeks with a handkerchief.

"It's almost like I designed it just for you," Thea said with a wink. "Why don't you step up onto the pedestal so we can get a proper look."

Elena picked up the front of the gown and stepped up onto the platform, exhaling sharply before looking at herself in the mirror. As she did, Anna noticed new details she hadn't seen before, like the way the back mirrored the V shape of the front, and the tiny pearls that embellished the lace underlay, giving it an almost sparkly effect.

Thea busied herself arranging the train and retrieving a veil from behind the curtain.

"Hair up or down?" Thea asked.

"Down," all the girls said in unison, and then giggled. The back was beautiful, but Elena's hair was a signature feature, and it wouldn't be her wedding day if she didn't have it out in full effect.

"Definitely down, but maybe pulled back a bit," Elena said. Thea pulled a couple of small sections back, pinned them just under the crown of Elena's head, and slid the comb of the veil into where the pins were. The barely-there material fell to around Elena's fingertips, creating a bit of a halo effect around her, punctuated only by the same tiny pearls from the dress, looking like they were floating.

"I feel so beautiful," she said, catching Anna's eye in the mirror. Anna stepped forward and grabbed Elena's hand, giving it a squeeze.

"You look it. Unbelievable."

"You can say that again," said a familiar voice from outside, and all the girls turned to see Nikos walking through the doorway.

"Nikos!" Elena gasped. "What are you doing here?" She looked at Anna as if to see if she had known he was coming.

"I'm wondering the same thing," Anna added as Nikos walked

up to where they were standing. He didn't take his eyes off Elena. It was a look of love – of family. They had grown up practically as siblings, and now the person who knew him best in the whole world was standing in front of him in the dress she would wear at her wedding. Anna melted to think of the affection he must be feeling.

Nikos stepped forward and took Elena by the hands as she stepped down from the pedestal to meet him.

"I made a promise to your mother when she got sick," he said. "She asked me to make sure you had everything you wanted when this day came. And Vasilis may be able to give you a dream venue and a dream honeymoon and whatever else, but this one's mine. Mine and your mother's."

Elena's lip was quivering at this point, and as Nikos brought her in for a hug, she fully lost it.

"Dab with the handkerchief, Elena," Thea said, then started fussing over her in Greek, trying to make sure she didn't get makeup on the dress. But the only garment in danger was Nikos's tee shirt where Elena's face was buried. Eventually she stood up and fixed her makeup in the mirror before turning back to her cousin.

"Thank you, Nikos. You've always taken such good care of me."

"That's what family is for." Then he kissed her on the forehead and stepped aside to let the others continue to gush over the bride.

"Alright Thea," Nikos said in a business-like tone, "how much is this gonna set me back?"

Thea stepped over to Anna and Nikos and lowered her voice. "Well, I was only going to charge Elena for materials, so not nearly as much as if she were someone else."

"Okay, so how much are we talking?"

Thea mumbled under her breath as she counted on her fingers. "Five grand."

Nikos's eyes went as wide and his mouth fell open. "Five thousand euros? For a dress?!"

"It's not my fault she picked the most expensive one," Thea said. "That lace was handmade by women in Athens, and the veil material isn't cheap either. If you were anyone else, you'd be paying three times that much, and I'd be having it mass-produced."

Nikos sighed. "It's fine," he said. "I have enough to cover it. Just send me details on how to pay and I'll get it to you this week. But don't you dare mass-produce Elena's dress unless she says you can."

Thea smiled meekly at Nikos. "I wouldn't dare," she said, then went back to Elena, pulling a pincushion and tape measure out of a drawer as she went.

Anna followed Nikos back out the door.

"You didn't tell me you were coming," Anna said. "We could have come together."

"No, it's okay," he said. "I knew I'd only be a couple of minutes. This isn't exactly my scene."

Normally, he would have said something cheesy like "but I could do with some time alone with you," and tried to find a quiet corner to cosy up in, especially if the last week were anything to go by. But instead, he looked uncomfortable, glancing past Anna every few seconds. She knew it wasn't about the dress shopping. He was nervous about Maria.

"Oh, you're not leaving just yet, are you Nikos?" Maria asked, strutting through the door.

Speak of the devil, Anna thought. *Or even think about her, apparently.*

Anna sighed and stepped back, bracing herself for whatever came next. She watched Nikos's face carefully. He didn't look scared or worried necessarily, but there was definitely discomfort there.

"Yeah, I'll let you girls have your fun," he said. "This trip has already cost me enough."

Maria went in for a hug, and though Nikos was never one to temper his affection with anyone, he slung one arm around Maria's shoulder for an awkward side hug. He was trying awfully hard to avoid looking overly friendly with her. Anna tried her hardest not to read too much into this.

Maria looked confused, half smiling and half cringing as she pulled away from him.

"I'll see you at home," he said, kissing Anna on the lips a bit more chastely than she would normally expect, even with people watching. And then he left.

Maria narrowed her eyes for a moment as she watched Nikos go, then glanced at Anna. Anna looked away, and Maria shook her head, shoulders and arms, as if to shake off the awkwardness. "So, what's with the fake-out dress?" she asked, pointing to Thea. "One of Elena's rejects?"

"No, this is going to be your bridesmaid dress!" Elena said, a huge smile on her face.

Anna looked around at the others to see if she was missing something about traditions here, but no one else looked as confused as she did. "But it's white…" she said, running her hand over the satin trailing down from Thea's hips. Surely Elena would be the last person to let someone else wear white to her wedding, right?

Of course Maria took the opportunity to contradict her. "I love it," she said. "Very trendy."

And Anna had to admit that they did look amazing together. The textures played off each other so well, and whilst the simpler one would probably be a wedding dress in its own right for someone like Anna, there would be no mistaking who the bride was when Elena emerged in her dress.

They spent the next hour getting their measurements taken –

Elena had given estimates to Thea ahead of time, but she only had one dress to test with.

"How are you going to get all of these done in time?" Maria asked as Thea measured her obnoxiously small waist.

"It'll all happen at the Athens production house," she said. "I've got a team of seamstresses there ready to work their magic."

Elena cleared her throat.

"Though, of course," Thea added, "only my hands touch Elena's dress. It will be a one-of-a-kind Thea Angelos original."

"Thank you," Elena said, handing Thea another glass of champagne and clinking hers against it.

Anna felt her wrist buzz, and she looked down at her watch to see an incoming call from Lizzy. She rifled around in her bag for her phone, barely catching it before it went to voicemail.

"Hey," she said, slipping out the door and walking over to the sofa.

"How's it going? You done with dress shopping yet?"

"It wasn't really shopping," Anna said. "Elena's bridesmaid Thea is a designer, so she brought a bunch of gowns to try on, and now we're getting fitted for our bridesmaid dresses."

"Very fun," Lizzy said and then paused. Anna could tell that she wasn't saying something. She could also tell from the way the voices echoed slightly that she was on speakerphone.

"What's going on?" Anna said. "Where are you?"

"Hello Anna," another voice said through the line. Grace.

"Hi, Mom," Anna said with a sigh.

"Don't sound so happy to talk to me."

"Sorry, Mother." Anna held her forehead in her hand and sighed. "Let me try again. Hello Mommy Dearest, I'm so delighted to be speaking with you today."

She could practically hear Grace rolling her eyes on the other end of the line. "Very nice, Anna. I'll leave you girls to it. Give your grandparents my love."

To anyone else this may have seemed nice, but Grace hated Greece and everything that came from it. She had met Anna's dad on a summer holiday, married him when they found out they were pregnant, made him move to Connecticut, and then had him deported less than a decade later to cover up her affair with someone else.

So when Grace Linton said to give Eirini and Christos her love, Anna knew it was a jab.

"Why are you at Mom's?" Anna asked after a few seconds.

"Martin and I had a bit of a thing," Lizzy said, having taken Anna off speakerphone.

"Oh Liz, I'm so sorry," Anna said. "You guys gonna be okay?"

"I'm sure we will," Lizzy said, "but enough about that. I'm thinking of coming a bit early."

Anna sat up straight. If Lizzy was going to pay to switch her plane ticket to avoid staying with their mom, things must have been really bad with Martin.

"Yeah, that's fine," Anna said. "I'm in Ireland and then London, next week, but any time other than that."

Elena poked her head out the door. "Is that Lizzy?" she asked. Anna nodded. "Ooh, great! Invite her please!"

"Invite me where?" Lizzy asked through the phone as Anna and Elena gave each other a thumbs-up and Elena went back inside.

"To her wedding."

"Well shit, Anna, I can't really afford two trips to Greece, can I?"

Anna laughed. "Well then, you're in luck, because she's getting married in less than three weeks."

Lizzy laughed so loudly that Anna had to move the phone away from her ear. "Of-freaking-course she is. That's the most Elena thing I've ever heard."

"I'll send you the details," Anna said, "but I'd better get back inside…" She looked through the window to see Maria hugging Elena a bit too enthusiastically. She couldn't help but sneer.

"What was that?" Lizzy asked. When Anna tried to brush it off, she pressed further. "Don't think I can't hear you being derisive from thousands of miles away."

Anna sighed. "Okay, you wanna hear me be the worst person ever?"

"Always."

Anna leaned back on the sofa, lowered her voice and told Lizzy everything about Maria. About the conversation she overheard, the time Maria and Nikos had been spending together, and even the weird flirtation attempts from earlier. By the time she was done, she was equal parts seething and embarrassed.

"I know it sounds ridiculous," she said. "I trust him so much. But do I sound crazy? Or is this something I should worry about?"

Lizzy chuckled. "I certainly don't think you sound crazy," she said. "But I'm not one to talk."

Anna wondered if the story had hit a little too close to home, and maybe the trouble with Martin wasn't just between the two of them.

"Wanna have it be your turn to vent?"

"Nope, I'm all good," Lizzy said, a little *too* forcefully. "Just be careful. Have your conversations, but don't use this girl as a bargaining chip. If you think something's happening, trust that feeling. But if you don't, then you're better off just forgetting about it altogether. You've got yourself a good one."

It definitely sounded like Lizzy knew what she was talking about, but Anna didn't want to pry. They'd be together in person soon enough – even sooner than she'd thought from the sound of it. Plus she hadn't told Lizzy about the rest of their conversations. The serious ones. The ones about their future.

"Love you, Liz."

"Love you, too. Have a great time."

"I'll try."

As Anna put down the phone, she looked back inside. The afternoon was starting to get hazy, and the light from the atelier perfectly illuminated the four women laughing and drinking inside.

Anna did feel like the odd one out, but not just in appearance. These women all had things in common that Anna would never have. A language, a culture, expectations for how their lives would look, an easy acceptance of white bridesmaid dresses… and they had those things in common with Nikos in a way Anna never would. And she couldn't help but feel like maybe, just maybe, Nikos would be happier with someone who had that shared understanding. Someone who understood the significance of every wedding ritual. Someone who knew all the right words to say. Someone who wasn't leaving Nikos alone every other week.

Someone like Maria. Who, apparently, had been by his side for the last four years when Anna wasn't. Maybe that was why she was so sensitive to it, and maybe it was why Nikos had kept it from her. Because both of them thought on some level that him being with someone like her made more logical sense.

Anna wasn't wishing it. She didn't want Nikos to want that. But she feared it might be true. And her time away wasn't just putting physical distance between them. Their lives were diverging, and she worried that unless she made some major changes, they would end up so far apart that there was no coming back together.

But what would she have to give up to keep him? And would she be willing to make the sacrifice? As she was coming to realise, there was only one way to find out.

Anna looked up at the sky, which was starting to change colours. In less than an hour, the sun would begin to set over the caldera, and when it did, she would be having a long overdue conversation with Nikos.

Chapter Ten

Nikos slipped the truck into park in front of the restaurant. It was a newly opened spot, but already it had been recommended to Anna three times, once even by someone not on the island. The cliff side building had floor-to-ceiling glass on three sides so that even whilst sitting in the truck, they could see the iconic view on the other side. It looked ultra-modern next to the traditional white and beige buildings on either side, all sharp angles and shine next to rounded corners and dust. There were only a few parking spots, to the point that cars were spilled out onto the street, but luckily someone had been leaving just as they'd arrived.

As she stepped out of the truck, Anna couldn't help but notice how nice all the other patrons in front of and inside the restaurant were dressed. She self-consciously tugged on the shirtdress she hadn't been given the chance to change out of.

When Anna had returned home, Nikos had been waiting at the gate fully ready to go. Despite how casual he'd been about their plans earlier, he was dressed up for a proper night out, making Anna feel severely underdressed – a feeling that was now increasing as they walked arm in arm into the restaurant. It was definitely more upscale than she'd anticipated, and she felt out of place. She'd tried to change at the house, but Nikos had insisted they were late, so Anna had only had time to run a brush through her hair and grab a summer scarf to tie around her ponytail.

Now, as the maitre d' asked for the reservation name, Anna and Nikos stared at each other, each waiting for the other to speak.

"Did you not make a booking?" Nikos asked, sounding surprised. "This was your idea."

"You're the one who said we were late," Anna replied. "I thought we'd just turn up and wait, but I assumed you'd booked based on how hurried you were. Otherwise, I would have changed."

Anna saw the maitre d' look her up and down as she said this, and she could have sworn she saw him smirk as he returned his gaze to the tablet in his hand. "No booking then?" He spoke in English, clearly viewing Anna as a tourist rather than a local. She didn't blame him.

Anna shook her head. "It seems not."

"I can seat you at nine," he said without looking up.

"That's nearly an hour from now," Nikos said, leaning in, his voice low. "Do you not have anything sooner?"

"We're all booked up for tonight," the man said in reply, again not even deigning to make eye contact. "I've had one cancellation for nine. Otherwise our next available table is on Thursday next week."

Anna gulped. "Let's just wait," she said. "I'm not that hungry yet."

"Speak for yourself," Nikos said, but he nodded at the maitre d', anyway. "Nine is fine," he said, then turned around to leave.

"I *was* speaking for myself," Anna muttered as she followed him out the door.

Anna followed Nikos as he paced over to a lookout where the

land dropped into the caldera, finding a bench to take in the view. At least they wouldn't miss the sunset; the sky was just starting to streak with pale yellows, and soon it would turn orange and pink as the sun sank over Thirasia to the west.

For minutes, they sat in silence, Anna replaying their last encounter in her mind. It had been awkward, sure, with Maria. But it hadn't been bad enough to warrant this level of hostility. Unless, of course, he had something to hide.

Anna had always been self-conscious because of her parents' story – her mother had come to Greece on holiday, fallen in love, and then created a relationship that was so toxic that she was willing to deport her own husband rather than admit that she'd had an affair. Anna had worked so hard to prove to her friends, her grandparents, and Nikos that she wasn't her mother; that she was committed, even when her work took her away.

But now, she began to wonder if Nikos was the one like her mother. Had he been unfaithful? Anna doubted it. But was he being sketchy about his friendship with Maria to the point that Anna distrusted him? Yes. And she worried that, should she press too hard, it would cost her everything she knew and loved – and yet, she couldn't shake the issue. Now that she'd met Maria, been confronted with the truth of how close they were, she couldn't put it out of her mind.

As if out of nowhere, Nikos turned to Anna and spoke.

"I've got several events coming up that I'd like you at if you can manage," he said. "Everyone else's partners come, at least when they're local, but, so far, you've not been to a single one. Not even when you're home."

Anna cringed. Of course the first thing said between them tonight was a fight, and Nikos was coming out of the gate strong. She'd assumed he'd be on the back foot because of Maria, but it seemed he was leading with something where he felt he had the high ground.

"We're going to London soon, doesn't that count?"

Nikos rolled his eyes. "One event. That's one event in two years of me doing this."

"I've offered before," Anna retorted. "You told me it would be a waste of time, and that you'd rather I spend time with Elena."

"That was one specific event, and it was over a year ago," he replied. "I've had dozens of events since then, and you haven't come to a single one."

Anna knew that was true, that she'd had plenty of opportunities, but he'd never given her any reason to think that he wanted her there.

"Well, at least you've got Maria there," she said, somewhat under her breath, but definitely loud enough for Nikos to hear. He pretended not to, though, or at least he didn't reply, glaring out at the sunset, instead. He was being childish, picking a fight with her and then retreating when she shot back at him.

But as she opened her mouth to say something to that effect, she felt a tap on her shoulder and jumped. The maitre d' was standing behind her.

"Excuse me, madam, sir, but we've had another cancellation. Would you like us to seat you now?"

Anna looked at Nikos, half of her wanting to call it off and go home. They could have it out in the privacy of the summer house rather than letting things simmer for longer because they were trying to keep cool. But she didn't get the chance to debate.

"Yes, please," Nikos said. "I'm starving."

So, Anna stood up and followed behind the two men as they went back into the restaurant. The maitre d' gestured towards what was arguably the worst table in the house, wedged between the hallway to the bathrooms and the entrance to the kitchen.

Anna sat down, smoothing her dress and draping her napkin over her lap to try to disguise the ratty denim. She had never noticed the spot on the chest pocket, likely from laundry detergent, which now seemed glaringly obvious. As a pair of women left the bathrooms and walked past, she saw one eye her up, and she considered going to the bathroom just to assess how bad it was, but that would help nothing.

"Is there a reason you wouldn't let me change tonight?" Anna asked as soon as they were alone – or at least as alone as they could be in the busiest thoroughfare of a crowded restaurant.

"What are you talking about? You could have changed if you wanted to." Nikos pretended not to be angry, though not very convincingly, as he browsed the menu. He hated a public fight, but she'd never seen him be this dismissive.

"I could not have. I tried to, but you told me we were in a hurry, so I didn't. I'm not sure how else I could have navigated that."

Nikos shrugged his shoulders. Anna sighed. She knew he didn't want to make a scene, but she couldn't be that couple – the ones who smile at each other over dinner all evening only to get home and have it out. It wasn't them. She didn't want to pretend with him.

"It's like you're punishing me. Why?"

"Well, in order for me to be punishing you, you'd have to have done something wrong. Are you suggesting that you've done something wrong, Anna?" Nikos raised an eyebrow at her, and she rolled her eyes. He was being so much pettier than usual. But this time, rather than taking the bait, Anna mirrored his action of scanning the menu in silence.

As the waiter came to take their order, Anna opened her mouth to speak. Normally, Nikos would hear what she was ordering, then order a wine to pair well, and then order something for himself that would pair well with the same wine. But this time he jumped in front of her, ordering his own food and a bottle of wine – one of the most expensive ones on the menu, in fact – then grimacing when she ordered the dish she'd selected.

"What's wrong with lamb?" she asked when they were alone.

"It won't exactly pair well with the wine," he said, pulling out his phone and scrolling through something. "I assumed you would order something fishy like usual at a place like this."

"Well perhaps if you'd waited for me to order first you would have known."

Nikos rolled his eyes. "I'm so sorry I didn't hold the metaphorical door for you."

"That's not what I meant," Anna said under her breath, but it sounded weak. "You didn't have to order the most expensive bottle on the menu."

Nikos didn't respond, but rather glanced at her without raising his head from his phone, the effect being a menacing glare. It was a warning. Not a threatening one, but an aware one. Anna knew that she should switch to small talk until they were in private, but the idea of talking about the weather with her partner of four years felt unbearable. So she went against her better judgment and returned to their conversation from outside.

"Why didn't you ask me to come to your events if you wanted me to?" Anna tried her best to stay calm and keep her voice even, but she could feel an edge creeping in.

"Well excuse me for not wanting to beg," he said, rolling his eyes and putting his phone down. At least now he was looking at Anna. "It would just be nice to feel supported. This is important to me."

"Well then, good thing you have Maria there to keep you company."

As soon as Anna said it, she instantly regretted it. She risked a look at Nikos. His body was rigid in his seat, far from the casual, laid-back demeanour he usually possessed.

"I knew that was going to be a thing," he said. "Is this because she tried to hug me at Thea's?"

Anna couldn't help it anymore. She rose to his challenge.

"Maybe it's because you've been spending every waking moment with her for the past year and a half, and somehow I knew nothing about her. You want me to be a supportive partner? How am I supposed to support you when I don't know what's going on in your life?"

She knew she was raising her voice, and she didn't want to make a scene, but everything she'd been feeling all day and for the past week was bubbling up inside her. She couldn't help it.

"You've had plenty of opportunities to be more involved in my life, but you've completely fucked off – and with Marcus of all people," Nikos said quietly. He always did this when they argued. Anna would get worked up in response to him, and he would get strangely quiet, as if he were trying to add contrast to her outburst to make her feel hysterical. Naturally it made her even angrier, and even her desire to avoid a public confrontation was no match for that anger now.

"Oh, I get it," she said. "I should step back from my career, my dream job, to spend more time with you while you learn to make wine. And if I don't, you'll find a gorgeous Greek placeholder, instead. Is that right?"

By now multiple tables were looking at them, but Anna didn't care.

"I never said that," Nikos said. "But it would be great if you prioritised our relationship over taking pictures every now and then."

Anna laughed. He was being intentionally condescending about her job, and the comeback was right there. He wanted her to pick it up and throw it back at him. To say that her "taking pictures" was what paid the bills. That maybe he'd forgotten what it was like to have a job, but Anna hadn't, and it was her work that paid for their house and their food and their date nights and their stupidly expensive bottles of wine.

But Anna wasn't going to go there. They had never argued

about money, and that's not what this was about. Just like she was angry about Maria, he was angry about… well, she wasn't fully sure. That she'd questioned why he wanted to get married? That she travelled so much? Who knew. Maybe he didn't even know himself. But that wasn't her problem, and she wasn't going to give him the satisfaction of being the one to pick a fight.

The idea of sitting across from Nikos for a meal neither of them would actually enjoy made Anna's stomach turn, and the childish part of her wanted to have the last word. So, instead of brushing it under the rug, instead of fawning until he came around, she stood up from the table, pulled a hundred euros in cash from her purse, and dropped it on the table between them.

"This should cover your wine," she said, meeting his gaze one last time before walking away. She was both heartbroken and vindicated to see that he looked hurt.

As Anna left the restaurant, she realised that she didn't have any way of getting home. They had come in the truck, and Anna didn't have the keys. So she turned down the street and began to walk.

The whirlwind of their argument washed over her as she examined every word said, the anger rising up in her anew with every passing moment, propelling her forward. And before she knew it, for the second time that day, she was running. She found a moment to be grateful that she was still in her trainers after all.

As her feet pounded the pavement and her legs propelled her through the hills, she thought about how unfair the fight had been. Nikos was holding her career against her in a way she hadn't thought him capable of. But then again, Anna was holding his friendship with Maria against him, too. She felt fully justified doing so, but maybe in his own way Nikos felt justified in his frustrations as well.

Maybe it was fair after all. Maybe they deserved each other. They'd certainly acted equally poorly tonight.

As Anna's breath began to shorten, she had to actively fight back tears. And as her body worked itself up through running, her emotions began to bubble to the surface until she couldn't hold it back anymore. She was running down the side of the road in a denim dress, a silk scarf in her hair, with tears running down her face. She got more than one concerned look from people driving past, but Anna was blind to their judgment.

To address the issues Nikos had with her travelling, Anna was going to need him to fess up about Maria, which he didn't seem willing to do right now. And as much time as Anna had spent away from him over the last month, she couldn't stand the thought of sleeping next to him tonight knowing that they were both boiling over with rage and resentment. So as she rounded the corner of the driveway up to the summer house and hobbled through the gate, she started making a mental packing list.

She pulled a backpack out of her wardrobe and shoved the first things she could find inside, then grabbed her keys and locked up, climbing on her Vespa and pointing it down the hill towards the other side of the island.

Let's see how Nikos feels about a few more days away from me.

Chapter Eleven

As Anna brought the hotel lobby into focus, she tried to blink away the tiredness from her eyes. She was never going to get a crisp shot if she couldn't even see clearly. She stood up, rubbed her eyes, and yawned. The world became a bit brighter, so she knelt back down and brought her viewfinder back to her eye.

She got the shot, took a few more for good measure, and then looked up when she heard footsteps clicking across the marble floor.

"It looks incredible in here," she said to Xenia as she stood up. Xenia was wearing an emerald-green power suit, perfect for her portraits, which were next.

KSR Hospitality Enterprises, Xenia's company, had taken over management of another hotel on the island. Her revival of Kamari Sands had been so successful that she had acquired six more hotels in other parts of Greece in the last four years, but this was her first other one on the island. And since Anna's photography of Kamari Sands had won them both an award, Xenia brought Anna to each new acquisition before relaunching. Iliou had been finished the week before, and it would be opening for the tourist season in a couple of weeks. It looked incredible. Xenia had taken the fact that it was less bright and open in most rooms and turned it into something that felt like an elegant cave, with textured walls that curved into domed ceilings, polished marble floors, and giant plants everywhere. Gold accents created a gilded glamour that she knew would be popular with influencers and travel publications alike. Based on the existing properties, those would be the two main drivers of bookings.

But of course, a Santorini hotel wouldn't be complete without a view. And whilst Iliou had a more limited view than some of the competition, Xenia had brilliantly designed it so the part of the hotel which did have a view was all about that view. In fact, Xenia had spent an exorbitant amount of money to open up the supporting wall on the north side of the building to create wall-to-wall, floor-to-ceiling windows on that side. It made you feel like you were underground when facing one way and like you were floating above the sea when facing the other.

"Seriously, you've done an amazing job as always," Anna said, leading Xenia over to a chaise lounge in the corner in front of some plants. Her suit would look perfect here. "I can't wait to shoot the honeymoon suite when it's ready."

"Thanks," Xenia answered, smoothing her trousers and running her fingers through her hair. "Since Kamari, I've tried to avoid renovating this close to the season, but I managed to get 40% capacity all summer on the CGIs alone, and the only thing more in need of TLC than the suites was the name. *Spíti* may mean home, but you can't market a resort to an English-speaking audience when the name has the word 'spit' in it."

Anna chuckled. "Well, what does Iliou mean?"

"Of the sun, so when it was *Spíti Iliou* it was called House of the Sun. Which is nice, but nice doesn't pay the bills. American tourists do. And nearly half of American tourists who chose the competition in the focus group did so largely because of the name."

Anna chuckled. "Fair enough. Well, I like Iliou. It sounds luxurious."

"Case and point," Xenia said, and then she went seamlessly into posing mode. Anna and Xenia always could mix work and friendship seamlessly, and today was no different.

An hour later, Anna had more shots from all over the hotel, from solo shots of Xenia to ones with the staff, and even some sweeping vistas of the view over the caldera. Clients like Xenia, who were prepared and up for anything Anna's creative eye dictated, were a dream to work with.

When they were done and the staff had said goodbye, they sat down at the bar, and Xenia busted out a bottle of champagne to celebrate being finished. She'd done this at every hotel they'd opened, so far.

"Ugh, I couldn't possibly," Anna said. "I feel like since I've come home, I've constantly been either drunk, hungover or exhausted."

"Just one sip for posterity," Xenia said, handing Anna a flute. "Then you can bail on the booze."

Anna obediently accepted the glass, clinked it against Xenia's, and took a sip. Then she set it behind the bar out of reach. As she sat it down, a wave of tiredness washed over her, and she couldn't help but yawn.

"Wow, you weren't kidding. You must be exhausted from that big trip and all the craziness since. How happy has Nikos been to have you back?" Xenia nudged Anna's knee with her own and winked.

"Very funny," Anna said. "Honestly, I wish he were. But things are a bit tense at the moment."

"Didn't you go out for some big romantic date the other night? After the dress fitting?"

Anna nodded. "You can take the fact that I'm staying at Kamari Sands right now as a sign of how that went."

Xenia frowned. "I saw your name in the guest book, but I assumed it was for Lizzy. Isn't she coming soon?"

"Yeah, but not until right before the wedding. No, that's me."

Xenia wasn't one to get involved in other people's conflicts, but even she looked concerned. Anna could see her deciding whether to press for more details. Then she seemed to make a decision.

"Do you want to tell me what went down?" she asked, sipping her champagne casually as if to let Anna know that there was no pressure to share. But Anna had always liked Xenia – trusted her, even. She was pragmatic. And since she didn't want to put a damper on Elena's wedding planning vibe, given how short it would be, she'd not had anyone to talk to about what was happening. No one but Lizzy, and she didn't know the people involved, so her advice was hardly objective.

So Anna told Xenia everything, just as she had told Lizzy a few nights earlier, including what they had both said at dinner. Anna hadn't even told her sister about that yet.

"I can't believe he said all that." She took another sip of her champagne, contemplating what Anna had shared. "So he didn't tell you about Maria at all?"

Anna shook her head. "I'm pretty sure the last time I heard her name come out of his mouth was when she first moved here the same summer I did."

"Well shit," Xenia said. "If I'd known he was keeping their friendship from you I would have said something. To you, but also to him. And probably to her."

"It's not your fault," Anna said. "I don't even think Elena knew he was keeping it from me. She might not even have known how close they are."

Xenia's eyes widened. "Oh, no, she knew. We all knew."

Anna frowned. "What's that supposed to mean?"

"Let's just say, that awkward side hug caught us all off guard. They're always pretty friendly. Never inappropriate, but definitely friendly."

Anna could feel tears welling up behind her eyes. That was exactly what she'd feared. Not that Nikos was more physically friendly with her – he was with everyone, so she'd never expected any differently – but that everyone else in her life knew something about her relationship that she didn't. How could she have been the only one kept out of the loop?

As if Nikos were whispering in her ear, she knew the answer. It was because she was gone so much. When you're only with someone a fraction of the time, it's easy to miss everything else going on in their life.

"He blames me travelling so much," Anna said. "And honestly? I'm starting to as well. I know nothing's happening, but how could my boyfriend have a bestie that I know nothing about?" Even Xenia knew, and she was gone almost as much as Anna was. "And can you believe we've been talking about getting married?"

Xenia's eyes narrowed. "Wait, really?"

Anna waved her hand dismissively. "Well, not really. I thought he was going to propose when Elena got engaged, and Marcus said something annoying about it, so Nikos got angry. But honestly, everything he said is weirdly accurate at the moment."

"What did he say?" Xenia didn't have the same visceral reaction to Marcus's name that Nikos and Elena shared, and Anna was grateful for that right now.

"Well, he said that people like us couldn't settle down long enough to make a marriage work. And obviously I'm nothing like him, but he was right that my work is getting in the way of my relationship."

Xenia paused, reached over the bar to grab Anna's champagne

flute, put it back in Anna's hand, and clinked it with her own. "I'll drink to that."

Anna took a small sip, her cheeks flushed. She had felt desperate to think about *anything* else for days now, and here was a lifeline. Xenia was giving her an out. She could have hugged her.

"You know, I don't think I know anything about your relationship history?"

Xenia shook her head. "You wouldn't. People on the island can be quite old-fashioned, so I keep it to myself. But I don't mind talking about it."

"When was the last time you dated someone?"

"Well, 'dated' is a strong word, but I was seeing someone over the winter. She lives in Agios, near the Nikiti resort we opened in February. I bought it from her parents, actually."

"I remember her! The one with the super long hair?"

"Yep. Her name's Dimitra. We actually got pretty serious."

"So what happened?"

Xenia shook her head. "She wanted me to stay. But I didn't want to. Because this is my home." She sighed as she drained the last of her champagne. "And also because I had to be in Siros for a couple of months to open the resort there. I asked her to come with me, but she didn't want to leave her life."

Anna felt tears welling up in her eyes. This was hitting pretty close to home. So much for a distraction. "That's heartbreaking."

"It's infuriating," Xenia said, staring at the bottom of her empty glass. "The fact that my life happens in lots of different places doesn't make it any less of a life. It doesn't mean I haven't worked just as hard to build it. And it certainly doesn't make me any more selfish than the person who stays in their hometown their whole life and expects others to want that, too."

Xenia had hit the nail on the head. All this time, Anna had been crushing it at work, only to feel like she'd somehow dropped the ball at home. She was made to feel like the time she spent cultivating her life didn't count if it took her away from Nikos. And like Xenia, she was sick of being made to feel that way. Because to her, it didn't feel like a distraction from her real life. It felt like an important, integral part of it. It was part of her, and Nikos rejecting it felt like he was rejecting her.

As a tear fell down Xenia's face, Anna realised she had started crying, too.

"Sorry if I struck a nerve," Xenia said, wiping her tears away and adjusting her blazer, clearly trying to regain composure. "I've been thinking about it a lot more since Elena got engaged."

"Me, too," Anna said. "It's certainly been a bit of a bombshell for people."

"I hope it hasn't blown up your life too badly."

Anna smiled half-heartedly. "Me, too. I don't even know what my life here is without him."

"Hey, that's not fair." Xenia caught Anna's gaze and held it. "Just like we all said all those years ago, your life on this island is more than just your relationship. We, your friends, are part of that life, too. And we're super proud of what you've done."

Anna remembered how conflicted she'd felt back then – like she needed everything to fall into place perfectly to compel her to stay. And, in fact, everything pretty much had. She hadn't really had to sacrifice anything, in the end. Maybe now it was time to pay the piper.

"Plus, if you want honesty, I'm definitely more your friend than Nikos's. So you'll always have me."

That made Anna smile, and she squeezed Xenia's hand briefly as a thanks.

Xenia stared at the rest of the bottle as if deciding whether to pour herself another glass. "Do you think you guys will make it?"

Anna swallowed hard, feeling like her throat was closing up. "Honestly, I don't know. Two weeks ago, I would have said absolutely yes. We've been so in love for almost four years. But for the first time, I'm finding myself wondering if that's enough."

"That's okay though," Xenia said. "You don't have to have everything figured out. You just have to show up and work at it."

Anna and Xenia sat for a moment in silence. They hadn't spent much time together over the last few years, but they shared a lot. They were kindred spirits; fellow ambitious wanderers surrounded by people who weren't quite like them.

The two women washed their glasses, packed away Anna's equipment and stashed it in a room – she'd be back in a few weeks to shoot the honeymoon suite, and she wouldn't need it before then since Marcus was arranging for some equipment in Ireland. Xenia turned out all the lights and locked up behind them.

The two women paused in the car park and hugged a bit longer than they normally would.

"Where are you headed now?" Xenia asked.

Anna shrugged. "I think I need to go home. Give you back your hotel room. Let some other American tourist check in."

Xenia laughed. "You're welcome for as long as you'd like, whenever you'd like, but I bet Nikos is ready to talk."

"I hope you're right," Anna said. She wasn't so convinced, but Xenia was never one to sugar-coat things. If she thought so, then maybe it was true.

"I'll see you soon," Xenia said. "We've got the hen do coming up, whenever Elena decides that is."

Anna laughed. "Yeah, I almost forgot about that," she said. Elena had asked for their availability a couple of days ago, but she hadn't heard anything since. "I'll see you then I guess."

Just as she was about to climb onto her Vespa, Anna felt her phone vibrate. When she saw who it was from, she looked up at Xenia, who was looking at her phone as well. It was the bridesmaids group chat.

"Right on cue," Xenia said. Anna laughed and opened the message.

> Thanks for the hookup X – we're booked in Nikiti NEXT THURSDAY (one week from today) for 2 nights for my HEN DO!! Flights on me, rooms on Xenia (thanks again!!!!) <3 <3 <3

"You gonna be okay?" Anna asked, thinking of Dimitra.

"Are *you* gonna be okay?" Xenia replied. She meant Maria.

Anna sighed. "I'll be your buffer if you'll be mine?"

"Deal." Xenia smiled ruefully and climbed into her car.

Chapter Twelve

Nikos

Nikos carefully aimed his spell at the orc grappling Kostas and released it. Okay, so it was more that he mashed the button on the controller until the orc crumpled to the ground, but released sounded so much more civilised.

"Thanks *malaka*," Kostas said with a grin, returning the favour by throwing his spear at the enemy approaching Nikos.

"Thanks yourself," Nikos said as a victory banner popped up on the screen.

"If you two are done," Vasilis said from across the room, "I could use some help choosing a wedding gift for Elena."

Kostas rolled his eyes as he turned off the console. "Honestly, you think we're the best people to help with that?"

"I don't mind," Nikos said, getting up off the beanbag he'd been sat on for the last few hours. "What did you have in mind?"

"I was thinking jewellery," Vasilis said, "but I don't want her to feel she has to wear it on the day if she has something else picked out."

Nikos looked over Vasilis's shoulder at the laptop in front of him. An Athenian jeweller's website was pulled up on the screen.

"I just want it to be perfect for her," Vasilis added quietly, just for Nikos. Kostas could be a bit childish about romance – maybe that was why he and Katerina had been together for over a decade with no sign of popping the question. But it seemed to work for them.

Nikos's heart swelled with affection as he heard the love for Elena in Vasilis's voice. To have someone love Elena so unconditionally and want the very best for her was everything.

Except, maybe, if he had it for himself. But he seemed to be doing everything in his power to make that impossible.

Nikos shook the thought from his head and focused on his friend.

"Do you want to pick it out so it's meaningful, or would you rather know that you've chosen the right thing even if you don't have as much say?"

Vasilis only considered his answer for a short moment. "You know the woman I'm marrying as well as I do. Definitely the latter."

The men laughed, and Nikos rested a hand on Vasilis's shoulder. "I've got you, brother."

Nikos took out his phone and snapped a picture of the website, then sent it along with a message: "Need wedding day gift for Elena". Then he sat down across from Vasilis at the table. Whilst he waited for a reply, he opened his phone and pulled up Anna's Instagram page out of habit. He often checked her Stories when she was away, hoping for a glimpse into the life she loved so much. He felt like she never shared details of it, but whether that was because it didn't occur to her or because she was trying to spare his feelings, he wasn't sure. Either way, he learned way more on Instagram than he did from her. Whilst she'd been in

Chile, he'd had enough snaps of her, Marcus and some guy named Patrick for a lifetime.

Today, however, there was very little to go off of – just a shot of the bar at Xenia's newest resort Iliou, with the location tagged.

Just as he was debating liking the Story, a banner popped up at the top of the screen. It was a text from Thea.

This will match the dress perfectly. Thanks for asking.

Underneath the message was a link. Nikos tapped on it, and a web page loaded, showing a white gold necklace with a small pearl drop. He turned the phone around and showed it to Vasilis.

"Dress designer approved," he said.

Vasilis squinted to look at the phone, then broke out into a huge smile. He turned his laptop around so Nikos could see the screen; the same necklace was pulled up in front of him.

"Perfect," he said, and Nikos agreed.

A few minutes later, Vasilis had ordered Elena's necklace, and Kostas had ordered a pizza. It was well past lunchtime, but Nikos wasn't in any hurry to get home. Anna had been staying at Kamari Sands for the last few days, and the summer house felt empty without her. Not that he didn't spend plenty of time there alone, but knowing that she was only a few miles away made it painful to be without her. So he'd spent plenty of time with the boys, instead.

"How are things with you and Anna?" Vasilis asked, and Nikos looked up to meet his eye. Vasilis did that a lot – it was like he could read people's minds. His uncanny ability to understand what was plaguing someone was part of what Nikos loved about him. He was one of the most empathetic people Nikos had ever met.

"Honestly, not great," Nikos said, putting his elbows on the table in front of him and holding his face. "She's been staying at the hotel since Monday."

Kostas grimaced. "What happened?"

Nikos thought back to their dinner Monday night. He'd been pretty terrible to Anna, and he knew it. He'd known it whilst it was happening. But every time the self-awareness crept in, the sanctimonious feeling of abandonment swatted it away, and the pettiness emerged. He'd rushed her out of the house unnecessarily. He'd made her feel bad about not making a reservation. He'd even given her a hard time about what she ordered at dinner, saying it didn't go with the wine he'd ordered, despite the fact that he'd jumped in before her, and despite the fact that he'd known from one glance at the menu what she would order. He hadn't even wanted seafood. He'd just wanted to spite her.

He wasn't proud of the way he'd behaved. But every time he thought about her standing up, slamming the cash on the table, and leaving him, he felt himself clench.

As his friends looked at him expectantly, Kostas as if he were ready for some gossip and Vasilis as if he might actually be able to help, Nikos sighed. If he couldn't speak to these guys, who could he speak to?

Well, Maria maybe, but that was a bit of a sore subject.

"Honestly, I was pretty horrible to her at dinner. She had every right to be angry. But I feel like I have a right to be mad, too."

"True that," Kostas said, nodding his head.

Vasilis, on the other hand, simply narrowed his eyes. "Why are you hurt?"

Nikos was pretty sure that Vasilis already knew the answer to this question, but he humoured him, anyway. "Because I feel like she's passing judgment on my friendship with Maria even though she fucks off around the world every chance she gets. If she's not going to be here, why does she care who I spend my time with?"

"Exactly," Kostas said. "If she's not going to be here, it's her own fault."

But again, Vasilis looked less impressed. "Did you ask her why she cared?"

Nikos shook his head. He was starting to feel a bit uncomfortable under Vasilis's gaze. "No, but she made it pretty clear that it was because she didn't know how close we were. Like, maybe she would know if she were here, you know?"

"Don't you talk about it?" Vasilis asked. He was pressing, but he wasn't accusing. If Nikos felt like he were on the stand, which he did, now that he thought about it, it was because Nikos wasn't saying everything. "It seems like Anna would pick up on how close you are given how much of a presence Maria is in your life."

Nikos sighed. Part of him wondered if Vasilis knew. "Well…" *Come on, he's your best mate. If you can't talk to him about this, who can you talk to?* "I don't exactly talk about Maria in front of Anna. Like, at all."

Vasilis breathed in deeply and nodded once. "So you've kept a close relationship with another woman a secret for years, and you think she's being unreasonable to be upset about that?" Again, his tone wasn't accusatory, or even firm. Vasilis was a remarkably even-tempered person, and that softness didn't relent, even now, when he could have just as easily called Nikos an idiot and left it at that.

"I suppose I see your point," Nikos said.

"I've not made a point," Vasilis replied. "This is your situation to navigate. I'm not offering advice or telling you what to do. I'm only trying to understand what happened, and how you feel about it, because clearly this is important to you."

Nikos rolled his eyes. Sometimes, Vasilis sounded like a wannabe-therapist, and it could be a little condescending. But he reminded himself that Vasilis didn't mean it that way. If he didn't believe he had a reason for Vasilis to talk down to him, he wouldn't be perceiving it as patronising.

"Listen, I get it," he said. "I've got no reason to be upset with her about Maria. She's definitely got the high ground there. But I feel like her being angry about that is keeping her from addressing the real issue, which is that she spends as much time away as humanly possible."

"Maybe Maria is the real issue for her," Vasilis said. "Or maybe it's a symptom for both of you."

"Yeah," Kostas said, chiming in. So far, he'd been looking back and forth between them like a verbal tennis match, but now he focused in on Nikos. "Maybe she's mad about Maria because she thinks you're getting back at her for being gone so much. And then you're mad about her being mad, because if she were around more then she wouldn't have anything to get mad at."

Nikos blinked several times. Kostas was being uncharacteristically wise. He was also right. "You're not wrong," he said, deciding that he needed to give Kostas a bit more credit.

"See, I knew that's why you and Maria were boning," he said, nodding and smiling in a self-satisfied way.

Nikos dropped his head into his hands. So much for giving him more credit.

"I am *not* sleeping with Maria!" he said. "We are *just friends.*"

Kostas's brow pressed together in confusion. "Wait, then why didn't you tell Anna about Maria?"

Vasilis chuckled. "Let's not let Kostas's characteristic oblivion cloud the fact that he was right just a moment ago. This isn't about Maria. So maybe it's time to focus on what it is about."

Nikos nodded. They were right. Both of them, sort of. Either way, he knew that he needed to have a chat with Anna. Plus, they were off to London in a couple of days, and he didn't want their frustrations bleeding into the trip. He had been planning it for months – not just the event, but their time together, too.

"I'll clear things up ahead of London," he said. His friends smiled.

"Show her what she's missing," Kostas said, and whilst Nikos knew from the wink and the cheeky grin that Kostas meant something very specific, it did give Nikos the seed of an idea. Maybe London would be the perfect place to remind Anna how happy they were when they were together, trying new things, without the pressure of the future or the weight of misunderstandings weighing down on them.

A couple of hours later, Nikos turned up the road towards the summer house, hoping Anna would be back that evening. Something in him felt that she would be. So as he drove, he rehearsed in his mind exactly what he would say. He would come clean about why he'd kept Maria a secret. He would make things right with Anna. And maybe, if things went well enough, he'd even take Kostas's approach to "show her what she's missing."

As he came around the corner just ahead of the drive, something darted in front of the truck. He slammed on the brakes mid-turn and felt the back wheels of the truck skid out from behind towards the hill on his left, and as the dust flew up around him and blocked his vision, the truck drifting, all he could see or think about was Anna.

Chapter Thirteen

Anna drove her motorbike home from the photoshoot, oscillating between feeling grateful that she didn't have to plan Elena's hen do and dreading spending it with Maria. She was sure Maria was lovely. Nikos wouldn't spend so much time with her if she weren't. But Anna couldn't get rid of the image she'd conjured of the two of them hanging out, laughing about how blind she was to their friendship. She knew it wasn't happening, that Nikos would never do that, but she couldn't help but picture it.

She'd calmed down a lot over the days she'd spent at the resort, and she even felt ready to address things calmly and constructively. But since she'd walked out on Nikos earlier that week, it seemed unlikely that he'd be as open. She hadn't heard a peep from him, though she knew he would be able to see that she was safe; they'd started using Find My Friends when Anna's trips abroad had become more frequent. Even so, what would his reaction be like when she went back? Assuming he was even there now.

As the main house came into view, Nikos was just coming

around the corner in the truck from the other direction. Anna knew he wouldn't be able to see her yet, and she wanted to avoid having to drive up behind him. Last time she had, she'd spent hours spitting dirt out of her mouth. She took a deep breath and held it, speeding up to pull into the drive ahead of him.

As she rounded the corner a few seconds ahead of him, her back tyre slipped just a little bit, but she easily righted herself and drove the rest of the way up the drive to the summer house, Nikos coming up the hill behind her. She heard him slam the truck into park.

"Are you insane?!" Nikos shouted as he got out, not even shutting the door behind him. "You could have come off the bike! And I nearly didn't see you!"

"I was fine," Anna said, "and I didn't relish the idea of eating your dust. Literally."

He was storming over to her, and she assumed he'd be checking the motorbike for damage, or even gearing up for a row. But instead, he beelined towards her and wrapped her in an impossibly tight hug, so close that it forced her head to the side.

Anna practically melted. After the last couple of days apart, with Anna spending most of her time working herself up over what was happening between them, she'd anticipated a rocky reunion. But this, how tightly he was holding her, how transparent his emotion was in this moment… she'd scared him, and he was beyond relieved.

Part of her was happy that it had happened because it had broken the ice between them. Maybe now it would be easier to connect without blowing up at each other.

"It's okay," she said, rubbing his back as he held her, his grip not relenting. "I'm sorry."

"Just don't do that," he said into her hair. "Beep at me and tell me to stop next time. My heart nearly stopped when I saw you slip."

He hugged her for a solid minute, not letting up at all, before she finally tapped him and ushered him inside. As he began putting away some leftovers – cheese, crackers, fruit – Anna was suddenly very hungry.

"How was your shoot with Xenia? That was today, right?" he asked.

"Yeah, really good," she said, plopping down on the couch. "How was your meeting?" It was Thursday, so he'd been at wine club. She didn't mention Maria, and she measured her voice carefully to make sure she didn't sound accusatory.

Nikos sighed. "It was good," he said. "I had a nice chat with Maria, actually."

Anna's entire body stiffened. "Yeah?"

He turned towards her, leaning against the worktop. "Yeah. She told me I was being an idiot."

Anna couldn't help but laugh. Even his side piece was annoyed with him.

"She said that I'm a chauvinist and an asshole if I resent you for having a successful career."

Anna didn't love hearing that he'd spoken to Maria about their problems, but it was nice that she was sticking up for her. Or at least for womankind in general.

"Do you?" Anna asked, picking at the skin on her fingers, avoiding eye contact. "Resent me for having a successful career?"

"Of course not," he said, his face collapsing as he sat down next to her. "And I'm so sorry that I made you feel like I do." He draped his arm across her shoulders, and she let her head rest against him.

"Good," she said. "Because I have everything I've ever wanted, and I would hate to think that our versions of happily ever after were so different."

He kissed the top of her head. "They're not." Then he straightened up and pulled Anna around to face him.

"But can you see my dilemma? Of course I'm happy for you. I love you, and nothing makes me happier than seeing you happy. But sometimes, I wish – admittedly, very selfishly – that you could be that happy without having to be far away from me so often."

Anna understood. Just like she hated the idea of him with Maria and her not knowing about it, he hated not being a part of her life, too. The only reason it felt chauvinistic was because he was the man and she was the woman. If it were the other way around, she'd feel completely justified in wanting him to be home more, and equally conflicted about expressing that desire.

Would she buddy up with a super hot Greek guy behind his back? Probably not.

"Why did you never tell me about Maria?" she asked, then took a deep breath, steeling herself, ready to get it all out in the open so they could put it behind them and move on.

"Honestly? It wasn't intentional." He fidgeted with his thumbs as he spoke, looking down at them. "Well, maybe at first a little bit. I knew it would be weird for you since she and I were supposed to go out all those years ago – when I stood her up because I was already in love with you – but I wasn't trying to keep her a secret. It just took us a while to get to know each other, and by the time we had, I just hadn't mentioned her, and so it felt easier to just keep not mentioning her."

Nikos trailed off towards the end, clearly hearing how that sounded. But after a few days of reflection, and after hearing how Maria had supported her cause, Anna was prepared to give him the benefit of the doubt.

"But still, why keep her from me? She's clearly been a big part of your life, at least lately."

Nikos took a deep breath and put his hands in his lap. His brow was furrowed, as if he were trying to remember something.

"It was a few months after I'd started wine club, after you got back from Australia. There was a wine club meeting where we paired up in a vineyard to go out and try to find the best bunch of grapes for a certain wine. Everyone else headed in the same direction, so we went the other way. It turns out it was super muddy, and we both ended up completely covered from the waist down."

Anna's face burned. She could practically fill in the blanks – *one thing led to another, and we were rolling around in the mud together.*

Nikos looked over at Anna and clearly noticed her distress. He quickly finished, "We changed into trousers from the gift shop while we washed ours in the laundry and went back to the group. Nothing happened between us."

Anna breathed a sigh of relief. But this clearly wasn't the end of the story, otherwise what was there to hide?

"When our trousers were dry, we put them back on, and I came home. And as I reached in my pocket for my keys, her underwear came out with them."

It took a moment to register, and then Anna cracked up. "I actually think I remember that," she said. "I was on the phone with some hotel receptionist in Melbourne when you came home. You looked panicked, but I was trying to track down my missing memory card, so I ignored it."

"I was *so* panicked," he said. "I knew nothing had happened, but I thought if you saw her underwear, you would think something had. So I hid it. And from that moment on, Maria felt like a secret. We had bonded over it, but I felt like I couldn't tell you because it looked bad. And the longer I went without saying anything, the harder it was to imagine bringing it up."

Anna nodded, thinking back to that night and the weeks that had followed. Had she known something was up?

As she reviewed the proceeding weeks, all of a sudden she froze, jumping to her feet.

"What is it?" Nikos asked, sounding nervous.

Anna walked over to the dresser and yanked open the top

drawer. She rummaged around until she found what she was looking for. She spun around and held out a black lace G-string.

"Did you stash Maria's underwear with mine?!" she shouted, waving them at him.

His eyes were wide and terrified. Anna could swear he was about to start crying. "I'm so sorry, I didn't know where to put them!"

Anna tried to keep a straight face for as long as possible, feigning outrage, but she couldn't help but laugh. Within a few seconds she was laughing so hard she could barely breathe. Nikos looked confused for a moment, but eventually, once he realised Anna was laughing and not having some kind of breakdown, he laughed along with her.

"Just to be clear," Anna said as she calmed down, "you come home with another girl's thong, and your first instinct is to throw them in with mine and hope I don't notice?"

"I know," Nikos said between gasps of laughter. "I'm an idiot."

"You're lucky Elena does so much of her washing here," she said, "otherwise the jig would have been up a *long* time ago."

"What, so you thought you were just keeping a pair of my cousin's underwear for fun?"

"I was gonna give them back," Anna said. "I just kept forgetting. I barely ever unpack my underwear. They go straight from the wash into my bag, so I never remembered."

Their laughter faded as Anna brought up her travel schedule.

"Also," she said, "don't hate me, but I have to take another trip. Elena's booked her hen do for next weekend."

Nikos nodded, surprisingly unbothered by this, at least as far as Anna could tell. Maybe because it was for Elena?

"That's fine," he said. "At least we have time together in London beforehand."

In just three days, Anna would leave to spend a couple of days in Ireland for a travel guide shoot, and then she would join Nikos in London for a big wine competition. They'd have a day together before and after the competition before she had to fly to Greece. Plus, she would finally get to experience Nikos's wine passion firsthand – he was entering one of his first bottles of the season to be judged.

"I'm so excited to try this year's vintage," Anna said, dropping her voice as she said "vintage" to sound as pretentious as possible. "I can't believe it won't be ready until right before you go. Isn't that a bit risky?"

"I mean, I'll try some beforehand, and if it's not good, I just won't bring any. We can still go to the event."

Anna pushed a strand of hair back off his face and tucked it behind his ear. "It will be wonderful," she said. "I know how hard you've worked, and I'm so, so proud of you."

"Back at ya," he said, kissing her softly.

Anna laughed with joy and wrapped her arms around Nikos's neck. As she looked her boyfriend up and down, she realised that, though a lot may have changed, and they certainly had their differences, she was still super in love with Nikolas Doukas. And pretty horny for him, too, it turned out, as his fingers danced along her spine.

Anna leaned in just a bit, biting her bottom lip, looking Nikos straight in the eye. She felt him tense as she pulled herself closer into him, her finger playing with the hair at the nape of his neck. As she moved forward slowly, his breathing grew heavier, until she was just an inch from his face. And then she kissed him.

The kiss deepened, and Nikos stood Anna up only to lean her back over the table. As he moved over her, propped up on his elbows, hovering over her, kissing her lightly all over and caressing her gently, she felt lighter than she had in weeks. They'd spent a lot of time since the engagement using sex as a distraction, but this wasn't that. Now, she felt like they were unburdened. Like they could finally, truly be together as one.

After, Anna rolled away from Nikos in bed, feeling absolutely weightless.

Nikos fell asleep almost immediately, so she got out of bed and grabbed her camera. She swapped out the memory card marked "Iliou" for the one marked "Home," then snapped a couple of pictures of Nikos's hair splayed out on the pillow. Then she scrolled back a few pictures to see the last photos she'd taken here at home. In the very next one, Nikos was wearing a hideous Christmas jumper, holding fake mistletoe over Anna's head whilst Anna held the camera out to take a selfie.

Could Christmas really be the last time she'd taken photos of her life here? She used to all the time. The further back she scrolled, the less time there was between the dates in the corner of the screen. She was glad Nikos was okay with her travel, but it hit her how much she missed the time she'd managed to spend here. She put her camera away, vowing to capture more of these moments with her family. They were important, and they deserved to feel important.

Anna snuggled back up next to Nikos and laid her head on his chest, hearing his heart beat. Maybe she would turn down a couple of the assignments she'd been offered for the autumn. What could it hurt? If it meant she got to spend more time where she was, cuddled up with the love of her life in the home they'd lovingly restored with their own hands, then it just might be worth it.

Chapter Fourteen

The next evening, Anna was still reflecting on the day before as she packed her bag. She was leaving for Northern Ireland soon, and then it was straight to London, and then straight to Nikiti for the hen do. She shuddered at the thought of having to check a bag, but, in the end, she managed to get everything into her trusty duffel. A couple of her outfits would just have to do double duty.

At eight o'clock, she sat down in front of her computer and pulled up her diary, layering Marcus's availability over hers. If his calendar was correct, he would be in his office right now. She placed her phone in the cradle in front of her and FaceTimed Marcus.

"Well if it isn't my superstar," he said as he answered, and Anna rolled her eyes. She could see that he was in his gallery in Manhattan, where she had worked as an assistant before moving to Greece.

"Hi, Marcus, I won't keep you. I've got a lot to do tonight." It wasn't exactly true, but Nikos wasn't Marcus's number one fan, and she didn't know when he'd be home. She tried to avoid the two of them coming face to face where possible.

Marcus tut-tutted. "Fine, straight down to business it is. Do you have everything ready for Friday?"

They spent the next few minutes going over everything she would need for the shoot: different equipment in different towns, different types of lenses, a million and one memory cards… the list felt infinite. Marcus would be flying over that evening to make sure that everything was in order before she arrived, and then they would spend a whirlwind forty-eight hours shooting before she flew to London.

Once everything was settled for the trip, their conversation turned to autumn bookings.

"We don't really have anything set in stone past this," he said. "I know you're taking some time off to be with your sister, but we really need to commit to a few of these jobs if we don't want them to move on."

Anna had been thinking a lot about this. Nikos was supportive of her career – he'd told her as much the day before. He wasn't asking her to give it up. But she also knew that her relationship and personal life were suffering because of it. So if she wanted to show Nikos that he was a priority, if she wanted to make sure he saw how supportive she could be, too, as supported as she'd felt when she came home to see her photograph hung on their wall as art, she knew she needed to make a change. She turned to face the picture for courage, pivoting Marcus with her.

"About that," Anna said, her face heating up a bit. Clearly, Marcus could tell, even on the tiny phone screen.

"No, no, no," he said. "You are not getting all soft on me. We're just building momentum!"

Anna sighed. "I know," she said, "but I'm spending too much time away from home. I've got friends and family and a relationship here that are being neglected."

Marcus shook his head. "If I'd known teasing you about what's-his-name would make you step back from work, I never would have said anything."

"You know his name is Nikos," Anna said defensively. "And it's got nothing to do with what you said."

"Oh bullshit. We both know it does."

Anna shrugged. "Well, I think it's the right thing for me."

Marcus sighed and rubbed his temples for a few seconds before replying. "Okay, so, what exactly does cutting back mean in this instance?"

Anna took a deep breath. "No more than two weeks away at one time, including travel, and I can't spend more than four weeks away in any three-month period." That would mean she would be home at least two-thirds of the time, and she should be able to come to Nikos's events regularly enough.

"*Are you shitting me?*" Marcus shouted, and Anna saw someone look up in the background. He wasn't exactly being private. "That's going to mean turning down eighty percent of these jobs!"

"Then turn them down," Anna said. "This is what I'm sticking with."

She heard the truck pull up the drive. Nikos was home.

"Listen, I've got to go, but we can debate specific jobs when I see you. Those are my terms moving forward. See you Friday."

Marcus opened his mouth to protest. "Anna, we've got to ta—" But Anna hung up on him mid-sentence just as she heard Nikos's footsteps on the path.

Chapter Fifteen

Anna shivered as the sea spray hit her again. She wasn't exactly dressed for cold weather. It was the beginning of summer, after all, and given that she'd just come from the Chilean winter not two weeks prior, she had expected it to be pretty mild. But she hadn't factored in how far north she'd be, and the fact that the best shots of the Giant's Causeway involved getting in the way of the ocean as it splashed onto the rocky shore. Anna crouched down between columns trying to get the right angle. It had a gorgeous, wild look to it, and her shots were going to be amazing, but her clothes were soaked.

She took a moment to breathe in the heavy seaside air, tasting the salt as she did. She could hear the waves crashing around her, literally at her feet, but she needed to stay steady. The damp between her toes from her wet socks made it difficult, but Anna pressed the balls of her feet down, feeling the unevenness of the ground through the thin soles of her trainers, and steadied herself. She inhaled, focused the shot, exhaled, and released the shutter. She continued exhaling for a count of three as the long exposure did its work. Then she stood up, opened the previewer on her camera screen, and celebrated internally.

She'd gotten the shot.

The water in the photo cascaded down over the columns of basalt, creating a smooth, calming effect. It wasn't right for the travel guide, who wanted to make it look as wild and untamed as possible, but it was one Anna wanted to add to her collection.

"Cool shot," Marcus said over her shoulder, "but I still can't believe you hung up on me." He hadn't stopped talking about their call since she'd touched down in Belfast the previous day.

"Can we please talk about this later?" Anna asked over her shoulder, gesturing to the rock formations. "I'm a little busy." She didn't really want to talk about it later, but she wanted to talk about it now even less. They were on a tight schedule. Plus, she wanted – no, needed – to stand firm on what she'd told Marcus on the phone before she'd left Greece.

The beauty of this shoot, which was to capture content for a new editorial-style travel guide, was that she didn't have to work around anyone else – no models, no directors, no product managers – but the downside was that Marcus was the only company she had.

"No, we'll talk about this now," he said, clearly getting worked up. "When we started working together, you said you wanted to do it all and see it all. I signed you because you were committed to doing this full out. And now a couple of years in, you're backing down? Right when you're hitting your stride? No way."

Anna grunted in frustration and lowered her camera. He wasn't going to drop this, was he? She stood up and spun around to face him.

"I did want that. I still do. But I've worked really hard to build a life for myself in Greece, and I don't want it to happen without me. So if your highness will allow it, I'll be making my own decisions about my career from now on."

She spun back around to start shooting again, but Marcus gently grabbed her arm. She was prepared to say something dramatic like "unhand me," but when she looked at him, he had a surprisingly worried look on his face, and she softened.

"Hey, is this about what I said on the last shoot?" he asked, removing his hand. "Because if so, you have to know I was just winding you up."

Anna sighed. This again. "I know you were. But you're not the only one who's said something like that to me lately. And I don't want to give things up completely, I promise, but if I don't change something, I'm afraid I'll lose him altogether. Maybe all of them. So I'm cutting back. And I think I can have both that way." She attempted to lighten things with a smile. "That's the modern woman's prerogative, right? To have it all?"

Marcus shook his head, not having any of it. "No. If you're going to quit, even a little bit, you should quit completely. Don't travel anymore. Because if you do this, if you insist on having both halfway, you'll get all the problems and none of the benefits of either one. Nikos will always say you need to stay home more, and you'll get frustrated when you're passed over for the jobs you do want because someone else is more flexible. So pick a lane and go full throttle, but don't idle in the middle like this."

Anna's eyes pricked with tears, but she hoped the sea spray hid her emotions. Everything Marcus was saying resonated with her – it seemed clear to her that he was right. But when the people and the life she loved, that she had actively chosen, were at stake, what choice did she have? She cleared her throat.

"You sound like you know what you're talking about," she said, trying to deflect onto him.

"Well, you weren't the first person I screwed, Anna." He put on an obnoxious fake swagger for his response, but almost immediately dropped it again. "I've been around the block. And I know what I'm talking about. So just be careful. Don't give up your dream unless you're completely confident that you want the alternative."

As she turned away and tried to find her light again, Anna couldn't shake the thought that his words were eerily similar to what Eirini had said to her as well. She wondered if maybe they were all three, despite their obvious differences, more alike than she'd thought.

Later that night, she sat in the bathtub in her Londonderry hotel room drinking a glass of wine from the bar downstairs. It was the kind of bath that was clearly meant for two people, but that made it all the more luxurious for Anna to soak in alone. She felt the heat from the water permeate all the way to her bones as they slowly thawed from the day of shooting. After the Giant's Causeway, they had visited a castle, a historic pub and what appeared to just be a stack of rocks in a field. It was a lot for one afternoon, especially with everything else Anna was holding in her mind, and she was exhausted.

The client always covered her room and board, but this hotel had thrown in a free bottle of wine and upgraded her room when they realised why she was there, probably hoping she'd have some pull regarding how prominently they were featured. So now here she was soaking in a gorgeous tub, letting the water warm her from the outside and the wine from the inside.

Just as she was finishing her glass and thinking about getting out, she saw her phone light up. It was Nikos, requesting a FaceTime.

She sat up, dried her hand on the towel behind her head, and answered.

"Oh hello," he said, his eyes widening as the picture loaded and he saw that she was naked. "You're lucky I'm alone."

"I suppose I am," she said, though she knew he couldn't see anything too exciting… yet.

Nikos was in his hotel room in London, where she would join him the following evening. He told her about his flight – a bit bumpy, but otherwise uneventful – and how the hotel receptionist had asked when his wife would be arriving.

Anna felt a smile play at her lips when he said that. She loved the idea of being Nikos's wife, at least when it wasn't hypothetically at the expense of her career. And maybe now she was on the road to having the best of both worlds.

"Did you correct her?" she asked, smiling playfully. Nikos shook his head. "Well, good. Maybe you should tell her we're on our honeymoon. See if we get an upgrade or a bottle of bubbly or something."

Nikos laughed. "Should I?" But even on FaceTime, she could tell that he wasn't looking at her face.

Anna nodded, becoming very aware of her body. She crossed her legs and bit her lip.

"What would we do if we were on our honeymoon?" she asked, angling the camera down a bit so it stopped just short of explicit. Anna knew she was a cliché – it only took one glass of wine to put her in the mood. And despite her conversation with Marcus earlier, she was definitely in the mood now. But they'd never done this over the phone before, despite all her travels. It felt naughty.

Nikos took the hint, taking his shirt off and sitting back against the headboard. There was a quick shuffle whilst he disrobed, but then he was there on her screen, all tanned and muscled, even more so than usual after all his time in the garden and the vineyard.

"Well, first I'd take you out and show you a good time," he said with a smirk. She could tell he was going to draw this out as much as possible. "Dinner, drinks, dancing…"

Anna pictured it in flashes. Him touching her leg under the table at dinner, inching his hand further north as the meal progressed; the taste of wine as he kissed her on a cobbled street, the cold air stinging her skin; their bodies pressed together on the dance floor, grinding against each other in time with flashing lights… she felt intoxicated just thinking about it. And it wasn't from the wine.

Her free hand floated up to her breast, massaging it as Nikos spoke.

"We'd barely even make it back to the hotel. In the elevator, I'd push you against the wall and kiss you, pressing my weight into you so you can feel how badly I want you."

With this, her hips began to rock gently in anticipation. She closed her eyes and pictured him whispering all this in her ear; imagined that it was his hand on her, reaching around and finding its way between her legs.

"I want you, too," she said, doing everything she could not to touch herself, but it was getting difficult. She clawed at her own thigh as she tried to resist.

"And then I'd lead you to the room, dim the lights, and take off your dress, slowly and carefully, your zipper cold on your skin."

Anna could picture it – he'd done it dozens of times, disrobing her slowly until she was practically begging for it – and a shiver ran up her spine.

"Then I'd gently kiss your neck, your shoulder, and all the way down to your hand. Then I'd put your middle finger in my mouth, close my lips around it, and suck it, hard."

"Fuck," Anna whispered, her eyes closing as she leaned back against the cold porcelain of the tub. She could practically feel her finger swelling as she imagined it in his mouth, his tongue tracing circles around it. She moved that finger between her legs, letting it explore how she knew Nikos would – how she'd felt him a hundred times before.

"Then I'd push you back onto the bed, tear your underwear off, and stare at you, taking you in, until you begged me to touch you," she heard him say, and she nodded.

"Yes please," she moaned, her fingers moving faster, the heat of the bathwater no match for the heat she could feel as she fingered herself, her whole body pulsing in time with her touches.

"Shit!" Anna shouted, feeling her orgasm build suddenly, like a wave in the ocean, surprising her. She rocked back and forth as she came, her body surrendering so fully that she had to fight to remember to keep her phone above water.

As the orgasm subsided, she slowly opened her eyes and looked down at her phone, where she saw Nikos smiling at her. She realised he was laughing softly.

"Hey, that's not very nice," she said, feeling her face go red, though she wasn't sure if it was from the heat or the embarrassment of how quickly she'd finished.

"No no, that was amazing," he said. "I didn't even get to the good stuff."

"Oh, I disagree, that was plenty good," she said, pulling the towel that had been behind her head up out of the bathwater where it had fallen. "Where have you been hiding that particular skill the last couple of years of FaceTimes?"

Nikos smiled. "I've been saving it for a rainy day."

"Well, let's just say you'll be in very high demand from here on out."

When they hung up a few minutes later, Anna found herself giddy at the thought that she would see him the next day. She hadn't felt that way in ages. It was amazing what a little phone sex could accomplish. Plus, she'd be able to tell him that she'd finally drawn a line with Marcus, and that she'd be home a lot more.

Anna climbed out of the bath and got ready for bed, reminding herself that she had a busy day ahead of her. She needed to be up and out by eight if she wanted to hit the other two stops on the list and still leave enough time to get to the airport. It wasn't an international flight, but she didn't want to chance anything.

But try as she might, she couldn't get to sleep. So just before eleven, she put on some jeans and a jumper, slipped on her shoes and went down to the bar. She figured she might as well try to get some more free wine out of the situation.

When she got down to the lobby, she saw Marcus at the bar chatting up a redheaded woman. She looked around for anywhere out of sight she could go. She didn't really fancy a late-night drink with him, but he saw her before she could sneak past.

"Anna!" he said, waving her over. She knew six-drink Marcus when she saw him. Or, rather, heard him. The southern accent he put on normally was slipping into a more generic American one, his real one, and he was living up to the stereotype in every way. Brash, loud and unaware of everything else around him.

"Hi, Marcus," she said, shooting an apologetic look at the girl for intruding. But the girl looked grateful, using Anna's arrival as an excuse to gather her things and leave. "Making an impression on the locals, I see?" Anna asked, nodding at the girl as she left.

"When in Rome," he said. "Or, should I say, when in Londonderry."

"No, you shouldn't," Anna said under her breath, but she took a seat next to him, anyway. She motioned for the bartender and ordered a large glass of Shiraz when he arrived.

Marcus was swivelling slightly on his barstool. He looked like the stereotype of an American gallerist; the guy the lead girl dates at the beginning of the romcom before she goes back to her hometown and finds someone she loves. How had she ever been attracted to him when there were men like Nikos out there?

She had been a different person back then. That was the answer. She hadn't even been a full person really. She hadn't known who she was. She felt instant gratitude that she'd managed to figure it out before things got any more serious than they had; that she'd managed to find herself after feeling so lost in the world for so long.

"Hey, sorry I got all serious earlier," he said.

"Makes for a nice change of pace," Anna said as her glass was placed in front of her. She took a sip and closed her eyes. Maybe by the time she finished, she'd be ready for bed.

"My ex-wife drank Shiraz, too."

Anna glanced at Marcus and made a noise of assent, then did a double-take. Marcus had never mentioned being married. Not once. Not even when they'd been dating.

"I managed to surprise you," he said with an air of self-satisfaction, raising his glass of whiskey to Anna before taking a gulp. She realised she was wearing her shock clearly on her face.

"Hardly," Anna said with a sneer, but then she softened. He was being more vulnerable on this trip than she'd ever seen him. Maybe she should return the favour and tone down the sarcasm. "What happened?"

"Exactly what I said would happen to you. I wanted success, she wanted to settle down. I tried to have both, but she was never happy, and neither was I, because no one was actually getting what they wanted. So I had to realise that I wanted artistic success more than I wanted her, and then I had to admit it. I wanted both, but push eventually came to shove. And I left her." He downed the rest of his drink and set it down loudly on the marble bar top. He waved to the bartender and pointed at his glass. Another one appeared shortly. "At least I had the sense to leave her before we had kids."

His blunt delivery made Anna wince. Clearly, from the way he talked about those things, he did want them. But this woman had made him feel like he couldn't have both.

"I didn't know," Anna said after a while.

"That's because I didn't tell you."

Maybe Marcus's ex had felt the same thing as Eirini; she didn't want to be left behind holding down the fort whilst Marcus lived his dream. This woman had probably been giving up dreams of her own to make things work, and it wasn't worth it anymore.

In a partnership, someone always had to pick up the slack. To carry the burden of keeping their life running. And if it wasn't Christos, Anna or Marcus, then it was Eirini, Nikos and Marcus's ex. And that wasn't fair to them.

Except Nikos wasn't sitting around cooking and cleaning all the time. Okay, he did a lot of cooking, but that was his choice. The point was, he wasn't just waiting around. He was getting to live his dream, too. He was getting to travel and learn new things and have new experiences.

No, that wasn't the problem. Marcus had said it. The tension is manageable when it's just the two of you. It's when you start thinking about what comes after that things start to break down. If Anna and Nikos had kids, who would look after them? Who would take a step back from their dreams to raise them? Based on their current arrangement, Anna would assume it would be Nikos.

Maybe that was why he was being so resistant. Because he didn't want to be a stay-at-home dad. She wouldn't know because she hadn't asked him. Maybe the issue was that Nikos had been thinking further ahead than she had realised.

"Were kids the issue?" Anna asked. She knew she was being nosy at this point, but she wanted to know. "Is that when the issues started?"

Marcus nodded. "There was always tension there, but when

we started talking about kids, it got way worse. She was a model – still is, as far as I know – and so she would have had to take a break from work, anyway, because of her body. She was happy to do that, and I was happy to let her. But I think she wanted to feel like I was willing to make the same level of sacrifice. But she was already making the sacrifice. Couldn't that have been enough for both of us? Why did I have to give something up too? Just for solidarity? That made no sense to me."

And honestly, Anna understood. If Nikos could work on the island and have a flexible schedule to raise a kid, why should Anna give up her travel? But just as Marcus's wife had, Anna knew that Nikos would feel unimportant and devalued if she ever said that to him, and she would feel the same if the roles were reversed.

Her post-orgasm high had definitely disappeared. She took a long sip of her wine and sighed. "This is all a bit too heavy for me tonight."

"Okay, well, how's this for a bit lighter," he said, reaching into the backpack he had leaning against the bar at his feet and pulling out a blue file folder. He dropped it on the bar top in front of her.

"That doesn't look very light," Anna said, pulling it towards her.

"No it isn't. Sorry."

She opened it up and saw a stack of paper thick enough to be a novella. Then as she leafed through them, she realised that each piece of paper was a job – one in Saint Kitts and Nevis, one in South Africa, several in the US, even one in the Galápagos – all costed, negotiated and detailed in front of her. There were travel schedules, a master calendar, expense sheets, commercial terms… all of the work was done.

Plus, the list of clients was as impressive as the destinations. Patagonia, BMW, REI, Hilton, Stella McCartney, The Hoxton, four different airlines, and... Anna's mouth fell open when she saw the last one.

"NASA?!" she said, practically squealing.

"The one and only." Marcus tipped an invisible hat to her.

"How the hell did you pull this off?" she asked, thumbing through the files, her mouth hanging open. She looked up at Marcus, who had a smug smile on his face.

"I pulled some strings," he said. "Mostly in the last forty-eight hours since you told me you wanted to quit on me. A bunch of these came from Patrick Farr, actually, the photographer you worked with in Chile."

Anna shot Marcus a look of disbelief. "I know who Patrick is. How did he get me these?"

"Seems he's ready to slow down," Marcus said, "because he's old and boring and has kids. Wants to give someone young and up-and-coming a chance. Someone like you..."

Anna rolled her eyes, but she felt a bit giddy inside. She'd loved working with Patrick, and clearly he'd felt she was up for the challenge.

"But all of those are happening in the next year."

Anna counted the number of jobs. "That's at least two jobs per month!"

"Sometimes, three," he said. "This is the opposite of what you asked for."

Anna shook her head. Nikos would never go for this – or, at least, he'd never be happy about it. He'd obviously never tell her she couldn't take them, but if pressed, he would say that she shouldn't.

But, at the same time, this was Anna's dream lineup. It had everything from fashion to travel to hospitality, and everything in between. So how could she say no?

This was a test. She knew that. Marcus wanted to show her exactly what she would be missing if she stepped back.

"When's the first one?" she said, flipping back to the beginning, trying to hunt down the earliest date of the bunch.

"Not until July."

Anna nodded. "Not until after the wedding then."

"What?!" Marcus barked. "You two aren't—"

Anna shook her head. "No, it's Elena. She's getting married in two weeks."

Marcus sighed. "Oh, that little minx," he said in a leering sort of way.

Anna chuckled, knowing that Elena would be furious to hear Marcus call her a "little minx" but too excited to call him out over it.

"And then my sister is in town until—"

"July eighth," he said, pointing to a job in Vancouver. "I remembered. That one starts on the twelfth."

Anna sighed. "Well, so much for a good night's sleep," she said. "I can't imagine I'll be sleeping again until I decide what to do."

Marcus was suspiciously quiet, and Anna looked at him, waiting for something. He cleared his throat.

"Not to add to the pressure, but there's something else."

Anna squinted her eyes. He sounded worryingly serious, as if he was about to tell her she was dying. She nodded for him to continue, and he took a deep breath.

"If you don't accept these," he said, "or at least most of them, I think we should terminate our partnership."

Anna frowned, her mouth agape. "Why?!"

"Because I've put a lot into working together," Marcus said. "I know we don't have the best history, but you have to know by now that I really care about you as an artist. And a lot of the time that we spend together on shoots, or organising those shoots, or networking on your behalf, is time I could be doing my own work."

"I never asked you to do that," Anna said. She'd known in the back of her mind how much Marcus was giving up for her. She'd idolised him when she first started studying photography. She'd gotten her big break at *his* Manhattan gallery and yet he was spending a huge portion of his time on Anna. She gave him a generous cut – almost as much as she made – for doing it, but she was also acutely aware of the opportunity cost to his own advancement within the industry.

"I know you didn't," Marcus said, holding his hands up. "I did it because I think you're insanely talented. And there's nothing more exciting than not only getting to watch a star on the rise but also to know that you're the one helping them along. I do it because I believe in you. But I can't justify it if you're not serious about taking advantage of these opportunities, because you'll look back in a few years and realise it was your peak. And if you haven't made the absolute most of your peak, you'll never forgive yourself."

Anna looked down at her glass. Every time she felt she'd made a decision, someone added something into the mix that felt important. And this certainly felt important.

Marcus put a tentative hand on hers and continued.

"And I wouldn't be able to forgive myself for putting my life on pause for a half-hearted effort. I've got my own career and reputation to consider. And as much as I enjoy working with you, I don't think we'll be a good fit if you're not one hundred percent committed to this work."

Anna nodded. She really did understand. It was only a couple of years ago that Anna was pining after Marcus because of his success, and now he was putting that on hold to help her.

"I never meant to make you feel like I wasn't grateful. You know I am, right?"

He nodded. "I know you are. And it's honestly a pleasure."

She paused for a moment, looking down at the folder. "You

know I have to think about this, right? I can't give you an answer here and now."

"I know," he said, nodding again. "Take the week. Even two. But Anna?"

"Yeah?"

"This is one decision you need to make alone."

Then he picked up his backpack, placed a hand briefly on Anna's shoulder, and left, leaving her sitting at the bar with a half glass of wine and a folder full of all her wildest dreams.

Well, all except one.

Chapter Sixteen

Anna's plane touched down at London City Airport twenty minutes early, which she felt was an auspicious start.

There was nothing fancy about London City Airport, but the idea that it was actually *in* London made it feel more decadent than when she'd flown into any of the other so-called London airports. She'd been at least a dozen times in the last four years, as a lot of Marcus's contacts were based there. She always felt a bit bedraggled by the time she actually managed to get into the city, and somehow the thirty minutes on the DLR felt far more manageable than a trek through Heathrow and an hour on the tourist-packed Piccadilly line.

Not that Anna wasn't a tourist. In fact, for the following day, Nikos had planned the most touristy day imaginable for them. But surrounded by the businessmen and the locals, she felt she was doing an okay job of blending in.

As she stepped out of the station at Bank and headed down Queen Victoria Street towards the hotel, she felt the sinking sun kiss her skin. Almost every time she'd been in London, it had been sunny, despite its reputation for gloomy weather. She had usually thought of it as a good omen. But as she cut down towards the Thames, she remembered the decision looming over her, and suddenly it felt less sunny.

It all went out of her mind when she saw Nikos.

He was sat on the brick wall between the path and the riverbank, leaned up against a black lamppost. With his yellow shirt and his long hair billowing in the breeze, he looked like Aquaman. The sexy one played by Jason Momoa, of course, not the cheesy comic book one. Anna started to laugh at the image of Nikos in tights.

As if sensing her mockery, he looked up from his phone and smiled. He hopped off the wall and trotted over to her, scooping her up in a hug and twirling her around before placing her back on her feet. He kissed her deeply, tilting her back as he did.

"Well, that was certainly a warm welcome," she said once she was vertical again.

"Well, I missed you," he said, continuing to plant kisses on her head, her cheeks and her mouth.

"I missed you, too," she said. "Marcus was a pain in the ass." *And he wants me to spend even more time away from you. But don't worry, it's just because he wants me to choose my career over our relationship.*

Nikos led Anna into the building and up to their room. He always unpacked his bag everywhere they went, and now was no different. She could see a pair of his pants peeking out of a drawer in the bedside table. Anna's things, on the other hand, would stay packed in her duffel bag until the moment they left.

"This place is nice," she said, looking around at the Scandi-chic decor and the minimalist art on the walls.

"It's pretty new," Nikos said. "Maria stayed here the last time she was in town."

Anna glanced at her phone. It had only taken twelve minutes for Maria to come up.

"Well, she clearly has good taste," Anna muttered under her breath, half hoping Nikos would catch the double meaning.

Either he didn't, or he did but ignored it. Instead, he launched into a debate over two different restaurants for dinner – the Indian fusion chain they had never been to but had a voucher for, or a trendy pizza place Anna loved but they would inevitably have to wait in line for.

"I don't mind waiting," Anna chimed in as she scrolled through her emails. "I'm not that hungry yet, and it's really nice outside."

Nikos made a joke about Anna having plenty of time to change, and she looked up at him, trying to judge if he was making a dig. But when she did, she saw that he was smiling, and it wasn't a condescending or sneering smile. It was an affectionate one. Maybe they had actually managed to make it through the argument after all. Which, of course, just made Anna's decision even more difficult.

"Good," she said, "because you won't want to miss what I brought for tonight."

Anna had brought a few different options for the trip: a crop-top and mini-skirt co-ord, a structured nude jumpsuit, and an emerald-green mini dress. She chose the dress. It was perfect for the flirty, girly mood she was in.

She took her entire bag into the bathroom to get ready, opting for her hair up and minimal makeup. The dress was perfect for the balmy sunshine, too: a wrap dress with thin straps over the shoulders, the back low and open. It reminded her a little of her bridesmaid dress, with the silky material, but unlike that dress, this one was short. Very, very short. The slit made by the wrap came up almost to her hip on one side, with a matching piece of green lace covering the space it exposed. She had to wear a thin, seamless nude thong to avoid it being seen, but it was better than the alternative of wearing nothing, which never turned out as sexy as one hoped. She chose flat sandals with thin straps that mirrored those of the dress, and a pair of dainty silver drop earrings.

When she stepped out of the bathroom, she couldn't help but laugh at Nikos's expression. He looked as close as a real human could to the cartoon cat with his eyes popping out of his head. She'd been saving this dress for a special occasion, and whilst she wasn't sure tonight counted as one, she was determined to make it feel special, if only to live up to the dress.

"You look insane," he said, stepping close, his eyes so obviously looking down Anna's dress that she couldn't help but laugh.

"Why thank you," she said, doing a little spin, and realising in the process that she had better watch her movements lest the entire square mile see her birthday suit. Nikos didn't seem to mind though, and it was everything Anna could do to get him out the door without a pit stop in bed.

An hour later, they strolled hand in hand into Neal's Yard as twilight fell.

Anna was always mesmerised by these little pockets of European cities. The courtyard was lined on all sides by colourful buildings and plenty of greenery, making it feel especially vibrant. A colourful hairdressers sat next to an upscale wine bar, which was sandwiched between the different storefronts owned by the iconic skincare brand that got its name from the tiny neighbourhood. And tucked right next to one of those eternally open massage parlours, which Anna was certain had to be a front for something, was the pizza place. And miraculously, there was no mass of people waiting outside.

Within a few minutes, Anna was snuggled up next to Nikos in a small booth, a carafe of red wine on the table in front of them. She rested her head on his shoulder as they read the blackboard full of specials, gawking at some of the more obscure toppings on offer, like air-dried Wagyu beef and Tenderstem broccoli.

Eventually they settled for Anna's usual: mushroom, ricotta, pumpkin seeds, chilli flakes, chives, and a soy truffle glaze. She didn't mention that the few times she'd been here had been with Marcus. She knew that wouldn't go down well, and she didn't want to start the next few days off on the wrong foot.

"I'm really glad you came with me," Nikos said, smiling as he poured Anna a glass of wine.

"Me, too," she said. "It's about time I came to one of these events."

Nikos graciously withheld his agreement, but she could see on his face that he did agree.

Before either of them had the chance to make it weird, Nikos launched into a story about the last event he went to – the "soil PH" course in Tuscany. He told her all about how he and Maria had shown up to the wrong vineyard, but because neither of them spoke Italian, they were halfway through a tour before they realised they were in the wrong place. By the time they noticed, it would have been rude not to finish the tour, so they tried to, but the man just kept adding stops because they were doing such a good job of seeming interested. Which they were, but eventually they had to fess up and leave so they didn't miss the start of the course.

Anna had already heard this story from Maria, but she was actually enjoying hearing it from his perspective. It sounded like the kind of hijinks she and Lizzy would have caused, and she forced herself to acknowledge that Nikos had found himself a pretty good friend.

In return, she took a chance and told him about a time she'd been shooting a vineyard near Melbourne, the one she'd been visiting just before the thong-in-pocket incident. She'd been photographing the same stop on the tour, in the part of the wine cellar where all the casks and barrels were, for nearly an hour. She'd been wondering why they had been there for so long, but she thought it must be important, so she didn't stop snapping. Eventually the man leading the tour looked over at her and asked if they could move on. It turned out he'd been dragging out that stop for ages because he thought Anna was trying to get a shot she hadn't managed to capture.

She knew that, sometimes, couples ran out of stories to tell each other, but usually that was reserved for those who spent all their time together. She should have had plenty of stories to tell Nikos, but usually he didn't like hearing about post-work drinks with Marcus or models she'd worked with in Los Angeles.

But something about the setting – a city that was comfortable for both of them but home for neither of them – put them more at ease. It had been forever since Anna and Nikos had laughed and swapped stories like this, especially without any awkwardness around the subject matter.

Three carafes of wine and dozens of anecdotes later, they were making out in the booth like teenagers.

Anna suppressed a giggle as Nikos's finger ran a trail just past the hem of her dress, just like in her fantasy from the night before. She could feel his hot breath on her face as they whispered to each other, taste the vinegary aftertaste of wine on his tongue, see the tinge of purple that had appeared on his teeth. Anna found this last detail particularly hilarious, and they took selfie after selfie on her phone, smiling to show off their wine teeth.

Eventually they found themselves stumbling through the streets of London, trying to walk with their arms around each other, clumsy as their bodies lurched back and forth but blissfully unaware of the clumsiness. They wandered through Seven Dials and past Covent Garden, eventually turning east to make their way towards St Paul's.

Anna smiled up at the landmarks as they passed, feeling closer to Nikos than she had in a long time. She paused in the middle of the pavement to admire him – the way his tee shirt rode up as he swung his arm, revealing a small patch of tanned, taut skin – and it took him a few seconds to register that she'd pulled away before he turned around.

"You okay babe?" he asked, taking the opportunity to check her out, and his gaze felt like it might bore right through her.

"I'm more than okay," she said, reaching out for his hand. "I'm just so fucking in love with you."

The smile dropped from Nikos's face, and for a moment, Anna's heart dropped. Was that the wrong thing to say? But as he stepped closer, Anna could see that it wasn't anger that was written across his face. No, she had seen this look before – on another drunken night, the summer they first met.

It was pure, undiluted lust.

Nikos walked forward until he was right in front of Anna, and he didn't stop. He kept stepping forward, driving Anna backwards, eyes locked the whole time, until she felt a wall against her back.

Nikos wasted no momentum. He grabbed her ass beneath her dress and lifted her up so she was on her tiptoes, their bodies perfectly aligned, him pressed against her so hard that she could have been fully off the ground and it would make no difference. She was too drunk to worry about what may or may not be on display right now. There was only Nikos.

She felt the brick scratch at her back where her skin was exposed, and she ran her hands up under Nikos's shirt to scratch him lightly, too. He kissed her hard and deep, his tongue running along hers, her hands clawing at the hair on the nape of his neck, their bodies fitting together perfectly, knowing exactly which buttons to press to add fuel to the fire.

He was so hard. She could feel him pressing more and more into her as he lifted one of her legs. She writhed her hips as he tried his best to close every gap between them, feeling the heat grow between them, even as the hot summer air formed beads of sweat on her chest and face. She wanted him so badly.

He pulled back for a moment and looked at her, his eyes so dilated Anna could see herself in them. He bit his lip and looked around frantically, settling his gaze on a gate next to them. He reached out and pushed on it lightly, and it swung open.

He stepped over and looked through, then back at Anna. She peered around the corner to see a dark alleyway running between otherwise empty office buildings. There was another gate at the other end. It was narrow. If she had been walking past, she never would have even noticed it.

She knew they were only a few minutes away from the hotel, but she didn't want to wait. She wanted this Nikos – the one who felt nothing but hunger and adoration for her – and she wanted him right the hell now.

She took his hand, pulled him through into the alley and pulled the gate shut behind her. He followed her until they were halfway along, shrouded completely in darkness. A doorway in one of the buildings offered some cover, and Anna decided this would do just fine.

Anna could no longer see Nikos's face, but she could hear his breathing, quick and shallow. It matched her own. Even in the darkness she could tell when she had locked eyes with him, and she held his gaze as she wrapped her arms around his neck and stepped backwards into the doorway.

Chapter Seventeen

The next morning, Anna awoke to a searing pain behind her eyes. The curtains were drawn, but the light seeping through the small gap at the bottom was enough to feel like it might blind her. She could feel Nikos's presence behind her, but the idea of rolling over to see him caused a wave of nausea to crash over her.

She lay there a few minutes, trying to see if things would get better, but they didn't. Eventually she felt Nikos begin to move.

"Morning," he croaked, at a volume that was probably hushed by normal standards but felt obscene to Anna.

"*Shhhh,* no yelling," she said, cringing. Even her own voice was causing problems.

Nikos rolled over and spooned Anna, and she felt for the first time how sweaty she was.

"No, babe, it's too hot for that," she said, feebly pushing him off.

Nikos laughed into her neck, adding even more heat to the equation. "Message received," he said, rolling away, the cool air left in his place a relief against Anna's back. She felt him swing his legs over the side of the bed and sit up.

"How would you feel about a shower?" Nikos asked.

Anna imagined cool water running over her shaky form and nearly said, "Yes, please," but then she pictured having to get up and get to that shower, waiting for the water to warm up, and she nearly lost it. She groaned and shook her head slightly. "Not right now."

"Okay, well I'm going to take a shower," Nikos said, standing up and walking around to the small kitchenette. He poured a glass of water and put it down on the bedside table in front of her, taking care to place it lightly so as not to make too much noise. "Please drink this," he said. "It will help."

Anna nodded and propped herself up delicately, adding a paracetamol to the mix from her toiletry bag on the floor. She gingerly placed the tablet in her mouth and picked up the glass. It was cold against her lips as she tipped the water slowly backwards, but the water had a sharp metallic taste.

She made a mental note to never drink red wine again. Then she remembered that she'd made similar vows to herself many times since Elena had gotten engaged. She would really have to watch the booze moving forward.

Then she looked over at her winemaker boyfriend turning on the shower and realised how unlikely that was. She wouldn't even be able to avoid it for this trip.

It was only eight, which was far earlier than Anna would usually try to revive herself when she felt like this, but Nikos was taking her to all his favourite touristy spots. And whilst she could think of a hundred things she'd rather do than walk anywhere right now, she knew the sun would be good for her. And clearly the trip had been good for the two of them.

Half an hour later, after she'd managed to drag herself to the shower, rinse off a small portion of her hangover, and barely keep down a croissant Nikos had brought up from the breakfast bar, she was as ready to go as she'd ever be. Nikos carried a large tote bag with him that he held protectively against his side, refusing to let Anna peek inside.

They started their ultra-touristy adventure by hopping on the Circle Line and making their way to Ladbroke Grove. They wandered through Portobello Road Market, stopping at stalls and trying on hats, sunglasses, and jewellery along the way. As they walked through the sunny morning and her hangover slowly dissipated, Anna found herself feeling hungrier, so Nikos led them to a donut shop with the most elaborate flavour options she'd seen. She chose a Ferrero Rocher doughnut, intending to munch on it as they walked, but they barely made it out of the shop before it was devoured. So she bought half a dozen more in other flavours to take with them, from red velvet cheesecake to chocolate milkshake and pistachio. Nikos denied having room in his tote bag for the box, but he produced a second tote out of the first, handing it to Anna.

"If you rack up this much baggage at every stop, you'll have to make a pit stop at the hotel," Nikos teased as he ate his own cookies and cream donut.

After the briefest wander through the streets of Notting Hill, with the requisite commentary on the unlikelihood of a bookshop owner ever being able to afford a home there, Nikos whisked them through Hyde Park and along the Serpentine, then through Green Park and past Buckingham Palace, and finally St James Park. Anna probably would have liked to move at a wandering pace to take some photos, but Nikos kept looking at his watch, trying to make sure they hit everything on his list, so it ended up being more of a power walk. They were enjoying each other's company, though, with Nikos sharing stories from his uni days in London and Anna telling him about her own college experience. They'd talked about all of this before, but the amicable atmosphere from the night before gave them a new sense of camaraderie that Anna realised they hadn't had for a while.

From the park they caught the Underground to the iconic Brick Lane, where they ate bagel sandwiches for lunch, the juice from the hot salt beef dripping down their fingers. Afterward, Nikos pulled Anna into a vintage record store as they passed, but instead of browsing the selection, he pulled her to a photo booth nestled in the corner. Despite the summer heat, they draped over each other in the tiny booth, making funny faces and kissing each other, spending far too much money on little strips of paper but having far too much fun to stop. Anna collected their prints as they left and chose a favourite – one where she was making a funny face at the camera, but Nikos was just staring at her, a huge smile on his face. He looked proud to be with her, and as she looked up at him, she felt the same.

"So, what's next?" Anna asked as they left the shop. Her legs were starting to cramp up from all the walking, and she made a big deal of rubbing them to get Nikos's attention.

"Oh come on, Linton, don't give out on me now. We've got a long way until Camden!"

Anna laughed. "There's absolutely no way I'm walking all the way to Camden from here. Can't we at least take a bus or something?"

Nikos shook his head, paused for a moment and then looked around dramatically. "No, I have something better in mind."

He jogged past Anna, and when she turned around and saw where he was headed, she laughed. He was standing in front of a bank of electric scooters for hire.

"There is no way I can drive one of those without crashing right now," Anna said, still feeling tender from their big night out.

"Don't worry, I can think of a way around that," Nikos said with a wink.

Two minutes later, they were tearing up the road, both of them on one scooter. Anna made herself as small as possible whilst she held onto the centre of the handlebars as Nikos stood behind her steering. Their tote bags flapped against their sides as they rode down the street, Anna worrying for the donuts in hers, and realising as it banged against her arm that Nikos had something quite hard in his. At least half a dozen cars beeped at them as they rode all the way to Camden High Street.

What would have taken them at least ninety minutes to walk had taken them less than half an hour on the scooter, leaving them with plenty of time and energy to weave through the strange and wonderful stalls of Camden Market. There was the obligatory Cyberdog stop, of course, with the flashing lights and neon clothes and random people dancing on platforms, but they also spent an inordinate amount of time in a Victorian art shop discussing which artistic period they'd most like to be a painter in, and even longer watching the canal boats passing through Camden Lock and making up stories about the people on board. After that, they found themselves passing a shop that seemed to be completely dedicated to the art of juggling.

"I'd have a conversation with you about which balls I'd use if I could juggle, but we both know that's laughable."

"Very true," Nikos replied, reaching up and pulling down a juggling pin. "I'm a pin man myself, anyway."

"Hilarious," Anna said. "All the better to drop on your head – or mine."

Nikos snapped his head up at her and smiled. Anna hadn't seen this particular expression before; his mouth was barely smiling, and his eyes were narrowed, as if he were on the verge of laughter. It was like someone had told a joke that she didn't get, which he would have expected her to understand.

Instead of explaining, he simply reached up, grabbed two more pins, and started to juggle them.

Anna's mouth dropped open.

"You can juggle?!" she shrieked, but it was a silly question, because not only was he juggling right in front of her, but he was actually looking directly at her, not at the clubs, whilst he did it.

It was a weird moment for Anna. Not because Nikos was juggling – though that was certainly unexpected – but because after all this time, there was something she didn't know about him. It was exciting, because it begged the question of what else there was left to explore about each other.

It was also strangely attractive, the juggling, his face all confident and playful, so she laughed and gestured for him to put them down before they ended up with a repeat of last night's alleyway incident. She suspected the afternoon crowd at Camden Market would frown on that.

By the time Anna's stomach began to grumble for dinner, most of the market was closing down for the day, but the post-work rush at the food stalls meant they were sticking it out. So Anna and Nikos took full advantage.

"Okay, we've got to be quick, because they'll be shutting down soon. What do you want?" Nikos asked, looking around at what was on offer.

"I don't know," Anna said, trying to take everything in but feeling overwhelmed by the options. "What's good?"

Nikos looked considerate for a moment, like he was going to answer, but, instead, he pulled out his wallet and extracted a stack of twenty pound notes. He handed two to Anna.

"You go that way"—he pointed behind her—"and I'll go the other. Get anything that looks good, then meet me back here and we'll take it to the park. Don't overthink it; the more random, the better."

Anna nodded and set off on her quest, trying to balance not wanting to stand in queues for too long with the fact that those were likely the best stalls. By the time she made it back to Nikos, she had her arms full of takeaway containers – a poke bowl, fried chicken, steak nachos, and a burrito made from a Yorkshire pudding. She'd seen a stall selling Philly cheesesteaks, but the line was too long, so she'd passed on that one.

As she approached the rendezvous point, she saw that Nikos had a similarly eclectic mix. It turned out to be a hot dog, an arepa, a burger, bubble tea, and some sushi. They managed to fit everything in the tote bags except the fried chicken, which they snacked on as they made their way out of the market. Anna followed Nikos down streets and over a bridge until they entered Primrose Hill.

As they wound up the paths, Anna turned to look behind her, and she realised she could see all of London laid out in front of her. The Shard, the Eye, the City, all of it. And clearly this was a well-known fact, as it seemed all of London had come here to watch the sunset. There was barely enough space for the blanket Nikos pulled out of his bag. But he managed to find a spot that was far enough away from the surrounding groups that they wouldn't have to pretend not to eavesdrop.

He also pulled out a bottle of wine, a corkscrew, and two plastic cups he'd clearly pilfered from the hotel. Together they laid out the spread of food and drink on the blanket, then sat down next to each other and tucked in.

If it hadn't been for the amount of walking they'd done, Anna doubted they would have been able to polish off all of the food, but they managed. Even now she was pretty sure Nikos would have to roll her down Primrose Hill to get her back to the hotel. The only thing left was the wine, and Nikos handed it to her.

"Are you sure you want me to open this?" she asked. "I'm not the best with a corkscrew, as you well know. And honestly, I probably shouldn't even have anything to drink after last night."

Nikos shook his head. "I do know you're not good with a corkscrew, and that's why I'll open it. But please look at the label. You're going to have to muscle through this one I'm afraid."

Anna dutifully brought it up closer to her. It had a beautiful label, with an illustrated image of a view that Anna would recognise anywhere – the caldera of Santorini. In a hand-lettered-style font, it said "Erastes".

"Is this from home?" Anna asked, admiring the label. The painting style looked so familiar.

Nikos nodded. "Brought it in my checked bag."

"I'm surprised it wasn't overweight. Didn't you have all your wine in there for the event?"

Anna looked up at Nikos and saw him smiling, tilting his head towards her as if waiting for her, and the penny dropped.

"Nikos, is this your wine?!"

He nodded and broke into a grin. "I wanted you to be the first to try it."

Her mouth hanging open, she turned the bottle over in her hands. On the back, she saw a credit for the artwork – Katerina. It was the same friend who had drawn the picture of her and her father. Of course, that's why she'd recognised the artwork!

She felt so proud in that moment, holding something made by the hands of the man she loved, in the place they called home, in a tribute to that place.

"What does it mean?" she asked, tracing the word Erastes with her finger.

"Lovers," he said. "I made it for you."

Anna looked at Nikos watching her, and she couldn't help but kiss him. The bottle dropped and rolled around between them as she launched over to him, caring little for the summer heat or their full bellies as she pressed her face to his. He reciprocated by moving the bottle out of the way so he could roll on top of her, his hair hanging down into her face, sending her into a fit of giggles.

They lay that way for a minute, him poised above her, her smiling up at him, planting little kisses on each other's lips every few seconds. Anna thought they felt like the embodiment of the word "lovers" in that moment: infatuated, intoxicated, single-minded in their affection.

"I'm so proud of you," she said, thinking of all the hard work that had gone into that bottle of wine.

"I'm proud of you, too," Nikos replied. "I know I don't say it enough, but I'm proud of how hard you work and how much you've achieved."

Anna smiled, her face flushing, and not from the heat. They were the exact words she needed to hear from Nikos.

"We're a bona fide power couple," he added, waggling his brow at her, sending her back into a fit of laughter. Eventually they pried themselves apart enough to open the bottle of wine and decant it into the plastic cups. Nikos handed her one and watched her take a sip.

Anna was no sommelier, but in the last four years, she'd learned what a good wine tasted like, and this was beyond good. It was incredible – a rich, oaky red with an almost cinnamon-y taste to it. Anna's eyes widened.

"Nikos, this is amazing," she said, immediately bringing it back to her mouth for another sip.

"You really think so?" His eyes were wide, his brow pressed together, his mouth in a slight frown. It was as if one word from Anna could make or break this dream of his.

"My opinion is hardly the most valid one here, but I love it," she said honestly, savouring the feel of it on her tongue as she spoke.

"I know you're just one person, but you're the one person whose opinion matters most to me." Nikos closed his eyes and leaned back on his elbows, smiling up at the sky. "Thank god you like it."

Anna could have melted. It was nice to know that Nikos cared so much what she thought. She cared about his opinion, too, always showing him the best shots after a trip, wondering if he understood why she'd made certain decisions. He always did. How lucky they both were to have someone who fancied them, shared their values, and understood them artistically.

But as the wine went to Anna's head, she meandered down the now-familiar path of questioning. If they had all of that going for them, how could it be that the issues they were experiencing now could feel so make-or-break? How could all of that be rendered pointless by the fact that their careers were both going somewhere, or that Nikos had a friend he hadn't told her about? Surely what they had together counted for more than that.

Just as she was starting to work herself up, Nikos put a hand on her leg.

"Stop that," he said.

"Stop what?" she asked, taking a deep breath and placing her hand on top, lacing her fingers through his.

"Whatever you're doing in that head of yours. Whatever is taking you away from me."

Anna sighed and looked up at him. *It's not that easy,* she thought. *Every time I think about how much I love you, I end up thinking about everything that's gone wrong lately. Everything that seems to be getting in the way.*

But she didn't say that out loud. She didn't want to burst the bubble. Instead she nodded at him and forced a smile.

"I know things haven't been great lately," he said. "But I do believe it's just a blip. You've got the summer at home, and I think you'll see that some quality time together will be exactly what we've needed."

And there it was. Nikos implying yet again that her travelling was the only real issue. But seeing how happy he was right now, how happy they could be when they were together, she couldn't do it. She wouldn't fight with him right now. So, instead, she mustered up a smile and snuggled up to him, sipping her lover's wine and watching the sunset over London.

Chapter Eighteen

Okay, deep breaths, Anna.

Anna took a look in the mirror and smoothed down her dress, a pale purple number that Elena had bought her for her birthday the first year after she'd moved to Santorini. She had picked it especially for today because she knew it was Nikos's favourite. That always made her laugh, because it was the farthest thing from a classically "sexy" dress – it was a lightweight knit material with a racerback cut, and whilst it did hug her curves, it also wasn't so tight that she couldn't get away with a sports bra and normal underwear. In fact, if not for the chunky gold jewellery and slicked back bun, it would have looked like athleisure more than anything else. She always wondered if he loved it so much because Elena had bought it for her, and he loved how close the two women were.

Anna was so excited to finally see Nikos in his element, but she couldn't help but feel nervous about being around Maria – or, more specifically, around Maria and Nikos together.

She knew she was being ridiculous; they had put the Maria issue behind them. But still, when she thought about how much time they'd spent together, she had to actively remind herself that nothing had happened between them.

Anna looked over her outfit, a quintessentially London summertime look, as she was coming to learn, of a midi dress and chunky trainers. After the event, they were headed out to some fun new Mexican restaurant, and then they were seeing the West End production of Hamilton. Anna and Nikos weren't huge fans of musicals, but they'd caught Hamilton when it started streaming, and since then, they'd been hooked. Each of them had been to London multiple times since then, but they'd always promised not to see it until they could see it together, and now was finally their chance. She wanted to look nice, but she also needed to be comfortable for the day, so she wore something that would work for both the walk to the venue and their night out later.

She opened her suitcase to put her wash bag back inside, but as she did, she saw the file Marcus had given her sitting nestled amongst her things. She picked it up and considered thumbing through it, but then she heard the door creak behind her, and she quickly stashed it in her tote whilst looking over her shoulder to make sure Nikos hadn't seen. She didn't want to go through this with him until she'd decided what to do.

"Almost ready?" he asked as he walked out of the bathroom, his blue floral short-sleeved shirt making him look like he was both perfectly coiffed and fully relaxed at the same time. But Anna could tell by the way he was wringing his hands that he was nervous. He began loading bottles of his wine into the tote bag he'd carried yesterday – apparently, he needed a few to make sure everyone got the chance to taste it.

"Ready," Anna said, stepping towards him and leaning in for a kiss. "You look very handsome."

"Back at ya," he said, but it fell flat. His mind was firmly on the events of the day, and Anna couldn't blame him.

They left the hotel and headed towards the venue, strolling along the river in the sunshine. They'd had a lovely, leisurely morning after their jam-packed day of sightseeing, opting for breakfast in bed rather than attempting the buffet. But now, as the heat of the day closed in, Nikos was clearly feeling wound up, and Anna was feeding off his nervous energy.

"So tell me what to expect," Anna asked, trying to get him talking.

"Well, Maria and Andreas will be there," he said, chancing a glance at Anna. She didn't give him any reaction. "Maria's just there for support, but Andreas has brought some bottles, too."

"Is his wine up against yours?"

Nikos shook his head. "No, his is a white. Which is more common on the island, not that there will be anyone else from Santorini there that I know of. There will be an overall winner of the day, but we'll be in separate categories."

Anna nodded along as he spoke. He sounded calmer already, so she knew she needed to keep him talking. "And how is it judged?"

"Well, the big competitions mostly use quality, value and package," he said, "but this one is just quality and package since a lot of people there don't sell their wines yet. So the quality will be about the wine itself, and the package will be about the bottle, the cork, the label, et cetera and how it complements the wine. It uses the Wine Spectator scoring, which is out of one hundred, but anything under eighty is considered mediocre or even undrinkable, so all the scores will be pretty high."

Anna grimaced. "Yikes. Have you ever seen one score that low?"

"Not at the big events, but at something like this there could be. Anyone could walk in with wine they made in their kitchen and enter."

She made a mental note to check with Nikos before tasting any of the other wines.

"So the judge's score will be worth sixty percent, and the attendees' will be forty."

"Attendees? Like, me attendees?"

Nikos laughed. "Yes, and me, and Maria. But we all have to taste blind so we don't lowball the competition. And we only weigh in on quality as a result."

Welp, there went my plan to avoid the home brews.

As they arrived at the wine bar, coming in through the front door and heading downstairs to where the event was being held, Anna's eyes went wide – and not just because it was nice inside, but because it was actually quite dark. The space was made up of a bunch of cave-like recesses, where folding tables were lined up to hold the various bottles of wine.

"Nikos!" someone called from across the room. Both Nikos and Anna turned to see who it was, but Anna knew before she looked, and she bet Nikos did, too. She'd recognise that voice anywhere. It was Maria.

Of course she looked gorgeous; she always looked gorgeous. Or at least, Anna imagined that she did. She'd only actually seen her twice, to be fair, and only once since she'd known who she was. But today she had on a tiny black minidress and four-inch gold heels. Sure she was short, but was that really necessary for a daytime event? It made Anna feel extremely underdressed again.

Nikos walked over and gave her a hug, and Anna noticed that it was definitely more friendly than the awkward side hug he'd given at the dress fitting. He pointed back at Anna as they spoke, and Maria caught Anna's gaze, giving her an enthusiastic wave. She followed Nikos over to where Anna was standing, next to a little table under the stairs.

"So glad you made it, Anna!" Maria said, pulling Anna in for a hug, which turned out to be kisses, actually, one on each cheek.

Anna stiffened at first, but she remembered to soften; she didn't have any reason to be hostile towards Maria, and she didn't want to be the one that came across as standoffish.

"Thank you," Anna said, reciprocating the hug. "It was about time, wasn't it?"

"I'm just so glad your schedule allowed for it. I know how busy you are," Maria said as she pulled away smiling, and Anna miraculously managed to abstain from rolling her eyes.

"Wouldn't miss it for the world," she muttered, but Nikos was already leaning in to talk wine. He and Maria reviewed the scoring, the other entrants, and how Maria thought he fared against the other entrants. Anna forced herself to stay engaged in the conversation, even when they were going a million miles a minute; she didn't come all this way to not participate and be supportive.

It seemed that the contest was only for independent winemakers, whatever that meant. As far as Anna could tell, it meant no established labels. This meant he was likely going up against other small-batch hobbyists and artisans rather than seasoned professionals.

The judge was going to be some famous sommelier from Australia, which Maria and Nikos seemed very excited about, even to the extent that it seemed some of Nikos's decisions around ageing and bottling were based on his judging history.

Just as they were getting into the specifics of the other entrants, Maria turned to face up the stairs and waved. Anna and Nikos followed her gaze, and Anna saw a tall, slender man whom she recognised from Elena's party. This must be Andreas.

As Maria got up to go greet him, Anna leaned in close to Nikos.

"Can I ask all my stupid questions now?"

Nikos laughed. "What do you mean stupid?"

"All the questions that I as your girlfriend should probably know the answers to, so I'm not asking them in front of other people."

Nikos nodded. "Go for it."

Anna took a deep breath. "Okay, so first of all, what makes this event so important? Don't you do these all the time? Why is this one worth changing your process for?"

"Well, I don't do these all the time," Nikos said, and Anna tilted her head to the side and frowned. Wasn't that what all of his travel was?

She asked as much.

"No, those are mostly educational, networking, or occasionally exhibiting. Some people have tried my previous vintages at those, but they've never been judged."

Previous vintages. It all sounded so legitimate. Anna felt her heart swell with pride.

"Okay, and what's the big deal with this Arthur guy?"

"Arthur Marsden. He's a sommelier and judge from Australia. They've got the best judging panels over there, and he's in town for a panel next week, so they managed to snag him for this event, too."

"And why is he such a big deal?"

"Well, he's one of the best connected people in the wine world, and he's got an unrivalled palette. Plus, he's got a reputation for being completely objective. That's why people will use his verdicts as a guideline because they know it's unbiased."

"Is he here yet?" Anna asked, looking around the space for someone with people congregating around them, but the crowd seemed pretty evenly dispersed.

"No, you'll know when he arrives though."

Anna leaned in even closer for the last question. "And whose ass do you really want to kick?" she asked, raising her eyebrows at Nikos.

He laughed at first, but then leaned in conspiratorially.

"Honestly, it's that guy over there," he said, subtly jerking his head towards the far corner. Anna chanced a look, and she saw a little old man – seriously, he couldn't have been younger than seventy-five or taller than five and a half feet – leaning against the bar.

"The old guy?!" she stage-whispered.

Nikos nodded. "That's Lorenzo Bonucci from Tuscany. He's been making small batches of wine on a one-acre vineyard for over fifty years. Maria took us to tour it last year."

"Short tour," Anna muttered, and Nikos chuckled quietly. Anna took in the persona that was Lorenzo Bonucci. Despite being of small stature, he was clearly very confident with a big grin plastered on his face. He was scanning the room and taking everything in. It was the smile of someone who was one hundred percent confident he was going to wipe the floor with the competition.

"There's a rumour going around that he's selling his land; that this is his last bottle."

Anna whipped her head back around. "That little old man is on his last bottle – the last vintage he'll ever make – and you want to kick his ass?" She shook her head in mock disdain. "Shame on you, Nikolas Doukas."

Nikos shrugged. "Listen, I doubt I'll even come close. And of course I want him to go out on a high. He's had an incredible career. But I'm just saying that beating him would be the ultimate victory. The man is a legend."

Just as they started to get into the particulars of the other people participating, Maria came by and told them things were getting started. Nikos stood up and walked over to a spot along the table closest to where they'd been sitting. Anna watched him take five bottles of wine out of his bag, examine each, and set one down on the table. The other ones were handed along with a piece of paper to Maria, who already held another bottle in her hand –

presumably Andreas's – and carried them both off towards a door. Anna assumed the kitchen was beyond that, given its proximity to the bar.

The crowd grew quiet as a group of people walked down the stairs. Anna couldn't quite see their faces from where she was sat, but as they reached the floor, everyone else began to clap softly, so she joined in.

"Thank you for joining us," a woman's voice said. "We are proud to welcome thirty-seven different winemakers to today's event, including several longtime friends"—several in the crowd turned to look at Lorenzo Bonucci—"and a record number of first-time participants. And of course, we are very honoured to welcome this year's head judge, Arthur Marsden."

The people filling the room clapped again, this time a bit louder. There was even a whistle from somewhere in the crowd.

"That's right," the voice continued, "we're very fortunate to have him amongst us this year, and I speak for all of us, including Mister Marsden, when I say how excited we are to sample your latest vintage. Now, a brief reminder of how today will unfold..."

The woman echoed what Nikos had told Anna, but one thing she was surprised by was the fact that the judges would taste the wine at the same time as the attendees. Whilst the judges would be using a more comprehensive scorecard, the attendees would simply submit their top ten by tasting them blind.

Almost as soon as the woman stopped speaking, a parade of waiters came out of the kitchen with wine glasses, water glasses, jugs of water, pads of paper, pencils, and what looked like little buckets. One of each was sat down in front of Anna, and she thanked the waiter who had placed them there. She wasn't sure where Nikos had gone, but she figured he would come over when he was done with whatever he was doing.

A few seconds later, another waiter approached carrying a bottle which had been wrapped in black tape with a big number two on it in white. She must have missed number one, but she was sure it would come around; she nodded at the waiter, who poured her a tiny portion of the golden white liquid and then moved on.

Anna did what she'd seen Nikos do each time he drank wine – she tilted it, swirled it, watched it drop down the sides, sniffed it, and then took a sip. Nikos always slurped it like he was eating soup, and Anna had always thought he was being distasteful, but she noticed others around her doing the same, so she did as well. She noticed the effect right away, the sweet and syrupy taste suddenly coming alive with citrusy flavours. She made a mental note to do this each time.

By the time she was done slurping, she didn't have any wine left – she doubted she would by the time she'd properly tasted things. Instead she poured a bit of water in the glass and swirled it around, draining that into the bucket. She also poured a glass for herself to drink and took a big sip, making sure to fully cleanse her palette.

Number one came around shortly after she was done, then number five, then three, then nine. She had to wave down the waiter carrying number eighteen. By the time she'd filled twenty slots with white wine, she was feeling incredibly tipsy. The water she'd drank was probably the only thing holding her back from being full-on drunk.

She looked around for Nikos. All this time he had been resenting her for not coming to these events, and now that she was at one, he was nowhere to be found. It made her wonder, did he actually want her here? Or did he just want to make sure that she wasn't off having fun without him?

She had wanted to avoid booze, and, instead, here she was, alone, after trying twenty different wines. She was too tipsy to be thinking about this, so, instead, she decided to lean in. She scanned her sheet to find which wine she'd scored the highest and flagged down the waiter carrying that bottle.

Chapter Nineteen

Nikos

After Nikos handed the bag with the rest of the bottles in it to Maria, he turned back to the one he'd set out on the table. It was the one Arthur would be judging later, so he wanted to make sure it was perfect. He'd already checked it a few times, but it didn't hurt to triple check. So he picked it up, gave it a once over, and wiped away a few fingerprints on the glass which were likely only just made. Satisfied, he placed it back on the table.

The nerves were getting to Nikos, and he desperately needed the bathroom, so he turned towards the back, scanning for signs for the toilet, when he saw Maria come through a door.

"Hey, Nikos, here's your bag," she said, and Nikos could see the bustle of the kitchen behind her. She held out Nikos's tote bag to her, but it didn't look empty. There was something weighing down the bottom.

"Didn't they need all the bottles?" Nikos asked. "I thought you said five?"

"They did," she said, but she was distracted, looking over

Nikos's shoulder and scanning the room. "It's just your paperwork left in there."

"What paperwork?" Nikos asked as he took the bag from her hand, but Maria was already off, clearly having spotted who she was looking for.

Maybe it's something from the event organisers? Nikos thought. He doubted it, but he wasn't sure what else it could be. So he stepped into the bathroom, where he found himself alone, opening the tote and looking down. Inside, he saw a blue file folder full of papers, some of which were coming loose. His first thought was that it must have been put in his bag by mistake in the kitchen – otherwise, wouldn't he have noticed it when he was unloading his wine? That said, he'd been quite distracted. His palms had been so sweaty, in fact, that he forced himself to hold each bottle with two hands so he wouldn't drop one.

Yes, it was entirely possible he had missed the folder earlier, but that still didn't solve the mystery of what it was. Perhaps it was Anna's? But how had it ended up in his bag? It definitely hadn't been there when he'd packed the picnic supplies the day before or unpacked them later that night. So what was it?

There was only one way to find out. Nikos pulled the folder out of the bag and opened it.

The first thing he noticed was Anna's handwriting scrawled across the top of the first page: "4 days after Lizzy leaves." So this was definitely hers.

Any doubt to that effect, had there been any, would have been eliminated when he read the actual printed contents of the page. It was a summary of a photoshoot in Vancouver – the client, the location, the equipment list, the coordinator, the fee.

Nikos felt like his eyes might pop out of his head when he saw the fee: six thousand dollars per day, plus travel expenses. He knew Anna wouldn't see all of that – she'd admitted once that Marcus took a larger than usual chunk for a manager because of how much of the work he did – but it still made his eyes water. He'd known that she was making good money, but this was next level. It was an eight-day shoot, meaning she and Marcus would make more on that shoot than he had in a year working for Christos. It was no wonder she squeezed in as much as possible. Then again, if she was making that much, she could certainly afford to stay home a bit more.

As Nikos thumbed through the pages, it became crystal clear that staying home more was not her intention. In fact, the jobs he was looking at would keep her away more than ever before. There were dozens of jobs, all of which looked objectively incredible. But Nikos didn't feel very objective, especially when he did the mental calculations and realised this would only have her at home forty-four days in the next six months. Only a week per month.

This file wasn't just some passing research. It was months and months of scoped out, genuine jobs. Nikos figured she must have been compiling it for weeks, if not longer. So every time he'd mentioned her staying home more, she had known that this existed. She had known that she had no intention of doing that. And yet she'd said nothing. She'd even brought the file with her, presumably to go over with Marcus whilst they were in Ireland. She was probably looking through them before he'd called her – had them just out of reach as she touched herself to the sound of his voice.

The pages began to blur, and Nikos realised he was crying. A few tears dropped onto the pages, so he packed them back in the folder, albeit not in order, and shoved it back in the tote. He took a few deep breaths to try to calm himself.

Just as he began to wonder what he would do, how he would approach this with Anna, he heard a woman's voice call everyone's attention outside. He wiped his face, checked the mirror to make sure he wasn't visibly upset, and then left the bathroom when he was confident he could pass for excited.

He stepped past a few people milling about and saw Anna, sat by herself at a small table, looking around for him. He considered walking up to her right then and confronting her about the file, but he couldn't do it. He didn't want to. Today was about him, and about how hard he'd worked on Erastes, not about her. Unlike every other day of their lives, today was about his dreams. And he wasn't going to let her ruin it.

But he also wasn't going to sit with her and pretend everything was okay.

So he ducked behind a group of people and made his way around to the other side of the stairs where she couldn't see him, sitting down at a table with Andreas. He would talk to Anna later. For now, he needed to focus on himself.

Chapter Twenty

It had been nearly forty-five minutes, and Anna still had seen no sign of Nikos. She decided she'd better get up to look for him before the reds came out. She wanted to be with him when she tried his. She hoped she would recognise it when she did.

As she peeked around the stairs, she was surprised to see Nikos at a table with Maria, Andreas, and another person she recognised. She took in the scene as she made her way across the room to them. The man was older than them by at least thirty years, with a tanned, wrinkled face and curly grey hair pulled back into a low ponytail. Maria was sat next to him, leaning towards him in a way that seemed intent on conveying nonchalance but was actually very intentional. They were all listening to Andreas as he described some misadventure involving a phone booth.

"Hey," Anna said, placing a hand on Nikos's shoulder.

"Hey," he said back, looking up at her briefly, then doing a double-take. "Okay, Drunky McDrunkerson."

Anna felt her mouth drop. "I am not drunk!" she protested,

perhaps a bit too loudly. Nikos laughed, but to Anna it sounded stilted. Tense.

"My love, have you been using the spittoon?"

Anna gave him a confused look, and Andreas pointed at the bucket in front of each of them. The realisation dawned on her.

"I thought that was for leftover wine!" she said, only now realising that it would be absurd to expect anyone to drink thirty-seven one-third portions of wine without falling over. Math wasn't her strong suit even at the soberest of times, but she was pretty sure that equated to over a dozen glasses of wine, more than half of which she'd already consumed.

The table erupted with laughter, except Nikos, who had a smile plastered on but didn't seem to be all that happy to see her.

"Oh don't you worry," Maria said, "I did the same thing at my first event. I always thought it was a shame the wine isn't enjoyed to the fullest." She stood up from her seat next to the older man and put a chummy arm around Anna – too chummy, perhaps, but Anna was tipsy enough to appreciate the support, both social and physical. She reminded herself that this woman was a friend of Nikos's, nothing more, and that she should make an effort to be friendly with her, too.

"Thank you," she said, crossing her arms and giving the gentlemen a look that said *See? I'm not the only one*. Even if she was very much the only one at the moment.

Nikos stood up and offered her his seat, but in a way that felt less like a question and more like a command. "I'm going to go get you something to eat," he said with a forced laugh. "I'm not having you missing my entry because you're too drunk to stomach it."

Anna waved him away jokingly, trying to ignore the jab about being drunk, and then turned her attention to the others at the table. Her gaze caught the older man, who was looking back at her as if he were trying to figure her out.

"Do I know you?" she asked, frowning.

"I doubt it," Maria said, back with that chummy arm, this time patting her hand. It was a bit condescending, but she'd allow it. "This is Arthur Marsden, today's head judge. Arthur, this is Nikos's lovely partner Anna."

Anna nodded and said "Oh, okay, nice to meet you," as Arthur reached out to shake her hand, but there was something bothering her, and she couldn't dismiss it. "Actually no, that's not it. I know I know you from somewhere."

Arthur smiled. "Yes, I believe we met at my winery outside Yarra Glen last year."

As Maria and Andreas turned to her with stunned expressions, Anna pieced together the rest of the puzzle. This was the owner of the winery where she'd spent an hour listening to the tour guide rattle on about different types of barrels. "Of course! You were doing a partnership with that travel brand."

"Arthur, darling, I'm going to get my feelings hurt," Maria said in mock sadness, hitting Arthur on the arm. "I've never even been invited."

"Well," he mused, smiling at Maria, "when you become an award-winning photographer hired by the brand I'm partnering with, I'll be sure to get you a press pass."

Maria rolled her eyes playfully, but her eyes briefly flickered back to Anna, and Anna thought she looked impressed.

"Actually," Arthur added, leaning in close to Maria, "if I recall correctly, I invited you to Yarra Glen last time we rendezvoused in Paris." He lowered his voice when he said "rendezvoused," and Anna realised what he meant. She tried to control her facial expression, but she could feel her eyes go wide, and clearly Andreas noticed.

"Oh, yes," he said softly, leaning over to Anna, "these two go way back. You'll notice that no other entrants are sat at a table with the head judge."

"But he must be twice her age!"

Andreas shrugged. "Doesn't seem to bother either of them."

Maria and Arthur continued to gaze at each other, and Anna suspected that the rest of the room had melted away.

Just then, Nikos arrived back at the table.

"Okay, I've got chips, bread, and a small cup of walnuts." He set the plate down in front of Anna, perhaps a bit too forcefully, and Anna descended on it immediately. She had enough wherewithal to know she should offer some to the others and eat delicately, but not enough to actually do that. She immediately scooped up a handful of chips, dunked them in mayonnaise and shoved them in her mouth.

"That's right, keep it up," Nikos said. "You've got seventeen wines left to try, mine included, and I need you with it." He pulled up another chair next to her, knocking her a bit as he scooted in.

At the same time, Arthur and Maria stood up and left the table without a word of explanation.

"Apparently they do that, sometimes," Nikos said in Anna's ear.

"Yes, so I've heard," she said through a mouthful of bread, nodding towards Andreas. "Was it cool getting to meet Arthur?"

Nikos grinned, despite whatever had him in a mood. "So cool. We've been talking about him being here for months, and to finally meet him is crazy. I wasn't prepared for how laid-back he would be."

Anna nodded, remembering how easy he was to work with in Australia. "Yeah, I get that from him, too," she said. "He's really knowledgeable, but not pretentious about it."

Within a couple of minutes, the food on her plate was gone. Her stomach gurgled, wanting more, and Nikos's comment about seventeen more wines played over in her mind.

"Where's the food table?" she asked Nikos, and he pointed her around the corner without a word, scrolling on his phone, instead.

She took her plate to the next room to see a huge spread laid out, with cheeses, cured meats, bread, olives, chips, breadsticks, crackers, nuts, sauces, pork pies, sausage rolls, fruit, and more. It was the charcuterie board of dreams.

She knew what Nikos would say – stay neutral to keep your palette clean – but she couldn't help but add a few sausage rolls to her plate alongside the breadsticks, crackers, and more chips. Just as she was debating adding some fruit as well, Arthur walked up to the table.

"I'd hold off on the fruit and cheese until after the reds," he said. "When you've picked your favourites, then you can try them with different foods."

Anna nodded and stepped away from the strawberries. "It's good to see you again," she said when he didn't move away.

"You as well," he said. "Working with you was great. I've been in front of the camera with some photographers who try to get you to do all sorts, but it was like having a normal, productive workday and then finding out someone had taken really good pictures of the whole thing."

Anna smiled. This was her favourite kind of feedback to get. Especially since the photos from that trip had been so good once Anna had gotten her memory card back that she'd been booked for three more jobs with the travel company who had hired her.

"Thank you," she said. "It was a great trip for me; I did a few jobs while I was there, but your vineyard was definitely the most beautiful setting."

"Will you be back in Australia anytime soon?" he asked, and Anna instantly thought of the folder Marcus had shown her a couple of days prior. Australia – Melbourne even – had been on the list.

"I'm not sure," she said. "Maybe."

"Well, we don't always have a huge budget to fly people in – I leave that kind of splashing out to the travel brands – but if you're in the country, it would be great to have you. Between you and me, we have a big rebrand coming up, and we could use new visuals to go with it."

Anna's initial reaction was to jump at the chance, but her conflict over whether to take the accelerated route with Marcus made her pause. Then again, if she might lose Marcus as a booking agent, she'd need to make her own connections, so either way she needed to say yes.

"I think I will be," she said, smiling. "And I'd love to work with you again."

As she spoke, she saw Nikos come up behind Arthur.

"Reds are coming out soon," he said, gesturing for them to follow. He smiled at Arthur, but as soon as he'd passed, his face dropped into a scowl.

"Are you okay?" Anna asked, touching his arm.

"Fine," he said, "but I'd be better if you could just take it easy with the wine please."

Anna followed him back to the table, wondering how she was meant to take it easy when half the wines were still to come, just as the reds began to circulate. Maria was already back in place, though the left pocket on her blazer was turned out. Anna discreetly tucked it back in for her as she sat down next to her, and Maria mouthed her thanks.

Any doubts Anna had that she would recognise Nikos's wine went out the door the moment she tried her sixth red. The cinnamon tinge, the weight of it on her tongue, the deep crimson colour, the lingering taste of blackberries... this was definitely Erastes. But she kept her enthusiasm to herself, not wanting to give anything away to Arthur. Nikos's wine would win on its own merit, not because they were sat at a table with the head judge.

"So, Nikos," Arthur asked as the last of the reds were cleared. "What made you choose to focus on red wine rather than white or dessert like most of the other Santorini winemakers?"

Nikos shrugged. "I'm a red wine drinker myself," he said, "and like you said, so many people are doing white wine well, including my friend here." He nodded at Andreas, who pressed his hands together and bowed his thanks to Nikos.

"And he thought he'd make his life more difficult," Maria added with a laugh.

Arthur opened his mouth to ask a follow-up question, but a woman came up next to him and whispered something in his ear.

"I'm afraid I must go play judge now," he said, standing up, "but thank you for the wonderful company." He looked Anna in the eyes. "Let's talk soon," he said.

Anna didn't want to miss the opportunity, and she didn't know how connected he and Maria actually were, so she reached down into her bag and pulled out her wallet, slipping out a single business card. She reached over the table to hand it to Arthur.

"Anytime."

Arthur nodded at all of them and then left, heading upstairs with the woman who had collected him.

Nikos turned his head to face Anna as soon as Arthur had disappeared up the stairs. "What the hell was that about?" he asked, a scowl on his face.

"We were talking about work," she said, feeling defensive. "Is that okay with you?"

Nikos sighed. "Honestly? It's a bit tasteless to flog your wares like that when we're in the middle of something important to me."

"I'm sorry, but he and I—"

"Could you not stop thinking about work for one week? Not even a week – just three days together? Is that too hard for you?"

Anna snapped her mouth shut. He was getting worked up, and despite the fact that she'd used her spittoon for the reds, she was still too drunk for this to go well. So, instead of biting back, she collected her things and stood up.

"I'm going to go back to my table if it's free. I think we both need a moment." She shot apologetic glances at Maria and Andreas, who nodded solemnly at her.

"You know what?" Nikos said, turning forward and putting his elbows on the table, his hands balled in front of his face, very much not looking at Anna. "I think you should just leave. I will meet you later."

As he said that, he bent down to grab something out of his bag, dropping the file from Marcus on the table in front of her.

At first, Anna was confused – how had he gotten it? Had he seen her earlier whilst she was looking at it? Had he gone through her stuff? But then, when she looked down at the bag he'd retrieved it from, she realised what she'd done. With two nearly identical bags, it was a mistake anyone could have made. But now it had cost her… well, she wasn't sure yet. But it had certainly cost her something. At least now his mood made sense.

Maria looked up at him. "Nikos, it's not actually—"

"No, it's okay, I'll go," Anna said, standing up. She didn't want to make a scene. She knew this was important to him. "I'm going to turn in my rankings, with Erastes firmly at the top, and then I'll meet you later. I love you, and I'm proud of you."

Then she picked up the file and her pad of paper and walked away.

Chapter Twenty-One

Nikos had said he would meet Anna later, but she had no idea what he meant by that. Did he mean at dinner? At the show? At the hotel? She didn't want to text him to find out, not after their almost-fight, so, instead, she found herself a coffee shop across from the Mexican restaurant where they'd made their booking. She ordered herself a latte and a slice of cake, put in one of her earbuds, and turned on a true crime podcast she'd seen someone rave about online.

In fact, she was so engrossed just over three hours later that she nearly missed Nikos's laugh bellowing across the street.

Her first reaction when she heard him – and she would recognise that laugh anywhere – was relief that he still wanted to eat dinner with her. But when she looked up, she saw him ushering someone through the door to the restaurant, gold heels glinting in the sunlight.

Anna froze in her seat, her mug halfway to her mouth. Surely he hadn't brought Maria on their date night.

Of course she'd known he might want to meet her at the theatre rather than at dinner, and she'd assumed he might go out to eat with Maria, instead. But bringing her to *their* booking, just inserting Maria into their plans, instead of her, felt like crossing a line. Was he going to take her to the show as well? Maybe move her into the summer house whilst he was at it?

She tried to tell herself that he didn't do it to hurt her – that he didn't know she'd be sat across the street waiting for him – but she couldn't quell the anger she felt at both of them, and part of her believed that he was actually being vindictive. After finding that file, she was sure he'd be furious. It was the opposite of what they'd talked about. But it was no excuse.

As the anger bubbled up inside of her, Anna went into autopilot. No thoughts, just movement. Up out of her seat, towards the front door after hastily gathering her things, across the street, through the door of the restaurant. By the time she got to the "Please wait here to be seated" sign, she still had zero idea of what she was going to say or do.

The hostess looked at her expectantly, but she blew right on past as if she belonged there.

The restaurant was dark, with mostly candlelight – quite romantic, in fact – but Anna could just about make out Nikos and Maria at a table up ahead. There was a slatted wall in the way, but Anna could see Maria's gold shoes crossed under her chair. As she got closer, barely concealed by the slats in front of her, Maria sighed. Then she began speaking in Greek.

Anna struggled to make out what Maria was saying, but she caught the gist.

"Just leave her," Maria was saying. "Stop being such a *mártyras* and leave. Then your *efiáltis* will be over for good."

Anna didn't know what mártyras meant, but assuming it wasn't a false cognate, Maria thought Nikos was being a martyr by staying with her. And she wanted him to leave her.

Had Nikos been complaining about Anna? Had they been secretly talking about her the whole time? Silly Anna who just doesn't get it, doesn't deserve what she has? How could he be having this conversation, sitting across from someone who clearly hated her if she was saying all of that?

All these thoughts flew through Anna's mind in half a second whilst Nikos and Maria sat silent, starting at each other, and yet again, Anna was frozen in place. She had three choices. She could stay and listen, but eventually they'd see her. She could leave, but where would she go? Or she could stay and confront them, but what would she say?

None of her options felt right, but something inside her decided she couldn't sit there and listen to Nikos's response, whatever it was going to be. If it wasn't what she wanted to hear, if he didn't shut her down and tell her to back off, she wasn't sure she'd be able to forgive him. So she turned around and left, shooting back past the hostess and out the door as quickly as she'd entered.

She made a split-second decision, fuelled by a heavy dose of embarrassment and a double measure of tipsiness, to go home. Even if she was jumping to conclusions, which she admitted was a possibility, she had had enough. She didn't want to be there. She didn't want to deal with it. So she went back to the hotel, and for the second time in the last week, she packed her bags to get away from Nikos. This time, though, she wrote him a note on the hotel stationery, leaving it on the dresser with the photo strip from the record store:

> This isn't the time or place to do this, and I can't fake a smile for the rest of the trip. Sorry about the show, but I'm just not up for it. See you at home.

The trip back had been difficult enough to make her seriously question her decision. Her journey started with the dreaded Piccadilly line journey to Heathrow. The ease of London City was a distant memory as she watched a man clearly on his stag do vomit on the platform. Even when she arrived at the airport, she barely made her flight, which was the last one of the night. She then landed in Athens at four in the morning, endured a three-hour layover in a practically desolate airport, and finally caught a horribly turbulent Ryanair flight to Thera with so little legroom that she came away with a slight bruise on one knee where it had been pressed against the tray table. The worst bit was that she would have to do the same journey back in just two days' time; her flight to Thessaloniki was from London, and the direct flights from Santorini had been completely sold out.

The next morning, Anna stepped out of a taxi in the driveway that led to the summer house. She paid the driver with a crisp banknote – she'd had to get cash out especially for the occasion – and watched him back up towards the road, trying to find the energy to carry her bag inside. Now, with just a few steps left to her house and her bed, the effort felt Herculean. She managed to drag her bag across the gravel and through the front door, barely pulling her shoes off before collapsing onto the bed, the door still cracked open.

Anna heard laughter coming from the main house, and the last thought that passed through her mind as she drifted off to sleep was that it sounded an awful lot like her sister.

Chapter Twenty-Two

Actually, the voice sounded exactly like her sister. Except now it wasn't laughter from a distance, it was an actual voice, and much closer. It almost sounded like it was standing over her.

"I know you think she should sleep, but she's not supposed to be here. I spoke to Elena, and she's meant to be in London right up until the girls' trip. Surely we should make sure everything is okay."

Then she heard her grandmother reply. "Wake her if you want to, Lizzy, but it seems to me she needs the rest."

But that didn't make any sense. Yaya never came in the summer house without being invited in, and Lizzy wasn't due in for more than a week.

Anna reluctantly opened her eyes, just a sliver, to see Lizzy sitting on the edge of her bed and Eirini propped against the doorframe. Lizzy looked back over at Anna, and when she saw that her eyes were open, she gasped.

"Anna, you're awake!" she said, and she fell onto Anna for a hug.

"You'd think I'd been in a coma or something," Anna muttered as she tried to sit up, but Lizzy was hugging her too tightly. She just propped herself halfway up with one arm, instead, and slung the other over her sister. "Wanna tell me what the hell you're doing here?"

Lizzy sat up. "Um, same for you it seems. Why aren't you in London with your boyfriend right now?"

Anna rolled her eyes. "Honestly, don't ask," she said, sparing a glance at Eirini, who had her arms crossed and her brow pressed together. "But don't worry, everything is fine," she added, more for Eirini's benefit than Lizzy's. She would see through it, anyway.

It seems Linton women have a knack for removing themselves from uncomfortable situations, she thought, thinking of her mother whilst looking at her sister, having just left her own partner for the second time in a week.

"Martin troubles?"

It was Lizzy's turn to roll her eyes. "Yeah, you don't ask about Martin and I won't ask about Nikos."

Anna nodded and lay back down. "Deal."

Lizzy lay down in the bed next to her, their arms linked together. After a couple of minutes discussing logistics, it was agreed that Lizzy would stay out in the summer house with Anna whilst Nikos was still away. Evening was still a way off. Anna had only managed two hours of sleep before being woken up by her concerned family, but, apparently, Lizzy had an impressive amount of baggage with her, which Eirini said was taking up the kitchen and keeping her from being able to make lunch. So Anna helped Lizzy haul her five bags out to the summer house, where they managed to take up nearly the entire living room area – and no, she wasn't allowed to ask why Lizzy had five bags worth of stuff with her for a trip that should have been only a few weeks – so the two stepped outside and sat down on the swing. The sun was now high in the sky, and they could already smell the aromas of lunch coming from the main house.

"The garden's looking incredible," Lizzy said, then winced as if to apologise for bringing up something related to Nikos.

"It's fine," Anna replied. "Yeah, it's incredible. It all tastes amazing, too. I honestly feel like you can tell how fresh and local it is."

Lizzy laughed. "Yeah, well, you literally can't get any more local than that." She pointed to the window between the kitchen and the garden, where Nikos often passed produce directly inside to avoid trailing any dirt through the house.

The two sat in silence for a moment. Anna felt weird not telling Lizzy everything that happened with Nikos, but it felt equally weird not to ask about what was going on with Martin and the million suitcases. She knew they had been having problems, but it wasn't like Lizzy to keep things to herself, and Anna certainly hadn't known that it was bad enough for a transatlantic escape.

Then again, she wasn't really one to talk at the moment.

"Okay, this is weird," she said, right as Lizzy started to say, "This is ridiculous."

Both laughed, and Anna put her head on Lizzy's shoulder. "You first," she said, hoping Lizzy would bite the bullet for both of them.

Lizzy took a deep breath. "Well, I think Martin and I may be splitting up."

Anna sat up and faced Lizzy. "Really? I didn't realise it was that bad."

Lizzy nodded. "It's been pretty bad for a while, but things finally came to a head." She paused and took another audible breath. "He cheated on me."

Anna frowned. That was shocking. Lizzy and Martin had been together since school, and never once had Anna doubted that Martin worshipped the ground Lizzy walked on. But clearly things had deteriorated more than she'd realised. In fact, she tried to remember the last time she'd seen Martin and came up short.

"There's more to the story, and I promise I'll tell you someday. But for right now, the only important thing is that I didn't leave him for nothing. I have my reasons. And they're good ones."

Lizzy was getting choked up, her words catching in her throat. Anna knew better than to physically comfort Lizzy when she was upset. She hated soothing touches, but she inched just a bit closer on the swing so their legs were a bit more pressed together. She just needed to let Lizzy know she was there, and that the past they shared was a non-factor in her eyes.

"You don't have to tell me that," she said. "I know you're not Mom. And I know you wouldn't leave him if it weren't for a good reason."

Lizzy nodded and wiped her face on her sleeve. "Thanks."

"So is that what you're doing? Leaving him?"

"I think so, yeah."

"Then you can stay as long as you need to," Anna said, chancing a quick squeeze around Lizzy's shoulders. "Nikos won't mind."

"Yeah, speaking of," Lizzy said, clearly keen to change the subject. "Aren't you meant to be having a romantic getaway in London right about now?"

Anna rolled her eyes. "Yeah, well, I wasn't exactly in the headspace for a romantic getaway anymore, and I don't think he was either."

"Wanna tell me about it?" Lizzy asked.

Normally, Anna wouldn't have hesitated to tell her sister everything. She was so firmly on Anna's side that she was an almost guaranteed ally in any situation. Today, however, something about the way she'd shown up and clearly been speaking to Elena gave her pause – a pause she didn't fully understand.

But Lizzy was Anna's closest confidante in the world, and there was no one else on the planet Anna wanted to speak to about this more. So she suppressed her doubts and decided to tell Lizzy everything.

Anna sighed. "Well, to start with, I'd basically decided to set some boundaries with work and tell Marcus I could only travel a little bit, but then he gave me a dossier of my absolute dream jobs that he's booked for me." Anna stood up and stepped through the door, grabbing the file from the table inside and handing it to Lizzy.

Lizzy thumbed through the papers, seeming just as excited about the jobs as Anna had been when she'd first seen them.

"Anna, these look amazing. Can't you just pick the best ones and do those? Even a handful of these would make for a hell of a year."

"Not exactly," she answered. "They came with an ultimatum. He doesn't want to put his own career on hold if I'm not all in. And these jobs only exist for me because of Marcus."

Lizzy didn't love Marcus, Anna knew that, and she expected a snide comment here, or to tell Anna to go around him and try to get the jobs directly, but Lizzy just nodded. "That does seem reasonable for him," she said, "though I can't imagine it's easy for you."

Anna shrugged. "And then while we were in London at Nikos's wine competition, the head judge ended up being a former client. And when Nikos saw me give him my business card, he freaked out about me not being able to switch off from work for just one day."

Lizzy nodded some more. "Definitely an overreaction, but I can see why that would happen based on everything else you've told me."

"Well, it turns out he'd found the file in my things, and I guess he thought that I'd decided to ignore what he wanted. And he sort of lost it."

Lizzy didn't reply, clearly able to tell that there was more. Anna took a deep breath before bringing up Maria – the part that, amongst the rest, felt somewhat petty and yet like the biggest stab in the back. "And then, after I left the bar, I waited at the restaurant where we had reservations, and he showed up with Maria. And she told him he was acting like a martyr by staying with me, and that he should leave me so his nightmare could be over."

At this, Lizzy was silent. Anna could practically see her cogs turning behind her eyes, but she couldn't tell what she was thinking.

"How do you know she told him that?" she asked after a moment.

"Um..." Anna knew this part was going to sound a bit unhinged, but this was Lizzy. There was no judgment here. "I heard it directly. I sort of followed them into the restaurant."

After a second of wide-eyed, shocked silence, Lizzy burst out laughing. "Okay Nancy Drew."

Anna chuckled uncomfortably. "Yeah, it was a bit much. But honestly I didn't mean to go in and spy. I meant to say something. It was only when I overheard them that I stopped."

As Lizzy's laughter died down, she took Anna by the hand. "Do you think it's possible that you misunderstood them?"

Anna frowned. "I mean, they were speaking in Greek, but I know what I heard." Anna had looked up the parts of the conversation she hadn't understood, and she was right about what Maria said. Plus, she'd learned the Greek word for nightmare.

Lizzy shook her head. "But that just doesn't make sense to me. From what I've heard, Maria is all about the girl power. It doesn't sound like her to put you down just to make a point to him, or for her to encourage him to leave you."

Anna froze. She pulled her hand away from Lizzy's, looking down at her feet as she spoke her next words. "What do you mean 'from what I've heard'?"

"You know, from Elena and stuff. When we talk."

"You've talked about Maria?"

"I mean, yeah, she's a pretty big part of Elena's life. Nikos's, too, from the sound of it. It seems like they're all pretty close."

Anna felt like she'd been punched in the gut. Her chest tightened, she could feel a pressure at the back of her throat, and she struggled to inhale. Not only had everyone else on the island known how close Nikos and Maria were, even her own sister, who had never met Maria and lived halfway around the world, had somehow picked up on it. Was Anna really that oblivious?

Even in the moment, she knew it didn't make sense, but her overwhelming emotion was fury towards Lizzy. It felt like a betrayal. Lizzy had sat there and listened to Anna complain about Maria whilst they were at the fitting, and yet she'd said nothing. No heads up, no context, no nothing.

"Why didn't you ever mention it to me?"

"Because honestly, Anna, until last week when you told me, I didn't even realise that you were out of the loop. And plus, it's not like I've met her or seen it with my own eyes."

"But you knew about it."

"I only knew what Elena told me, which was that they hung out from time to time. All of them, together. On their cousin nights, or whatever."

"Cousin nights?" Anna searched her memory for Elena or Nikos ever having used the phrase, but she came up dry.

"Yeah, their nights just the four of them. Elena's cousin and Vasilis's."

"So you mean a double date."

Lizzy pursed her lips. "No, I mean like cousin nights. You know they don't mean it as a date."

"No," Anna said, "I don't know what they mean, because I've never heard of these 'cousin nights.'"

Lizzy frowned. "I assumed you would have."

Anna rolled her eyes. "Well, you assumed wrong."

"Clearly." Lizzy stood up off the swing. "Listen, it's fine if you want to be mad at me about it. I know you're hurting, and I can see how it would feel weird to find out about all this after so long. But I don't think anything untoward is going on, and I think you should give both of them the benefit of the doubt."

"But she just told Nikos to leave me! How am I meant to spin that in a positive way?"

"I don't know," Lizzy said, annoyingly calm, like she had no idea why Anna was so bothered. She stretched her arms over her head, then pulled her phone out of her pocket and checked the time. "Now, Elena will be here in under an hour. I'm going to take a shower, you're going to make us some lunch, and then we're going with her to some wedding appointment, and we're going to forget all about this for a while, okay?"

Anna stared off into space as Lizzy walked away, trying to process what she'd heard and how she felt about it.

Not only was Lizzy closer to Elena than Anna had realised, but she'd been more in the loop about Anna's own home life than even Anna was. And even worse, the one person she could always count on as an ally seemed to be less firmly on her side than she'd thought.

When Anna heard the shower start, she walked inside and opened the refrigerator to start working on lunch. Inside there was a casserole dish full of something that smelled lemony and garlicky, so she scooped some out into a bowl and put it in the microwave. Out of habit, she mentally thanked Nikos for having the foresight to prep some food, and then she reminded herself of everything that had happened. Being angry with him was difficult – there was so much consideration and love contrasting the hurt.

For a moment, Anna felt a pang of guilt over leaving him like she did, and she felt she should at least let him know she was okay. She wondered what he had done last night, and what time he'd discovered that she had left.

As the bowl of food spun around in the microwave, she pulled out her phone. As she went to open the phone app, she saw that she had an Instagram notification, so she opened it up. It was a message from an influencer who was travelling to Santorini over the summer and wanted some pictures taken.

When she'd first moved to the island, she'd made good pocket money taking pictures of tourists and influencers in Oia and at other landmarks. She hadn't done it for a while, but sometimes, she missed doing portraits. It was far more dynamic and fleeting than landscapes and products – more challenging. She decided to respond and see when the influencer would be in town. Maybe she could make it work. Again, depending on what she decided to do with the jobs in Marcus's file, she may need some backups lined up.

As she closed the message and returned to her feed, Nikos's name jumped out at her – his Story was the first in the queue. She tapped the green ring around his photo, one she'd taken in the garden last summer, and smiled when she saw what came up. Nikos had won second at the wine competition, and the picture was of him shaking Arthur's hand.

> Massive honour to place second today! Thanks to @mariamerlot89 for helping make Erastes a reality!

He must have come in second only to Lorenzo Bonucci. Anna knew that Nikos would view this as a win. She felt a swell of pride as she held her finger on the screen to look at the image for longer. She quickly rummaged through a cabinet one-handed to find a bottle of champagne and popped it into the fridge for when he got home.

The next photo, however, nearly made Anna drop her phone. It was reposted from Maria and showed her and Nikos in a selfie in front of a stage. Anna knew from watching it online that this was Hamilton. Worse still, Anna could see Nikos's hand wrapped firmly around Maria's waist.

Anna must have stared at the image for nearly half a minute when the microwave beeped and jolted her out of her mini fugue state.

She quickly took a screenshot and pocketed her phone. Her phone call to Nikos seemed irrelevant now. She needed a bit more time apart to think.

Chapter Twenty-Three

As Anna looked out across the water from the bow of Vasilis's speedboat, her icy mood had officially thawed. After collecting them from the summer house, with much gushing and hugging between her and Lizzy, Elena led them down to Athinios harbour where the boat was kept. The road down to the harbour was full of switchbacks and crowded with large trucks bringing shipments up from the freighters, so Elena had to concentrate. This meant she didn't ask Anna why she was there, or what had happened with Nikos. Anna had briefly thought that it may be because she had already heard from Maria, but she shook that thought away. It had been a while since she'd had an adventure with Elena, much less with Lizzy along for the ride, and she didn't want a raincloud hanging over their time together.

Now, as droplets of salt water stuck to her face and her hair, Anna could feel all those worries and thoughts disappearing in the wind.

So far, even though Anna knew they were tagging along on a wedding-related appointment, they didn't seem to have a specific destination; they were just circling the island, taking in the sights.

They'd first headed north through the caldera and past Oia before rounding the northern side of the island and heading down the eastern coast. As they went, Anna could hear Elena and Lizzy chatting from the front seats, but she couldn't make out what they were saying, and she didn't try. Instead she stayed in the bow. It was a quintessential Santorini summer's day without a cloud in the sky, so she tilted her head back, her golden hair billowing behind her, the sun shining warm on her face and shoulders.

About half an hour after they passed Kamari Sands, Elena pulled into Blychada Marina, which had a long curved pier sheltering a tiny harbour. Anna only knew what it was called from the sign at the end of the pier; she'd never been to this part of the island before.

"Where are we?" she asked Elena as they stepped off the boat.

"It's the southernmost part of the island," Elena replied, leading them along the curved pier towards a large white building set into the cliff side. "It would have been much faster to sail around Akrotiri, or especially faster to drive, but where's the fun in that?"

"I would have been sorely disappointed if I'd not been chauffeured here by boat, and I fully expect it for the rest of my visit," Lizzy replied, laughing and taking Elena's hand. The two of them walked along the pier side by side with their long, dark hair and olive skin shining in the sun. Lizzy had always looked more like their Greek father, whilst Anna was the picture of her WASPy mother. But seeing Lizzy here, it struck her that she looked so much more like she belonged than Anna did. No one would automatically hand her a tourist menu in restaurants, or question when she said her father was from here, or roll their eyes every time she lifted a camera to her face, all of which happened to Anna on the regular.

"So what exactly are we doing?" Anna asked as they walked

through the doors of the large white building, which was clearly a hotel.

"Eating cake, of course," Elena said as she walked straight through the lobby and into what looked like a ballroom of sorts, the Linton sisters in tow. "Xenia said the best wedding cake baker on the island works here, so she's arranged for us to do a tasting."

Anna smiled, and Lizzy jumped up and down and clapped her hands together. "Oh, yay!" she said. "I didn't think I'd get to do any fun wedding stuff."

"Don't be silly," Elena said. "You'll come on my hen do this week, too, right?"

Lizzy looked back at Anna.

"Don't look at me," Anna said. "I'd love to have you there, and I've obviously got no plans for you." She stepped up to join the other two and put a hand on the shoulder of each of them. "Plus, the bride always gets her way."

Elena laughed. "Damn straight. Now, let's eat some cake, shall we?"

"Wait, shouldn't Vasilis be here for this?" Lizzy asked, following Elena across the ballroom.

"He's in Athens again, tying up some work before the wedding. He'll be back this weekend. Plus, cake is much more my domain."

As they walked through another door into the kitchen, Anna's mouth almost instantly began to water. In front of her, on a massive stainless-steel workbench, were three full-sized wedding cakes. Each stood three tiers high, with perfectly smooth frosting – possibly fondant – and stunning decoration.

The first was a gorgeous white-and pink ombré with petals cascading down one side, so lightly placed that they looked like butterflies that had landed on the cake for just a split second. It was feminine and delicate and light in a way Anna wouldn't have thought a massive wedding cake could be.

The second cake was a striking black square with silvery shards of what Anna assumed was chocolate stuck into the side like fans. She took a step towards this one, looking closely at the shards to try to understand how they were defying gravity by staying in the cake.

But the final one, Anna knew immediately, was the cake Elena would love the most. The bottom layer was covered in a fluted frosting with what looked like pressed flowers in various vignettes all over, except the flowers were all white and gold. The middle layer wasn't cake at all, but a fully transparent resin layer with flakes of gold throughout. The top layer was covered entirely in brushed gold leaf, and on top of all of it were dainty white and gold mini macarons. Clearly, the cakemaker had known what she was doing, too, because this one was front and centre as they walked in the door.

"Holy shit," Lizzy said, staring at all of them. Anna looked at Elena, and she could see she had been right. As she stared at the one in the middle, her eyes were practically popping out of her head.

"How did I do?" a voice asked from behind them, and all three of them spun around at once to see a petite Greek woman standing in the doorway.

"They're amazing, Magda," Elena said. "Just like I knew they would be. And thank you for allowing the extra guests."

Magda waved her hand. "No worries. I lived in the US for nearly ten years, so English is fine by me. And the more the merrier."

"Are these all for weddings this weekend?" Lizzy asked, pointing at the cakes.

"Two of them are," Magda said. "Can you guess which one isn't?"

"That depends," Anna said. "What's different about the other one?"

Elena was smiling slyly, so clearly she knew the answer already. "One of them is just frosted Styrofoam," she said.

Anna looked from Magda to the cakes and back again. "One of these is fake?"

Magda shrugged. "The decorations are real, just not the cake. Go on, see if you can find the fake one."

Anna looked back at the cakes, inspecting them for a giveaway, but she couldn't see anything obvious. The only thing she could think was that it might be easier to get Styrofoam into a square shape, and maybe that was why the shards could look as if they were levitating. So she pointed to that one.

"Nope," Magda said, smiling proudly. "That one's on its way to Fira for a wedding tomorrow night. The middle one's the imposter."

As Anna looked over the most impressive of the three, everything made sense. Of course it looked tailor made for Elena, because it had been.

"Well, you've certainly nailed Elena," Anna said, still gawping at the cake.

"She most certainly has," Elena said. "They're all gorgeous, Magda, as I knew they would be, but it's definitely this one."

Magda grinned. "I thought it might be. And the size is fine? This should do you up to sixty guests."

Elena nodded. "That'll cut it close, but should be fine. Could we do some extra macarons?"

"Of course you can. We have displays which we can bring to go on either side of the cake."

"Cake and macarons, all gilded!" Lizzy said. "How very decadent. Feels very regal."

"Whatever the bride wants, the bride gets," she said, unknowingly echoing Anna's earlier words as she ushered them around to the other side of the workbench. They stood in front of what looked like an assembly line setup behind the cakes. There were large bowls full of cubes of different cakes, smaller bowls of what looked like sauces and jams, a few deli containers of what Anna thought might be toppings, and a huge metal bin of teaspoons with an empty plastic bin beside it. There was also a large pitcher of water with four glasses, plus three pads of paper and three pencils.

Magda explained the process to the girls. They should use the teaspoons to spread the filling of their choice on the cake of their choice, using the crumbs as desired and putting each dirty spoon in the plastic bin. Then they could take notes in their notebooks and cleanse their palettes with the water.

They didn't need much encouragement; as soon as Magda had finished instructing them, all three women jumped straight in with the tasting. Anna briefly flashed back to the previous day's wine tasting process – god, had it really *only* been a day? – but then she got distracted by a heavenly cookies and cream cake and coffee ganache filling combo. On a whim, she added some of the malt crumbs to the second bite, and as she put it in her mouth, she could feel her eyes roll back in her head.

It was so good. More importantly, it reminded Anna of a grown-up version of a snack Elena asked her to bring back from the States every time she visited – Oreos and Ovaltine.

"Elena, try this one," she said, pointing her to the right combination. Elena's reaction was almost identical to Anna's, her eyes going wide and her feet tapping on the floor in a frenzy. She tapped Lizzy on the shoulder and, when she turned, put the second bite straight into Lizzy's mouth. Lizzy paused as she tasted it, then shimmied her shoulders somewhere between a shiver and a dance.

Magda laughed. "I take it we have a shortlist candidate?" she asked, and after enthusiastic nods from all three of them, she made a note on a tablet she was holding.

After just twenty minutes of tasting, they had incredibly full bellies and an incredibly full shortlist to match. It took them a further ten minutes to whittle it down to a final three: the cookies and cream, coffee and malt one Anna had built, a brown sugar sponge with a cinnamon apple butter filling that Magda had suggested, and a white chocolate sponge and cherry filling option Elena had constructed. Apparently cherry was Vasilis's favourite, and all three agreed that it was delicious enough for that to matter in this instance.

"How will we decide?" Elena asked, looking down at the three options in front of her.

"Remember," Magda said, "you can have different flavours in different tiers."

"But there's only two tiers," Lizzy said, sounding genuinely distressed, and Anna didn't blame her. All three were equally delicious, and it seemed a shame to leave any of them out.

Magda frowned as she looked at the options. "Hmmm, let me check something," she said after a moment, walking over to an industrial-sized fridge. She rummaged around and then pulled out a piping bag of something white and a zipper bag of what looked like extra macaron shells. She came back to the workbench and layered a macaron shell with a ring of what Anna could now see was a white chocolate ganache, filling the centre with the cherry preserves before topping it with another shell. She did this three more times, then distributed a finished macaron to each of them, keeping one for herself.

"Cheers," Lizzy said, lifting hers up. The other three lifted theirs in response before taking a bite.

Elena chewed for a moment, nodding her head, before speaking. "Well I'll be damned if that isn't the tastiest deciding factor I've ever had," she said, sighing contentedly. "We have a winner."

"Good choices," Magda said, and Anna and Lizzy agreed. They had just started discussing the logistics for the big day when

Anna felt her watch buzz. She looked down at it to see "Incoming call: NIKOS" flashing up on the screen.

Half an hour later, Anna was walking back down to the marina to meet Nikos. He had called her from the airport, having come back a day early, and whilst Anna could tell he was trying to play it cool, she could also hear a tinge of desperation in his voice. So she told him where she was and said he could meet her there if he wanted to. Now, as she came to the bottom of the steps, she saw him sitting on the edge of the pier with his feet hanging over the water.

"Hey," she said as she came close. When he saw her, he gave her a look, his mouth smiling but his eyes telling a different story. He didn't get up, so Anna sat down beside him. The pier was too high for their feet to touch the water, but Anna could feel the cooler air coming off it whilst the sun hit her back. They sat side by side in silence for a solid minute before either spoke.

"Why did you leave?" Nikos asked without looking at her. "I was an ass to you at the competition. I know that. But I wouldn't have thought that you would get on a plane as a result."

Anna weighed up how she wanted to approach this. She felt like she'd spent enough time justifying the things that had annoyed her, and she was tired of it. She decided to be honest.

"You were an ass," Anna said. "But you're right, that's not what made me leave. In fact, I waited to go to dinner and the show with you."

This warranted a look from Nikos.

"What do you mean?"

"I mean that I was there," Anna said, studying Nikos's face to see his reaction. "I was at the restaurant. Or, well, at the coffee shop across the street. And then when I saw you go in with Maria,

I followed you in to say something. And that's when I heard her tell you to leave me."

Nikos paused, an incredulous look on his face, and then shook his head. "It didn't happen that way."

"Oh, so you didn't take her to see Hamilton instead of me?"

"Only because you'd already left. I found your note at the hotel."

"What, and you didn't feel like calling me, or even texting me?"

Nikos scowled. "I was hurt, Anna!"

Anna pulled up the screenshot she'd taken earlier and pushed her phone close to Nikos's face. "Yeah, you look really eaten up about it."

Nikos pushed her phone aside. "Except that I was. You know as well as anyone that one picture doesn't mean anything." His words had a venom that took Anna right back to the wine bar. Her eyes narrowed.

"I know as well as anyone that a picture is worth a thousand words. And your actions speak for themselves."

Nikos waved his hands around, gesturing at where they were. "And what about you? You want me to believe you're eaten up about it when you're literally eating cake on a boat trip?"

"My sister is here," she said. "I don't have a choice but to put on a smile and carry on. Plus, there's only so much time to spend with Elena before the wedding."

By the shocked look on Nikos's face, she could tell he didn't know about her sister. "Lizzy's here? But I thought she wasn't due to arrive until next week?"

Anna remembered Eirini's words from earlier. "Yeah, well, it seems there are two Linton women who needed a bit of a break from their men."

Nikos rolled his eyes and muttered under his breath,

"Typical." Anna tried not to take it personally. She knew he didn't mean it as deeply as she took it. But it still stung.

"Anna, why wouldn't you tell me about the jobs?" he asked. "If you were never going to cut back at work, I'd rather you had just told me."

"I wasn't sure what I wanted to do," Anna said, though that wasn't strictly true. "I only found out about those jobs when I was in Ireland. Marcus had been working for weeks to put together a roster, and I didn't know anything about it." She looked into his eyes, trying to read the multitude of emotions she saw brewing. "Besides, what would you have said if I did decide to take them?"

Nikos didn't reply, and Anna held his gaze, hoping – and fearing – that the truth would pass between them unspoken. She wasn't sure if he were trying to convey this or she was projecting it, but she thought she could tell what he was thinking in that moment. That if she'd told him she planned to take all those jobs, that something would break between them, maybe irreparably so.

"That's what I thought," she said, standing up and wiping off the back of her shorts. She didn't want to give him the chance to articulate it. Then the damage would truly be done. "Listen, I know we need to have a talk. Clearly, there's a lot going on here." She moved her finger in a circle between them. "But this isn't the time, just like it wasn't in London. Now that Lizzy is here, I need to focus on her. She's not having the best time right now either."

Nikos nodded. "I get it, I guess. Is she staying with us?"

Anna cringed. Whoops, she'd forgotten about that. "Oh, yeah," she said, "I'm so sorry, I told Eirini she could stay in the summer house until you were back. I thought you wouldn't be back until tomorrow, and by then we'll be gone on the hen do. Her bags are all over the place."

"No that's okay," he said, standing up as well. "I can stay at Elena's." He looked at Anna, and she could see remorse in his eyes. He was clearly still hurting, but there was still love there, too. "But Anna, please let me know when you're ready to talk. I can't stand that things are like this between us."

"I know," Anna replied. "Me either. But I also don't think we can brush this under the rug anymore. There's a bit of a pile starting to form."

He nodded. "I just don't want us hashing it out to end up hurting one or both of us."

Anna fixed her eyes out to sea. A sailboat was moving just along the horizon, to the point that it looked a bit like it was floating. So far she and Nikos had been beating around the bush trying to protect each other, making assumptions to avoid confrontation, and where had it gotten them? Nowhere, that's where. Maybe it was time for a bit more brutal honesty after all.

"I think it's a bit late for that, don't you?"

Chapter Twenty-Four

The next morning, Anna waved goodbye to Lizzy at the airport entrance. She, Elena and Xenia wouldn't fly out for another few hours, but they would get there hours ahead of her, and Anna kicked herself for not paying the change fee. Last night had been a girl's night for the books, complete with a cheesy romcom to cap off the night. In the end, Anna only managed a couple of hours of sleep before having to wake up and head to the airport.

After another bumpy Ryanair flight to Athens and a less bumpy but surprisingly still cramped connection to London, she had barely enough time for the coach connection to Stansted Airport, where yet another Ryanair flight waited for her. Finally, at ten o'clock at night, she touched down in Thessaloniki. She was used to multi-leg journeys for some of the jobs she took, but this was brutal.

As she was waiting for the hoard of people to get off the plane and trying to remember how close the car rental agency was to the international arrivals area, she heard a voice she recognised.

"Yes darling, I can do that, but not until next week. I'm off on a hen do."

A shiver ran up Anna's spine as Maria stepped past her in the aisle. As she hung up her call and reached to put her phone back in her bag, Anna looked away to try to avoid eye contact, but the movement must have given her away.

"Oh my god, Anna, there you are," Maria said, playfully batting at Anna's shoulder.

"Yep, here I am!" Anna said through gritted teeth. "I didn't know you were on this flight."

"Didn't you?" she asked. "We're meant to be carpooling to the resort."

"Oh, are we? Sorry, I didn't realise."

As if on cue, Anna's phone went off, her messages finally loading after turning it back on. One was from Elena:

Sorry, forgot to say that Maria is on your flight – can you two share your ride to the resort? It's in your name. See you soon! xxxxxxxxxx

And then another from Xenia:

Elena told me you're sharing a ride with Maria. Sorry, I would have stayed behind to ride with you if I'd known. But it's less than an hour, and drinks are on me when you get here.

And finally, one from Nikos:

Have fun my love. No matter what's going on, I still love you, and I hope you have a fantastic couple of days. Spoil Elena for me please.

"Sure enough," Anna said to Maria, standing up in the aisle

and reaching into the overhead compartment for her duffel. "Elena said there's a rental car reservation in my name, so, hopefully, it'll be nice and easy."

In the end it was quite seamless, other than the fact that it was an eight-seater SUV, which felt a bit excessive for the two of them. But by the time Anna pulled up to the resort at nearly midnight, she felt less than thrilled about spending the next couple of days with Maria.

It wasn't just *that* she talked the entire car ride, even when Anna had conspicuously turned on the radio, but *what* she talked about. Her relationship with Arthur (apparently, they'd had sex in over two dozen wine cellars around the world!), her relationship with Elena and Vasilis ("They're my absolute best friends," she'd said, making Anna roll her eyes in the darkness), and, of course, her relationship with Nikos.

It was this last point that ground Anna's gears the most. Maria seemed to have an endless stream of anecdotes involving Nikos, none of which Anna had heard. Except, notably, the story about them ending up in the mud, which Maria told in a far more sensual way than Nikos had, down to the two of them trying to hose each other off outside first. And every time Maria spoke, Anna just remembered that same voice telling Nikos to leave her, and rage would bubble up all over again.

By the time they pulled off the highway and turned down the road where the resort was, Anna felt like she must surely know every single detail of her boyfriend's relationship with this woman. And, whilst this should have made her feel better – with what was, hopefully, every moment out on the table and not an inappropriate act in the bunch – instead, she felt even more uncomfortable. She would have struggled to fill a one-hour car ride with stories about everything noteworthy she and Nikos had done together in the last four years, and that, combined with what she heard in London, made her defensive.

But it was the last story that made Anna tip over the edge.

"And don't even get me started on Hamilton the other night," she said. "I'm so sorry you weren't feeling well. What a nightmare! Trust me, it's so much better in person. You absolutely *must* see it the next time you're in London."

Anna slammed on the brakes as they pulled into the car park, throwing the car into park so hard that it made Maria wince.

"I wasn't unwell," she said, her voice trembling as she tried to keep it just below a proper yell. "I was angry. That after a massive and hugely personal conflict, Nikos would opt for a night out with you, instead of trying to make amends."

Maria sat back in her seat, pressed against the door as if Anna had tried to attack her. She looked genuinely shocked at Anna's reaction. Anna expected her to backpedal, but what she said instead made Anna seethe even more.

"When you remove yourself from the situation, you don't get to dictate how the other person spends their time. The tickets would have gone to waste otherwise."

Anna rolled her eyes and opened the car door. She wasn't going to have this conversation with Maria. Despite what Lizzy said, she clearly wasn't "all about the girl power." Not only had she told Nikos to leave Anna, but she had no qualms about inserting herself into his plans the second she was gone.

Anna grabbed her duffel bag out of the back, shut the doors a bit too hard, handed the keys to the valet and headed inside. She could hear Maria's heels clicking on the cobbles behind her, but she didn't look back or offer to help. And just as Anna was wondering how they would find the rest of the group, she saw a chalkboard sign pointing down a hallway to the right, advertising two-for-one cocktails until midnight on Thursdays. Anna checked her phone: 11:56 PM. This was where they would be.

Anna took a deep breath just as Maria caught up, promising herself that she wouldn't let Maria ruin the hen do. Anna had been distracted enough throughout the wedding planning process. She didn't need Maria making things worse with Elena as well as Nikos.

They followed the sign to the hotel bar, which was decked out more like a club, with blue and purple lights washing over them as they stepped inside. The bar was relatively busy, but Elena was impossible to miss in her white tulle minidress and golden "Bride" sash, partly because she, Thea and Lizzy were currently dancing on a table. Xenia was perched against the bar next to them, looking up with an expression of both amusement and concern.

Maria threw her hands up in the air and let out a loud "*Wooooo!*", leaving her suitcase next to Anna as she ran up to the table, using a chair as a step to join them. Anna considered leaving Maria's bag in the middle of the bar, but, in the end, she decided it was the diplomatic thing to do was to drag it over to the bar, where Xenia was waving her over. She caught the attention of the bartender and asked for four of the special, some sort of rum punch concoction, getting in on the two-for-one a mere minute before it ended.

"How was the journey?" Xenia asked, glancing at Maria as she did, making it clear she was asking about more than just the traffic conditions.

Anna rolled her eyes. "That girl can talk. And mostly about my boyfriend."

Xenia laughed. "That's true. But she means well. No major arguments to report?"

Anna winced a bit – not only because there had been, but also because she wondered, was that how Xenia, and probably Lizzy, felt? Like Anna was just one flippant comment from Maria away from a smackdown? Not that she'd done a very good job of contradicting that.

As the bartender set four cocktails in front of her, she tapped her card on the machine he held out, grabbed one, and took a sip. They certainly hadn't been stingy with the rum element of the rum punch. She instantly felt more relaxed.

"I can be reasonable," she said. "Though I'm grateful for the buffer now."

"I met Lizzy," Xenia said, nodding at Anna's sister who was currently dancing with Thea. "She's great."

Anna smiled, then tilted her head in confusion as she tried to tell what dance move Lizzy was aiming for. "Yeah, she really is. Though not at twerking, it would seem."

"I heard that!" Lizzy called, motioning for Anna to join her. When Anna shook her head, Lizzy came down to floor level and over to Anna, giving her a hug and trying to guide her towards the table.

"Absolutely not," Anna said. "I need at least three of these before I'll be at that point. And I won't be going that hard tonight."

Lizzy rolled her eyes and shifted focus to Xenia. "Any sign of her yet?"

Xenia shook her head. "Not yet. But it's only a matter of time."

"Do you mean Dimitra?" Anna asked, looking around.

Xenia nodded. "Yep, she's working tonight, apparently. But, hopefully, we'll miss her."

Anna was a bit surprised that Xenia had told Lizzy about Dimitra after how guarded she'd seemed about it, but she was also glad Xenia had more people looking out for her this weekend.

"Don't worry," Lizzy said. "I'll be your bodyguard."

Xenia laughed and took a sip of her drink, but then her face dropped as she looked up.

Anna turned her head and saw a familiar-looking girl standing at the door, swivelling her head, clearly looking for someone. Looking for Xenia.

"I knew someone would tell her," Xenia said, barely audible over the music.

"Do you want to talk to her?" Anna asked, seeing the sudden change come over her friend. She looked paralysed.

"Honestly? Not really."

Dimitra was getting closer, and Anna wracked her brain for what to do. They couldn't go anywhere. They were literally backed into a corner. She made eye contact with Lizzy, who nodded at her, indicating that she had a plan.

Anna grabbed her cocktails, assuming they were making a run for it, but before she knew what was happening, Lizzy grabbed Xenia's drink from her hand, put it on the bar, wrapped her hands around Xenia's face and kissed her.

Like, really kissed her. With tongue, Anna noticed with a cringe. She didn't particularly need to know how her sister kissed.

Anna stared in shock for a few seconds, but then she remembered Dimitra. She turned around to see the girl standing in the middle of the bar, watching Xenia kiss Lizzy, her face slowly transitioning from the same shock Anna felt to a sadness and betrayal Anna could sympathise with – the same sadness and betrayal she'd felt when she'd seen the photo of Nikos and Maria at the show. Then she turned around and left the room, seemingly in a hurry.

"You're good," she said over her shoulder, but when she turned around, Xenia and Lizzy were still going at it, Lizzy pressing Xenia up against the bar, Xenia with Lizzy's hair wrapped around her hands.

"Guys!" Anna said, a bit louder this time, and they broke apart laughing.

"Yep, well, that'll do it," Xenia said, wiping her brow dramatically.

"I told you I'd be your bodyguard," Lizzy said with a wink. Anna laughed uncomfortably – not because of the kiss, but because Lizzy was acting weird. She wasn't the type of person to kiss a friend. She barely let Anna touch her.

"I'm sorry, did I just see Lizzy and Xenia making out?" Elena said from behind them. The others were down off the table now, the song having changed to something a bit less dancey.

"Making Dimitra jealous," Anna said, hugging her friend. "You look wonderful, by the way." As always, Elena was dressed impeccably, somehow having made it onto and off of a table in six-inch heels.

Elena flipped her hair in response. "Thank you, darling. Thea brought me the dress."

"Well done," Anna said to Thea, who had joined them, the rest of the group closing into a tight circle. "So what's the plan?"

Elena held her hands out like she was preparing to say something important.

"Now, don't faint when I tell you this," she said, "but I'm thinking an early night."

Every single woman in the circle gasped dramatically in unison, and then they all laughed.

"Okay, it's not that shocking, is it?"

"It's not," Anna said. "It's also not exactly early. It's already after midnight."

Elena waved off this comment. "Early for those of us who enjoy a little nightlife, my dear. Now listen, we've got a big day tomorrow. We've got spa bookings in the morning thanks to Xenia, then a private lunch with an important chef thanks to Maria, and then some kind of exciting evening activity courtesy of Thea."

It struck Anna that, other than Lizzy, who had been a last-minute invite, Anna was the only one who hadn't contributed something. Why hadn't Elena asked her?

But also, she wondered as she looked at the bar, what was she going to do now with four cocktails if they were going to bed?

She managed to foist a drink each on Elena, Thea and Lizzy, and the four of them emptied their glasses in record, and likely inadvisable, time. Then she handed Maria her bag with a forced smile and followed the others out of the bar.

"So the original plan was for Xenia to have her own room," Elena said, "but now with Lizzy here, should I stay with you, Xen?"

Xenia shook her head. "Lizzy's already dumped her stuff in my room, so the original plans should be fine," she said.

Lizzy nodded her agreement and looked at Anna. "As long as that's okay with you?"

"Yeah, of course," she said, looking forward to sharing a room with Elena. She snored less than Lizzy, and besides, it had been a while since they'd had any time just the two of them.

As they walked down the hall towards the rooms, they heard a voice behind them.

"Xenia?"

They all turned around to see Dimitra standing in a doorway they'd just passed.

Xenia let out a deep breath and turned back to the group. "Well, it was only a matter of time."

"Do you want me to stay?" Anna asked quietly, making eye contact with Xenia. She shook her head.

"No, it's okay, I can't put it off forever." She turned to Lizzy. "I'll see you in the room?"

Lizzy nodded. "I'm going to go get a bit of fresh air, so I'll see you back there in a bit."

Anna saw something in her sister's eyes as she held her gaze. It was like she was experiencing the heartbreak of Martin all over again. She wondered if it was seeing Xenia and Dimitra together that reminded her, but either way, she knew Lizzy was hurting right now. She would want to lick her wounds.

Anna grabbed her hand and whispered to her, "Do you want me to stay with you?"

"I'm alright," Lizzy said. "You get some sleep. I'll see you in the morning."

Anna smiled at her, hoping Lizzy was doing alright. She had been doing a great job so far of putting on a good front, but Anna hadn't forgotten that she was only there because her husband had cheated on her.

As Anna and Elena stepped into their room, Anna smiled. The rooms were gorgeous, with a turquoise blue effect on the wall behind the bed to mirror the ocean, which would be mere metres outside the huge picture window and French doors during the day, and a big stone-carved fireplace in the corner. Not that they'd need it in Greece in June, but it made the room feel extra luxurious. And when Anna had come to photograph the hotel in February, she'd taken full advantage of it.

Elena stepped out onto the balcony to FaceTime with Vasilis, incurring just a bit of teasing from Anna. "You're not supposed to talk to your fiancé on your hen do," she said, but she also smiled as Elena stepped outside, a giddy schoolgirl grin on her face. It was always great to see the people she loved experience so much love.

Anna decided to take advantage of the huge rain shower after a long day of travel, letting the hot water wash all the air from the plane, the car and the bar off of her. Despite Maria, she was determined to enjoy this trip. She had such amazing women in her life, and the presence of one she wasn't so crazy about shouldn't detract from that. Plus, they were all here for the same reason – to celebrate Elena.

Anna came out of the bathroom, wrapped in the big, fluffy bathrobe that had been on the towel warmer, at the same time Elena came back in. They both changed into their pyjamas and headed for bed, swapping travel stories as they did. It felt like their sleepovers at the summer house, and not for the first time that summer, Anna vowed to do more of that moving forward. She didn't want life or anything to get in the way of this feeling of family.

Just as they were ready to turn off the lights, as they quieted down, they heard a noise coming through the wall to their left. Anna stood up and walked over, pressing her ear against the cold wall.

"Oh my god," a voice moaned. "Don't stop, please, don't stop!"

Anna's eyes widened, and she motioned Elena over, holding a finger up to her mouth.

"That's Xenia's room," Elena whispered, pointing dramatically.

Anna's mouth gaped. Clearly, her conversation with Dimitra hadn't been about closure after all, unless this was their "one last time."

Whoever was on the receiving end of that exchange was clearly enjoying herself, and the moans and cries continued to escalate. Anna and Elena both stood there, hands over their mouths, frozen in place. It was super voyeuristic to stay, but surely they would be able to hear it from the bed at this point, anyway?

"Fuck!" the voice cried, repeating it over and over, getting quieter, clearly satisfied.

Anna and Elena scurried back over to the bed, giggling as they slipped under the covers.

"Good for her," Elena said.

Anna reached for her phone and sent a text to Lizzy:

> Might want to give X a minute – seems she's not alone in the room! Let me know if you want me to come keep you company.

She put her phone on the charger and turned over to Elena.

"I'm really happy to be here," she said, thinking about their plans for the next day. "But why didn't you ask me to plan anything? I totally would have if I'd known everyone else was contributing."

Elena shrugged. "I mean, I didn't ask anyone, they all just offered. Xenia asked if I wanted to choose a resort to come to, and then Thea was telling me about the woman we'll meet tomorrow night, so I decided this was the place. Maria only texted me yesterday to set up the lunch."

It made sense, and Anna knew that if she had any connections nearby, she would have done the same. But she also wondered if maybe, as the maid of honour, she should have been a bit more proactive about the hen do. Wasn't it usually the maid of honour's job to plan it altogether?

"I'm really sorry if I've been distracted," she said. "This time should be really special for you, and I've been all over the place."

Elena nodded. "You can tell me about it if you want?"

Anna did consider this, but after her conversation with Lizzy the day before, she was a bit wary of bringing up Maria to Elena. Especially knowing they all had to spend the next two days together. So instead, she shook her head.

"This weekend is all about you. And I can't wait for whatever tomorrow brings."

"I'm especially excited about lunch," Elena said, rubbing her hands together in delight like a giddy schoolgirl. "Maria must have really charmed this chef. Apparently, she selected the wine pairings for his last seasonal menu, and they got on like a house on fire. Which isn't surprising, given how she takes to men like that."

Anna had bristled initially at the mention of Maria, but she took a twisted pleasure in hearing Elena gossip about her.

"Men like what?"

"You know," Elena said, drawing it out as if Anna should indeed know, then continued when it was clear she didn't. "Let's just say Maria loves a silver fox, especially when he's internationally renowned for something."

Anna thought back to Arthur. It made sense; there was a certain gravitas to men like that, especially those with natural charisma, or the confidence that a Scrooge McDuck-style pile of cash could give them. She wondered which of those the chef had, if not both. She sank back into the pillow feeling satisfied that she understood Maria just a little bit more.

As Elena turned the lights off, Anna waited for her phone to light up with a response from Lizzy, but part of her knew it wouldn't come. Lizzy would want to be alone right now. Eventually Anna couldn't keep her eyes open any longer, and she drifted off to sleep to the sound of the waves outside.

Chapter Twenty-Five

Anna yawned as the waiter put a latte down in front of her. She looked up and thanked him, then drank it so quickly that she burned the top of her mouth. She reached in her bag for her sunglasses; she'd avoided them earlier in an attempt to let the sun wake her up, but it was really quite bright out on the terrace, even with the vines on the trellis above the table offering some dappled shade.

It wasn't that she didn't sleep well – in fact, the bed had been like a cloud, and she'd slept all the way through the night. Plus, now she had some caffeine in front of her, and at least she wasn't hungover this time. But the last few days of travel were catching up with her, and she felt like she could sleep all day. In fact, she had slept through most of her massage, which was disappointing, but based on how loose she felt after, she suspected it hadn't been a waste.

Elena, on the other hand, was chipper as always, currently raving about the meal they were going to be having shortly. Apparently one of the most famous chefs in Greece had a holiday home nearby, and Maria, who was with Xenia collecting bottles of wine from the cellar, had managed to convince him to disrupt his summer holiday to cook them lunch at the hotel. The girls were discussing it, with Thea saying how hard it must have been to tear him away from the beach on such a gorgeous day.

"Yes, well, she does have a way with men of that age, doesn't she," Anna said with a chuckle.

The whole table looked at her, but none of them were laughing.

"That's a bit mean, Anna," Lizzy said after a moment.

Anna smarted as if Lizzy had smacked her. "Is it? I mean, I was sort of kidding, but Elena said that last night."

"That's not really fair," Elena said. "I told you she was attracted to ambition."

"And silver foxes," Anna said in defence. "I didn't even mention how she was with the head judge at Nikos's competition."

Thea rolled her eyes, clearly knowing who Anna was referring to. "Maria has known Arthur for years. They see each other all the time. And Maria isn't sleeping with the chef."

"It was just a joke, I'm sorry." Anna felt her face flush. She had assumed that everyone else saw Maria as a bit of an obnoxious flirt like she did, especially after her conversation with Elena, but their reaction had proven otherwise. Even Lizzy's.

"It's fine," Elena said. "Besides, without Maria, we wouldn't be having this gorgeous lunch."

As she said this, she looked Anna in the eye, her eyes narrowed, her gaze probing. She looked concerned.

"Did I hear my name?" Maria asked as she emerged from the hotel onto the terrace, the stems of six wine glasses tucked into the spaces between her fingers. Xenia followed with four bottles of wine.

"Yes!" Elena called back, tearing her gaze away from Anna.

"And not a moment too soon. Let's pour the wine so we can cheers to you for setting this up."

Xenia opened the bottles and handed them to Maria, who expertly poured them into the glasses. Anna would have assumed that she would pour small measures, being one who enjoyed wine more as a hobby than an intoxicant, but Maria seemed to know her audience, and she went through a bottle and a half between them all.

Anna half-heartedly raised her glass as Elena offered her thanks to Maria. She was still cowering after being chastised by the group. It was Lizzy's reaction that had shocked her the most – she knew Elena was close with Maria, and Thea didn't know Anna well enough to know her intentions, but Anna's own sister? Anna found herself thinking for the first time that maybe she was being a little bit harsh on Maria. There seemed to be some invisible line she had crossed without realising, and she wondered if maybe she'd been a bit hasty to latch onto the first criticism of Maria she'd heard. In fact, Elena hadn't actually criticised Maria. It was Anna who'd turned what she said into a negative – something worth making a joke about.

But as she watched Maria smile and cover her face in affected modesty as she was praised and thanked, she remembered what Maria had said to her in the car, and her stomach turned. She decided she didn't actually feel that bad about her comment after all. She'd just keep it to herself next time.

The lunch was just as delicious as promised. Anna had experienced very little fine dining in her life, and never in Greece, so she wasn't sure if it was just the novelty of the experience, but she thought it may be the best meal she'd ever had. It was a smorgasbord of things she'd never even imagined trying, and didn't sound like anything she'd had in Greece, so far – dishes like sea urchin pasta with black truffle cream, crayfish tartare with caviar, and sea bream with Jerusalem artichoke and smoked bacon

– yet they all felt completely at home in the setting she was in, with the waves of the Aegean crashing nearby, the summer sun shining down on the group, and the grape vines climbing overhead.

And, Anna had to admit, Maria had chosen the perfect wine to pair with the menu, with the zest of the white wine adding a new dimension to the seafood on the plate and vice versa.

"That was incredible," Anna said as their plates were cleared. "And," she forced herself to add, "the wine pairing was next level."

"Thank you," Maria said, but when she looked into Anna's eyes, the over-the-top friendliness was gone. Perhaps one of the others had filled her in on Anna's comment, or perhaps she was still thinking about Anna's outburst the night before. Anna searched herself to see if she was more embarrassed to have been caught out, annoyed at not being universally liked, or gratified that her disdain had finally been perceived.

The embarrassment won out, and she could feel her face go red. At least she had the sunshine and the wine to blame it on should anyone notice.

From there, the women spent a couple of hours on the beach, some of them tanning on the loungers whilst Lizzy and Xenia splashed in the waves. Anna found herself musing that they could really do with a mother hen type on this trip, as they really shouldn't be playing in the water after how much wine they'd had, but she didn't have it in her to ruin the fun. They were all adults.

As Lizzy and Xenia wandered further and further down the shoreline, clambering over the boulders that made up the tall groins, she felt herself growing more and more uneasy.

Then, as the two women reached a groin far out past the last of the sun loungers, Anna watched as Lizzy moved too quickly to join Xenia in the water below and toppled off the rock. She squealed as she went down, and Anna saw a splash, and then nothing.

Anna bolted out of her chair and ran down the beach. They were a good hundred metres away, and she had a belly full of food and wine, but she willed her legs to move as quickly as possible. By the time she reached the groin where Lizzy had fallen, she could feel her lunch threatening to make an appearance, and her chest felt like it might explode. She braced herself for something bad as she rounded the corner and dashed into the water, but she couldn't have been prepared for what she saw.

Lizzy was laid back on a rock, her legs splayed apart. Standing between them was Xenia, who had one hand on a rock and the other down Lizzy's swimsuit bottoms. Lizzy had her head thrown back in pleasure. Anna watched as Xenia leaned over and put her mouth to Lizzy's chest, kissing her way all over and continuing to move her hand beneath the bikini.

Still lost in the moment, Lizzy turned her head to the side, and as she opened her eyes, she saw Anna standing ankle-deep in the water. She shrieked and pulled away from Xenia, standing up as quickly as she could. Xenia looked over at Anna to see what had happened and then quickly turned around to face the sea, one hand still on Lizzy's stomach. Anna could see from her shoulders that she was laughing. But Lizzy wasn't.

Lizzy was looking at Anna as if her whole life had flashed before her eyes. She was terrified.

Anna didn't know what to say or do, but she certainly didn't want to seem like she was judging what she'd seen. So, instead, she offered a feeble smile, nodded, and turned back towards the populated end of the beach. She walked a few paces until she was out of sight, then sat down on the closest chair and waited.

A couple of minutes later, she saw Xenia swim past in the sea, and a moment later Lizzy came around the groin on the beach. Anna could see that she was using her arms to try to cover herself – one arm across her chest, the other across her stomach – and she walked slowly towards Anna.

Anna stood up, closed the distance between her and her sister, and wrapped her in a hug.

"I love you," she said as she squeezed her sister tight, not caring that Lizzy would normally hate being hugged. "And you don't have to be afraid to be your whole self around me, whatever that looks like."

And in an uncharacteristic moment of affection, Lizzy accepted her sister's sympathetic touch, wrapping her own arms around Anna.

"Thank you," she said, and Anna could tell she was crying from the way her voice broke. They stood there, unmoving and unrelenting in their embrace, for at least a minute before they broke it. Anna led Lizzy to the lounger she had been sat on a few moments earlier.

After a couple more minutes of silence, Anna asked the question that had been spinning around in her mind since the second after she'd seen them together.

"Is this why you left Martin?"

Lizzy laughed. "Not really?" she said, the question mark obvious in the way she spoke. "I've known for a while that I was into women, but I've always been into him, too. And we were monogamous, so it didn't matter who else I was attracted to. I was with him."

Anna could sense a "but" coming.

"But then he surprised me with a threesome for my birthday."

Anna grimaced. "Okay, not sure I need to be hearing this."

"It's relevant, I promise," she said, an apologetic smile flashing on her face. "And plus, I think it was as much for him as it was for me, because it turns out my super woke husband is just a pervy straight guy like all the rest and just wanted to see me get with another woman because it's 'sexy.'" She put air quotes around the word "sexy," and the frown on her face told Anna exactly how she felt about that.

Anna waited for Lizzy to continue.

"Then things got really weird. He kept asking me if I wanted to do it again, and I said yes, because it *was* fun. The first few times, anyway. But it was always with this same girl who worked on another farm nearby. That was weird for me, so I said I didn't want to do it anymore, because something felt off. And then one day I came home and he was with her all by himself."

Anna could practically feel her heart breaking for her sister. She knew what it was like to see the man you were with in the throws of passion with someone else – the image of Marcus fucking someone against a window would forever be burned into her brain – but she and Marcus hadn't been married. They hadn't been childhood sweethearts. They hadn't even been in love. This… well, this was something Anna hoped she would never have to experience, and yet here her sister was grappling with it.

"He just assumed because I was bi that I wanted to sleep around; that being attracted to multiple genders would make me attracted to everyone. But I only ever wanted him when we were together. I wanted our life together. I wanted to be monogamous. And he took my sexuality and used it as an excuse to manipulate me, and then to leave me for someone else."

"Wait, you don't mean—"

"Oh, yeah, they're together," Lizzy said with an eye roll. "I moved out about two weeks ago, and when I went back to pack my things, her stuff was moved in and mine was in boxes in the hayloft."

Anna's jaw dropped. "What a prick."

"Tell me about it," Lizzy said, and Anna could hear the energy change in her voice. She was done being sad for now.

"So how did you and Xenia even get together?" Anna asked, trying to piece together the timeline in her mind.

"It was only last night, after Dimitra. The kiss was… well, pretty enlightening, to say the least." Lizzy made a suggestive face, and Anna rolled her eyes. "After she was done talking to Dimitra, we went to bed, and things just sort of happened from there."

"Yeah, about that…" Anna replied, cringing. "After just now, I've seen more than I ever wanted to of your sex life, and now I've heard more than enough of it as well."

Lizzy turned to Anna, her eyes wide. "What do you mean?"

"I mean," Anna said, "that yours and Xenia's room is right next to mine and Elena's."

Lizzy clapped her hand over her mouth.

"Oh Anna, I'm so sorry, that's so weird." Her words and her laughter were muffled beneath her hand. Anna joined in laughing, actively trying not to picture what had happened in that hotel room.

"Just do me a favour and be kind to Xenia. Dimitra really messed her around, so just be clear about what you want and don't want."

Lizzy nodded. "Yeah, I know. I'm trying to be really open. But I'm just two weeks out of a decades-long relationship, so I'm not really sure what I want. Makes it pretty hard to articulate that to someone else."

"That's fine, just make sure she knows that."

Lizzy looked at Anna for a moment, then hugged her again. Anna was shocked, but she didn't waste a moment. A hug from Lizzy in a tender moment was rare, so she pulled her in close and made the most of it.

Chapter Twenty-Six

As Anna and Lizzy walked back down the beach together, they saw the rest of the party packing up, ready to go back and get ready for the evening. Thea kept reiterating that they had a long drive and an active night ahead of them, so Anna had to repurpose her airplane outfit for the next day, having expected to dress up. It seemed Elena, however, had an endless supply of white outfits for every occasion with her, emerging from the bathroom in white leggings and a white sports bra that looked less sporty and more showy, with its many straps zigzagging across her back. Anna thought that it was a good thing she wasn't wearing it out in the sun, otherwise she'd have some weird tan lines for her wedding.

The six of them piled into the car Anna had hired – now it made sense why Elena had reserved such a giant car – and headed inland. Thea drove, since she knew where they were going. Everyone had offered Elena the front seat, but she seemed far more interested in being in the middle of everything, so she hopped in the back with Anna. Lizzy and Xenia went in the very back, and Maria nabbed the front seat and immediately connected her phone to the Bluetooth. She put on some pop song that Anna had never heard before.

"What's this?" she asked, directing the question more at Elena than anyone else, but Maria responded, calling back over her shoulder louder than was strictly necessary.

"It's Antique," she said as she danced along. "They were a pop group in the nineties. They did Eurovision and everything."

"Eurovision is so overrated," Elena said, and everyone except Thea turned to look at her. Elena not liking Eurovision may have been the most out of character thing possible.

"That surprises me," Anna said. "It feels like exactly your kind of thing."

"It's also bullshit," Maria said, laughing. "Nikos told me you used to put on shows for your family because you wanted to practice your future Eurovision audition."

Everyone else laughed, and Anna forced herself to join in. After the comment at lunch, she wasn't about to lower herself to comment on anything Maria said, despite the fact that Nikos had never told her that story. But Lizzy caught Anna's gaze, and she knew she wasn't the only one that had picked up on the subtle Nikos reference. She smiled a quick, thin grin to show Lizzy that she was fine, and then turned to stare out the window.

As they drove back through Thessaloniki and then up into the Grecian countryside, Anna counted four different Nikos stories, one story of being overly flirtatious with wealthy older men, and at least three humble brags. Anna added her laugh to the chorus where appropriate, but mostly she kept her eyes focused on the landscape outside. After a couple of hours, they climbed into some low mountains, the roads growing narrower and more winding. The forest around them grew denser, until all of a sudden Thea turned off the road onto a narrow lane, and the landscape opened up before them.

A small stone cottage sat before them, situated on a tiny lake.

To the left, a cliff rose up immediately behind the house, as if the cottage had crushed the landscape into submission. To the right, the hills cascaded down into a much larger lake and the floodplains beyond.

As they got out of the car, Anna looked at the house and was reminded of the summer house. There was a swing out front, a kitchen garden off to the side, and even the same roof tiles she had back home. It was absolutely charming, and she felt instantly at home. It made her proud of how others must feel coming to her own house. This brought with it a fresh pang of sadness that her home was less welcoming at the moment given what was happening with Nikos.

Thea gathered the group around her, speaking in a hushed tone.

"The woman you're about to meet is an oracle," she said, eliciting squeals from Maria, Lizzy and Elena, which Thea quickly hushed. Anna smiled, but her forehead pressed together into a sceptical look at the same time. Xenia just rolled her eyes.

"She used to live near Delphi, so she calls herself Pythia after the Oracle at Delphi. It's not her real name, or at least I don't think, but let me tell you, this woman is scary accurate. I met her last year at a gala in Athens, and she told me exactly what would happen with a job I had coming up. She said the birds told her. And it played out *exactly* like she said."

Elena was clapping her hands together quietly. This was exactly her kind of thing.

"So, do we call her Pythia?" Anna asked.

Thea looked at her and scowled. "Just be respectful."

"Are we having our fortunes read or something?" Anna wasn't trying to be difficult, she was genuinely trying to understand how she was supposed to behave.

Thea smiled thinly, and Maria lowered her gaze and smiled. Anna got the impression she was saying all the wrong things.

"You'll see," Thea said, then turned around and waved them towards the front door, knocking timidly. There was a clear reverence in the way she waited, perfectly poised, at the closed door.

"If she were clairvoyant, don't you think she would see us coming?" Xenia whispered to Anna, clearly trying to cheer her up. Anna stifled a laugh, but, apparently, not well enough, as Thea threw both of them a look of pure daggers. Xenia straightened up exaggeratedly, and Anna barely kept herself from laughing again.

Just as Thea turned back around, the door creaked open. Anna had been expecting someone ancient based on the deference Thea had shown, but the woman who was standing just inside the door couldn't have been more than a decade older than them. She had wiry, curly hair, a bit lighter than typical for a Greek woman, which was piled on her head and wrapped in a head scarf, though tiny sprigs were poking out from nearly every fold. Anna thought the scarf was polka dotted at first, but as the woman stepped through the door to greet them and passed by Anna, she could see it was actually an evil eye motif. Her stone-coloured kaftan brushed Anna's legs as she passed, and Anna caught a whiff of dried herbs and marijuana.

"I did see you coming," the woman said as she stepped around them, aiming her words directly at Xenia. "But only because I have cameras on the road and the house." She pointed up at a small black dome nestled in a trellis of flowers off to the right. "Now please, come with me," she said, ushering them away from the house and towards the cliff to the left. They followed her through a gate and along the contour of the mountain.

"It's lovely to see you again," Thea said to the woman, trying to keep up with her.

The woman looked at Thea and narrowed her eyes. "Oh, yes, you, too," she said over her shoulder, waving her hand dismissively, not taking her focus away from the path in front of them. Clearly, she had no idea who Thea was.

After a minute or so of walking, the path turned sharply around a large rock ahead of them, leading to a cave entrance. The passage was lit by oil lanterns mounted on one wall; they needed their light as they walked further into the hill, the air growing damper and colder and darker around them. Elena had to pause to untie her sweatshirt from her waist and pull it on over her head. Anna shivered and wished she'd brought one, too.

Eventually they came to a small circular cavern with two exits, one on either side, and a bench carved into the walls. In the centre of the room was a table with a water jug and six glasses, right next to a huge stalagmite that looked like a large white crystal. Anna thought it must be bigger than she was. The space reminded her of a steam room or sauna, but it was perfectly dry and as chilly as the hallway had been.

"This is salt," Thea whispered, pointing to the crystal. "It's meant to ease your breathing, clear your skin, and remove psychic debris from your energy body before the reading." She sounded like she was reading from some New Age website, and Anna could see Lizzy rolling her eyes in her periphery. But Elena was hooked.

"Oh my god, I had no idea salt worked like other crystals," she said, looking at the formation in amazement. "How cool."

"It does work like other crystals," Lizzy whispered, "in that it does absolutely nothing."

The woman gestured for them to sit on the bench.

"I'll be back in half an hour to start your sessions," she said. "We'll start, of course, with our bride to be." She held her hands out to Elena and smiled, and Elena did a little pageant wave. Then the woman closed the door they'd come through before leaving through the opposite exit, closing that door behind her as well. As she did, the only source of light was a red glow coming from the crystal. Anna hadn't noticed it before.

"What sessions?" Anna whispered to Xenia, who was sat next to her.

"Oh, you know, to remove our psychic debris. Maybe with one of those little suction things like at the dentist?"

Anna chuckled, and Thea shot her a look. "Say what you want," she said, "but people have been using salt caves since Ancient Greece."

"I think it's lovely," Maria said. "Tell us about the sessions then, Thea," she added with a nod to Xenia.

"Well, she's an oracle, so I guess she does tell us the future? But she uses books and energy reading to do it, not a crystal ball or anything."

"Not very on brand then," Lizzy said, gesturing to the large crystal in the centre, and again Anna laughed.

"Salt isn't used to tell the future," Thea retorted, though she was glaring at Anna, not Lizzy. "If she pretended to use a crystal ball, that would be phony."

"And wouldn't that be a shame," Lizzy muttered under her breath. Luckily, Anna was the only one to hear her that time.

After a few minutes, Anna noticed that the room was actually beginning to feel quite warm. It started with a dryness in her mouth. When Elena brought this up as well, Thea shared that salt was meant to help clear up mucous, which was why they felt dryer.

"If you keep drinking your water, you'll be fine," she said, topping everyone's up.

A couple minutes after that, there was a definite band of sweat under Anna's boobs and across her forehead. She figured the open doors had been ventilating the room, and now they were sitting in a sweatbox. The doors were far from airtight, with the light from the oil lamps visible through cracks at the top and bottom, so

Anna told herself the air would be fine. And sure enough, she did feel like she was breathing more easily than she'd expect to in a cramped space with a rising temperature.

The others spoke around her, laughing and joking, but Anna felt unable to engage. The heat was becoming oppressive – worse than any Australian outback or Amazonian rainforest she'd experienced – made worse by the fact that she felt trapped. But she didn't want to make a scene after what had happened at lunch, so she just kept to herself and tried to put a relaxed expression on her face, closing her eyes and leaning her head against the hard wall behind her.

After a couple of minutes, Elena came to join her.

"Are you doing okay?" she asked as she took a sip of water. "You seem a bit quieter than usual today."

Anna nodded, smiling through the discomfort. "I'm fine," she said. "Just tired from travelling."

Elena frowned. "I know I didn't ask you what happened in London, but I have heard the digest version."

Anna rolled her eyes at that. "From who? Maria? Great, glad to know my relationship is a go-to topic of conversation for her."

"*Oi!*" Elena said, snapping her fingers at Anna. "First of all, Maria didn't tell me anything. Nikos did. Remember him? My cousin? The person I'm closest to in the world?"

"Oh," Anna said weakly, feeling a flush of embarrassment. Or maybe it was the heat? "I'm sorry."

"Which brings me to my second point," Elena said, carefully measuring her tone, her voice low but with a hard edge to it. "What is with this hostility towards Maria? Where has it come from?"

Anna considered answering her honestly. *Oh, you know, maybe from the fact that she's been my stand-in for the last few years in all of my relationships, and no one told me?* But she bit her tongue, not wanting to cause another scene. She would have to give Elena an answer – she knew brushing it off was unlikely to work – but she didn't want to get into it here. Not in front of the others, and certainly not in front of Maria herself. Especially not when she felt like she may melt onto the bench at any moment.

"I don't have a problem with Maria. She's not someone I'd ever be best friends with, but she's fine. I'm just a bit sensitive to her relationship with Nikos. I'm sorry, I'll try to look past it."

She'd hoped that Elena would accept her weak apology and move on, keeping the peace for the sake of her own party. But it seemed the fiery temperatures were heating up her fiery friend, too.

"Well that feels thoroughly unfair," Elena said, louder than the hushed tone they had been speaking in, so far, putting her water down on the bench next to her.

Anna looked at her, both surprised and exasperated. She was brash, sure, but she wasn't confrontational. Especially not in public. But she had said that last bit loudly enough that Lizzy was looking over at the two of them, concerned.

"Elena, let's talk about this later please," she said, looking around the room.

As Elena sat back and took another sip of water, a bit huffier this time than before, Anna began to doubt they'd be able to move on peacefully. Anna had seen Elena get angry like this before, but she'd never been on the receiving end of it.

A moment passed, and Anna held her breath, hoping she'd gotten away with it. But then Elena sat forward again.

"No, I think let's do this now." Her voice was still quiet enough, but when Anna looked into Elena's eyes, she saw that she was angry. "My cousin is not faultless. Is it a bit weird that he didn't tell you about Maria? Yes, it is. But you've discussed that now. You told him you were past it. Yet you keep bringing it up."

"Because it's still an issue," Anna said. "He keeps choosing her over me."

Elena shook her head. "No, he keeps spending time with her when you choose something else over him. Do you see the difference?" Her voice was a bit louder now, and the other women were watching them. Except Maria, that is, who was looking down at her feet.

"Do you expect him to sit around and stare at the wall when you choose to be somewhere else?"

"No, of course not."

Anna silently willed Elena to stop. She could feel it all bubbling up now, her threshold for pretending having been broken down in the heat. She could see beads of sweat on Elena's forehead, too.

"Good, because he's not going to." Elena stood up, towering over Anna, who tried her best to dissolve into the bench. "Nikos is a social person. Of course he would always rather be with you, but if he can't, he's got other friends. Maria is his friend, just like Kostas or Vasilis or me. And to suggest that him hanging out with her is any different than with us just because she's a beautiful woman is a bit old-fashioned, don't you think? So stop using Maria as the scapegoat for the real issue, which is that you and Nikos want different things. The sooner you realise that, the sooner you can work it out. But leave my friend out of it please."

Elena wasn't wrong. The Maria issue had started as a cover for the real argument – the fact that Nikos wanted her to give up travelling but wouldn't outright ask her to do it. But that didn't mean it was meaningless. Anna had heard Maria on two separate occasions saying something negative about her to Nikos. And Anna had no self-control left in this oppressive place to filter her response.

"I'd leave your friend out of it if she didn't keep inserting herself into my relationship," Anna said, standing up, not caring that everyone was now openly staring at them. "I've overheard two separate conversations where she's talked shit about me to him. She even told him to leave me."

Elena stared wide-eyed at Anna, flicking her eyes back and forth from Maria, who was bent over with her head in her hands. This part was clearly news to Elena.

Anna was long past making a scene and had moved on to a full-on defence. She was seeing red, literally and figuratively. If everyone was going to stare, she at least wanted them to know that she wasn't acting crazy for no reason. She might be crazy, and she certainly felt it in that moment, but that's because she'd been driven there, by their behaviour and by the environment and by this fucking heat. She was angry and embarrassed and scared – scared that in an attempt to avoid pushing Elena away, she was doing so even more – all at once.

"So no, I can't leave your friend out of it, because she keeps dropping herself in it."

The cave went quiet for a long moment as Anna's words sunk in, and then Maria sat up straight.

"Does anyone want to know what I think?" she asked, her tone loud and firm, any friendliness long gone from her voice. "Because no one's bothered to ask me yet."

Anna rolled her eyes, but she dropped her gaze.

"Yes, go on please," Elena said, nodding at Maria, who stood up and faced Anna directly.

"I think that Nikos is being a child about the whole situation," she said, and Anna snapped her head to look at her, surprised. "I think he's expecting you to read his mind about what he wants, which is pretty unreasonable, and then he's sulking when he doesn't magically get his way. And honestly, I think it's super weird that he never told you about me. We spend a lot of time together, maybe even more than the two of you, sometimes, and it feels odd and a bit manipulative – to both of us, actually – that he's never mentioned that."

Anna nodded. Maria was absolutely right, and she felt relieved to have someone else validate the frustration she had been experiencing. She just wished it were anyone else, in any other setting.

"I also think he massively overreacted in London. He's very sensitive to your work right now, Anna, but that doesn't give him an excuse to blow up at you in public, no matter what. And I promise, I wouldn't have gone with him to the show if I'd known that it was part of this big argument. I don't want to be in the middle of that."

Anna swallowed, her dry throat making it difficult.

"However—"

Ah yes, here we go, Anna thought, steeling herself for the indignation she'd been expecting from the beginning.

"Whilst I think you're in an incredibly difficult situation that every feminist who's ever been in love should understand…" She looked around the room, and all four of the other women nodded along. "I think you're also being unfair to use me as the catalyst for your conflict. Just like you, Nikos has crossed no boundaries that you've set, as far as I know. If you feel he has, you need to communicate them better, just like he does. But honestly, things have been exceedingly platonic between us, and if your boundaries don't allow for that, I'd question you as a woman."

Her words and tone were even and measured. Clearly, Maria had been thinking about what she would say, and Anna wondered if maybe Maria's mind had been as consumed by the situation as hers had since their brief exchange the night before.

"What I don't appreciate," Maria said, taking a few steps forward around the salt crystal so she was directly in front of Anna, her voice dropping lower, taking on an almost menacing quality, "are the eye rolls, and the snide comments, and the judgment. I'm not the villain in your story. Think whatever you want about my lifestyle and my taste in men, but I'd appreciate if you'd stop making your disdain so obvious and making the rest of us uncomfortable in the process – especially me. I'm just trying to live my life like anyone else."

Anna kept her eyes cast towards the floor of the cavern, unable to meet Maria's gaze. She wanted to look up at Lizzy to get reassurance or encouragement, but after the way she'd defended Maria at lunch and back at the summer house, she wasn't confident she'd get it.

Maria moved to step past Anna, but then she paused shoulder to shoulder with her, and Anna could feel the heat intensify as she stepped close, their bodies nearly touching.

"And for the record," she added in a whisper, "I wasn't telling Nikos that I thought he *should* leave you. I was telling him that he either needed to leave you or shut up about it, because I was done listening to him complain about how successful you were. And to be clear, I was hoping he would do the latter."

As Maria stepped away, Anna felt a shiver roll down her spine.

Chapter Twenty-Seven

Over an hour after Elena's turn, Anna went in to see the oracle. She was the last one to go in. The oracle had entered the room just after Maria sat down, clearly sensing the psychic debris flying through the air. She hadn't even explained what was happening, just ushered Elena through the door, leaving the rest of them as they were. Anna could have cried when she shut the door behind her, desperate for a bit of fresh air, but the space stayed hot and sticky.

No one had said a word to each other since the argument. They all sat in silence, intermittently sipping their water and clearing their throats. At one point, Anna watched Xenia consider saying something, open her mouth to speak, then decide better of it. Then Thea was called back, and then Lizzy, and then Xenia, leaving Anna and Maria alone in the cavern for nearly twenty silent, sweaty minutes. Every time the door opened there was a quick breeze, a slight reprieve, and then the heat would build again. By the time Anna was left alone, she was genuinely concerned about being by herself. But she obviously wasn't about to ask Maria to stay with her, so she just closed her eyes and focused on her breath.

Eventually, the woman emerged and waved for Anna to follow her through the second passageway. The hall was much cooler but also less frequently lit, meaning there were stretches of more dimly lit walking, and Anna took close care to not trip and fall into the woman, whom she was following quite closely. At least she wasn't burning alive anymore, though, and she felt her sweat turn cold as they seemed to head deeper into the mountain.

The woman turned suddenly into a doorway in the wall, and Anna struggled to react quickly enough to turn with her.

They stepped into what looked like a fairly modern office with a sleek white desk, a rolling chair tucked underneath it on one side, and a plush armchair on the other. The woman motioned for her to sit. There was even a modern-looking glass light fixture hanging from the ceiling. Anna followed the cord until it disappeared behind a bookcase and wondered why, if she could get electricity in here, the hallways were lined with oil lamps – or why anyone would choose to have an office in here at all, for that matter – but she supposed the ambience was meant to be part of the experience. Adding to said ambience were the seemingly countless books lining the shelves that bordered the room, all of them looking like they could easily be hundreds of years old.

"Sorry," Anna said as she turned her gaze to the woman, "but what should I call you? Thea didn't tell us what your actual name was."

"You can call me Danai," she replied as she paced along the perimeter of the space, running her fingers along the rows of tomes. "Have you ever worked with an oracle before?"

Anna shook her head. "Nope."

Danai stopped and turned towards Anna, a leatherbound volume in her hand. "I like to work with books. My intuition guides me to the passages relevant to you. But books can be limited."

She sat down in the rolling chair and placed the book in front of her, all the while staring deep into Anna's eyes.

"Usually as a last resort, simply because it can bring up quite a lot of emotion, I can intuit the truth from bodily contact. Not the past or the future, just the truth of what is at present. Do you understand?"

Anna nodded. "Books, future. Bodies, present. Got it."

Danai nodded back at Anna, but her eyes were narrowed, and a smile played at her lips. "You don't believe in my gift."

Anna shrugged. "I don't know. I'm not ready to write it off." What she didn't say but was running through her mind was, *I would believe anything you said was divine prophecy if you just told me what to do.*

Danai wagged her finger. "That wasn't a question. You don't believe. But never mind, it doesn't make a difference to me. It's a bit like a horoscope – you can make sense of it, or you can dismiss it, but either way it's there. You don't have to believe for me to get what I need, and you can make meaning out of anything you'd like. Deal?"

"Deal." Anna gulped. "And what about the heat in the salt cavern? Is that meant to help in some way?"

Danai smiled knowingly. "It may get a bit stuffy in there, but there's no heat element. It never gets above a normal body temperature, even with a room full of people."

"That's not possible," Anna countered. "I was sweating my ass off in there."

"Well then, clearly you had a lot weighing you down that needed to be cleansed. You'll be very ready. Anyway, let's start with the books, shall we?" She closed her eyes and ran her palms over the pages. Anna half expected her to start chanting or moaning, but none of that happened. In fact, it was only a few seconds before the woman nodded her head, picked up a pair of reading glasses from the desk and put them on, squinting to read the text on the page she had opened.

"Give me a moment," she said. "I'll need to translate to English." She squinted at the text, mumbling to herself in Greek before nodding. "Okay. This is a gardening text from the region. It says most flowers of this type can be planted in any kind of soil, or a mix of soil types. How you cultivate it, however, depends on where you choose to plant it." She put the book down. "Does that mean anything to you?"

Anna considered it for a moment. It could mean that Anna's relationship would survive no matter where she was. Or maybe it meant she needed to choose the right way to cultivate her life if she wanted to flourish.

Or, of course, it could mean that the first book Danai picked up was some Ancient Greek gardening book, and it had no bearing on Anna's life at all.

"Maybe," she said with a shrug. "It's a bit too vague to tell."

Danai nodded. "I agree," she said. "Let's keep going."

She stood and picked up a smaller volume from the shelf, this one with gold metal corners on the cover. She opened it seemingly at random and ran her finger over the page with her eyes closed until she stopped. Then she opened her eyes and read, eventually shaking her head and discarding the book.

Then she picked up a small, plain book made of black leather. She opened to one of the earliest pages, her eyes glinting and the corners of her mouth turning up with recognition.

"This one is an old children's story about a painter who travelled the world, bringing his lover paintings from every place he visited. When he would ask his lover where she wanted a painting from next, she would give him the name of a new far-flung destination, and he would be gone for as long as it took to find the spot and paint the picture. He would bring them home and give them to her, and she would put them in a locked box in her room. Then one day, after decades of this, when he came home from his longest time away yet, he looked in the place where she always put his gifts. But, instead of his paintings, it was full of a child's drawings. When he asked her about the drawings, he discovered that she had been living a full life without him, even bearing his child, whilst he was gone. When he asked why she kept sending him away, she said it was because she knew how much he loved to paint."

Anna felt like all the air had been knocked out of her. The metaphor couldn't be more obvious – Nikos was holding back from telling her about what he wanted because he didn't want to take away the thing she loved. But that wasn't stopping him from living his life without her. And if nothing changed, then either he would grow to resent her, or, like in the story, she would start to miss out on more and more, because it would get easier and easier to be away. She could even picture the double bowl of memory cards at home, a collection of images of faraway places, whilst the things that mattered most to Nikos fit on a single card or hadn't been captured at all.

"That one's a bit more relevant," she said, barely getting the words out.

Danai smiled slightly. "That's good. We're on the right track then. But if it's alright with you, I'd like to try a bit of body reading."

At Anna's agreement, Danai stood up and came around the desk, motioning for Anna to stand and face her. She did, pushing the armchair away, then wishing she still had it for support. She was still weak from the heat, or maybe from the story. She didn't know what "bodily contact" meant in this context, so she tried to brace herself for anything from holding hands to a sumo tackle.

"Do you consent to be touched?" Danai asked gently, standing up straight and looking Anna directly in the eye.

"Sure," Anna replied, having to actively stop herself from assuming a defensive position.

But, instead of tackling her or taking her hand, Danai stepped in and hugged Anna, wrapping one arm around her waist and the other around her shoulder, with no regard for how sweaty Anna still was from the salt cave. Anna stood stiff for a moment, then decided it probably worked best if she reciprocated, so she mirrored Danai's grasp and sank into the hug. They exhaled in unison, and Anna felt herself relax into the embrace, her head resting on the arm wrapped around her shoulder. Danai did the same.

After a few deep breaths – which could have been seconds or minutes, it was difficult to tell – Danai began muttering something under her breath. Anna piqued her attention at first, but her attention drifted when she realised the words were in Greek. Within a couple of minutes, though, the words clarified into English, and Anna realised she was speaking to her, whispering in her ear.

"Your feet are firmly planted in two domains, dragged towards one but drawn to the other. To be fully in one or the other would require sacrificing part of yourself. But to stay rooted in both requires those dragging you to choose to root themselves with you. This is a decision only they can make. But you can show them where the light is."

The woman suddenly broke away from Anna, who felt tears run down her face. And all of a sudden she was sobbing, unable to hold back the emotion. She fell to her knees, the stone floor rough beneath her, as she cried for everything that had happened.

Nikos keeping Maria from her and taking her out in London. Making her feel guilty about her career. All the jabs she made about Marcus, and about her mother, and when he compared her to either of them. Stealing the joy out of her best friend's engagement and wedding planning because she was so worried about him. Embarrassing her in front of Arthur. Jumping to conclusions about the file. Not giving her the benefit of the doubt. Not trusting her. Not loving the thing that made her feel more alive than anything else ever had. The weight of it all piled on her as she sank further down towards the floor, her tears mixing with the sweat on her thighs as they fell.

But then a funny thing happened. As Anna cried, she began to feel a calm wash over her. And whether it was the catharsis of the cry or her brain shutting down to the emotional overload she'd experienced, she knew she was going to be okay for now. But she needed some time to herself.

By the time she caught her breath, Danai was waiting for her by the entrance to the room, clearly content that she had given Anna what she needed. Anna followed her down the hallway in silence, not thinking about anything in particular, just focusing on putting one foot in front of the other.

As they came out of the cave into the night air, they were on the hillside just a few metres down from where they'd first entered. Anna could see the lights on in the house up ahead, and as they grew closer, she could hear her friends chatting and laughing. But, instead of joining them, she walked over to the car, which Thea had left unlocked. She pulled the back door open and grabbed her phone, opening the notes app and quickly tapping out what Danai had said to her. She may not have known what it meant now, but she could tell it was important. Then she headed down to the lake, the full moon bright in the sky to light her way.

The lake was bordered on this side by a cluster of rocks. Anna leaned against one to take off her shoes, then began to climb over them to get to the water's edge. It occurred to her that her clothes were unlikely to dry before they left in the morning, but she needed to get in the water. She needed to wash off the sweat and tears. She needed to float in the water with her ears below the surface where the noise of the world couldn't reach her. So she stripped off her leggings and tee shirt, draped her bra and underwear over a rock, and swam out to the middle of the lake where the laughter from the cottage couldn't reach her anymore.

Chapter Twenty-Eight

The next morning, Anna awoke to find Elena already gone.

She rolled over and looked at her phone. The time read 07:12. The sun was filtering gently through the curtains, and she could see the bright blue sea through the bit of window that was visible.

Anna groaned. There was no sore head this time – skipping dinner had meant skipping wine – but the memory of last night's drama washed over her with the same pain as if she were hungover.

After she'd skipped dinner the night before, the group had been almost silent on the way back, and whilst part of her felt guilty for bringing down the mood, she was also fully in her head about everything the oracle had said, and what had happened with Maria. Anna had known deep down that there was nothing going on between Nikos and Maria. But now she'd heard how Maria had been standing up for her, and whilst it should have made her feel better, it simply clarified the fact that the only thing wrong between Anna and Nikos was, in fact, Anna and Nikos. And now, Anna felt sick to her stomach every time she remembered how serious that issue felt when Danai was speaking to her. And now, though she was stone-cold sober and had been the night before, she felt sick and embarrassed enough that part of her wished she had partaken.

Today was, thankfully, to be quite low-key. They would have breakfast in the main dining room, and then they'd leave the hotel in Anna's rental car to drive back to the airport. Anna felt pretty secure in the idea that those would be drama-free settings, which was good, because she wasn't sure she could take much more. Hopefully everyone else was as ready to brush things aside and move on as she was.

She heard laughing from the room next door and sighed. In last night's commotion, she'd completely forgotten about Lizzy's revelation yesterday. At least no one was making a big deal out of that; Anna hoped that nonchalance would continue back on Santorini and with their grandparents.

Anna pulled herself out of bed and slowly gathered her things, changing into joggers and a tee shirt, unconcerned about looks for the day. Plus, her moderately cute airplane outfit had been worn last night. She found a few of Elena's things as she cleaned up, but her suitcase was gone, so Anna tucked them into her own to take back with her.

After washing her face and brushing her teeth, she was ready, but she still had nearly half an hour until breakfast would start. So she dragged her suitcase to the lobby, curled up in a lounge chair, and pulled out the detective novel she'd started reading in London.

It was a while before anyone she knew walked past, and her stomach dropped when she saw that the first person who came by was Thea. Not that she had any issues with Thea, but she had firmly been on Maria's side in every instance, and they'd been sharing a room all weekend.

"Morning," Anna said, meeting Thea's gaze over her book.

Thea nodded at her and began to sit down in the chair opposite. When she didn't immediately pull out her phone or something else to keep her busy, Anna packed away her book.

"No, don't stop reading on my account," Thea said, but her tone was clearly sneering, as if Anna had offended her.

"Sorry," Anna said, though she wasn't sure what she was apologising for.

Thea simply shrugged. The two sat in silence for nearly a minute, and whilst Anna definitely would have plucked up a conversation in any other situation, she felt for some reason that she was walking in a minefield now.

"So are you headed back to Athens now?" she asked, feeling that small talk was the safest course of action.

Thea nodded.

"That must be a short flight, right?"

"Less than an hour," Thea said. "But it beats having to drive for six hours."

Another long pause followed. Thea uncrossed her legs and then re-crossed them the other way.

"And how's Elena's dress coming along?" Anna asked, desperate to fill the silence.

Thea nodded again. "Well," she said. "It's just the lace to go now. I've left it in the hands of some very capable seamstresses in Athens."

"That sounds really glamorous," Anna said, picturing a life full of tulle and sequins and lace. "Did you always want to design wedding dresses?"

A sigh escaped Thea's lips. "We don't have to do this, you know. You can just sit there and read while we wait for the others."

Anna frowned. "Do what?"

Thea looked around and half smiled as if it were obvious. "You know, pretend to be friends."

Anna shifted uncomfortably in her seat. This was already a bit too reminiscent of last night. "I'm not sure what I did to make you think we couldn't be friends, but either way, we don't have to be friends to be friendly, do we?"

Thea laughed – a singular "ha!" – as if the idea were ludicrous. "You should have kept that in mind last night then," she said.

"Listen," Anna replied, leaning forward and lowering her voice. She refused to make a scene in yet another public place, especially one owned by one of her friends. "I know last night was uncomfortable, and I feel really bad about Maria. But I'm not sure what I did to offend you personally."

"I'm just not a big fan of women who pit themselves against other women," Thea responded, sitting back and crossing her arms. Her body language seemed to force Anna to come to her, to explain herself.

Anna sighed. "I'm not pitting myself against Maria. It's a complicated situation involving more than just the two of us."

"Complicated, sure." Thea rolled her eyes. Anna wasn't going to get anywhere with her. She saw the others approaching, all four of them in a group, and she put on a smile, determined not to drag the rest of the group into this – again.

"Just remember," Thea said quietly, "that Maria is a person. With a life, and with feelings, and with ambitions. And she doesn't deserve to be reduced to fit your story."

Breakfast with the girls brought with it an uncomfortable forced jollity that set Anna on edge. Even Lizzy wasn't really looking at her, and whilst no one was outright excluding her, there was a clear sense of being on the outside. She was sat at the end of the table, all of the conversation was oriented in the other direction, and not once did anyone ask her a question. To be fair, she didn't contribute much either, preferring to eat in silence to avoid putting her foot in her mouth for a third time.

As they got up to leave, Anna decided the safest course of action was to offer to drive back to the airport so that she wouldn't have to engage with the conversation and risk making anyone uncomfortable.

As everyone began to pile into the car, with Maria and Thea in the far back as Anna would have expected, it quickly became clear that no one planned to sit shotgun with Anna. Not even Lizzy moved to the front. They all preferred to sit tightly together.

There was a brief moment of quiet as they all silently acknowledged what had happened, and Elena briefly caught Anna's eye in the rear-view mirror, but she quickly looked away and started up a conversation about the flowers she had been mentally designing ahead of her appointment later that day. Anna focused her gaze on the ignition, starting the car and putting it into gear, then tried her best to concentrate on the road.

As she listened to all of them laugh and joke in the back seats, her driving them back to the airport like a chauffeur, she felt, just as she had at lunch the day before, just like she had at breakfast and in the salt cave and even at the fitting, like she could feel her friendships slipping through her fingers along with everything else at stake. The only thing she was grateful for was that no one was paying close enough attention to her to notice the tears threatening to spill from her eyes.

Chapter Twenty-Nine

The summer house looked as picturesque as ever when she got home. The pink bougainvillea cascading down over the porch swing, the garden full and luscious, the blue shutters on the front window where Nikos's herb garden box hung – as she was greeted by the familiar sight, she felt herself lighten.

Anna was alone. Lizzy had gone back with Xenia, Nikos seemed to be out, and Elena was at home. She may not have her sister, or her friend, or even her boyfriend, but as she took in the sight of her favourite place in the world, she felt grateful that at least she had her summer house and the memories of her father it held.

And, she remembered as she heard the truck coming up the drive behind her, she had her grandparents. Her perpetually loving Yaya and Pappouli.

Anna could hear them bickering in Greek as they got out of the truck, one door closing quietly and the other slamming. Actually, she could hear a solid stream of Greek coming from Eirini's mouth – Christos, on the other hand, was clearly trying to hold back a smile, grunting and throwing his hands up every now and then. Anna stepped back through the gate.

"Hi, guys," she said, and they both looked over at her.

"Hello, darling Anna," Christos said, walking towards her with his arms outstretched. She went towards him to accept the hug – nothing would feel better right now than a Christos hug – but she stopped short when he got just a few inches away, turning up her nose.

"Christos, you smell horrible," she said with a laugh, noting the sweat stains on his grey sleeveless top. Or, rather, one large sweat stain that covered virtually the whole top. "What have you been up to this time?"

"Don't ask," Eirini said, glaring at Christos, who just smiled.

"Oh come on," Anna said after a moment, when it was clear neither was talking. "You can't just leave me in suspense like that."

They shared a look between them, and Eirini rolled her eyes and nodded at him. Christos looked Anna dead in the eye and smiled wider than she'd seen him smile in years.

"Pole dancing."

Anna blinked as she tried to process what Christos had just said. "I'm sorry, what?"

Christos just kept smiling at her, looking like he was about to explode with laughter, giggling like a caught schoolboy. Anna looked at Eirini for confirmation.

"Your reaction is better than mine was," she said. "I got a call to pick him up – note that he didn't ask me to drop him off – and I walked into the studio to find him spinning around a pole with a class full of supermodel wannabes from America."

Anna suppressed a laugh at the mental image she conjured of excitable bridesmaids sticking singles in her grandfather's sweaty waistband as he attempted his best slut drop. Somehow she managed to hold it in.

"Pappouli, I'm shocked. I just got back from Elena's hen do, and even I didn't do that."

"It was fun!" he said, giving a big grin and a big thumbs-up to match.

Eirini rolled her eyes again. "Go inside and shower, you old tart."

Christos squinted at her with incomprehension. "Tart?"

She translated into Greek, and he let out a mighty laugh.

"Tart!" he repeated, over and over again as he walked inside. "Tart, tart, tart, tart, tart."

"Well, look on the bright side," Anna said as the door to the main house closed behind him. "At least this one's a skill he can use to financially contribute to the household again."

Eirini swatted Anna's arm with the back of her hand, but she was laughing as well now.

"When I tell you that he was actually hanging upside down from the ceiling when I walked inside – oh Anna, it was such a delight. This is so much better than the stupid sandcastles."

Anna joined in with her grandmother's laughter. "Why do you give him such a hard time then?"

"Oh, he knows I don't really mind," she said. "The day I stop talking is the day I'm truly upset. As long as we're talking, we're fine, even if we're arguing."

Anna nodded. She knew what that was like. She thought back to the moments she and Nikos had sat next to each other, neither of them saying how they truly felt.

"Is everything okay, Anna?" Eirini asked, sensing Anna's sombre mood.

She tried to nod in response, but she could feel herself tearing up.

Maybe Anna's grandmother had spoken to Lizzy already, or maybe she had seen the conflict coming, but Eirini put a firm hand on Anna's shoulder and smiled at her. "If someone can't see that you're the kindest, most thoughtful person among them, then they don't really know you at all, and good riddance." Then Eirini wrapped Anna in a big hug.

She had been wrong. The only thing better than a Christos hug right now was an Eirini hug. As she relaxed into her grandmother's embrace, she felt the emotion of the last few days – hell, even the last few weeks – pour through her yet again. She had thought she'd cried every tear she had in her with the oracle, but clearly she was wrong, and as she sobbed into Eirini's chest, she knew that there was likely more to come between now and the wedding.

Through it all, Eirini just hugged her ever closer, ever tighter, ever stronger.

A few minutes later, as the two women swayed gently, a clattering noise came from the main house. Anna stepped back and gestured towards it. "Sorry, I didn't mean to keep you for so long."

"No, don't you worry, Anna. Christos is a grown man. He can fend for himself. I'm here as long as you need or want me to be."

Anna smiled gratefully and decided that this time she would take the support being offered to her. She invited Eirini into the summer house, and for the first time since she'd moved to Santorini four years prior, she sat her grandmother down in her kitchen and made her dinner. It was nothing fancy, just a simple pasta dish that she knew she would have the ingredients for. Nikos was the real cook. But Eirini ate it as if it were the best meal she'd ever had, and she drank her wine as if it were the sweetest nectar.

Throughout dinner, the conversation stayed on lighter topics: what Christos's next hobby might be, what the weather was going to be like for the wedding, what Eirini was going to wear. But as they sat down on the swing outside with a cup of tea, Anna knew she wanted to get her grandmother's perspective – the perspective of someone who loved her, and who respected her enough to tell her the truth, no matter what. So she told Eirini everything about Ireland, London and the hen do, sparing no detail except for the parts about Lizzy and Xenia. That wasn't her story to tell.

Eirini didn't chime in with questions or comments; she simply sipped her drink and listened throughout the whole thing. When Anna was done, she sat quietly for a few more minutes, nodding her head as she thought.

"You must feel so lonely," she said, finally meeting Anna's eye.

Anna nodded. "I really do," she said. "It feels like no one in the situation is on my side. I thought Lizzy at least would be, but even she seems to think I'm in the wrong here." It went unspoken between them that Eirini was on Anna's side.

"From what you've told me she said earlier, I would think it's more that she doesn't understand the hostility towards Maria. But from the rest of what you've told me, I understand why you feel that way. I would, too."

Anna smiled. It was nice to feel like someone understood why she'd let Maria become the bad guy, but she was still embarrassed she'd done it.

"Have you seen Nikos since you got back?" Eirini asked.

"No, I came straight here. I got back only a few moments before you did."

"Do you know what you're going to say?"

Anna shook her head. "Honestly, I have no idea. Maria may not have been after him, or vice versa, but the main issue hasn't really changed. If anything, it's gotten worse. Nikos wants me to stay here more than I want to be here based on the opportunities I've been given. They're not always going to be there, and I don't want them to pass me by."

Eirini nodded, considering what Anna was saying. "You're lucky, women of today, because you have such choice. But in this situation, I doubt that choice feels very lucky."

"Nope." Anna pressed her lips together. Of course she felt lucky to have the work opportunities – not everyone did. The idea of being a professional photographer was ambitious enough, never mind the idea of having people all over the globe want to work with her. She was exceedingly fortunate. But having to choose between a quiet, cosy life with the man she loved and the opportunity others could only dream of? That didn't feel quite so lucky.

"Anna, you know we love Nikos, and he will always be like a grandson to us. He has been since long before you met him. But you are so much more than just his partner to us, you're our grandchild. Our flesh and blood. And if you really want these jobs—"

"I really do, Yaya."

Eirini nodded. "Then you must take them, regardless of how it makes Nikos feel."

Anna stared at her grandmother, half in disbelief, and half knowing that she was always going to say exactly that. Of course she wanted the best for Anna. And after what she'd shared before about wishing she'd had the same opportunities as Christos, much less Anna? Well, it made sense that she didn't want Anna settling to appease Nikos's feelings. Of course she didn't.

It hadn't exactly made Anna's mind up for her, but she felt a sort of peace knowing that, no matter what her decision was, she would still have Eirini and Christos on her side. They were still her family, and this was still her home. And they were rooting for her.

Her interest piqued, Eirini asked more about the jobs, and Anna went inside to get the folder and show her. She had to dig it out of her bag. She hadn't been able to bring herself to look at it since she'd picked it up off the table at the wine bar after Nikos had dropped it there. Looking through it now, she saw that there were some jobs inside that Anna hadn't even noticed the first time around, including one for the Santorini Tourism Board right there on the island. Marcus really had created quite a collection.

"What are you two looking at?" a voice said from the gate, and Anna looked up to see Nikos standing just inside it. Her instinct was to hide it away, but she remembered that wasn't necessary. "Never mind," he mumbled as he realised what she had in her hands.

Anna could tell that he was exhausted. His normally bright eyes were ringed with dark, baggy skin. His face was covered in stubble that had gone far past his standard five o'clock shadow, and his hair was greasy as he ran his hands through it. He'd clearly not been doing well since their chat at the marina.

Eirini stood from the swing and gave Nikos a brief kiss on the cheek. "Drinks in an hour," she said. "Full family affair. Lizzy is bringing her new girlfriend."

Life came to Nikos's face as he did a double-take, looking first at Eirini and then at Anna. "I'm sorry, what?"

Anna put a hand on his arm. "I'll fill you in later," she said. "Let's go inside."

At least that answered the question of how Eirini would react to Lizzy's news. With food and wine, of course.

As Eirini walked back to the main house, Anna grabbed Nikos's hand and led him inside. But, instead of collapsing into bed or flirting in the kitchen before ending up in each other's arms like every other time she'd tried to do this, they simply sat facing each other, her cross-legged on the bed and him leaning against the kitchen counter all the way on the other side of the room.

They stared at each other for long, silent minutes. Anna had gotten used to awkward, pregnant pauses over the last few weeks, but this wasn't that. It was empty. Barren. Like neither of them could find any words to say, and neither was trying. Like all of the words had been said that could be said, and yet nothing had changed.

Every other conflict they'd faced, they'd been able to fix. But this was different. Because neither of them was wrong in what they wanted for themselves, and neither could begrudge the other for what they wanted. There was no misunderstanding between them anymore. Just sadness.

"What are you going to do?" Nikos asked, plain as that. No preamble, no explanation. Just, "What are you going to do?"

And Anna knew what he meant. He was asking if she was going to take the jobs. And she also knew what the answer was. She'd known all along. But she couldn't bring herself to say it. She couldn't say to him, "I'm going to keep leaving you, no matter what that means for us." Because the man in front of her was the man she loved and saying that would only hurt him. So instead, she lied to him for what she hoped was the last time, but she had a sinking feeling wouldn't be.

"I don't know. What are you going to do?"

Nikos shrugged. "What can I do?"

Anna shrugged back.

Another couple of minutes passed in silence. Anna knew she was the one who would have to bring them out of this stalemate. She just wasn't ready to do what she knew she needed to do.

"I'll figure it out, I guess," she said. "Let's just get through the wedding, and then we'll figure it out."

He nodded. "Through the wedding," he agreed.

The wedding was one week away. Anna had one week to figure out if there was a way to get what she knew she wanted – what she needed for herself – without it causing the end of her relationship. But as she looked at the tired, dejected man in front of her and felt the vastness of the silence between them, she wondered if they were already too far gone.

Chapter Thirty

Every time Anna passed by a gap in the buildings and caught a glimpse of the caldera to her left, she fell in love with Santorini all over again. Golden light bounced off the waves as the sun rose in the sky, creating a sea of sparkles, like reflections off a disco ball. She could see the white buildings of Oia in the distance, contrasting with the still-shadowy cliff side on the west of the island.

Despite the wedding festivities and everything happening with Nikos, Anna was determined to make sure Lizzy got the full Santorini experience whilst she was here. She was only in town for another week. She was due to fly home just after the wedding, but when Anna had asked over dinner last night what that meant for her and Martin, or for her and Xenia, Lizzy had shrugged the question off and asked what they were going to be doing in the morning.

Anna and Nikos had created a detailed list of must-dos, half of which had to be scrapped because of the wedding. There were still a few "non-negotiable" items on the list, but Anna planned to tick very few of them off today. Now that Nikos had bowed out to help Elena, Anna was throwing out the list. She herself had fallen in love with the island on a very similar mission four years ago, undertaken by Nikos to make sure they left no stone unturned, and she wanted her sister to get the same feeling she got way back then. The feeling of being at home. She knew exactly how to do that for her sister, but it was going to look a bit different from her own experience.

Lizzy wobbled on her Vespa a few metres behind Anna. She was less than confident as a driver, despite her claims to the contrary, so Anna was making sure to drive extra slowly. She'd offered to have Lizzy on the back of hers, but her big sister had insisted on driving herself, so they'd paid an extortionate amount to hire one from one of the tourist shops. She'd actually wanted one of the ATVs that were popular with visitors, but Anna had insisted that if she was going to hire something, it would be something Anna was familiar with. It was only seven in the morning, so the roads were fairly quiet, but Anna was still nervous watching her sister inadvertently bob and weave behind her.

As the roads began to twist and they rounded the curve of the island, the view disappeared, and Anna could see in her wing mirror that Lizzy was craning her neck to try to find it again. She was hooked.

The rest of the traffic turned off the main road into Oia town, but Anna veered right, and Lizzy followed obediently. The road twisted away from town and downhill, looping back on itself in a couple of switchbacks until they arrived at Ammoudi Bay. There, a passenger ferry was waiting – though calling it a passenger ferry seemed generous, given that it looked like it would hold a dozen people at most. It was impossible to tell, because there was no one else there except the man who Anna presumed to be the captain, leaning up against the piling the boat was tied to and scrolling on his phone.

"Where are we going?" Lizzy asked, hopping off her Vespa as Anna did and pushing it along the pier.

Anna ignored her sister. "Two tickets to Thirasia," she said to the man, who looked up at her, took the money from her outstretched hand, and nodded her onto the boat. She looked down at her Vespa and back up at the man, who looked around as if expecting more passengers to materialise. When none did, he looked back at her and nodded.

"What's Thirasia?" Lizzy asked, stepping onto the boat behind her sister, their Vespas barely navigable on the small ramp.

"That is," Anna said, pointing at a smaller island across the caldera. From here, though, it was close enough that it looked practically like an extension of the main island.

"Why are we going there? Isn't all the touristy stuff here?"

"You'll see," Anna said with a smile. The man started the boat and untied it from the piling, pulling away. They were still the only people on board.

Anna had visited Thirasia for the first time only a year earlier. She'd gone with her grandmother, treating her to a birthday lunch out. She'd asked Eirini where she wanted to go, anywhere on the island, and she'd asked for a small cafe on Thirasia – literally, a place called Small Cafe. Anna had arranged it, and the two had shared a wonderful day taking in the views and exploring the island. Anna realised as they climbed the hills side by side, Eirini's breath far more even than Anna's own, how much life Eirini still had in her. This was clearly a woman who had grown up here.

Now, Anna took advantage of the noise of the boat to stare out to sea and avoid conversation. Things had been a bit awkward with Lizzy since the hen do. Anna couldn't stop remembering how she'd taken Maria's side, or at least the group's, in the salt cavern. There was so much going on that Anna and Lizzy would normally talk through together – with Nikos, with Lizzy's marriage, with Xenia – but every time they'd been together, there had been a tension that held Anna back as much as it frustrated her. So now she sat as close to the noise of the engine as possible, making it as difficult as she could for Lizzy to attempt a conversation. In the end, she didn't even try.

The crossing took less than ten minutes. On arrival, they pushed their Vespas off the ferry and immediately found themselves in a small fishing village, with signs pointing off to different Thirasia attractions.

"Welcome," Anna said, holding up her arms and spinning around to face Lizzy, "to the village of Agia Eirini."

"No way," Lizzy said. "As in, Yaya's name?"

Anna nodded. "One and the same. It's where her name came from."

"That's so cool!" Lizzy said, smiling and looking around, taking in the little harbourside buildings and the colourful fishing boats. "Is she from here?"

"Not far. Do you want to see?"

Lizzy nodded, and Anna motioned for her to get back on and follow her. They headed north, turning right onto the road, and within a couple of minutes, they stopped in front of a small white house nestled into the rocks.

"This is where Eirini grew up," Anna said when Lizzy pulled up beside her. They turned off the Vespas and walked a few paces up the drive. "She's the one who knew I'd be able to get the Vespas on the boat, because her family used to run them back and forth from Oia."

"Does anyone still live here?" Lizzy asked, nodding at the house. The front door was slightly off its hinges, and the grass had grown up tall around it.

Anna shook her head. "When her parents died, she didn't have any other family on the island, so she sold it. When we came last year, she told me the person who had bought the land hadn't even bothered tearing the house down. But at least this way she can come back and see it."

"That's so sad," Lizzy said, her eyes fixed on the building, and Anna had a flash of inspiration. For the first time since Ireland, Anna pulled her camera out of her bag, quickly adjusted the settings, and raised it.

Anna instantly felt herself relax into the position, her camera in front of her face, looking through the viewfinder, bending at the knees to get the best angle. The first picture she'd ever taken for school photography class had been of her sister, and she'd been in love with the art ever since. Now four of her favourite things had come together in one moment: her sister, her grandmother, her home, and her passion.

The light was still growing as the sun rose higher in the sky, and after a moment, half of Lizzy's face was covered in a golden ray. It was what Anna had been waiting for. She snapped the photo and immediately put the camera away. She didn't even look at the image on the screen; she knew she'd gotten the shot. She'd felt it as the shutter clicked.

After a few moments, Anna and Lizzy continued on down the road. They drove with the hills on their left and the open sea on their right, and Anna knew that just out of sight, about twenty-five miles north and northwest of Thirasia, were the islands of Ios, Sikinos and Folegandros. Then, as they turned inland towards the town of Thirasia, they began to climb upward, eventually cresting the top of the hill, where they could see the rest of the island falling away in front of them, then the caldera with the smaller volcanic islands in its centre and Santorini beyond.

"Wow!" Lizzy said, almost under her breath, as she and Anna stopped to take in the view.

"I know," Anna said. "There are a lot of good views *on* Santorini, but this might be the best view *of* Santorini."

"I can't believe you get to live here," Lizzy said. "This is so much better than rural Georgia."

"Yeah, I mean, it's stunning," Anna replied. "But I don't just *get* to live here. I *chose* to live here. I've built a life here. Anyone could do it."

"Yeah, but you actually did. And it's really great."

Anna smiled. It was pretty great when things were going well. She'd had the career, the man, and the gorgeous home. But it hadn't been so great lately, to the point that it made her wonder if she'd actually had all of those things to begin with.

She opened her mouth to say all of this to Lizzy, but something stopped her. The moment she went to speak, she felt the sweaty palms and the flushed skin and the sweat of the salt cave, despite the breeze she was feeling on her face. And she couldn't do it.

"Thanks," she said quietly, instead.

When they reached the seafront at the bottom of the hill, Anna led Lizzy on foot along the beach, pushing their Vespas through the gravel, until they reached Small Cafe where Anna had eaten lunch with her grandmother the year before. The cafe was a small white building with a veranda cut into the middle of it. The sun filtered through the thatched cover in tiny slivers, most of it well shaded, which was good since the sun was getting higher in the sky. A woman came through the door between the cafe and the veranda with a bucket of cutlery, clearly opening up for the day.

"Coffee?" Anna asked, and Lizzy nodded. She popped her head in and ordered two lattes, then joined Lizzy in the shade as she looked out at the view. The sea was remarkably blue as usual, and the striated cliffs of Thirasia closed in on them on both sides of the little marina in shades of red and brown. The sky was peppered with wispy white clouds, which were slowly blowing south in the wind.

"Thank you for bringing me here," Lizzy said. "I thought we would be doing a bunch of touristy stuff, which I was excited about, but getting to see where Yaya is from has been incredible. I feel so much more connected to this place."

"I mean, everything is touristy here," Anna said with a laugh. "And don't get me wrong, you've got a touristy day ahead of you. Nikos would kill me otherwise."

Lizzy laughed. "You know what I mean."

"I do," Anna said, smiling at her sister. And she did. Anna and Lizzy had grown up in a house where traditions and connections were overlooked in favour of appearances, which Anna suspected was part of why Lizzy had overcorrected by moving to a rural farm in the middle of nowhere. She had been obsessed since childhood with the idea of connecting with the Earth; to the place she chose to call home. The best way for her to feel at home in Santorini was to help her create that connection. She'd already done it in the garden at the summer house, but their family history was so much richer than that, and Anna was proud to be able to share that with her sister the way Eirini had for her.

The woman emerged with their coffees and set them down on the table. Anna nodded her thanks.

"So how are things going?" Lizzy asked. "With Nikos, that is."

"Not great, to be honest," Anna said, dipping a toe in the conversational water to see how Lizzy would react. She wanted so desperately to talk to her sister, who had always been her best friend, but she wasn't sure she'd be able to take it if Lizzy set herself against Anna again.

"He seemed fine at drinks the other night."

"Yeah, well, he was on his best behaviour."

"Because of me and Xenia?"

Anna looked up at Lizzy, and she could see trepidation in her eyes. She didn't say more, but it looked like she was holding back – her lips were pressed together as if to open her mouth would mean that all her feelings would come tumbling out. Anna realised that, as much as she wanted to clear the air to talk about what was going on in her own life, Lizzy probably wanted that just as badly for herself. She took a sip of her coffee and considered the best way to move forward.

Anna may have been the little sister, but she knew she was going to have to take the lead if they were going to get anywhere. That seemed to be a theme in her life. Maybe being brave and vulnerable with Lizzy would help her do it with Nikos, too.

She took a deep breath.

"Listen, Liz, we've both got a lot of shit going on right now. And I'm pretty hurt about how things went down on the trip, but I'm also pretty embarrassed about it. So can we just draw a line under it for now so that we can help each other out?"

Anna watched Lizzy's shoulders drop, as if she'd been a balloon about to pop, and someone had let the air out just in time. Relief flooded her face.

"I would love that," she said. "But can I go first? I am dying to gush about my crush, and I haven't got friends on the island like you do."

"Please do," Anna said, though she wasn't sure she had as many connections as Lizzy thought. She gestured for Lizzy to go on as she sat back to sip her coffee.

Lizzy leaned forward and pressed her palms together, wrinkling her forehead and pressing it up against her two forefingers, her chin resting on her thumbs. It had always been her thinking face. Then she exhaled and nodded at the same time, clearly having decided what she wanted to say.

"I really like Xenia," she said, "but I'm worried she doesn't feel the same way. We just made out at first to make her ex jealous, and I feel like maybe she never moved on from that mindset."

Anna nodded as she considered what to say. She couldn't help but feeling like they'd skipped a crucial part of the conversation.

"Is your marriage that clearly over that you're thinking about moving on altogether?" she asked tentatively, keeping an eye on

Lizzy's expression to make sure she hadn't touched a nerve. She knew Martin had really hurt Lizzy, and she didn't want Lizzy to feel like she had to defend herself to her own sister.

But to Anna's surprise, Lizzy just smiled.

"It really is," she said. "And of course I'm sad about that. Martin and I were together for more than half our lives. But when I'm with Xen, I don't feel any of that. I just feel..." Lizzy got a wistful look in her eye as she trailed off. "I feel hopeful."

She was smiling shyly, and Anna could see a touch of colour coming to her olive cheeks.

"That's great," Anna said, reaching out for her sister's hand. "I'm really happy you've managed to find something hopeful in this mess."

Lizzy rolled her eyes. "Yeah, I know, vom. But it's how I feel."

"Not vom," Anna said, catching Lizzy's eye. "Not vom at all. Very good. Very encouraging for sad saps like me. And as for Xenia, just talk to her. She's a reasonable person."

"That is so much easier said than done, and you know it."

Anna laughed. "I know, but Xenia's seriously the most chill person I know. And even if she doesn't want what you want right now, she wouldn't reject you because of it."

Based on how they'd behaved at dinner, Anna would have been surprised if Xenia rejected Lizzy for any reason at all. They were clearly trying to keep their distance, presumably for Eirini and Christos's sake, but they could barely keep their hands off each other. Anna had never seen Xenia drop her professional, put-together demeanour, not even for a second, but she acted like a giddy schoolgirl around Lizzy, all furtive glances and blushing and batting of eyelashes and hand holding under the table.

Lizzy considered what Anna had said, then nodded. "You're probably right," she said. "I just need to find a good moment. Maybe at the wedding so she's feeling all mushy."

Now it was Anna's turn to roll her eyes. "Whatever you think is best, but do *not* cause a scene at the wedding."

"Yeah, you've been doing enough of that for the both of us," Lizzy said, and Anna looked at her to see a smirk on her face. Anna must have given her a look of disdain because she added, "What, too soon?"

"A bit," Anna said, but she did so with a laugh.

"Do you want to talk about that?" Lizzy asked, more seriously this time. Anna considered for a moment. Did she? She'd spoken enough about the problems she had with Nikos, and mostly to people other than Nikos, and she wasn't sure if she actually wanted to anymore. It would be good to get Lizzy's support, but what could she tell Anna that would change things? What could she say that Anna didn't already know?

"You know I always have your side," Lizzy added before Anna could respond. She reached across the table and took Anna's hand. "I'm your big sister. And I'll always call you out if I think you're being a dick, but I'm always in your corner. Especially on this. Especially when there's so much at stake."

Anna smiled, her mind made up. All she needed was to know that Lizzy was there for her. The rest could remain unspoken.

"Thanks," she said, giving Lizzy's hand a squeeze. "There's nothing to say, really. It's all been said at this point. But I really do appreciate that you're here for me." Then she gestured around her. "And I do mean *here*!"

Lizzy scooted her chair around so it was just an inch from Anna's, leaning her head on Anna's shoulder.

"Love you, Banana," she said.

Anna leaned her head on Lizzy's in kind. "Love you, too, Lizard."

They stayed in that moment for a while, looking out at the caldera, sipping their coffee, not breaking the link between them, as the sun filtered down through the veranda. Anna had no idea what was going to happen with Nikos – not the next day, or the next week at the wedding, or certainly the next few months when the dream jobs were scheduled. But she knew that right now, she had more than most people, and for that she was grateful, even as it all threatened to fall apart.

Anna and Lizzy spent the rest of the day ticking more touristy things off the list: cliff jumping at Ammoudi Bay, hiking from Oia to Fira, visiting the ruins at ancient Thera. For lunch, they had Anna's favourite, super-authentic meal that went all the way back to her first day on the island – McDonald's. After living on an organic farm, Lizzy hadn't had fast food in years, and Anna decided it was time to break that streak.

They then spent the rest of the afternoon lounging on Kamari Beach, and despite Anna's goading, Lizzy refused to use that time to talk to Xenia, even though she would be on-site that day. Anna knew this because she'd seen Xenia's car, but she would have known, anyway, from the way Lizzy wouldn't just relax, instead making sure she was posed at every moment, her bikini straps perfectly positioned and her back slightly arched as she sunbathed.

After a couple of hours, Anna went inside to get them some drinks. She knew from experience that the bar on the beach charged twice as much during peak beach hours. As she walked into the lobby, she saw Xenia behind the front desk, frowning at a computer screen.

"Something wrong?" Anna asked as she walked up, putting her elbows on the countertop and resting her chin in the crook of one arm.

Xenia looked up suddenly, and her face softened into a smile.

"Oh, hi, Anna," she said. "Yeah, everything's fine. Just pulling some data to compare for a new project I'm considering."

As she spoke, Xenia looked over Anna's shoulder and around the lobby.

"She's on the beach," Anna said with a smile.

Xenia nodded, then immediately straightened her spine, putting on an innocent face. "Who is?"

Anna laughed. "Very funny."

Xenia sighed and shook her head. "I'm hopeless," she said. "I haven't spoken to her since drinks at your grandparents' house, and I can't tell if she wants me to reach out. She's obviously got a lot going on."

Anna felt an intense internal struggle between keeping her sister's confidence and orchestrating something on her behalf. In the tradition of sisters everywhere, she meddled.

"I promise you, she wants you to reach out."

Xenia blushed. "You really think so?"

"I know so," Anna said. "And I've had a morning of 'Xenia this, Xenia that' to prove it."

"I just don't want to overstep my bounds," Xenia said, frowning.

"Honestly, I don't think that's possible right now."

Xenia nodded. "Noted," she said, clearly doing some mental calculations to determine what was appropriate versus what she wanted. Anna remembered that tension – wanting someone so badly but not wanting to cause drama – and she smiled.

"You'll be fine," she said, then decided any further meddling would be crossing the line. So she said goodbye to Xenia, grabbed some drinks from the bar, and headed back out to Lizzy.

"What took you so long?" Lizzy asked, sitting up and taking the drink Anna offered her.

"I went inside, and then I got talking to Xenia."

Lizzy smacked Anna's arm, nearly knocking her drink out of her hand. "You didn't say anything to her, did you?"

Anna rolled her eyes. "Um, let's see, I said hi, I asked her what she was doing, and…" She looked up at Lizzy as she trailed off, seeing that she was, quite literally, on the edge of her seat. "Oh, and that you were head over heels in love with her. Hope that was okay?"

Anna laughed as Lizzy groaned and collapsed back into her seat on the sun lounger.

"So not funny," she said, pulling her towel over her face to hide her growing redness.

"I thought it was," Anna said, sitting back in her own seat.

Was it too much to hope that Xenia and Lizzy would actually fall in love? It was so good to have Lizzy here, and if her marriage was really over and her home invaded by this other woman, then what did she have to go back to? Maybe she would stay here, and they could all live happily ever after together.

That was, of course, if she could manage to get her own happily ever after.

In her excitement for Lizzy, she'd almost forgotten that her own relationship was on the brink. The wedding was just a few days away, and Marcus's deadline fell just after that. And if it all fell apart… well, Anna didn't even want to think about what that would mean for her happily ever after.

Chapter Thirty-One

Nikos

"Stupid sugary piece of shit," Elena shouted, throwing the pouch she'd been working on for over a minute down in front of her. The candy-coated nuts spilled out of the gauzy material and scattered over the glass surface of the coffee table, clinking against it, making the spill sound far more dramatic than it actually was.

Nikos laughed. He'd been watching Elena try to tie the little ribbons together neatly, and he was honestly surprised she'd lasted as long as she had. He took a self-satisfied look at the not-so-small pile of perfectly tied pouches on the floor next to him and then smirked at Elena.

"Very funny, Jack-be-nimble over there. I don't understand how you're so freakishly good at this." She sank deeper into the sofa and rested her head on the back, shutting her eyes.

"I think it's more that you're freakishly bad," Nikos said, tying another one with ease and adding it to the pile. He watched as

Elena took a deep breath, exhaling it out in a sigh. "You okay? I can't imagine it's the *koufeta* stressing you out this much. I really don't mind doing all of them." They'd been getting the *koufeta*, the tiny bags of sugared almonds, ready for hours now. He knew that wasn't what was bothering Elena, but he wasn't sure what was. He decided to push it just a bit. It was her wedding week, after all, and if there were something he could help with, he wanted to. For her.

"Honestly?" she asked, looking up at him.

"Honestly," he said, holding her gaze, and he meant it.

"You and Anna are stressing me the fuck out," she said, sitting forward, tossing her hands about as she spoke. "She and Maria really got into it on my hen weekend, and now she's being all smiley and weird like nothing's going on, but she's not being herself. And the last time I saw her like that was when you two first got together and she thought I was going to dump her as a friend if she hurt you. Like she was walking on eggshells but trying to act natural."

Nikos balked. Sure, Anna was trying to keep the peace, but he hadn't known how weird it had gotten at the hen party.

"What do you mean she and Maria got into it?" he asked.

"I mean, she acted like she'd never heard a word about Maria and accused Maria of trying to break you guys up. And then Maria told her she thought you were being ridiculous, but that Anna needed to leave her out of things."

Nikos exhaled a large whoosh of air. "Well, that explains this," he said, pulling his phone out and opening his texts with Maria. Right below him messaging a few days before to ask about their next wine club event, she'd sent him in return:

> Whatever is going on between you and Anna, please leave me the fuck out of it. I don't need the drama, and I don't enjoy feeling like a pawn in your relationship when I thought we were friends.

He tipped the phone to Elena so she could see, and she let out a whistle.

"That woman is a force to be reckoned with," she said. "I actually think she and Anna would have been friends if you hadn't fully fucked that one up."

Nikos nodded, but his mouth formed into a grimace. She was probably right; Anna and Maria would have gotten along perfectly under normal circumstances. It was another reminder of how Nikos had made things worse. And now, apparently, that decision had ruined Elena's bachelorette weekend.

"I'm so sorry," he said, looking up at his cousin. "I didn't mean for my actions to ruin your trip."

"Yeah, you're an idiot," she said back to him, "but don't worry, it wasn't ruined. I actually quite enjoyed seeing them duke it out. I love Anna, she's my bestie, but she was *owned*. It was kind of funny."

Elena laughed, and Nikos let himself crack a smile. He hated the idea of Anna being uncomfortable, especially because of something he'd done, but he also couldn't help but feel a swell of pride towards Elena. Everyone always joked that she was the centre of the universe and that she loved attention, but Nikos knew that the best thing about her was that she couldn't care less who was in focus at any given time. She was her best, most fabulous self, anyway. Nikos knew that came from a childhood with a mother who would choose if and when to give her attention, doting on her half the time and completely ignoring her the rest. For anyone else, it might have made them fawn at anyone who would give them the time of day. But, for Elena, it just made her find an internal source of confidence. Nikos wished he were more like her; Elena would never jeopardise her whole life and relationship because of something she was too afraid to say out loud.

"What are you thinking?" she asked, and Nikos realised he'd been staring down at a pouch for quite some time.

"I'm just worried about Anna and me," he replied, tying up the pouch.

"I thought you said things were better this week?"

Nikos had said that when Elena asked him earlier, and on the surface they had seemed better. Their decision to pause the conversation until after the wedding seemed to give them both an excuse to pause their frustrations, too, and things had been pleasant. More than pleasant, even. But Nikos knew it was a veneer.

For one, Anna was throwing herself into wedding prep. Every spare moment, she was helping Elena with something else. This didn't seem overly weird for a maid of honour to do, but Nikos knew that normally Anna would be doing some sort of work. In fact, he'd seen the "Ireland" memory card sitting at the top of her to-be-processed bowl for days.

And second, they hadn't had sex. In fact, they'd barely touched each other since their drunken alleyway moment in London. Not a cuddle, not a kiss, not a tender hand on the arm since they'd gotten home… it was like a wall was up between them.

"They've seemed better, but I can tell it's not," Nikos said. "She's hardly speaking to me and definitely not getting anywhere near me romantically. I don't know. Maybe she's distancing herself to make it easier to break up with me before her tour de force at work."

It wasn't the first time the idea had occurred to Nikos – that Anna might be distancing herself not to keep the peace but to start the separation process – but the thought still felt like a stab to the heart. Had he screwed things up so monumentally by hiding Maria from her that she was ready to take Marcus up on his offer and more? Was she ready to walk away entirely?

"What tour de force?" Elena asked, frowning.

For a moment, Nikos was surprised. Elena was always the first to hear about exciting new jobs. But then again, if Anna had been keeping it from him, she was unlikely to tell Elena. He told his cousin all about the file of jobs he'd found in the tote bag, and how Marcus was trying to lure her away.

"Well, I wouldn't say that," Elena said, stopping him. "Marcus may be a bit of a skeeze, but since he and Anna started working together, he's only had her career in mind. He wouldn't put his own name on the line to screw you over."

"But he might if he thought I was holding Anna back."

"Well, are you?"

Nikos paused to consider what she meant. "You mean, am I holding Anna back?"

Elena nodded.

"I mean, maybe," he said. "Is it wrong to say I hope so?"

Elena smiled and moved onto the floor next to Nikos. She took one of his hands in both of hers and held it to her cheek. "Kind of," she said, "but I don't think that's what you really mean."

"What do I mean then?" Nikos wasn't being challenging; he was pleading. It was like he was too close to the situation to see it clearly anymore. And Elena knew him better than anyone.

"You mean that you wish Anna would prioritise you over work, sometimes," Elena said with a smile. "Not that you hope your relationship is curbing her success."

Nikos nodded. That was exactly right. Why couldn't he articulate his own feelings that well to himself, much less to Anna?

"Exactly," he said. "I just feel like a second choice. And I'd feel that way regardless of how successful she was because of the decisions she's making."

Elena's mouth pressed into a thin line, and her brows creased together. "Not quite. Why don't you try again."

Nikos leaned back just a bit. "What do you mean 'not quite?'"

Elena sighed and released Nikos's hand. "I mean that you don't feel that way because of the decisions she's making. You feel that way because of your own fear of abandonment. Your insecurity about not being enough, and being left, like Giorgos was and like you almost were four years ago."

Nikos could practically hear the collective cishet male population of Greece laugh at what Elena was saying. Men around here didn't talk about fear of abandonment or insecurity or trauma. But Nikos had been lucky enough to grow up with Elena, and she had always been one to tell it like it was. He thought, not for the first time, not even that day, that she would make a good therapist.

She was right, of course. He was terrified that Anna would decide that this life wasn't enough for her. That she needed more; deserved more. And every time she proved him wrong by staying, by committing, he told himself it was a fluke, that he'd gotten lucky. And every time she left, every time she chose to be away, he took it as confirmation that she wasn't happy. That he and his little life on this little island weren't enough to fulfil her.

He'd been having this fight with himself for four years, but until Elena got engaged and he found that stupid file, he hadn't realised he was still in the thick of it. He hadn't realised how much it was eating away at him and at their relationship.

"What are you thinking in that big ol' head of yours?" Elena asked, smiling at Nikos.

"I'm not sure," Nikos said, attempting to smile back, but it fell flat. "I just feel like I need to know once and for all that she's committed to me. To our life together."

Elena's smile melted into a scowl. "But can you ask that of her if you aren't fully committed to her?"

Nikos scowled back. "What do you mean? Of course I'm committed to her."

"No, you're committed to an idea of a life together. But what about Anna, the actual, whole person? The woman who loves what she does? Who wants big things for herself? Who doesn't give into things like imposter syndrome or fear? She's incredible, and I'm pretty sure she's the one you fell in love with, right?"

Nikos nodded. "Yes, of course," he said. Anna's passion for her art and her refusal to ever quit was part of what drew him to her – both in the beginning and still to this day.

"Well, you're not acting very committed to that person right now," she said, standing up. "Now, I have to make a phone call. Wedding stuff. But you need to have a good hard think about which Anna you want in your life – the one who's full of life and passion, who you fell in love with, or the one who gives those things up for some guy."

"Hey," Nikos said, a bit jokingly, but it did sting.

Elena shrugged. "That's what you are in this equation. She may love you, but you're still just some guy unless you can step the fuck up."

Elena grabbed her phone off the coffee table and left the room. Nikos wasn't sure why she would leave her flat to make the call – maybe to leave Nikos to stew in what she'd just said – but he took the opportunity to finish tying the *koufeta* in silence, thinking with every knot he tied about the mess he'd made.

Of course Elena was right. He'd fallen in love with the Anna who would absolutely take the opportunity Marcus was offering her. But was it so wrong of him to hope that a four-year relationship had moved the goalpost? It certainly had for him.

Then again, over the last couple of years, he'd begun to develop his own passions, taking trips with the wine club and keeping busy in the vineyard. How would he feel if Anna asked him to give all of that up for her?

And there was the problem. Nikos knew that, if Anna asked

him to, he would give it all up for her. If he thought it was hurting her, he'd do it in a heartbeat. And maybe that was why he had never told her about Maria.

So why wasn't she prepared to do the same for him?

Chapter Thirty-Two

The sun was just beginning to rise as Anna walked up to the resort where the wedding was taking place. It wasn't even seven in the morning, but she was already a few minutes late. Still, though, she took a moment to admire the view before going in. It wasn't often these days that she got to see a Santorini sunrise. She was always admiring the sunsets, but this side of the day was equally gorgeous, with soft pinks and oranges lighting up the thin clouds overhead, hinting at the imminent arrival of the sun as it sat stubbornly below the horizon.

The last few days since her day out with Lizzy had passed relatively uneventfully. Anna was stuck between wanting to resolve things and wanting to give people space, herself included. She felt some distance would help. Plus, she was keenly aware that she had been doing a poor job of celebrating her friend, who was getting married the very next day.

So, instead of resolving things, Anna had become the faithful servant. She'd driven the truck all over the island collecting archways and flowers and candles. She'd hand-tied the boutonnieres when the florist fell ill. She'd even cleaned Elena and

Vasilis's flat the day before once they'd checked in so that it would be tidy when they got back from their honeymoon, and she'd packed Elena's bag so that the destination Vasilis had chosen (the Maldives) would stay a secret. The whole time, she'd spoken barely a word to anyone that wasn't about the wedding. It seemed to be keeping the drama at bay for now.

This included Nikos, who had been pleasant yet distant. A few times Anna had lain next to him in bed debating whether they should be hashing it out, but her fear of the outcome, and of further stirring the pot before the wedding, held her back. So they'd smiled through meals and slept without cuddling and limited their conversation to logistics.

She'd also declined more calls than she could count from Marcus. The first few times she'd wondered if there was something important, but she figured he would email her if anything job-related came up, and she didn't need him clouding her mind any further. She had enough to deal with right where she was, and she didn't feel she could give him an answer until she'd decided things with Nikos.

Now, standing in the hallway of the resort with Elena's large suitcase in one hand and her own bag for the next two nights in the other, she braced herself to interact with Thea and Maria for the first time since the hen do.

The moment she entered the bridal suite, she was met with a flurry of activity. Maria and Xenia were standing in the middle of the room with their bridesmaid dresses on and their hands over their heads, Thea was spastically darting around them with several pins in her mouth, Lizzy was curled up on a chaise lounge in the corner, possibly asleep, and Elena – wait, where was Elena?

"Hi," Anna said to the room in general. Xenia waved at Anna's reflection in the mirror in front of her, and Anna waved back. She dared a moment of eye contact with Maria in the mirror, too, who just nodded at her.

"Hi, Anna!" Lizzy called, her voice clearly strained, as if she'd just woken up. She never had been much of a morning person, and Anna laughed at the thought of her having to decide between sleeping in and spending every possible second with Xenia.

"Thank god you're here," Thea said. "Can you please put your dress on?"

Thea's voice was urgent, and even though Anna had a couple more loads to bring in from the car, she wasn't about to decline the order. So she stashed the suitcases in a corner and slipped into the bathroom, grabbing the hanger holding her dress from Thea's outstretched hand as she went.

The dress seemed to fit perfectly, which was lucky because she didn't fancy being Thea's pincushion. She turned around to admire the draping. Thea really did make a good dress. Anna wondered, not for the first time, how much it would set her back if it weren't for Elena (or, more likely, Vasilis) generously covering the cost. She changed out of it, careful to avoid the water on the floor, suspecting it would stain.

Just as she was about to leave the bathroom, she heard a yelp from outside. A moment later the door burst open, and Maria rushed in. She hurried over to the vanity and held out her arm over the basin, and Anna saw a thin pinprick of blood forming on the underside. Without thinking, she lunged for the toilet roll, wadded up a small piece and pressed it to Maria's arm before the blood could spread or drip.

"Thank you," Maria said, somewhat awkwardly, but her face told Anna that she meant it.

"It's not on the dress, is it?" a voice asked, and Anna turned around to see Thea poking her head through the door.

"No, we caught it," Anna said, and Thea disappeared as quickly as she'd appeared.

Anna moved the tissue just a bit to see if the wound was minor enough to get away with, but as she did, she saw that a large spot of blood had formed and was continuing to grow.

"She really nicked you," Anna said. "Hold this for a moment." She guided Maria's hand to the tissue, then stuck her head out into the suite.

She called for Lizzy, who suddenly sat up straight as if Anna had awoken her.

"Lizzy, please go get the clear box from the truck," she said, thinking of the emergency kit Eirini had prepared for her. It had a first aid kit, some snacks, deodorant, and even "spare" stockings (as if any of them would be wearing stockings to begin with), amongst other things Eirini deemed potentially helpful.

Lizzy grunted her assent and rolled off the chaise, disappearing out of the room.

Anna turned back to the bathroom and tore off a new wad of toilet roll for Maria, then found a clean white towel and helped Maria wrap it around herself to protect the dress. They both sat down on the bench against the wall.

"Thanks for your help," Maria said. "Honestly I'm sure Thea would have killed me if I'd bled on the dress, despite the fact that she's the one who stabbed me!"

Anna laughed. "What happened to the team of seamstresses she was supposedly bringing with her?"

"Oh, they exist, but they're stuck in Athens. The ferry was cancelled."

Anna pulled a face. "The ferry? Why wouldn't they fly in?"

Maria cringed. "Because they have Elena's dress."

Anna's eyes went wide. "The wedding dress is stuck in Athens the day before the wedding?!"

Maria nodded solemnly. "Yep. Which is why Elena's not here for the fitting. We figured she could have a lie-in rather than sit around and watch us get fitted."

"Seems sensible." Anna nodded as she considered the possible implications of the news, though if she knew anything at all, she knew Elena was most certainly not having a lie-in at that moment. She was either up worrying with the rest of them, or Vasilis was getting an early wedding present.

Lizzy arrived back at that exact moment, passing the first aid kit to Anna. She also noticed that Lizzy had helped herself to a pot of hummus and a pita, but she didn't say anything. She dug around in the box for a plaster and affixed it to Maria's arm, holding her hand underneath it until they were both certain it wouldn't leak. Both women sighed in relief when it didn't.

"What will happen if the dress doesn't make it?"

Maria shrugged. "I'm not sure. I don't think there's a backup."

"Well, I think we'd better find one then," she said, standing up. "I don't know about you, but my dress fits fine, especially if the alternative is our bride not having one."

Maria stood up, too. "My pinning is done," she said. "I'll help you."

Anna helped Maria change into her sundress, which involved some shielding of eyes and some crossing of boundaries, but a couple of minutes later, they emerged from the bathroom in the clothes they'd arrived in.

"My dress was beautiful," Anna said to Thea, who opened her mouth to protest. "I promise to let you poke and prod me later if you don't agree. But for now, we're going to sort out a plan B for Elena. Is that alright?"

Thea nodded and gestured towards the door. "Get on with it then."

A moment later, Anna and Maria, the unlikeliest of duos, were sat in the truck ready to go. And then it hit them both at the same time.

"Where the hell are we going to go?" Anna asked.

"It's only seven in the morning!" Maria said. They both laughed.

Anna looked out at the sun, which had now peeked above the horizon, and thought for a moment. If she were looking for something on the island, who better to ask than someone who had lived here for more than half a century and knew every inch of it like the back of her hand?

"We're going to see my grandmother."

Eirini was, of course, already awake. She woke up promptly at six thirty every morning, every day of every week, which Anna knew because Eirini would bring it up every time she was confronted with the fact that Anna did not share her penchant for early mornings.

As it was, Anna and Maria found her sipping her coffee in the courtyard of the main house.

"Hello Anna," she said, and then saw Maria behind. "And who is this?"

"This is Maria," Anna said, and only she would have seen the look of acknowledgement her grandmother offered her before greeting the other woman.

"Pleasure to meet you, Eirini," Maria said.

"Yaya, we have a bit of a situation," Anna said, then told Eirini all about the cancelled ferry and the still absent wedding dress.

Eirini stood up and walked inside, Anna and Maria on her heels, muttering to herself in Greek as she went. She walked over to the wall calendar and paged backwards, month after month, clearly looking for something. Then she pulled out an old-fashioned rolodex, flipping through the cards with purpose.

"Here," she said, stopping on a card. "Stela Papaioannou's daughter got married last year, and she bought four dresses for that ridiculous wedding. She wore one of them, but the other three have just collected dust. Her daughter asked her to sell them, but she wouldn't even know where to begin, so they're just sitting in the house."

Anna and Maria looked at each other. It wasn't ideal, but it was certainly a start. "Thank you, Yaya," Anna said. "Where does Stela live?"

"All the way in Baxedes," she said with a sigh. She removed the card from the rolodex and handed it to Anna. "But it should only be twenty minutes at this time of day. It's a good thing you're here, Maria, because Stela doesn't speak a word of English."

"Do we know if she'll be up?" Maria asked, but Eirini answered with a laugh.

"Not everyone sleeps in until the day is half gone like you young girls. She will be up. I'll phone her now to make sure she's expecting you."

"Thank you so much," Maria said, already walking out the door.

"Good luck, girls," Eirini said. "You know where to find me if you need anything else."

Anna leaned in to kiss her grandmother on the cheek, and she and Maria headed out to the truck.

"This is crazy," she said as she put the truck in gear. "I can't believe we're driving across the island as the sun rises to buy an old wedding dress the day before Elena's wedding."

Maria laughed. "Yeah, life's funny that way," she said. And maybe it was just Anna's imagination, but she could almost hear an unspoken "especially with you" tacked onto the end.

Anna considered saying something. She'd been thinking for days what she might say to Maria if given the opportunity. But she didn't want to be the one to drag her drama into today.

In the end, it was Maria who brought it up.

"Hey, I'm sorry everyone was really weird to you on the hen do," Maria said. "It was between you and me, and they didn't need to gang up on you like they did."

Anna felt her face go hot. "It's okay," she said. "I was being pretty childish." She kept her eyes on the road in front of her, but she saw Maria shake her head out of the corner of her eye.

"No, I don't think you were," she said. "I think you were hurt, and the others lured it out of you. Don't be too hard on yourself. You tried to brush Elena off, remember?"

Anna nodded. That was true. She really had tried to keep the peace, especially for Elena's sake.

But there was one more thing nagging at her.

"Can I ask you about something you said to Nikos at the party?" she asked, and Maria nodded for her to continue. "You told Nikos that I was batshit crazy if I didn't want the same life he did."

Maria sighed. "I did say that, but that's not quite what it meant. Did he tell you about it?"

Anna felt her cheeks go hot. She had basically just outed herself. "Honestly, no, I overheard you on the porch swing."

Maria nodded again. "That makes the way you acted at the fitting make way more sense."

"Sorry about that," Anna said. "It was super awkward because Nikos still hadn't told me about you. I thought maybe…" Anna trailed off, not wanting to finish the sentence, but Maria finished it for her.

"You thought maybe there was something going on between Nikos and me?"

"Yes," Anna replied, practically at a whisper. "Or at least I was afraid there could be."

"Well, as you know, there wasn't. Never has been. And when I said you were batshit crazy, I wasn't actually calling you crazy. I was just reassuring my friend, letting him know that I saw how much he loved you, and wanted him to know that he deserved someone who was worthy of that love, who could get to the same place he was at."

Anna nodded along as Maria spoke. That made sense. Maria hadn't had any idea at that point that there was anything weird going on. She'd just been giving Nikos a pep talk.

"Which, by the way, I wouldn't say to him now that I know you and know what's been going on," Maria added. "I'd tell him to either leave you or stop complaining, but to shut the fuck up about it either way, just like I did in London. I have no sympathy for that boy anymore."

Anna found herself laughing. "Being angry about everything would be so much easier if you sucked."

"Yeah, well, tough shit," she said. "I'm delightful."

They both laughed together, and Anna nodded. "That you are. It's no wonder Nikos enjoys your company so much."

The laughter ebbed, and Anna thought she might have made it awkward again. But Maria didn't miss a beat.

"Honestly, that whole thing is really weird," she said. "I didn't ask to be anybody's dirty little secret, especially if nothing dirty is happening. I hope you know that. In fact, it's made me question our entire friendship. Made me wonder if he's just been using me to make you jealous; to make you stay."

Anna felt Maria's gaze on her face, and she turned to her briefly. "And I'm sure that's not what was happening at all," she said, and she meant it. "Nikos would never intentionally use someone like that. Like I said, he seems to really enjoy your company from what I've heard – at least since I've found out. The problems Nikos and I have go way beyond one weird lie of omission."

A brief moment of silence passed, and Anna could tell Maria was weighing up saying something.

"Do you want to talk about it?"

Anna considered before answering. Honestly? Yeah, she did want to talk about it. She'd been holding it in since that conversation with Eirini. Lizzy had been shacked up with Xenia for days, Nikos had been keeping their interactions to a few words at a time, Elena was understandably tied up with wedding things… and Anna had had a lot of time to think. And here next to her was someone who not only knew Nikos incredibly well but also had been hurt by him in all of this. Maybe this was her chance to finally have a productive conversation about it.

"Would it be weird if I said yes?"

Maria laughed. "Probably, but I offered for a reason."

Anna took a deep breath and went for it.

"Okay, so the issue boils down to this: I love my job, and I don't want to slow down when things are going so well. But every time I come home, Nikos makes me feel guilty for not spending more time there. He's not asked me outright to stop travelling, but he's been pretty blatant in expressing how he feels about it."

"You do spend a lot of time away," Maria said. "Like, nearly half your time, if not more."

"Yeah, I do, and I know that must be really hard on him," Anna said, and she took a moment to properly acknowledge that.

"Also," Maria added, "just to clarify, Nikos doesn't hate your work. In fact, he doesn't shut up about it."

"Really?" Anna asked, frowning.

"Yes really," Maria said, rolling her eyes. "I must get a WhatsApp at least once a month of some picture you've taken somewhere, or a link to some campaign you've shot, or some award you've won. When I got my new office at work, he sent me at least a dozen of your pictures and asked me which one I wanted as my office-warming present."

"Did you get one?" Anna asked, struggling to picture Maria working beneath an Anna Linton original every single day.

"I've got a lovely portrait of the winemaker who started the vineyard hung in pride of place," Maria said.

Anna knew which picture she meant. It was one of the first jobs she'd had on the island. One she'd shown in her first collection at Marcus's gallery. The fact that Nikos remembered it enough to send it meant a lot.

"But if he loves my work so much, why does he resent me going away to do it?" Anna asked, exasperated, and she could feel the pinpricks of tears in her eyes.

"Nobody likes feeling left behind," Maria said. "But honestly, Anna, it's not your job to make sure he's okay with your success. He fell in love with a creative, successful woman. This is par for the course. And that's what I keep telling him."

Something about the weight of Maria's words told Anna that she was speaking from experience.

"We've all got a past," Maria said when Anna asked. "All I know is that my future involves making no apologies for my ambitions, and so should yours."

Anna wondered what Maria's ambitions were, and who had made her feel like she couldn't pursue them. Maybe that was why she liked older, more successful men, because they didn't get insecure about her success. But before Anna could say anything, they arrived at Stela's house, and they slipped back into bridesmaid mode.

They walked up the narrow path to Stela's, which was positioned right on the beachfront road, steps from the sea. They knocked quietly, careful to not wake anyone in the house who may still be asleep, but they needn't have worried. Stela answered the door with the enthusiasm of a party host greeting her first guests. After a couple minutes of small talk, they headed to Stela's back bedroom, where she had laid out three dresses on the bed.

"She says that the fourth is the one her daughter actually wore," Maria said, translating for Stela. "These three are practically brand new."

Anna looked over the dresses and felt her stomach drop. They certainly weren't custom designer gowns. They also couldn't have been more different – one was a strapless princess gown with a skirt made entirely of cheap tulle, one was a fluted lace number with a floral strap meant to be worn diagonally over one shoulder, and one was covered head to toe in white sequins, a couple of which were hanging loose from the dress.

It was dire, but what other option did they have? As Elena had rightly pointed out during the first fitting, there were no real bridal shops on the island, and they didn't have any other options. At least they looked to be about the right size.

Anna paid Stela for the dresses, and it was some consolation that they spent so little – only fifty euros per dress. But just as they were picking up the dresses off the bed, Anna's watch vibrated. Maria's phone pinged just a few seconds later.

"It's the group chat," Maria said, checking her phone whilst Anna held the dresses. Her face relaxed into a smile. "The seamstresses have just got on the next ferry out. The dress is en route."

Anna breathed a deep sigh of relief. Then she looked at Stela, who was grinning at them, not understanding a lick of what they'd just said. But rather than try to give the dresses back, they just thanked her and headed out. At least they'd done a good deed for the day by ticking something off Stela's list.

The day was already getting warm as they tucked the dresses into the cab of the truck.

"Thank you," Anna said, "for coming with me, and for the chat."

Maria smiled. "The funny thing is, I think you and I could have been friends if not for all this."

"Well, there's still time," Anna said, climbing into the truck. "Don't rule it out yet." She paused halfway, with one leg still on the ground. "Hey Maria?"

"Yeah?" Maria asked, standing on the other side with her door open.

Anna's voice was low as she continued. "Do you think there's any hope for Nikos and me?"

Maria sighed. "Do you want the honest answer?"

Anna nodded. People never said that if what they were going to say was good, but she needed honesty from someone who knew him. She needed something she could actually use.

"There's always hope. But I think you both need to be willing to say what you want, and right now what you both want seems to be incompatible. And of course, once you say what you want out loud, you can't take that back, whatever the implications."

She knew that was right. In fact, it was probably why Nikos hadn't outright told her what he wanted from her. He knew that if he did, there would be no coming back.

Anna rolled Maria's words over in her mind, trying to distil the advice into a Magic 8 Ball answer.

"So you're saying there's a chance, but it seems unlikely?"

Maria laughed, but her smile was fleeting. "What I'm saying is that, honestly, you both have more important things to pursue right now than each other. And if you don't focus on that, you've got no chance of making each other happy."

Chapter Thirty-Three

When Anna and Maria arrived back at the hotel, the first people they saw were Nikos and Vasilis, sitting on the pool deck with a drink.

"You boys know it's super early in the morning, right?" Maria said as they approached. As the boys looked up at them, Anna saw Nikos's brow press together as he looked back and forth between Anna and Maria. He didn't look upset, just confused.

"It's a Bloody Mary," he said. "It's a brunch drink. So it doesn't count."

"Whatever you say," Maria said, touching Anna subtly but intentionally on the hand as she took the dresses out of her arms. "I'll see you inside?"

Anna nodded and then went to sit with Nikos on the sun lounger. He welcomed her with open arms, pulling her in for a hug, which caught Anna off guard. It was more affection than she'd had from him all week.

"I need to go wash pants," Vasilis said, standing up suddenly and heading inside.

Nikos laughed. "Okay, that sounded like a really bad excuse to leave, but he does actually need to wash some pants. Elena had a go at him about his trousers for tonight being the wrong colour, so he needs to wash the ones he wore to the stag do."

Anna hadn't heard much about the stag do from the night before other than the fact that it was supposedly very innocent. Elena had said in the group chat that she was convinced the boys had stayed in and watched a film, instead of going out, despite her setting up a tab for them at Vasilis's favourite bar.

"Did you have fun?"

"Not as much fun as you and I could have on this sun lounger right now," Nikos said, grabbing Anna around the waist and leaning her back onto him. He kissed the side of her face from behind, and Anna could smell the booze coming off his breath.

"Very funny," she said. "Maybe it's time to cut off the brunch drinks." She looked around for evidence of how much he'd had, but she only saw one glass. He always had been such a lightweight. Plus, weddings made him sentimental. And rather horny, to be honest.

"Sorry," he said, laughing and laying back, tilting his face towards the sun, which was already a good deal higher in the sky. "We had the brilliant idea of trying to treat the hangover with hair of the dog, but now I suspect I'll just be hungover by lunch, instead."

"You seem in a good mood," Anna said, smiling affectionately at him.

"I am," he said. "You know weddings are my favourite."

Anna met his gaze for a moment, then looked away. She didn't have it in her to pretend everything was okay, no matter how sentimental he was feeling.

"Well, I'd better get back to Elena. What's your schedule like today?" Anna thought through her own – trying her dress on again for Thea, helping Elena finalise the seating chart, and taking some bridal portraits at sunset.

"Pretty chill," he said, highlighting the stark difference in duties between a maid of honour and a best man. "You?"

"Decidedly less chill," she said. "But I've got lunch free if you do? Midday?"

He nodded and planted a kiss on her shoulder. "Looking forward to it already," he said. "Meet you right here?"

"Sure," she said, and she smiled. This was the Nikos she loved; the Nikos she missed when she went away. She was excited to have him back, if only for the moment. She leaned in and kissed him on the mouth, lingering for a moment, sinking into his warmth. He seemed to do the same. She could have stayed right there, just like that, forever.

But the kiss ended. No noise startling them apart, or person interrupting them; the warmth just faded, and their lips parted naturally. It ended like most kisses did.

Anna stood up to leave, then looked back down at Nikos. He was looking back at her, his drunkenly honest face full of questions. She just needed to figure out what the answers would be.

As she walked inside, she heard the other girls before she saw them. The frantic energy of this morning had been replaced with pure excitement. The bridal suite was clear of all Thea's kit which had been strewn about the room, and, instead, there were bottles of champagne chilling on the side as the girls sat on the bed and sofas whilst Maria held the backup wedding dresses in front of them. Elena was cringing at the one with the loose sequins.

"We can laugh now," Thea said to Elena, "but I hope you realise how close you were to actually having to wear one of these tomorrow."

Elena waved her hand. "Not close at all. It certainly would

have arrived before the wedding tomorrow. The final fitting was a nice-to-have; I trust your measurements."

"Oh, it's not optional. I'll have a bride walk down the aisle naked before having her wear a poor fitting dress."

"Ooh, naked. There's an idea." Elena pretended to think about it, and the rest of the girls giggled.

Maria noticed Anna in the doorway and waved her in. Elena smiled, and as she caught Anna's eye, it was clear she was picking up on the improved energy between them. Anna nodded and smiled back.

"Great, well, let's look at the seating chart," Elena said, pulling out a giant board with table diagrams on it. Then she handed each girl a stack of paper flags with names written on them.

"Who's got Vasilis and me?" she asked, putting her finger on a small round table at the top of the diagram.

"I do," Lizzy said, holding out two flags. Elena took them and placed them at the centre of the tiny top table, then stood back and looked at them before swapping them around.

"Okay, and who's got the wedding party?"

Anna looked down at her own hand, seeing her name, Nikos's, Maria's, and the rest of the bridesmaids and groomsmen. "I do," she said.

"Which table do you want to be at?" Elena asked Anna.

She looked back at the board, choosing the table closest to where Elena was sitting. Nikos would want to be as close by as possible. "There."

Elena smiled and nodded. "Yes, that'll be good," she said. First she placed Nikos in the seat furthest from her, and Anna almost said something, but then she realised that this way they'd be able to see each other the whole time. She wished, not for the first time, that Elena had more family with her, but she was also grateful that Elena and Nikos had each other.

Elena arranged the rest of the flags around the table – Anna on one side, Lizzy on the other, then Xenia, then Thea, Thea's partner, and finally Maria. There was an empty seat between Anna and Maria.

"Who's going to sit there?" Anna asked, and the others leaned in to see what she was referring to.

"If I've messed up the seating chart by being here, I can sit somewhere else," Lizzy offered, but Elena quickly shut her down.

"I have a mystery guest coming," she said, giving a mischievous half grin.

Anna narrowed her eyes at Elena, wondering who it could be. She was pretty sure, having sorted through all the RSVPs earlier in the week, that everyone she'd ever heard Elena mention either would be there or had declined the invitation. Who could she have invited?

"Don't bother guessing, because you never will," she said. "Just prepare to be surprised." She pantomimed twirling a moustache as if she were a villain planning a train heist. She did love a scheme.

The rest of the seating chart came together relatively easily, though there was some debate over whether Eirini and Christos should be forced to sit with Vasilis's insufferable grandparents. Anna saw a brief twinge of grief in Elena's eyes over her lack of family on the seating chart. She would have to ask Nikos to look after Elena and make sure she felt particularly loved and supported. She knew Vasilis's family had been super accepting and welcoming to Elena, but Anna couldn't imagine that was the same as having your own family there. She knew she would feel that way if she ever got married; she'd be thinking about her father the whole time.

Anna reflected, not for the first time, on the fact that Nikos was the link to family for both her and Elena. Maybe that was why the three of them had always been so close – they had all suffered so much loss, and they knew the value of family. When Elena and

Nikos could no longer have that with the rest of their family, they clung tightly to each other, and they formed deep, immovable bonds with others in their life. They loved hard, and they loved for good.

Anna had always felt honoured to be a part of their little family. But now, she knew that sense of family was part of what made her decision so difficult.

After the seating chart was done, Elena left for a pre-wedding couple's massage with Vasilis, and Anna tried on her dress for Thea. What she'd thought was a perfect fit apparently wasn't, and Thea pinned a few bits as they stood there, albeit much more carefully than she had been working earlier. Then Anna was free to go and meet Nikos for lunch.

The resort had a restaurant inside, but when Anna got to the pool deck, she found that Nikos had a picnic spread out ready for them to enjoy. Though they'd had a picnic recently in London, this one instantly made her think of the one they'd shared when she first came to Santorini, out on the smaller island of Aspronisi, where she'd first shared her love of photography with Nikos. If she were reading into things – and she had been doing a lot of that lately in lieu of anything else to work from – this could be his way of telling her that he supported her decision to keep working as much as she could. As much as she wanted to.

Or it could just be a picnic. It was probably just a picnic.

Either way, Anna was glad they weren't sat inside. It was a beautiful sunny day with a refreshing breeze as they sat atop the island, looking out over both the caldera and the eastern shore. The island stretched out before them, white and blue buildings glimmering in the sunshine. It was like a postcard come to life, and it would be a shame to be anywhere else in the world at that moment.

Anna sat down next to Nikos and popped an olive into her mouth. "This looks amazing," she said, admiring the spread of spanakopita, meatballs, pork souvlaki, aubergine, calamari, humous, pita and, of course, Anna's favourite, bougatsa.

"I wanted to have a picnic," Nikos said, "because the first time you and I had one was the first time I learned how important photography was to you."

Anna beamed. Of course it wasn't just a picnic. Nikos had always been the more thoughtful of the two of them, so if it occurred to her, it had occurred to him. He turned to her and took her hand in his.

"In case it's not clear, I want you to know how proud I am of you. I think you're the most talented person I've ever met, and I feel so lucky to have you in my life. I know you have a lot of decisions to make, but I want you to know that I don't begrudge your success. If anything, I'm in awe of it."

Anna choked back tears as she heard Nikos say such beautiful things to her. It was amazing to hear him finally validating all the hard work she'd put into her career over the last few years. Of course he'd told her in little moments he was proud of her and celebrated her wins, but this was the first time he'd taken the time to acknowledge that him missing her didn't diminish his pride in what she'd achieved.

But, then again, he hadn't exactly said what he wanted yet, either. So he was proud of her. Great. But what did that mean for their situation?

"Thank you," she said, and she could tell from the way his face fell slightly that her words carried less warmth than he'd hoped. But she couldn't help it. He could make all the grand gestures he wanted, but nothing had actually changed between them until he said what he wanted from her.

Nikos asked how the morning had gone, and his interest was piqued slightly at the mention of Elena's mystery guest (he assured Anna he had no idea who it could be), but otherwise there seemed to be very little to say. Not that Anna couldn't think of anything to talk about, but everything seemed to either carry the weight of the dilemma they were in or felt trivial in light of everything else going on. So they stuck to wedding talk – small talk. And that broke Anna's heart.

By one in the afternoon, Anna had stuck it out with him as long as she could manage. Any more awkward silence and she would end up confronting him, and they'd agreed to leave it until after the wedding. So she got up to leave, claiming she was needed back in the bridal suite.

"Are we okay?" Nikos asked as she did.

"What?" she replied, honestly shocked. She had thought their standoff was clear: that Nikos was feeling the tension between them just like she was, but didn't want to cause drama because of the wedding.

"I said, are we okay? You're acting a bit off," he said, and Anna could tell from his face that his question was genuine. She couldn't help but laugh.

"No, Nikos, we're not fucking okay. You've been avoiding telling me to stop working so you don't have to be the bad guy, but you've kind of backed me into a corner."

Nikos held his hands up as if in surrender. "Okay, can we not do this now?"

Anna shook her head. "Unbelievable, Nikos," she said, her breath coming quicker. If she didn't get out of here now, she was going to properly lose it. "You're the one who asked if we were okay. So please, don't ask questions you don't want the answers to right now." And then she turned around and strode back into the hotel, leaving Nikos slack-jawed on the picnic blanket.

Chapter Thirty-Four

A couple of hours later, Anna was sat cross-legged on the floor of the bridal suite with a tiny sandwich between her fingers. As if they hadn't spent loads of time together over the past week, Elena, apparently, wanted all the girls to sit down and enjoy high tea for a couple of hours. Now that the air had cleared with Maria, Anna didn't mind. In fact, it was nice to take a break from the frustration that her picnic with Nikos had surfaced. The conversation was light-hearted and now that Anna wasn't viewing Maria as some evil temptress trying to steal her boyfriend, she found that she genuinely enjoyed her company. She was annoyed with herself yet again that she'd painted Maria in such a negative light, but mostly she was just enjoying getting to know the woman so beloved by the people in her life.

As they finished their tea, the seamstresses arrived with Elena's dress in hand. Everyone cheered when they arrived, except Thea, who had the dress unwrapped and on Elena's body in less than two minutes. But she needn't have worried – the dress fit like a glove.

"Oh wow," Anna said, catching her friend's eye in the mirror. "Thea, you've really nailed it."

"I know, I know," Thea said, waving her hands and putting them on her heart as if accepting an award.

It was about three in the afternoon, too early to take decent photos in any of the touristy spots, but Elena had given Anna full creative freedom over her bridal portraits, and Anna had an idea.

"Elena, how would you feel about having your shoot now?" she asked, and Elena clapped her hands together. Thea, however, shot her a look.

"Must you?" she said. "I would hate for anything to happen to the dress." Her words came out like a warning, and Anna understood it perfectly. One speck of dirt, and there would be no wedding for Anna, because Thea would destroy her.

"I promise you we'll be careful," Anna said. "In fact, you can come along if you'd like."

Thea looked up hopefully at Elena, who shook her head.

"Nonsense, Thea's got plenty to do here, and you and I are perfectly capable of being careful."

Elena motioned for Thea to unlace her dress, and within another couple of minutes, she was out of it again, Thea zipping it into its protective bag and barking instructions at Anna for how to keep it from creasing. Elena's hair was already perfectly curled for the fitting – though when was it not – so all she needed to do was touch up her makeup, and they were ready to go. Anna carried the perfectly packed wedding dress in her arms, along with one of the spares, as they made their way to the truck.

A few minutes later, they turned onto the road running along Kamari Beach.

Elena frowned. "You're not doing my portraits on the beach, are you?" she asked, crumpling her nose.

"Absolutely not," Anna replied with a laugh. "For starters, I've got something far less basic in mind. But also, Thea would kill me if I let you on the black sand in your dress. No, I've got something else in mind."

They drove along the seafront to a small church nestled in the spot where the beach gave way to sweeping cliffs, forming the base of ancient Thera. They parked the truck next to the church entrance, then got out and started walking along a wide path carved into the cliff side. Anna carried a wicker basket she'd stashed in the back of the truck. After a minute, they arrived at a large alcove carved into the side of the cliff, beyond which were some roughly carved steps down to a lower section of cliff closer to the waves, which lapped gently against the rocks below. There was almost no sea spray, and it was late enough in the day that the cliff side fell into shadow, but the light reflected off the ocean gave it a sort of glow. It was perfect for pictures.

Clearly, Elena agreed, because she turned to Anna with a wide smile. "Thank you," she said. "This is perfect!"

Anna helped her undress and put on her wedding dress, careful not to let her lean or brush against anything dirty. Luckily the rocks were incredibly smooth here, so there was no loose dirt or mud to be seen. Should she probably have waited until after the wedding to do these portraits? Sure. But Elena seemed up for it, so she was willing to risk it.

For the next hour, they spent maybe a third of their time actually taking pictures and the rest navigating the cliff side without compromising Elena's dress. At one point, Anna put the backup dress behind Elena on a particularly wet spot so that her own wouldn't get dirty, and she had to do some creative positioning to make sure it looked like part of Elena's dress.

But it was absolutely worth it because what they ended up with was stunning. The pictures were moody, dynamic, and absolutely not your typical bridal portraits. And the best part was that the dress was completely spotless.

Just as she had finished getting her lenses packed away, she saw Elena hunched over her dress bag, texting furiously on her phone.

"What are you doing?" she said, looking over Elena's shoulder. She could see the message "We're headed back to Carpe Diem – meet us there!!!!!" but Elena hit send and turned off the phone before Anna could see more.

"Nothing," she said, stashing it quickly.

"You think I'm going to push you off the cliffs?" Anna asked with a laugh, and Elena chuckled.

"No, of course not. I'm just letting Vasilis know where we are."

Anna laughed. "You two should really give it a rest, if only for the night before the wedding," she said as they grabbed their things and walked back down towards the church.

"Oh please," Elena said, flipping her hair. "That tradition is sexist and puritanical. I will be pleasuring my husband-to-be as much as possible this evening."

Anna made a fake gagging noise, then laughed as she climbed into the truck.

As they arrived back at the resort and entered the bridal suite, Anna was surprised to find it completely empty. After the hubbub of the morning, she'd expected at least a few of the girls to be milling around. But she took advantage of the quiet and relative tidiness to get a few shots of the dress, hanging it up in the window so the light peeked through the lace. As she brought the viewfinder to her eye, Elena opened the door.

"Thanks for meeting us here," Anna heard her say.

Thinking it was Vasilis, Anna panicked, pulling the duvet off the bed and holding it in front of the dress, shouting, "Don't come any closer!"

But the voice that laughed back at her wasn't Vasilis's, and the English was much better.

"Don't worry, sweetheart, I didn't see a thing."

It was Marcus.

Chapter Thirty-Five

"Decided to make this a habit?" Anna asked, walking towards Marcus. This wasn't the first time he'd shown up unannounced when she was in the midst of a big decision.

"Not if I can help it," Marcus said, "but I do think we need to talk."

The hostility between Anna and Marcus had long since dissipated, but she was still annoyed that he would just show up, especially whilst she was spending precious time with Elena before the wedding. To just walk up on them like that… come to think of it, how did he know where they were?

Anna whipped her head around to look at Elena. "You!"

Elena put her hands up in a "don't shoot" motion and laughed. "You got me," she said. "I invited him."

Anna gestured at Marcus behind her. "This is your mystery guest?!"

"Hey," Marcus said, protesting her incredulous tone, "she could do worse."

"Yes, he is," Elena said. "He reached out to make sure you

were okay, and I told him to come, because I think you need to talk to him about your future."

"I've already spoken to him about my future," Anna said. "I speak to him about the future all the time."

"I've tried calling," Marcus said, "but it seemed like you were freezing me out. I thought one last plea might work in my favour."

Anna put her hands over her face and breathed in sharply. She had been pushing all this away so well over the last week, and Elena had only gone and invited her problems to the wedding.

"I don't need this right now," she said to Marcus through gritted teeth. "I'm trying really hard to focus on this wedding, and you're making it impossible."

"Hey, it's my wedding, remember?" Elena said, wrapping an arm around Anna. "So if I think it's worth addressing here and now, maybe I'm onto something."

Anna's breath became shorter and shorter, and she could feel panic rising up inside her. She'd tried so hard over the last week to put this off until after the wedding, but here it was, chasing her down.

Elena grabbed Anna by the shoulders, squeezing her tight.

"Hey, it's okay," she said, breathing in deep, and Anna tried her best to mirror the rise and fall of Elena's chest. After a few breaths, she felt her shoulders start to drop, and as the tension and panic released, so did her tears.

"Why don't you give us a minute," Elena said to Marcus, leading Anna over to the bed. Marcus nodded and left the room without a word.

"Why did you invite him here?" Anna asked, wiping the tears from her face. "No one here can stand the sight of him, and him being here isn't going to change the way I feel about work one way or the other."

"Because," Elena replied, "despite how I've felt about him in the past, I actually think Marcus has your best interests at heart."

"But he thinks I should ditch Nikos and travel with him all over the world. Do you think that's in my best interest?"

"To be fair, it sounds like he wants the second part of that, but I don't think he cares whether you're with Nikos or not."

"Well, Nikos has made it pretty clear that I can't have both. And surely you aren't suggesting I leave him."

When Elena didn't immediately reply, Anna looked up at her. She was doing a great job of admiring her own feet.

"You don't think I should leave Nikos, do you?" she asked slowly. When Elena didn't respond, she ducked her head down to catch her friend's eye. Elena's eyes widened for a split second, and then she set her mouth into a thin line and nodded.

"I think you have to do what Marcus has offered," she said. "Nikos told me about the file. You have to do it, Anna, because you wouldn't be you – gorgeous, talented, brilliant, passionate you – if you didn't take on an opportunity like this. Even if it means leaving a man behind. Even if that man is my dear cousin, my favourite person in the world. And even if he's the love of your life."

She grabbed Anna's hands in hers and squeezed.

"You can't love him well if you don't love yourself first, and this is how you do that."

Anna's chest went tight as Elena's words and their repercussions sunk in. At the same time, Anna knew that they were true. She knew that if she didn't do this, she might never forgive herself. A tear slid down her face as she held Elena's gaze.

"Did you just paraphrase RuPaul?" she asked with a laugh. Elena laughed, too.

"I guess I did," she said. "Mama Ru is full of sage advice."

As their laughter subsided, Elena finally let Anna's hands go, leaning in, instead, to hug her.

"By the way," she said as she pulled away, "I know I said a long time ago that I would choose Nikos if you hurt him… but I want to be clear: you're my family. And if you choose yourself, that won't change anything between us."

Anna smiled, and fresh tears pricked at her eyes. Relief washed over her as she realised that, whilst there were still so many things at stake, her friendship with Elena wasn't one of them. "Thank you," she said. "You can't possibly know how good it is to hear that." She wiped her face on the back of her hand. "I'm sorry I've not done a very good job of honouring you. I'm a terrible maid of honour."

"Girl," Elena said, leaning back, "yes you are. But I forgive you."

Anna laughed and stood up. She'd just had the thought that they should go find Marcus when she heard shouts coming from the hallway. She exchanged looks with Elena and ran for the door.

"I know you've been trying to lure her away with all these fancy jobs," Nikos was saying as they opened the door. Neither man seemed to notice them.

"If Anna takes those jobs, it's because she wants them," Marcus said, his face mere inches from Nikos, "not because I've manipulated her. It's you who seems to be doing that from what I've heard."

"You know what's manipulative?" Nikos spat. "Showing up out of the blue. You always do shit like this. Why are you even here at my cousin's wedding?" Anna caught herself thinking if this were an enemies-to-lovers romance, Marcus and Nikos would start making out at any moment. But she was worried it was trending less romantic and more violent.

"I'm not gatecrashing, I was invited."

"Oh, yeah, by who?"

"By me," Elena said, and both men finally turned to look at her.

"Um, why would you do that?"

"Because of me," Anna said, stepping forward past her friend. She was done beating around the bush. She couldn't put this off any longer, not for the sake of the wedding. Not when the bride herself was, quite literally, behind her.

"How is this helpful for you?" Nikos said, stepping towards Anna and dropping his voice. "I know you have a lot of decisions to make, but surely you're better off doing that without him distracting or putting pressure on you?"

Anna saw Marcus roll his eyes over Nikos's shoulder. She took a deep breath and looked back up at Nikos.

"You keep saying that. That I have a lot of decisions to make. What do you mean?"

Nikos looked around and half smiled. "You know, about work, right? What you're going to do moving forward?"

Anna shook her head. "I wouldn't know what decisions you expect me to be making because you haven't actually asked me for anything, have you?"

"Don't be ridiculous," Nikos said. "I haven't exactly been subtle about how I feel about your work life."

"No, you certainly have not," she said. "But you haven't actually asked for anything either."

"What do you want me to say?"

Anna stepped forward onto her toes, her face close to his. "I think if you're going to expect me to give up my dreams for you, you should at least have the balls to ask for it."

"Okay!" he shouted, throwing his hands up. "Fine, I'll ask it. Anna, please stop leaving me for work every chance you get. Please stop insinuating that your 'dreams' are something other than me. Please quit choosing your job over our relationship every fucking time. Is that what you want to hear?"

Anna exhaled, and she felt like she might float away. There it was. She hadn't been reading into things, or being sensitive, or villainising him. She'd known exactly how he felt, and now he'd finally admitted it.

All four of them were silent for a long moment, and it was lucky that they had the whole hotel for the weekend. If anyone else were around, they were wisely staying well away.

"Honestly, yes, it is," she said, calmly and quietly. "But I'm not the one with a decision to make, Nikos." She put her hand on his arm, but he flinched away. His face immediately dropped into a scowl.

"What are you saying?" he asked, stepping back slightly.

"I'm saying," Anna said, taking another deep breath, "that I'm going to take the jobs Marcus has lined up for me. All of them. And it's you who needs to decide if you're going to be okay with that."

Nikos looked like Anna had smacked him across the face. "Oh, so you're just going to hand out an ultimatum?"

Anna gave a sort of half-sigh, half-laugh. "Honestly, it's about time one of us did. About time that we were honest about what we want, even if we know it's to the other person's detriment."

"That's not fair," Nikos said. "I just meant that—"

"That I needed to be the only one to sacrifice something for this relationship," she said. "That my dreams are negotiable, but yours aren't. Whatever you meant, that's what you've said by asking me to give this up. But at least you've finally asked me."

Nikos's shoulders dropped, and he shook his head. "This isn't happening," he said. "I refuse to believe it's happening like this."

Anna couldn't believe it was happening like this either. In fact, as she floated back to Earth, her emotional high wearing off, she saw Elena and Marcus aghast at what was unfolding in front of them. She and Nikos were in a hallway of a resort the day before their darling Elena's wedding, and they were – what, breaking up? No, it wasn't going to happen like this. There was too much love between them.

Anna stepped forward and took Nikos's hand in hers, catching his gaze. He didn't flinch away from her this time. Instead, he wrapped his fingers through hers as his lip trembled.

"No, it's not happening," she said. "Not right now. But Nikos, we need to take some time apart to think. And I think it needs to be now."

She turned around to face Elena.

"I think I need the night," she said, and Elena nodded. "I'm sorry, I promise I'll be back in plenty of time for the wedding tomorrow. I just need to process all of this."

"Please do," Elena said. "When you stand up by my side tomorrow, I want the real you – the you who wouldn't compromise your dreams for anyone or anything."

Anna held her friend's gaze and her resolve steeled. With Elena by her side, and her grandparents, and Lizzy and Xenia and Marcus and, hell, maybe even Maria, she knew that she had the strength to do what she needed to do. She gave Elena a quick hug, grabbed her bag from the corner where it still sat from that morning, and turned back to Nikos.

"We'll talk tomorrow. I promise. But you need to have a long, hard think about what *you're* willing to compromise on to keep me in your life, because I'm telling you right now that you're going to lose me if you don't. And I'll be doing the same."

He opened his mouth to say something, but thought better of it, closed it again, and nodded, tears forming in his eyes.

Anna shrugged her duffel strap up onto her shoulder, nodded at Marcus, waving for him to follow her, and strode out of the resort.

Chapter Thirty-Six

Nikos

The wedding should have started nearly an hour ago, but Anna was nowhere to be seen.

As Nikos paced the aisle, checking the stairs up to the resort each time he did, he knew he should be worried about Elena. It was her wedding after all. But Nikos was convinced that it wasn't Elena holding things up. Even Vasilis seemed to be unworried, laughing casually with the other groomsmen.

No, this was about Anna. Elena would want to wait as long as possible for her to return. But she wouldn't wait forever, and Nikos was convinced that Anna wasn't coming.

When she'd left last night, her sleazy ex-boyfriend in tow, Nikos was sure that their relationship was over. She said they needed to take some time, but the whole time she said it, it felt like goodbye. And as much as he'd known in that moment that he didn't want her to go, that she was the love of his life, he also felt that too much of the bridge between them had been burned to come back from. And it broke him.

His first stop had been their hotel room.

After Anna snapped at him at the picnic, he'd known that he needed to make a gesture, but he didn't know what he could do to make it better. The last time he'd thought things were over between them, he'd been able to fly to New York and tell her he wanted to be with her. But that was before they had built a life together; before they'd accumulated so much history. And the issue wasn't that cut and dry this time.

She was right. He'd been avoiding asking her outright to stay. He could feel her slipping away, and he was afraid that she was so far gone that it might push her away for good if he did. So he'd made petty and snide comments, feeling simultaneously desperate for her to stay and angry that she didn't take the initiative to make the decision on her own. He hated feeling like he was asking her for anything, much less to give up something so important to her, but at the same time he felt like he was being perfectly reasonable. He was only in the same country as the love of his life half the time, and it was getting to him.

The best thing he knew to do was to take a moment to call Eirini. He wasn't sure if he should, as he didn't want to worry her if Anna had gone somewhere else, but he knew that Anna might need a shoulder, and Eirini was the most supportive person they knew. And if he knew Anna at all, she'd be headed for the summer house.

All night, he'd lain awake, staring at the ceiling of their room. After all these years of her travelling, he was used to sleeping alone; but this time, the bed truly felt empty without her. Would that be how it would feel forever now? Had he fucked this up beyond repair?

He lay there until the sun rose, the night giving way to a brilliant, endless blue sky, and still he lay there thinking to himself, *I don't know what to do to make it better. To go back to the way things used to be.*

Except he did know. The realisation dropped into his lap, as obvious as the blue sky outside, and he sat straight up in bed. He did know how to fix it. And that was to take it back.

It seemed so simple, but he'd been so angry and hurt that he hadn't seen it right in front of him. The answer was that he didn't actually want Anna to give up her career. He just wanted to feel like she wanted to be with him. But when had she ever said that she didn't?

To him, the fact that she went abroad so much felt like she was running away from him. But she'd never once made him feel unloved or unconsidered when they were together. As people – okay, Maria – started to ask questions, somehow he'd gotten it in his head that Anna was less committed than he was. But that wasn't true, and she'd given him no reason to believe that.

Of course he wished she could be with him more. But if it was at the expense of doing what made her happy, he didn't want that. And he felt so ashamed that he'd ever made her feel like he did. Even if he only had her half the time, it would be the real her, as Elena had said. The her that felt whole. And that's who he wanted to be with.

His confidence was shaken, though, when, just two hours before the ceremony was meant to start, Nikos delivered Vasilis's gift to Elena, only to discover that Anna was still nowhere to be found.

"I don't know where she is," Elena said, reading Nikos's face even though he didn't want to bring it up. "But she'll be here."

"I'm not so sure," he'd muttered, and he'd had to force himself to focus as he helped Vasilis get ready, with Nikos shaving him and the rest of the groomsmen helping to dress him, as per tradition.

Nikos's nerves got worse as the morning pressed on. As they

walked down to the ceremony site, he saw no truck in the car park, and Lizzy, sitting two rows back, seemed to know just as little as he did. A few minutes after things were meant to start, he saw Marcus sneak in the back, but when Nikos made eye contact with him, he simply shrugged.

And as he paced up and down the aisle of the dunes forty-seven minutes after the ceremony should have started, he felt less and less confident that she was coming. He didn't blame her. He'd been cruel and unfair, and she deserved better. He simultaneously hoped she believed that and also hoped she'd ignore that belief and come back to him.

Just as he was beginning to get really worried, the coordinator came down the stairs and whispered into the violinist's ear. The string quartet picked up their instruments and began to play.

As Nikos took his place next to Vasilis, he put a hand on his friend's shoulder. He may have been mentally wherever Anna was, but he also needed to be there for his friend, and for his dear cousin. Vasilis turned and smiled at him, and then turned back to the front to await his bride.

Nikos saw Maria coming down the steps and his breath caught; not because of Maria – no matter what anyone thought, there had never been any feelings there on his part – but because every step she took was one moment closer to him finding out whether Anna would come back to him. Finding out whether there was still a chance to make things right.

She took an excruciatingly long time to reach them – did everyone else feel like this was excessively slow? – and Xenia didn't even appear until Maria was almost at the front. She walked equally slowly, and Nikos became convinced that Elena was having them drag it out as long as possible for maximum suspense before she appeared. That would be a very Elena thing to do.

As Xenia reached the dunes, Nikos ran through the

possibilities in his mind. There were three outcomes he could imagine: Anna arrived and was ready to forgive him (unlikely given his behaviour), Anna arrived and decided to ignore him (which would devastate him), or she didn't come at all. Both the latter options meant the doors were closed to him and Anna, so he decided to focus on the one that didn't – the idea of her appearing at the top of the stairs, coming down to him, and giving him a look that let him know she was in. He imagined it so hard that he told himself he must be manifesting it.

Please Anna. I'm begging you, come down those stairs to me, and I'll never make you feel torn in two again.

Thea walked towards them, and time slowed again to a crawl. Now Nikos knew it was all in his head. His heart felt like it was beating at a million beats per second, and his breath was shallow and quick. He could feel the heat from the sun even as it sank in the sky, and a tiny bead of sweat formed at his hairline, moving slowly down his forehead, tickling in the light breeze, and settling on his brow.

Nikos felt himself freeze. His whole body went numb, and his stomach pushed up into his chest, like he was speeding over a hill and momentarily feeling weightless. For that split second, everything was up in the air. It was like the universe had tossed a coin and he was just waiting to see where it would land.

As he saw a flash of white at the top of the stairs, the coin landed, and he let out a deep breath.

He knew what he wanted. He wanted Anna, whatever it took. However much she would let him have.

And now it was time to find out if she felt the same.

Chapter Thirty-Seven

22 hours earlier

"That was so badass," Marcus said as they climbed into the truck. "Way to go."

"Shut up," Anna said as she turned the ignition. "I wasn't trying to be badass, I was trying to resolve a very serious conflict that you know nothing about."

Anna paused and remembered what Marcus had told her about his past. "Okay, maybe not nothing," she added, "but still, I don't want to hear anything about it."

"That's fine," Marcus said, putting his hands up. "I'll drop it. But if you want my input, I'm happy to give it. All joking aside."

As they drove, Anna considered his offer. But really, she'd already had tons of input. From Eirini, from Elena, from Maria, from Lizzy, from Xenia, and finally, at long last, from Nikos himself… and at the end of the day, she had to figure out what she wanted, separate from all of their input. What was the life that she wanted for herself, and what could she do to make it happen?

She'd told Nikos that he was the one with a decision to make now, but she couldn't shake the feeling that there was more she could do – a solution she hadn't figured out yet. Her mind and her heart didn't like ultimatums, and no matter how many people told her she couldn't have her cake and eat it, too, she wanted to find a way.

Anna pulled up outside of Kamari Sands. "This is your stop," she said, gesturing for Marcus to get out of the car.

He looked at her incredulously. "What, you're going to fly me all the way here and then not talk to me? What am I supposed to do?"

"Correction, Elena flew you out here, not me." Anna continued to point towards the door. "And I stand by the fact that I need to make this decision myself. If I need your input, I'll come ask for it. Otherwise, I'll see you at the wedding tomorrow."

Marcus nodded and got out of the car. "Good luck," he said. "I really am rooting for you, Anna. I want you to be happy, whatever you choose to do with your life." He caught her eye, and there was a rare tenderness in his gaze.

"I know you are," she said, and in that moment, she knew she could rely on him.

There was no question of where Anna would go. She had hunted down every picturesque and private spot on the island for photos over the last four years, but there was nowhere quite as wonderful as her summer house. So she drove home, walked through the front door, put her bag down on the bed and took a deep breath.

In this summer house, she could fully be herself. She and Nikos had refurbished it with their own two hands. Decades before, her father had built it with his. He'd lived in it until the day he died, and there was nowhere on the planet that Anna felt more connected to him. Connected to her family. This was where she needed to be to make the decision that would be best for her.

She grabbed a few things that felt important – her camera with the "Home" memory card inside it, the file of jobs Marcus had given her, the letters her father had written her – and she climbed into her favourite place in the summer house: the bathtub.

As the sun set over the caldera, she thought about all the people she'd built a life with here.

Nikos, of course, who had been campaigning from day one for her to stay on the island. Maybe that was why he felt his request was reasonable. She'd agreed to stay, but then she'd left time and time again, and now she'd had nearly four years of adventures, whilst he was still waiting on the life he'd wanted all along.

Then there was Elena, who had always remained the same, but whose ultimate allegiance had always been to Nikos. Since that very first summer, every time there had been a conflict between her and Nikos, she had been terrified that Elena would want nothing to do with her if she'd hurt him. It had made her fearful; timid when she wanted to be bold. It was a game changer for her to hear that she'd been wrong and that Elena would still be there for her no matter what. Of course it wouldn't be the same – so much of their friendship revolved around Nikos, too – but she no longer felt afraid of Elena abandoning her.

And then there was her gorgeous family. Eirini and Christos were the one constant she never had to worry about. As soon as they had gotten over the fear that Anna was there to take part of their home away from them after her father died, they'd welcomed her with open arms, and over the last four years, she had never felt more at home than she did with them. And having longed for that sense of family her whole life, she never once took them for granted.

So, knowing that she would still have her friends and family by her side, Anna let herself imagine for just a moment what her life would actually look like without Nikos.

She would be alone in the summer house. Memories of him would be everywhere – in every tile they'd laid, every flower in the garden, every window she'd peeked through to see him working, the photos he'd had printed and hung on the walls – and she'd never be able to go anywhere on the island without thinking of him and wondering if she might bump into him. She'd have Elena, but she'd feel like she couldn't ask questions about Nikos, and given how close they were, that was bound to feel awkward. And then there was Eirini and Christos, who, yes, were firmly on Anna's side, but who had a long history with Nikos, too – much longer than with Anna. He was like a son to them. And it would break their hearts to feel like they had to choose.

Anna saw how this would play out. She would feel increasingly isolated on her short trips home until she decided it was more reasonable to find a different home base. She'd keep the summer house, not wanting to sell it off, vowing to come back to visit as much as possible. But after a few years unoccupied, it would slip back into the state of disrepair it had been in when she'd arrived.

No, Anna knew she didn't want that future. Their relationship may have been turbulent over the last few weeks, but there was so much love and respect between them. They had bonded over their grief at the start, but they had grown a joyful, hopeful life together on the island. To simply say goodbye to that would feel impossible.

As she looked out the window from her beautiful home, even just thinking about this option broke her heart, forming a tightness in her chest that made her grip the sides of the tub. It was so distressing, in fact, that she was sure she couldn't do it. She found herself thinking that maybe, if Nikos said he couldn't do it anymore, that she would give in and call off her bourgeoning career just to keep it from happening.

Which led her to the other option – Nikos deciding he could live with it, and them carrying on as they had been. Yes, they'd cleared up the Maria issue, but undoubtedly there would be more miscommunications and resentments along the way. And what happened if and when they decided they wanted children? Would Anna keep travelling whilst Nikos stayed home with a baby? Anna didn't want that, and she knew Nikos didn't either. She doubted that, in all his imaginings of the future, he'd imagined raising a child largely alone. They'd have to postpone that decision until her career began to ebb, at which point Anna knew she would feel like she'd been forced out.

No, maybe it was better in the end to leave whilst she was on a high. To know that she was in demand enough to get almost any job she wanted, but to decide to leave it all behind. To give Nikos what he wanted. But even as she thought it, Anna knew that wasn't an option. She'd regret it for the rest of her life, and like Elena had said, she would be betraying a core part of herself to do it. Once she did that, it would be one wound she could never fully heal. Plus, with Nikos's career taking off at the same time, she knew she would resent him and that wouldn't be fair to either of them.

Two shitty options sat before Anna, neither of them making much sense to her. She thought back to how happy they'd been on that day in London. Had it all been a lie? Was it impossible to actually sustain the kind of passion and adventure they'd felt with each other, both then and when they first met?

No matter how many times she looked at the folder of dream jobs, scrolled through the pictures of her life with Nikos, or read through her father's letters for advice, she had no more clarity than she did before. Unlike all those years ago, there was no piece of advice she could unearth to make things clearer.

Except… maybe there was something.

The only thing that seemed to hold any weight were the words the oracle had whispered to her just a week before. She'd been so focused on the obvious parallels with the story of the painter, but now this last uttering felt more urgent. She pulled up the note on her phone where she'd recorded it that night.

"Your feet are firmly planted in two domains, dragged towards one but drawn to the other. To be fully in one or the other would require sacrificing one leg. To stay rooted in both requires those dragging you to root themselves with you. This is a decision only they can make. But you can show them where the light is."

Originally, Anna had thought it meant she would have to sacrifice Nikos to fully commit to her work or sacrifice work to fully commit to Nikos. But now, thinking it over, it seemed like there must be a third option there. If only she could figure out what it was.

Anna knew she was probably grasping at straws, but she was desperate. And as she watched the light fade from the sky outside her window, she knew that she was running out of time.

Then she heard a soft, tentative knock on the door.

"Come in," she called, and Eirini stepped through the door into the summer house.

Anna braced herself to stand up, but Eirini waved at her to stay where she was. She came into the bathroom with her, sat down on the floor and leaned up against the bathtub.

"I saw you come in a couple of hours ago," she said, "but I didn't know why you were here, and I didn't want to disturb you."

Anna smiled. "But you decided to, anyway?" she joked.

"Nikos called me," she said. "He told me you were taking some time to yourself this evening. He said he was pretty sure you would come here, and that you might need some food or some comfort."

Anna nodded. Nikos really did know her inside and out. And if he called Eirini, it meant he wanted the best for her, even in that moment. Her heart swelled with love for him yet again.

Eirini looked at Anna, inviting her to explain, but before she could answer, Anna felt herself burst into sobs. It was unexpected, and the tears came so fast Anna wondered if she'd been crying before and just not noticed.

"My dear, it's okay," Eirini said. "Whatever happens, you're okay. You're a talented, intelligent, kind, and very loved woman. And you'll be okay no matter what."

Anna nodded. She knew Eirini was right. She knew that no matter what happened, things would be okay, but when she'd been living her dream for so long, both at work and at home, the idea of having something that was just "okay" felt devastating.

"I just feel like there should be a third option," Anna said between sobs. Eirini nodded as if she knew what Anna was talking about. "I don't want to be sat around watching Nikos succeed and chase his dream like you and Christos. But I also don't want to lose him."

At that last part, at the thought of losing Nikos, the tears fell harder and faster, and Eirini's face quivered as if she might join in. She reached out and stroked Anna's hair as she tried to calm her.

"Oh, no," she said, "that won't happen. I know it won't happen."

"How can you say that?" Anna asked, her desperation welling up.

"Because," Eirini said, "you are not me. And Nikos is not Christos. You are your own people, and your story is not ours. You two have so much love for each other that I think you'll manage to find a way."

And then the penny dropped.

Suddenly Anna froze. She felt the truth clarify in her mind and confidence radiate through her body, calming her instantly. A smile erupted on her face.

"Yaya, you're a genius," she said. "You're absolutely right."

Eirini sat back and crossed her arms. "Well of course," she said. "Yaya is always right." But she looked surprised, too.

Anna stood up suddenly and climbed out of the tub, kissing Eirini on the cheek. If she were right, she had a lot of work to do tonight, and a lot of phone calls to make. The first would be to Marcus.

"Get to the summer house now," she said when he picked up. "I need your help with option three."

Now

Marcus cursed as the gears of the truck ground against each other yet again, causing it to lurch.

"Careful," Anna said as she sat still, mascara wand halfway to her eye. The last thing she needed was a face full of black mascara – or worse, an actual eye injury – when she was already hideously late. The ceremony was meant to start any minute. "Don't forget, you need to take the stuff straight to my room before you go to the wedding," she said. "I need it there when I talk to Nikos."

Marcus confirmed the plan as he finally managed to get over the hill, bringing Carpe Diem within sight.

"Thank you for everything," Anna said, putting the final touches on her makeup and packing it all into her wash bag.

"Yeah, well, this better work," Marcus said. "I've called in a lot of favours for you."

Anna rolled her eyes as Marcus pulled up to the front. He grabbed her arm before she could get out.

"I really do hope it works, Anna."

She nodded, holding his gaze. "Yeah, me, too."

She really was grateful for everything Marcus had done for her over the past day, but for now, she needed to hustle. So she jumped out, grabbed her bag, and ran into the hotel as fast as she could.

When she burst into the bridal suite, she was met with pure chaos – Thea still making tweaks to the dress, Xenia trying to curl Thea's hair as she did, Vasilis's mother and aunt sitting in the corner and shouting corrections at Thea, the seamstresses trying to help Thea but having their hands slapped away…

"We're running super late," Maria said, spotting Anna from across the room and handing her a glass of champagne. "You'll want this."

Anna nodded her thanks as she took one big sip, then another.

"Wouldn't be Elena if there wasn't a little bit of drama," Anna said with a fond smile. "She's gotta make an entrance, after all."

Maria laughed. "Yes, well, tell that to the venue coordinator, who seems to be really concerned that it's somehow her fault."

Anna sighed. "And where is she?"

Maria pointed at a small woman huddled in the corner with a clipboard, looking around at everything going on and shaking. The woman was actually visibly shaking. Surely this wasn't the worst bridal party she'd encountered?

Now was her moment to prove that she wasn't a completely worthless maid of honour. Anna knew what to do. She stepped up to the terrified woman and leaned in conspiratorially.

"First wedding?" Anna asked her, and she nodded. "Well, I'd imagine this is par for the course. The good news is that nobody else is at the resort this weekend, so all you can do is just wait for her to be ready, and then you can call ahead to everyone else and prepare them. Okay?"

The woman nodded again, looking over her list. "But what about the canapés for cocktail hour? The ceremony is meant to be so short that they've already put them out, but if we're late then they'll sit out for too long."

"Let's get those put back inside," Anna said, "and you can get a team to set them out as soon as you know we're ready for the ceremony."

The coordinator looked up and bobbed her head as if doing some mental calculations, then pulled out her phone. "Thank you," she said. "Will they all be like this?"

Anna nodded. "Yeah, probably," she said, thinking back to the handful of Greek weddings she'd been to. "Better get used to it."

She scurried from the room, and Anna turned back to find the rest of the group looking at her. Elena had a huge smile plastered across her face.

"Maid of honour to the rescue," she said. "Good to have you back. We've been trying to get rid of her for hours."

Elena gave her a loaded look – it was like she was trying to probe into Anna's mind to see how things had gone. But she didn't ask, and her attention quickly drifted to what was happening behind her. Only then did Anna notice the stack of empty champagne bottles by the mirror. She realised this was probably why they were so late, and why Elena was so easily distracted.

"What can I do to help?" Anna asked, and Elena opened her mouth, presumably to tell Anna to get some more champagne, but Thea cut her off.

"You can start by getting in your dress please," she said. "I haven't even seen the alterations on you yet, because somebody disappeared last night…"

"I sent her on a secret mission," Elena said, winking at Anna in the mirror. "There's a difference."

Anna and Elena smiled fondly at each other for a moment before Thea snapped her fingers at Anna, making her jump. She took the dress from the seamstress who was holding it out to her, then headed to the bathroom.

Surprising no one, the dress fit impeccably. Anna had thought it was good yesterday, but today it was the most flattering thing she'd ever put on her body. It was like a sleeker, off-white version of Kate Hudson's yellow dress in *How to Lose a Guy in 10 Days*. As she spun back and forth, watching the way the small train barely swept the ground behind her, admiring the way it dipped down her back just low enough to be sexy and just high enough to be tasteful, she thought to herself that she could see herself getting married in a dress like that. But now she was getting ahead of herself. Option three had to work before she could even think about things like that. They needed to rebuild their foundation before trying to add in a conversation about marriage.

As she stepped out a few minutes later, her hair and makeup fully in place, she was met with whoops and whistles, including from Vasilis's family in the corner. Anna did a little spin for them, posing dramatically, before Thea called for them all to get back to work.

"You're fine," Elena said. "You're just faffing now."

"Am not," Thea said. "Your bustle will have to be done with needle and thread if I stop now."

Elena rolled her eyes. "If only I had someone here who was good with a needle and thread!"

Thea laughed. "Fair enough. As long as you promise to let me do it the second your pictures are done so you don't tear the train trying to dance."

Elena did the sign of the cross and nodded. "I promise."

"Very well then," Thea said with a sigh. "I think we're done."

Anna ran back out to find the coordinator, who had only just started getting the canapés brought back in. She sighed and rolled her eyes, then told the servers to put the trays back out again, and she was met with groans all around.

Twenty minutes later, they were stood on the pool deck waiting for the music to start, the sun just managing to kiss their shoulders before the breeze blew away the sting. It was the perfect day for a wedding.

As Maria started down the stairs, Anna let herself take just a moment to slip out of bridesmaid mode and into thinking about Nikos. He would be waiting at the bottom of those stairs, at the end of that aisle, watching her come down in what was essentially a wedding dress, not knowing what their future held. She wished she knew herself.

Xenia went down after Maria, and then Thea. Before Anna knew it, it was her turn, and she put her foot on the top step, her thoughts pinging back and forth between "Don't fall, don't fall" and "I'm not ready for this."

She walked down the steps slowly, not just because she had been instructed to, but because she was so afraid of falling down the steps and making even more of a scene than she had already this week. Her eyes stayed on her feet, and she focused on each step, not letting her mind wander until she reached the bottom and looked up, locking eyes with Nikos at the other end of the aisle.

Chapter Thirty-Eight

As Anna got closer, holding Nikos's gaze all the while, she tried to decipher the emotions she saw playing across his face. She saw flickers of relief in the way his forehead relaxed as he exhaled, then confusion as it pressed together. Anna knew he was trying to gauge what she was thinking. She tried to keep her own face blank. This was Elena's moment, and she desperately wanted to be present for her friend. But she was looking her own future in the face – hopefully, anyway – and she struggled to stay neutral.

As she reached the end of the aisle, she turned away from Nikos and let out a deep breath. She sucked in a big gulp of air, feeling like she'd had all the wind knocked out of her.

By then the attendees were all stood up and facing the stairway, where Elena was descending. So whilst everyone else was looking away, Anna chanced one more look at Nikos, but now he was looking at his cousin, and Anna could see tears in his eyes. She wondered if they were joy at seeing Elena on her wedding day or sadness over how up in the air his own relationship was. She suspected that, like the night of the proposal, it was a complicated mix of both. The more joy he felt for Elena, the more sorrow he would be feeling for himself, knowing what elation was possible, whilst also knowing that it was slightly out of grasp. Anna knew exactly how he felt in that moment because she'd been feeling it, too, all summer.

Anna was surprised at how traditional the ceremony was – she'd expected personalised vows and as many cheesy additions as possible. They drank from the common cup, accompanied by the reading about Jesus turning water into wine. They weren't being married by a priest, but Anna knew the symbolism was still important to Elena, just like it was to Nikos. Anna knew from Nikos that Elena's parents had had quite a traditional wedding, and this was likely her way of connecting to them, just like Anna did with her father whenever she could.

As soon as Elena and Vasilis were pronounced husband and wife and Vasilis dipped Elena back elegantly for a kiss, the crowd erupted with applause. Elena and Vasilis were the kind of couple that people really rooted for. They were always there for those around them, and they deserved every ounce of happiness and affection directed at them.

Anna avoided Nikos's eye as they recessed back up the aisle and up the steps linked together, but she swore she could feel his heart beat even through his arm. Or maybe that was hers – she felt like her heart might beat out of her chest. She even managed to avoid speaking to him whilst they took photos, his arm wrapped around her waist as they posed with Elena, Vasilis, and the rest of the wedding party.

But the moment Elena and Vasilis went off to take pictures of the two of them, Anna grabbed Nikos's arm and led him straight past the canapés and cocktails and down the hall to their room. As they walked through the door, she saw her duffel bag on the chair in the corner and sent a silent thanks Marcus's way.

The door shut softly behind them, and Anna turned around

and looked at Nikos in the eye for the first time since walking up the aisle. She instantly melted. Looking back at her was the love of her life, nearly in tears.

"You look incredible," he said to her, letting out a deep breath.

"You're not so bad yourself," she said, feeling the emotion welling up in her already. She closed her eyes and exhaled slowly, trying to calm herself down enough to start. But before she could, Nikos took the lead.

"Anna, I screwed up," he said, taking a step towards her. "I never meant to make you feel like I didn't want the absolute best for you."

He took her hands in his, bringing them close to his face as if to kiss them.

"It's hard, Anna. Really hard. Being away from you so much is awful. I'm not going to pretend like it isn't. But knowing that you're doing what you love most makes it bearable. No, not just bearable, worthwhile. Because it's what makes you whole. I've known how important your art is to you since our first picnic together, and I would never forgive myself if I thought that I was holding you back from what we both know you're capable of."

Anna nodded as tears began to spill from her eyes. This was exactly what she'd hoped to hear all summer. And if she had, that might have been it.

But Anna had played through this scenario last night. And she knew that Nikos was ready to try to make it work, but she also knew that nothing he did would make it okay. They had no real future together that way.

"I know," she said. "As soon as I gave you that ultimatum last night, I knew you wouldn't leave me. But Nikos, you were right, too. We can't go on like this."

Anna saw betrayal flash across Nikos's face as she said that, but she carried on talking before he could react. She had to say all of this.

"I spoke to Eirini earlier in the summer about Christos's hobby hopping, and she was so sad, Nikos. She felt like she'd been forced to hold down the fort whilst he discovers his passions, despite the fact that she has so much she wants to do beyond being his housewife. And every time you talked about me pulling back at work, I felt like Eirini. I was so afraid of being my mother that I was willing to become my grandmother."

"But I don't want that for you," Nikos said, pleading, and tears were streaming from his eyes now. "I don't want our lives to stay the same forever. I would never want that. I want to grow and explore and change with you. And I know you're not your mother, no matter what stupid comments I may have made. Please believe that."

"I do," Anna said, putting one hand to the side of Nikos's face, his tears wet against her palm. "Of course I do."

She held his face for a moment as he sobbed, leaning into her hand, and she cried with him, the weight of all their grief and baggage weighing down on them together.

But that would not be their story.

"Eirini reminded me of something last night. She told me that I'm not her, and you're not Christos. In fact, if anything, I think that I've been Christos, and you've been Eirini, feeling eclipsed by what I want for my future."

Nikos looked up at her and pressed his lips together. She knew he would want to deny this but couldn't anymore. Not honestly; not with all their cards on the table. It was how he felt, whether he thought it fair or not, and it was written all over his face, in the sad way he met her gaze.

But there was something else in his eyes as well. Hope.

Anna took a deep breath. This next part was the gamble.

"But Nikos, Eirini never wanted Christos to stop following his passions."

"I don't want that either," Nikos said. "I know I said it earlier, but that's not how I really feel, I promise. Your work is such a fundamental part of who you are. I still remember the day you first showed me your work, and how your entire body lit up as you told me why you love it. I would never want you to give that up – not for me, not for anything."

"I know," Anna said. "What I'm saying is, the only thing Eirini wants is to be asked to join him as he explores. She wants them to share the adventure of finding happiness. So Nikos, please… come with me."

Nikos's face held a shocked expression for a moment. He hadn't seen this coming – she knew he hadn't. And she didn't wait for him to respond.

"Come with me," she said again, stepping closer to him. "I've been off on these trips doing something I love, but half my life is happening without me, and I know you feel the same as well. But I don't want to take pictures of the world alone anymore. I want us to do it together." She was holding his face with both her hands now, willing her sincerity and desperation through her hands so he might understand how this was the best way, the only way.

He opened his mouth to speak.

"How?"

Anna knew what he meant. How could they make that work? How would that solve the issue of him feeling like his dreams were second fiddle to hers? How could he keep pursuing those dreams if he dropped everything to come with Anna?

Luckily, she had answers for all of it.

She moved over to the bed and unzipped her duffel, pulling out the folder of dream jobs. Nikos winced at first, and Anna didn't blame him. This damn file had caused so much hurt between them over the last couple of weeks.

Except now, it was different. Some of the jobs had been removed. Some new ones had been added in tentatively. And for those that were there now, Anna's and Marcus's handwriting was scrawled all over them – agreements from the organisers to pay for Nikos's travel, too, nearby vineyards or wholesalers for Nikos to visit, even some meetings with top wine industry names.

"This is what Marcus and I have been working on," she said. "It's not my folder of dream jobs anymore. It's *our* folder of dream jobs."

She flipped through some of the pages, showing them to Nikos and explaining the decisions they'd made. His face stayed frozen in surprise the entire time.

"Nikos, my dream isn't just to be good at my job. It's you, too. And as much as I'm not willing to give up my work, I'm not willing to give you up, either. Remember how happy we were in London, adventuring together? Sharing the experience? This way we can have that all the time, and both get to pursue our passions, too."

Nikos smiled, then took a moment of consideration. "But what about my vineyard?" he asked eventually.

"It would all be covered," Anna said, pulling a budget table out of the folder and showing it to Nikos. "We can easily afford to hire someone to run it while you're away, but you'd also be back enough to still run it the way you want."

Anna locked eyes with Nikos, begging him to see how much she believed that this was right. That this would give them both everything they had ever wanted.

"This is it, Nikos. I really believe that. I love you, and I want the best for you. And I want it for me, too. For both of us together. Our dreams don't have to be at odds with each other anymore. So root yourself with me. I'm telling you this is where the light is."

Nikos was silent for a moment, taking it all in. But eventually, his face spread into a wide grin, and he picked Anna up and spun her around. "Yes," he said, kissing her cheek, her jaw, her eyes, her ear. "Yes, I'll come with you. Thank you so much for asking me."

Anna felt more tears stream down her face as she kissed him

back, her body weightless, feeling like she might float away if she didn't anchor herself right here with him. She didn't have to say goodbye to Nikos, and, hopefully, never would, but she didn't have to say goodbye to part of herself, either. She could stay whole.

She could feel all the frustration and anger and hurt of the last four weeks rush through her body to her lips, their kiss turning them to passion and joy and hope. And as it built, their kisses turned more frantic, desperate after such a long time in standoff, neither of them willing to let go ever again. She clawed at his shirt, a voice in the back of her mind warning her not to rip the buttons, but her body taking over and wrenching the fabric back until she could reach her hands around to his back and sink her nails in. His hands grabbed at her arms, her ass, the hair at the nape of her neck, and she wrapped her arms as tightly as she could around his neck, expecting him to ask her to loosen up, but he never did.

Nikos pushed Anna against the closed door, bunching her dress up in his hands until he was able to reach beneath it and touch her, his tongue tracing along her collarbone as his hand worked below to create a friction that rivalled their kiss. Anna pressed into it, trying to move her hands between them to unbuckle his trousers, but neither of them would relinquish their proximity to the other.

As Anna finally managed to release his belt buckle, Nikos removed his hand, to Anna's protest in the form of a moan, to slip the straps of her dress down over her shoulders. The barely-there material fell away immediately, leaving Anna's breasts exposed, and Nikos wasted no time, bringing his mouth down to kiss them, bite them, run his tongue along the swell of them. Anna wiggled to let her dress fall the rest of the way, then reached her hand out to slip beneath the waistband of his underwear and hold him firmly.

Nikos let out a low growl as he bit down hard in response, and

Anna couldn't take it anymore. She yanked Nikos's pants to the ground, her own following quickly after, and pushed him over to the bed, sitting down on top of him before his head even landed.

The moment she slid him inside of her and began to move, she moaned in ecstasy. She had missed him so much – she'd been with him like this a lot this summer, but this time there was no distraction, or posturing, or lies – she knew exactly what it meant. It meant forever.

"Fuck Anna," Nikos whispered, his eyes shut tight.

"Come with me," Anna said to him again, and as she caught his eye and began to move faster, a look of understanding flashed across his face, and he smiled. And just as a rush of pleasure began to rise through her body, Anna felt Nikos come, and they both cried out, riding the wave until they both crashed into each other, grasping at each other's flesh, holding on tightly to one another, their chests rising and falling in synchronicity.

If she'd thought she felt whole before when he agreed to travel with her, she'd been wrong. This was it. This was everything. Now she was whole. Now she was home.

Chapter Thirty-Nine

Anna laughed as she rolled away from Nikos. This was not how she'd expected the conversation to go, but she certainly wasn't complaining. She planted a kiss on his chest before heading to the bathroom to clean up. Her makeup was in surprisingly good condition considering the tears she'd shed earlier, and the benefit of her liaison was even more tussled-looking hair.

As she headed back into the room, she saw that Nikos was already putting his clothes back on.

"Where are you going?"

"Don't forget we've still got a wedding to attend. I seem to remember us being best man and maid of honour or something like that?"

Anna laughed and gently pushed him back onto the bed, sitting down beside him and running a finger along his spine. "Elena's going to be at least another hour before she's back. I reckon we have nearly half an hour to ourselves still."

Nikos sighed. "I don't think I have another round in me, Anna. That really took it out of me."

Anna laughed again. "Not what I meant," she said. "Actually, there's a lot more work that Marcus and I did last night if you want to see it?"

Nikos smiled and nodded, and Anna picked the folder up off the ground, flipping to the back few pages. It wasn't lost on her that this was the first time she'd ever mentioned something Marcus had done without Nikos saying or doing something to show he was annoyed. There was progress already.

"Well, first of all, we're going to start prioritising jobs based in Europe, but especially Greece."

He nodded along as she spoke. "Is there enough demand for that?"

"Well, we're planning on partnering with some local and national sites and attractions to put together commercial hire packages. It'll be its own business venture, actually."

"That sounds like a lot to do," Nikos said, frowning. "Won't that get in the way of your other work?"

Anna shook her head. "Marcus is going to handle it."

"All the way from New York? That feels nonsensical if the idea is to be in Greece."

Anna grimaced. This was the part that she suspected Nikos wouldn't like.

"Well, actually, Marcus is going to buy a home here and work from the island part-time."

Nikos looked at her in shock. "He actually agreed to that?"

"It was his idea," Anna said. "I was as surprised as you are. But he said that he'd crunched the numbers, and if I was willing to commit to a long-term partnership, then it made sense. Plus, I think he's ready for a change in pace."

Nikos rolled his eyes. "You mean he's sick of pretending to be some high-flying artist with a girl on each arm?"

"Actually, yeah," Anna said. "All the travel has made him

want somewhere to settle down, and it seems he doesn't think New York is the place to do that."

Anna had been taken aback when Marcus had suggested it the night before, but from the way he'd spoken about the gallery and his own work, Anna realised that, just as she was worried hers might, his career had officially waned. He wasn't nearly as in demand as a photographer as he was for his management and consultation. So if he could work with Anna and branch out a bit, it might let him stay connected to an art form he loved without trying to resurrect something that no longer felt worth saving.

"Honestly, babe…"

Anna braced herself for what he would say next, but she didn't expect what came out of his mouth.

"Good for him."

Anna eyed Nikos cautiously. "Yeah, good for him, and good for us," she said, not sure where the magnanimity was coming from, but she wasn't about to question it.

"Oh, and look at what the first one is," Anna said, pulling the first sheet out of the folder and handing it to Nikos. When he saw what was on it, his eyes went wide.

"We're going to work with Arthur?!" he asked, pulling it closer as if to make sure he hadn't hallucinated it.

After a long call with Arthur that morning, Anna and Marcus had convinced him, though it hadn't taken much, that a two-for-one was better for him. Anna would take pictures of the rebrand, and Nikos would get to learn from Arthur in exchange for a short-term exclusivity deal with Arthur's distribution company whenever Erastes was ready to go to market. Maria had offered some helpful input on that side of the deal, and Nikos seemed more than thrilled with the terms they'd noted down on the sheet. They'd scrapped the Vancouver trip for this one, so they would be leaving in just a few weeks.

Anna and Nikos spent another few minutes flipping through

some of the plans, and Anna was pleased to see that Nikos was getting just as excited about the projects as she was. She could tell that they'd absolutely nailed some of the trips and meetings they'd arranged, and for the destinations where there weren't any, Nikos almost always knew of something that could be added.

"Plus, you don't have to come on every trip if you don't want to," Anna said, but Nikos grabbed her hand.

"Anna, I want to be with you anywhere and everywhere."

They kissed again, and then they heard a cheer from somewhere outside the room.

"Oh shit," Anna said. "That's probably them. We'd better go."

She smoothed her hands over her dress, hoping Thea wouldn't notice a couple of the wrinkles that had formed whilst it had been on the ground, and they hurried out of the room. They came out onto the pool deck just in time to catch the first dance.

As they watched Vasilis twirl Elena around in what was clearly a choreographed dance, Anna found herself able to fully sink into the happiness she felt for her friend. She couldn't believe how fortunate they'd been to find each other in a world full of strangers, each of them as kind and passionate as the other. Elena had literally plucked Vasilis from the street to use as a human prop in her photos, and now here they were, married, dancing into their future together.

She looked around the room at a crowd of people all fully enamoured with the bride and groom – all except for Xenia and Lizzy, who were locked in an embrace.

Here she and Nikos were, hand in hand, with their own shiny future ahead of them. She didn't know what life would look like beyond the next few months, but it didn't matter. She had Nikos, and her career, and her family and friends, and her home on this beautiful island. And that was more than she could ever have hoped for.

Epilogue

5 years later

As Anna stepped onto the tarmac and into the Santorini heat, she knew she was home. She'd done it so many times at this point that she could tell exactly how long it would take to get to the arrivals lobby based on what gate she arrived into. She sent off a quick text: "30 mins. See you soon."

Everyone else had already deplaned and she jogged to catch up. As a luggage carrier pulled out of the way, she saw someone waiting for her, curly black hair blowing in the wind, tanned skin glistening in the sun. She reached out and took her in her arms, spinning her around.

"Did Daddy forget to put your sun hat on again?" Anna asked her, planting a kiss on the top of her head.

"She'll only be in the sun for a minute," Nikos said. "Won't you, little G?"

Georgia wriggled in Anna's arms, keen to walk by herself. She'd taken her first steps only two months ago, and already she was walking all over the place. She'd even insisted on walking through the plane on her own, threatening tears every time they tried to speed things along by picking her up, so they'd let her toddle, much to the frustration of the other passengers.

Anna ushered them through the door into the airport, aware that Georgia needed very little time in the sun before she overheated. Their time in Mumbai last month had proven that, when Georgia had gotten sick and they'd become a little too familiar with the Indian medical system. But Nikos was right; she was fine. She twisted Anna's blonde hair around her chubby little fingers, babbling nonsense as she did.

Nikos checked his phone. "We're going to be late."

"No we won't," Anna said in a sing-song voice as if talking to Georgia. "Auntie Xenia drives like a maniac."

Georgia perked up at Xenia's mention. She loved Xenia almost as much as Xenia hated babies. It was like she could sense the resistance and welcomed the challenge with open arms. Xenia tolerated Georgia, but preferred to admire from a distance; one expensive suit had been ruined by spit-up when Georgia was a couple of months old, and that had been warning enough.

"Elena will kill us if we're late," Nikos said.

"We won't be late," Anna repeated.

It was Elena and Vasilis's fifth wedding anniversary today. They made a big deal of their wedding day every year, having lavish parties that were just as mandatory as the actual wedding had been, but five years was actually quite exciting. So much had changed for all of them that day.

A lot had happened in those five years, and yet so many things were still the same. To start with, Nikos kept his word and came on almost all her shoots with her. Even Marcus warmed to it when he saw how much more willing she was to be away from home, as long as Nikos was with her.

And Nikos hadn't just been holding her camera bag, either. With Marcus, Xenia and Maria's help, he'd become very well connected in the hospitality industry, getting his wines stocked by hotels and resorts all over the world. On this particular trip to California – which happened to be part of a collaboration with Arthur, who was now a close friend and colleague – he'd even managed to get a meeting with the Head of Food and Beverage Procurement for a group of over fifty resorts worldwide, securing a major deal for Erastes.

During the first two years after their new arrangement, Anna and Nikos had travelled to over two dozen countries on more than forty jobs. Nikos missed very few of them, and yet they managed to spend enough time in Santorini for him to keep the winery not just running but thriving. Just as they'd planned, he hired Andreas to oversee the day-to-day so that he wouldn't have to stop travelling, and he even paid one of the people who worked at the vineyard to look after the summer house garden when they were away for long stretches. He kept Maria on retainer as well, and she worked with Marcus to make sure the destinations they travelled to had opportunities for him as well.

Marcus and Maria had grown very close, in fact. Marcus's intention to settle down had been the subject of a lot of scepticism, but he really took to the Greek lifestyle, and he rarely visited New York these days. But his ambition never waned, and he poured all of that into Anna's career. That ambition was, of course, immensely attractive to Maria, and after years of casual flirtation, they gave in and began seeing each other. Just six months before, they'd finally moved in together in Marcus's cliff-side villa, which was sold just as quickly in favour of something more child-friendly when Maria found out she was pregnant.

When Marcus had said Anna's star was on the rise, he'd had no idea how right he would be. She became so in demand within the business that companies would organise their shoots around her schedule, and they paid her more than enough to bring Nikos along. They'd started the incentive programme they had dreamed up together, but Anna and Nikos ended up enjoying the far-flung destinations so much, and it benefitted both of their careers immensely, so they never were able to stick close to home.

As both began to put money away, they talked about trying to buy a bigger, nicer house on the island, but they couldn't imagine leaving their little summer house. So, instead, Anna invested some money in Xenia's business, which at that point was nearing thirty properties all over the Mediterranean.

And then, nearly two years into their adventures, Christos died.

He had still been exploring his passions – the latest being model trains – when he passed away in his sleep from a stroke, resulting from a heart condition none of them knew he had. The medical report indicated the condition had likely been present since right around the time Christos retired. Whether he knew about the condition and didn't tell anyone, or something in his subconscious told him he needed to live his life more fully whilst he had the chance, they would never know. But they took comfort in the fact that the last few years of his life were full of more joy, family and love than ever before.

Losing Christos rocked Anna and Nikos to their cores. Yet again, a family patriarch who was equally important to both of them had passed away unexpectedly. Their grief over Anna's father Giorgos, also Nikos's best friend, had brought them together in the first place. Now that they had each other, mourning Christos wasn't easy, but it wasn't as brutal, either.

It was Anna who brought up having children about a month after the funeral. They'd discussed it casually on and off over the years, but it was the first time they'd spoken about it in earnest.

"I don't want to wait until things have settled down," Anna said. "They might never settle down. And we don't know how long either of us has."

Nikos shook his head. "I don't know, Anna. I want this, too.

You know how badly. Bringing your partner on shoots is one thing, but a baby?"

Anna nodded. "I know. It'll definitely take a lot more planning. But think about it. If your options were to carry on as we are and not have a baby, or to do all of this with a baby, even if it came with extra logistics and sleepless nights, and it meant we were singing lullabies at ten PM, instead of sitting in a wine bar somewhere, which would you prefer?"

Nikos thought for a moment. "I think I'd actually prefer the lullabies."

Anna nodded. "Me, too."

The next day, Anna stopped taking her birth control. It took them more than a year of trying, but eventually Anna read a pregnancy test in the bathroom of the summer house that said she was pregnant.

Eirini mourned Christos for months and months, barely leaving the house, much less the island. But on the first anniversary of his death, she came to Anna with a proposition – that Anna buy the house from her so she could finally see the world. She still had a number of good years left in her, and she wanted to have the adventures she'd never been able to, for both of them now.

Anna didn't even think twice. She bought the house outright and paid for a round-the-world ticket for her grandmother to boot.

In the following year, Eirini met up with Anna and Nikos a handful of times in mutual destinations, including one trip to Banff that involved a cold-water swim challenge Anna had to artfully get out of because nobody knew about the baby yet. Anna had never seen Eirini look so alive, and she felt grateful that after the heartache of losing her son and then her husband, she was finally able to get what she'd longed for all those years, even if Anna had to watch from the sidelines.

When the baby came, a beautiful, bouncy girl, there was only one name that felt right: Georgia, named for Anna's father.

They had every intention of moving into the main house, but whilst Anna was breastfeeding, the summer house was actually the easiest solution. For everyone but Nikos, that is, who availed himself of the guest room when he had a long day at the vineyard ahead of him. When Georgia started sleeping on her own, however, they finally pulled the trigger and moved into the main house full-time. The summer house became Anna's workshop, and it was still the place where she felt most at ease in all the world.

Anna took a hard and exhausting ten months off from any serious travel when Georgia was born, though she couldn't resist accepting a few local jobs and even taking a couple of quick trips. Then they were right back at it, this time with a baby in tow. Georgia took it like a champ, acclimatising to travel faster than they could have hoped for. Now it had been two months of almost nonstop action, and they were ready for a few weeks of uninterrupted home time.

As they passed through the doors to the arrivals lobby fifteen minutes later than she thought – she hadn't quite gotten used to all the checked luggage a baby requires – they saw some friendly faces waving a sign. But it wasn't for Anna or Nikos. It said "GEORGIA" in big letters.

"She can't even read yet," Nikos said, repositioning Georgia, whose arms were outstretched towards her favourite auntie.

"So what?" Lizzy replied, squeezing her fingers in and out until she had Georgia in her arms. "Let's not pretend I'm anywhere near as interested in collecting you guys. You could have taken the bus for all I care."

"Hey Liz," Anna said, leaning into her sister.

"Hey Banana." Lizzy wrapped her arms around her sister, Georgia pressed between them, wriggling with glee.

"Thanks for the lift, Xenia," Nikos said, hugging Xenia, who had the sign tucked under her arm and was gesturing for Anna's bags. Anna accepted the help so she could click Georgia's stroller fully into place.

"Ready everyone?" Lizzy asked, directing her words mostly to Georgia, who was resisting being lowered into the stroller with admirable ferocity.

"Let's go," Nikos said, giving her his patented stern dad look, which Anna found remarkably adorable.

"He thinks we're going to be late," Anna clarified.

"Not the way this one drives." Lizzy gestures a thumb at Xenia, who rolled her eyes. "Just kidding," Lizzy added, with a peck on Xenia's mouth. They each pulled a suitcase with one hand, holding their free hands together as they walked. Lizzy had never really left after Elena's wedding, and though she and Xenia had orbited around each other for a while with no real plans, after a year they finally made it official and moved in together. They'd been inseparable ever since.

They loaded up the car and drove straight to the hotel where the party was taking place – Iliou, the hotel Xenia had opened up just a few years prior. The only stop they made was to drop the now-sleeping Georgia off with Eirini, who now lived in a stylish apartment in the centre of town.

Despite Nikos's worries, they were actually slightly early. Thankfully, that is, as Anna still needed to change. They checked into the hotel room they'd treated themselves to for the night, and Anna changed into her bridesmaid dress for their annual photos, per Elena's request. It was a bit snug around the chest thanks to Georgia, whom Anna was still breastfeeding, but thankfully it still fit otherwise. She had always loved this dress, and part of her was glad Elena had decided not to have the girls shorten them for the photos they took each year. Secretly, she thought that if she and Nikos ever did get married, she would wear it. Nikos had loved it so much, and it was still in perfect condition. She would have to remember to thank Lizzy for picking it up for her.

They'd talked about getting married a few times over the years, especially when they were trying for Georgia. Anna knew that the big celebration was something Nikos still wanted. But when she brought it up, and she was usually the one to do so, he said that he was happy with their life, and he didn't think it was necessary. And in trying to make sure Nikos was okay without all those things he'd wanted for so long, Anna had started to understand why he had wanted them to begin with, and even to want them for herself.

But as Georgia suddenly and completely took over their life, and Anna got back in the swing of things at work, the idea of planning the kind of wedding they would want felt overwhelming, and they'd never even bothered to get engaged. Anna told herself they didn't need it, that their life together was everything she'd ever wanted, and mostly it was. But sometimes, she would see a dress in a window or a photo online and think, *I wouldn't mind that*.

But for now, she would settle for playing dress-up for the most extravagant engagement party ever. Elena would be in her wedding dress again as well, at least for pictures. Anna personally thought it was incredibly over the top to have basically a second wedding reception for your fifth anniversary, but in nine years of having Elena as a best friend, she'd learned that, if anything, that would only encourage her. So she curled her hair just as it had been on that day five years ago and left the room.

As she headed through the lobby, she could see all of the guests on the terrace, the glistening infinity pool stretching out towards the endless blue of water and sky. She felt the breeze blow in and tickle her shoulders; she could smell the salt on the air.

Everyone had champagne in their hands, but no one was drinking it – like they were waiting for something. Anna thought they must be waiting for Elena and Vasilis, but then she saw Elena stroll up to Maria and give her a hug. Elena was wearing pink.

Anna had known Elena for nearly a decade, and if there's one thing she was certain of, it was that Elena would always take the opportunity to wear white. So why wasn't she now? Plus, if she wasn't in her wedding dress, why was Anna in her bridesmaid dress? Had Anna misunderstood when things would be happening?

Just as the wheels began turning, Anna felt a tap on her shoulder. She turned around to see her mother, poised as ever.

"Mom," she said, kissing her mother on both cheeks, too shocked to say or do anything else. Grace had made more of an appearance since Georgia had been born, but she still wasn't exactly a central figure in Anna's life, and she certainly wasn't expected. Not by Anna, at least.

"Anna, love, good to see you." They'd certainly come a long way from cold greetings and verbal jabs. Grace stepped back to look Anna over. "Don't you look lovely."

"Thanks, Mom," Anna said, still not quite putting together what was happening. Finally, she found the wherewithal to ask. "I mean this with all the love in the world, but what are you doing here?"

Grace smiled and *hmmmm*'d – the closest she ever came to pleasant laughter. "Well, I don't believe it's my place to discuss that, but I also don't fancy a crowd, so I thought I'd come say hello before you join the party. I'll be at the bar if you want to chat after."

Anna watched her mom walk away as quickly as she'd

appeared. "After what?" she asked as an afterthought, but Grace didn't acknowledge it.

As the pieces of the puzzle began to fall into place in Anna's mind, she turned back around to see Nikos coming through the door. He was all dressed up in a suit and tie, and not the one he'd worn to Elena and Vasilis's wedding. This one was black, very James Bond, and he was looking at her like she'd hung the moon.

"You look incredible," he said, taking her hands and eyeing her up and down. Anna glanced over his shoulder at the terrace, where people were doing a very poor job of pretending not to watch them. When Lizzy saw Anna looking, she actually turned around and waved a bunch of other people away.

"What's going on?" Anna asked, but she already knew the answer, and her lip began to quiver. Becoming a mother had turned her into even more of a crier, and she gave silent thanks for the foresight to wear waterproof makeup.

Nikos grinned at her and pulled her close, bringing her hands together in front of his chest.

"My darling Anna, since the moment I laid eyes on you more than nine years ago, I've been hopelessly yours."

Yep, that was all it took. Anna felt the tears welling up.

"I've had a lot of important people in my life taken from me, and not because either of us wanted it. Because it was their time. My parents, Elena's parents, your father, Christos…"

Nikos paused for a moment, and Anna could tell she wasn't the only one getting emotional. A tear slipped down her cheek, and Nikos took a deep breath.

"When I realised how important you were to me, I clung on tight – so tight that it hurt both of us at times. But despite your own past, you never ran. Not once. You held onto me, too. We've always been willing to fight for each other, and that's how we've built the incredible life – the incredible family that we have now.

And I can't wait to keep having adventures with you and Georgia for the rest of our lives."

As he said "the rest of our lives," Nikos got down on one knee, and the full waterworks were unleashed. He pulled a small black box out of his jacket pocket and opened it to reveal the most stunning ring she'd ever seen – a trio of diamonds set in a gold band. She didn't even have to ask to know it was meant to represent her, Nikos, and Georgia.

There was a time when she would have questioned this – wondering if Nikos's motivations were right, or if she was cut out to be with him forever, or if their idea of the future lined up – but their hearts and souls were so intertwined at that point that saying yes to him was going to be as easy as breathing. So she held her breath until he asked a question she could say yes to.

"Will you continue to make me the happiest man on planet Earth and be my wife?"

"Yes," she exhaled. "The easiest yes I've ever said."

The party outside erupted in cheers, but Anna couldn't take her eyes from Nikos. His big beautiful brown eyes were full of tears as he took the ring from the box and slipped it on her trembling finger. It fit perfectly.

Nikos shot up off the ground, causing Anna to gasp as he lifted her off her feet and spun her around. They kissed, and the crowd cheered again.

As Nikos set Anna down, she noticed that he suddenly had a very serious look on his face.

"What?" she asked, cupping his face in her hands.

"So, there's a second part," he said, grimacing.

"A second part to this??" Anna said, holding her hand in front of his face, and then she took a moment to admire the ring again.

"Well, yes, a second part to that."

Anna frowned. "Well, go on then."

The crowd went quiet in anticipation. Clearly, they had caught on, even if she hadn't.

"If you'll have me, I'd very much like to marry you—"

"Nikos, I already said I wo—"

"Right now."

Anna paused, blinking fast as if it would help clear the confusion. "Right now?"

"Right now."

"As in, right here, right now?"

"The one and only," he said, nodding his head.

Anna looked back out at the crowd and began focusing in on faces. These weren't Elena's guests, they were hers. Elena and Vasilis, Lizzy and Xenia, Kostas and Katerina, her mother… of course, now her mother being here made perfect sense. The only people missing were—

As if on cue, Nikos waved his hand, and Eirini and Georgia walked through the door. Anna rushed forward to scoop Georgia into her arms, wondering if she could sense the excitement of what had just happened. She looked adorable in a white tulle dress with her hair pulled into a tiny ponytail, a pink flower pinned in it.

Pink like Elena's dress.

And Lizzy's, now that she noticed, despite the fact that Lizzy hated pink. They were wearing the same dress.

Pink like the flowers she could now see on all the tables outside, which she realised were the same as in their garden at the summer house.

Nikos had thought this through.

"Everyone's here?" she asked.

Nikos nodded.

"You've got cake?"

"Magda's finest. She's not on the island, but Grace brought it over on the ferry this morning."

Anna swivelled her head until she found the bar where Grace was sat, and she raised a glass towards Anna. Anna nodded at her mother and mouthed the words "thank you." Grace nodded and took a sip.

She made a show of thinking about it for a moment, but really this was the second easiest yes she'd said that day. "You've got my people, my cake, and my dress. What more could a girl need?"

Nikos let out a cheer. "Let's do this!" he yelled, taking Georgia and putting her back in Eirini's arms so he could grab Anna around the waist, dip her low, and kiss her.

As the guests took their seats and a pianist began to play, Nikos grabbed Anna's hand and pulled her towards the door, facing her in the threshold.

"You ready for this?" he asked, placing a gentle kiss on her forehead.

"So ready," Anna said. "Thank you for doing all of this. You know me so well."

"Don't I ever," Nikos said. "Here's to many years of digging even deeper."

"Let's do it," Anna said, squeezing his hand and turning towards the door. He winked at her and faced the party as well.

Anna and Nikos stepped confidently out onto the terrace, hand in hand, to the people that represented their past and their future; to the beautiful rolling hills of Santorini; to the endless blue horizon of happily ever after.

Acknowledgments

This book took me a really long time to write. Life hasn't been easy for most of us over the last couple of years, but we've had a few particularly jarring moments that made it feel hard to keep going at times. Coming back to this book pulled me out of a difficult place, and for that I'm immensely grateful. I hope it helps provide you with a bit of respite, no matter what you're going through.

As always, thank you so much to the brilliant team at One More Chapter. To Jennie, my editor, working with you on this book has been incredible, and I can't wait to tell more stories together. To the design team, the marketing team, and everyone else working hard to create wonderful stories, I feel so lucky that my books are among them. To Charlotte, you're one of the best people I know, and I feel so lucky to have you as a publisher and friend. *pulls glasses forward* That's all.

To my mom Lisa, thank you for always being my champion. Your belief in me and your encouragement has always inspired me, and I can't wait for you to read this one. Just skip the sex scenes, please, and maybe tell dad to sit this one out.

To my beta reader and friend Jaye, thank you for being my ultimate hype girl as I worked on this book.

To my gorgeous and long suffering husband Alex, thank you for always making space for my dreams, and always encouraging me without making me feel pressured. Our marriage is the greatest joy of my life, and every time I write about love, I'm pulling from the well you are constantly filling.

To my grandmother Velma, who I hope would have been proud of the kinds of stories I've chosen to tell using her name. I think about you every single day.

And of course, thank you to all of you who have chosen to continue on Anna's journey with me. Your messages and posts have been so encouraging over the last few years, and I promise you that every single one meant the world to me. I hope I've done right by you when writing the end of Anna's story, and I can't wait to show you what else I've been working on for you.

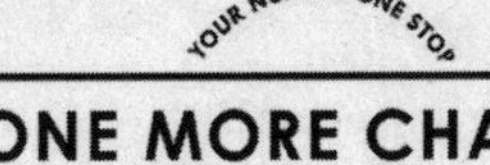
YOUR NUMBER ONE STOP
ONE MORE CHAPTER

FOR PAGETURNING BOOKS